A KID CALLED CHATTER

UNIVERSITY OF CALGARY
Press

A KID CALLED CHATTER

CHRIS KELLY

Brave & Brilliant Series
ISSN 2371-7238 (Print) ISSN 2371-7246 (Online)

University of Calgary Press
2500 University Drive NW
Calgary, Alberta
Canada T2N 1N4
press.ucalgary.ca

LIBRARY AND ARCHIVES CANADA CATALOGUING IN PUBLICATION

Title: A kid called Chatter / Chris Kelly.
Names: Kelly, Chris (Christopher Robert), author.
Series: Brave & brilliant series ; no. 24.
Description: Series statement: Brave & brilliant series ; no. 24
Identifiers: Canadiana (print) 20210360240 | Canadiana (ebook) 20210360259 | ISBN
    9781773852645 (softcover) | ISBN 9781773852652 (PDF) | ISBN 9781773852669 (EPUB)
Classification: LCC PS8621.E44147 K53 2022 | DDC C813/.6—dc23

The University of Calgary Press acknowledges the support of the Government of Alberta
through the Alberta Media Fund for our publications. We acknowledge the financial support
of the Government of Canada. We acknowledge the financial support of the Canada Council
for the Arts for our publishing program.

Printed and bound in Canada by Marquis
This book is printed on Rolland Opaque Smooth pur white paper

Editing by Naomi K. Lewis
Cover image: Colourbox #31898099
Cover design, page design, and typesetting by Melina Cusano

for Katherine,
with all the love in my tin heart.

CHAPTER 1

A white-furred jackrabbit crawled under the fence boards. Taller than the kid, she crept forward with her odd jackrabbit gait, a pause then tilt, a pause then tilt, on limbs stiff as porcelain. When she was close to where he sat in the grass, her forelegs failed, and she collapsed between the kid's feet. Little more than a toddler, the kid had no notion of death, but he noticed the shiver in his chest fade. For the rest of his life, whenever his thoughts strayed into hope, he would recall her muscles loosening under her skin. He would remember pushing his fingers into the bunched fur at the base of the hare's neck, and the shadow that fell over him. He never forgot the gasp.

Later, when he was called an orphan, the kid came to suspect he was unnatural. Whenever that hateful notion arose in his mind, he returned to the shadow, the flurry of motion above him. The gasp, the single sound to which he ascribed the title Parent. He fostered the tone at night, stretching it into a full scene, a contested exchange of words in a nearby room. There was fear in the voice, he felt sure of that. On better nights, he didn't even blame the voice. Fear is natural to life, he told himself. Other nights, however, when his inside voice grew hard and angry and coherent, he cornered himself with the inescapable question: *How long would anyone keep a baby that attracts dying jackrabbits?*

When he wearied of this line of inquiry, his thoughts turned to the only other aspect of the memory to which he was attached: the unmistakable feeling in his chest. The

call-and-answer in his heart as the hare neared, overwhelming
the kid as she came close enough to touch. It was this, perhaps,
that encouraged him to reach out, to lay his hand upon her
fur, this dislodged sensation that longed for completion. The
kid pondered the shiver, placing it against the outwardness
of the gasp, and learned something about himself, about the
secret, the wordless nameless, which was as part of him as an
organ. Before he accepted a name, he accepted this. He would
sooner strip off his skin than rid himself of the shiver. It was his
first instinct, his always instinct, to attribute the shiver to the
approach of another dying jackrabbit.

Occasionally, the shiver in his heart preceded a different
animal. Several species entered the city, unmistakably headed
towards whichever orphanage housed the kid. Many, growing
lost, succumbed on the way; he was always unsure if the corpses
in the gutters were meant for him. Of the common species,
the dried husks of squirrels and robins and crows, he found
speculation pointless. When he came across a weasel, however,
or a badger, or a tire-treaded falcon, he dared wonder. Was this
proof? Those animals, saddled with their nameless plagues,
or bearing wounds that cruelly permitted travel, only entered
the city to die. So, the dead, discovered in the streets, became
barbs of failure. He wasn't sure if his presence comforted, but as
he accepted his affliction, the kid felt glad for the animals that
reached him.

Once, when he was eight, a black bear died in a lane a half-
mile away from His Holy Rules, the last of the kid's orphanages.
One of the boys there, a gangly blond named Sandy Bixby,
claimed to have seen the creature collapse, and mimicked the
shake of its limbs and its laboured breath. *Huff huff huff*, Sandy
said, and then paused. *Huff huff huff*.

The sound replaced the parental gasp in the kid's nights
for months. He pictured the bear through its last paroxysm,
or speculated about what he would have done if the animal
reached him. In this way, the jackrabbits became a balm for

his fear. Whenever the kid felt an approaching animal, he was overcome with relief when it resolved itself into a pitiful, dying hare.

This is how the kid came to love the jackrabbits.

CHAPTER 2

When the kid came to All's Well Boys Dormitory, an admitting nurse, who'd spent the afternoon at the grocer, named him Custard. He went unnoticed by most of the staff because of his habit of sleeping for fourteen-hour stretches. He was judged three years old. The custodian at the All's Well, Selwyn de la Rosa, found the first jackrabbit three days later. A leveret, its head too big for its body. Thin with winter sickness, it collapsed near Selwyn's woodshed.

Selwyn collected the corpse and neglected to burn it for two days. His head buzzed. He thought of his mother, Alexandria de la Rosa, the final in a line of Andalusian soothsayers. Her whole life, she'd considered herself a failure for not bearing daughters. Men merely muted the family talent. Selwyn never doubted his mother's love, but grew up with the fact of his inferiority. He drew solace from being her favourite. She granted him the duty of cleaning her hutch and feeding the family of European hares she kept as familiars.

The leveret was the closest Selwyn had come to the wild animals that sheltered in the distant river valley. While he kept the leveret, Selwyn rarely left his room next to the boilers. From time to time, he reached out his hand and corrected the jackrabbit's head on its paws. He burned the body in a private ceremony.

By the end of the month, Selwyn had cremated three more jackrabbits. He kept their skulls after speaking with a huge skeletal hare in a dream, believing this a message from his mother. His clumsy hands, however, collapsed brainpans and cheekbones. He cracked the jaw of another. After three weeks Selwyn destroyed the skulls and the shrine beside the water boiler, in a rage meant to wipe away his sacrilegious fumbling.

In the course of regular eavesdropping, Selwyn learned that Custard also unsettled the staff. One of the nurses discovered that Custard didn't sleep for fourteen hours at a stretch, but instead lay awake, his eyes pressed closed. *"Listening,"* whispered the nurse loud enough for the room to hear. The kid wasn't adopted once in his first or second year at All's Well, despite his relative health and plainness. Couples meeting with him sensed the staff's unease. Although five years of age, he didn't speak, and gazed upon prospective parents until they felt the need to answer an unasked question.

Selwyn's mind hummed. He watched the boy.

His suspicious were confirmed after an April sun shower the following year. That clear and dry morning, Selwyn removed a section of the gutters in order to replace rusted rivets. He worked through the lunch hour, and was close to finishing when a pocket of rain swept over the grounds. Selwyn hauled the repaired section up the ladder, desperate to preserve what remained of the gardenia patches. He slipped once, and almost lost his life. The rain passed as he fit the trough into the joists and set it into place. It was then, as he admired his work, that motion on the grounds caught his attention. A jackrabbit emerged from the birch near the mowing shed.

A sharp creak split the air, the shunt and slide of a metal door. Custard slipped out of All's Well, his little head and little hand first in view. He crept across the courtyard, bent almost double. Avoiding, Selwyn realized with a flush of anger, the line of windows where his minders might have spotted him. Sure enough, the kid hunched his shoulders, and he scampered away from sightlines. Such intention, such flagrancy, incensed Selwyn, and he felt about to shout, when the kid's eyes flicked upwards, from the gardenias to the ladder to Selwyn. Custard shivered, Selwyn saw it, a shiver and shock and his spine straightened in panic. The kid's eyes went wide, and he beat a retreat into the orphanage. He'd gone far enough into the courtyard by that point, however. Selwyn saw his face. He knew it wasn't a mistake. Custard sought the jackrabbit.

The very next week, Selwyn went on strike. Overturned books and crumpled pages soon littered the hallways; sheets of dust drifted through slanting sunbeams. The orphans adapted quickly, and invented games of avoidance in each upset hall, but the staff of All's Well were in a constant state of stumble. A few days after this, a jackrabbit died in the field. Four days later, another corpse was found in the concrete courtyard.

Summoned by the most official tone of Missus Bliss, the director of All's Well, Selwyn spoke of his mother and the hares of his childhood. He described how their fur smelled in mountain rain. He held up his hand and used the lines of his palm to show how big their paws grew. When Selwyn detailed the jackrabbits that died at All's Well, and the three years of private ceremonies he'd held in the basement, Missus Bliss was surprised at the wetness of her cheeks. Selwyn shook his head, he stared forlornly at the mountainous horizon. "Why isn't someone doing something about this?" he wondered. Missus Bliss, unsure the question was posed to her, put on her fieriest manner, and commanded Custard brought posthaste.

Custard came into the office with his eyes rooted on the webbed and curling cream tiles. He kept his hands clasped before him and didn't even raise his head when Missus Bliss said his name. Not even when she repeated it. The kid clung to this quiet, even when the noise in Selwyn's head grew, even in the face of Missus Bliss' questions. Did he have a whistle that called the jackrabbits? Was he taught a trick when young? Missus Bliss couldn't find evidence of his parentage; she seemed not, even, to know how the kid arrived at All's Well, other than the year of admittance, 1928, which, she admitted, revealed nothing. And still the kid was quiet. As silent as the animals, whose open faces proclaimed so loudly, while their manners were rooted in a primordial wordlessness that, so it seemed to Selwyn, was dangerously contagious. The kid wouldn't answer any of Missus Bliss' concerns; each accusation drove him further into himself. He wouldn't raise his eyes. Selwyn felt himself begin to shake. If only the kid could admit to his oddity. Even that would reinforce his humanity. But the kid kept quiet. As silent as suffering.

Selwyn only stopped shouting when Missus Bliss's hand smacked flat on her desk, upsetting a yellow pencil holder and a cup stained with dry coffee. She warned Selwyn that she was not so crippled as the city. Thousands had lost their jobs after the market collapse, and she could easily find another custodian amidst those unwilling to join the bristling relief camps in the countryside. Selwyn made to respond, but the only sound that emerged was wordless, the inarticulate noise of a defeated animal.

Each of them, after the length of a moment, turned their attention to the kid called Custard. He kept his eyes on the cream tile. He stayed silent.

CHAPTER 3

The orphanage named Slatterly was famous for the wide grass field that separated it from the sloping prairie shelf. Mrs. Anders, the administrator, often bragged about her charges, pointing out fit and tanned boys as exemplars of her charity of nature. Indeed, the boys of Slatterly spent most of the spring, summer, and fall outside, although neither the field, nor administrative vigour, were the reason. Slatterly, built of stones from the nearby river, had functioned as an asylum for fifty years, until the building was deemed Cruel and Unusual. This was because of the constant moisture in the walls. No administrator, not even Mrs. Anders, offered to explain this, but a common myth amidst the orphans claimed the stones seeped centuries of absorbed river water. Dampness had plagued the lungs and joints, caused falls in the hallways, and drove the invalids mad with an unremitting applause of ceiling-stone rain. After the building stood unused for two decades, the city converted Slatterly into an orphanage to counter the growing numbers of abandoned children. A skeleton staff of janitors, cooks, and three nurses cycled through their *On Wet* duties in the main building. Mrs. Anders never mentioned the insistent moisture, and directed visitors to nearby buildings that offered a grand view of both the field and the prairie horizon.

The kid called Custard arrived early in the alphabetical rotation, and received the name Aaron when he arrived, though later he was renamed Clot by Macy Sullivan, a cafeteria worker recently hired. Macy named the kid Clot because of what she witnessed in Slatterly's famous field.

The kid called Aaron was six, and faced the largest shift of routine in his life. He'd grown comfortable at All's Well. The 05:45 bell hardly shook his heart, and he felt sure the eggs and oily mash at breakfast were on the cusp of nourishment. The boys of Slatterly, however, housed in a single dormitory, woke each other in the mornings, after the vigourous Mr. Hollis shook the oldest boy, Neils, at 05:30. The kid woke to an elbow in his stomach the first morning, in a bed surrounded by laughing boys. Slatterly's breakfast was cold porridge, believed by Mr. Hollis to provide all necessary nutrition. They ate this every day, with a dollop of honey on Sundays, for which they assiduously thanked the Lord. The porridge chilled the kid's tongue, and he ate little of it the first day. When Mr. Hollis noted this, he called it to the attention of the rest. For a week, the boys of Slatterly called the kid a *Waster*.

No one prayed at All's Well either. The boys of Slatterly were subjected to Morning Service from 08:00 to 08:45 by Mrs. Anders, the headmistress, who made a point of telling others she was ordained whenever she wasn't wearing her white and blue robes with a yellow sash. She wore her robes often enough, though, long after Morning Service each day. She wielded her religion like a cudgel of Redemption, and centred the faith of the boys on those she called the *Saved*, who, to the boys, were merely holy people once as dirty as the rest.

Despite the bounty in her book, Mrs. Anders avoided stories of martyrs. She knew the subject matter would interest the boys, but Mrs. Anders felt the notion of martyrdom, with its apotheosis of suffering, gave the wrong impression of faith. Her figures found enlightenment in their Lord whilst they lingered in the lost world, administering to the wretched. Every morning she evoked the wearied Saved, who toiled amidst filth and decay, and she could not be helped if, every once in a while, she gestured to herself. The boys noticed this, and, before they grew insensate to it, knew she saw them as the scum in which she waded, saintly.

Yet such wallowing figures made little sense to the boys. They saw no worth in being Saved, if you weren't also spirited away. What reward was a view of the sky, they asked, if you remained in the mud? Not one of the boys wanted to be Saved; none imagined they could endure it. In fact, this was the first advice the kid received at Slatterly: "When Mrs. Anders asks if you want to be saved, say no."

The kid fell in with one group of boys, then another. He found the different vocabularies confusing. Some camps called Hardheart Wynston a saint of athleticism, others, a dirty masochist. Most wanted to scrimmage like the bigger boys, and spent their time shadowing—falling, punching, and yelling like the rest—glad for a distracted glance from Mr. Hollis. The kid knew to stay away from these boys, and recognized something of his own nature in the instinct. Nor did he choose individual friendships with the quiet boys, those intimate, enduring bonds the battered few formed in their suffering. He saw danger in those sorts as well.

Mostly, while the boys of Slatterly ran in the field, the kid used the distraction to scan the tall prairie grasses beyond its border. He'd wait inside, the shiver growing in his chest, for Mr. Hollis to kick open the field door with his customary exuberance, then slink as quick as he could to the distant corner, where he felt sure he could kneel unobserved. He was excited at the shiver, eager for company, once he'd properly shed the boys and their unminding minder. He'd slip into the tall grasses, tailing the swell of the shiver, until he found an ailing hare, crouched, the whites of its eyes exposed, still as a stone. Without a thought, he held out his hand and pressed his fingers into dew-soft fur.

He found his first intimacies in the tumult of blades, those moments as comforting as claustrophobic, his hand settled on an animal's back, rising and falling with the rhythm of its breathing, when he felt better able to understand the no-language of the hares. Better, at least, than the languages of the boys. He did pause, whenever he knelt in cold mud, or the hateful spatter of rain, and considered Mrs. Anders' notions of the Saved. He paid attention to his pains, the discomfort he endured, sometimes kneeling for hours, while the hare died. Was this similar to the stories Mrs. Anders shared in the mornings? The kid didn't know. He'd stopped listening long before, and retained only a notion of suffering and forbearance. Yet he understood why the Saved held out their hands. He understood where they dwelt.

One afternoon, after a year of quiet in the grass, the kid ignored the vigourous voice of Mr. Hollis. He sat cross-legged in an open patch pressed down by sleeping deer. He didn't move, content amidst the musk of fur, as Mr. Hollis called the boys back in the building. The kid closed his eyes and counted to one hundred without cheating, then peered overtop the grass. The field was empty.

He felt the shiver of an animal as clearly as he saw the sky, a sudden flare in his chest, as familiar as the rest, yet tinged with a distinctiveness he'd never experienced. Immediately, the kid knew something was wrong. The shiver was involved with a hollowness, an echo without source, which fomented a rot that climbed his throat and settled in his sinuses. White specks crowded the corners of his eyes. He tried to force a sneeze, but nothing came of it. Still, the shiver worsened, the animal drew closer. The kid risked standing again, but couldn't make out a distinct motion against the sway of the grass.

His head spun with the rot after he stood. Fear, wriggled from the deep, shook the kid's mind, and with each moment of approach, it resolved itself into an acute terror. A rustle of the grass sent darts of dread through his heart, and he scrambled in the opposite direction.

The fear, he realized dimly, was not owed to the approaching animal, but to something else, to a sense he got when he stood. Only it wasn't a sense so much as an absence. The rot emphasized it, the silence of the landscape, the great vacancy of the sky as it fell to the horizon. The immensity of the land, quiet and unmoving, became threatening, an abundance that served to conceal. For the kid knew then, in the moment his eyes swept over the tall grasses and wooded slopes of the distant river valley, that something watched him. The point of horror, this figure that threatened to emerge from obscurity, was not shaken by the kid's presence. In fact, the kid wondered, in his most secret voice, if this intolerable patience sought him out.

The kid wanted to shout, but he knew his own voice would be all he heard, only paler, quieter. An echo with almost no source. The silence terrified the kid. He knew it would not yield.

The kid scrambled. His heart thundered in disgrace. He stumbled into the mown field, but refused to turn. The only victory, he told himself, would be closing the steel door of Slatterly with unquivering hands. He wouldn't run in the open field. He would not.

He broke into a sprint midfield, but stopped after a few paces. The shiver and the rot swelled in thunderous synergy, and made him so dizzy he tripped. Humiliated, he wriggled on the ground to confront the attack.

A small hare with a light brown coat crawled out of the prairie grass. It held a lamed foreleg to its chest. One of its ears hung limp, as though the afterthought of a careless creator. A cluster of knife wounds blackened by blood marred its flank.

The kid swooned. He had never seen an animal in this condition. So clearly marred by the work of human hands. Revulsion and compassion whorled. The kid went to hold out his hand, but he did not hold out his hand. He kept his warm wrist pressed to his chest. He faltered for a moment that shamed the rest of his life. Years later, he decided the first test was the unhesitating approach.

The kid hesitated.

The crippled hare was beyond fear, and settled forward when the kid reached out. He laid his hands on the jackrabbit's body, despite the gore. He thought of shouldering through tall grass, mulch and dew a fine compost in his nostrils. Surges of excitement pulsed down his arms, the sensation of thrust, of power building in the deep reserves of his thighs. Happinesses he presumed all hares shared.

The kid's finger slipped under a flap of skin as the animal leaned into the touch. His hand recoiled in disgust. The hare yawled at the sudden jolt, and leapt back into the grass. It was the first time the kid had heard the voice of a jackrabbit.

With the clap of a wave in a deep cavern of his self, the kid knew he wasn't one of the Saved. Not once, not in any of the stories, did the Saved recoil. Shame, worse than his hesitation, overtook the kid. He was such a goon he couldn't handle the icky feeling on his precious hand. And the hare was gone, too. Shot a trail into the grass where it would die, alone, shivering, dead from morning dew. The kid clenched his fists until his nails dug into his palms and the skin went corpse white.

He got to his feet, his right hand warm with blood. The beat of the hare's heart lingered. Blood smoothed the creases in his palm, wiped away his past and future. He dragged it in the grass until a voice startled him.

"What did you do?"

A woman who worked in the cafeteria stood nearby. Her name was Macy Sullivan; she looked worn out by a life she was half-way through. She had washed the dishes at Slatterly for three weeks. She searched the kid, eyes wide with terror.

"What did you do?" she stammered again.

CHAPTER 4

For a month, Macy Sullivan kept her visitors secret. The first two women were introduced as great aunts avoiding fumigation. The kitchen supervisor, Auggie, found this reasonable, and offered the women comfortable places near the ovens rather than the cramped nook called dish pit, but they declined, and spent the day staring out a small window at the verdant field of Slatterly. Macy's excuse extended to the next batch. Uncles, second cousins, aunts-once-removed, and great-great- greats took turns at the window. Auggie's suspicions grew, but the shell of government that oversaw their territories refused to subsidize further employees, particularly in the damp of Slatterly.

Auggie waited a month to speak to Macy.

But the past week he'd seen a great-great-grandfather crying, *crying*, real tears and snot and all, and later a group of women drinking tea from matching cups. Tea! Twice he'd found little garbage items strewn along the windowsill. A pink plastic rabbit, the kind bought in a corner store for a penny, several beads, and bundled wheat stocks tied with a blue ribbon.

The night before, Auggie found an expired tealight and a photograph, a yellowed wallet-sized picture of an infant. The infant looked neither happy nor sad, and Auggie felt uncomfortable staring. The decision to throw away the photo haunted his whole evening.

Macy fessed up when confronted. She told Auggie that the boy named Clot healed with his hands. She'd seen it through her window. She watched the boys in the field as respite from her duties, she explained, and kept a second eye on their numbers as they lined up to leave and ran out. One day, the kid she called Clot disappeared in the grass, and Macy noticed he didn't return. She kept watching out of *concern*, she said. She'd waited until the kid emerged.

Macy nodded solemnly. "First I thought he's a little sick," she said, "like that's why he's here, why he's abandoned. I thought he's sneaking out to the field because he's hurting them animals. I told you, I seen blood on his hands. So, I ask him, I said, *What you doing?* And he says, *I'm saving them.* Says that. And believes it; I seen it in his eyes. Some sort of natural fear at what's happened. He ain't hurting them, I watched. He don't ever go after them, he just waits. No, not harming, not a boy that precious. I seen him since go and go again into those grasses. Sometimes he's bloody hands, sometimes not. But he always looks afraid after."

"Why do your people cry?" asked Auggie.

Macy pointed to her window. In the distance, a dead jackrabbit marred the expanse of the field. "He don't know enough to save them all yet," Macy said.

Under the combined effort of Auggie Mariner and Macy Sullivan, Mrs. Anders did not find out about the string of visitors for three months.

Auggie convinced Macy to charge the visitors two dollars. He called it *token* first, then *collection*, which the visitors appreciated more. Tea and an umbrella ran a further two dollars, he and Macy decided, or thirty cents each. Macy brought visitors through the side door, in between the cook's cigarette breaks. She maintained the fumigation story with the rest of the staff.

Once a week, after lunch, the kid called Clot helped bring the three grey plastic tubs of dishes from the dining hall to the kitchen. On these days, Auggie made sure the boy was gone for no longer than fifteen minutes. He didn't know if the kid was even aware of what was happening. Children, he assumed, weren't even human until age ten. But Auggie didn't wonder. He simply knew that such days doubled the fee.

This bothered him considerably less than the photo with the infant.

CHAPTER 5

The dishwasher's people called him *Clot* when they knelt. The kid wasn't sure, at first, if this wasn't just a sound of praise. Some shook while they spoke. A boy named Maul accompanied him the first time it occurred, and ever after, the kid's name was Clot, whispered with breathless wonder. The boys woke him in the mornings with a collective gasp.

Clot once gave a grey tray to an old man wearing a turtle-green vest, and the old man said, "Thank you, Lord," same as Mrs. Anders before and after every meal. Clot nodded, and repeated the blessing, but the old man's face flushed red, and Clot knew he'd made a mistake.

Clot lay awake after Mr. Hollis turned out the light that evening. He didn't know what the word Clot meant. It sounded like the noise made by horse hooves. He wished he had someone to ask. Mr. Hollis wouldn't know. He employed language to direct, to admonish, he hurled words like they were balls for boys to chase after. Nor would Clot find answers with the teachers who cycled through the classroom, each of them more suited to caring for small children, and who countered questions like noisome flies. Clot wouldn't ask any of the other orphans; they would only make a game of exposing his ignorance. He couldn't understand their language most times, anyway. The words they used were plain enough, but he had the sense they carried a double meaning of which he was unaware, a secondary language that all the other boys seemed to understand. Silences followed their speaking, glances, and the boys seemed to know without conferring what each of the others thought. But Clot was never privy to what transferred. He only felt it spool out, reaching everyone else in the room. Clot turned in his bed. He turned and turned. He thought about his loneliness until it made him sick.

The old man in the vest trembled at the word *Lord*. Mrs. Anders' second favourite after *Saved*. The concept confused Clot. The Lord, Mrs. Anders told them, was owed everything. All human effort. Clot wondered at the efforts of animals, if their little lives meant anything to a Lord. That animals didn't have a Lord was obvious. Clot couldn't imagine a Saved badger. What filth did animals live amongst? They lived in the dirt, sure, but Clot knew this wasn't the same as filth. Perhaps that's why humans needed a Lord, because they created so much filth. But humans weren't any better than animals. Most were just as quiet.

Mrs. Anders swore they owed the Lord everything, but each orphan knew exactly what absent parents were due. And what did the Lord do? The Lord forced the Saved onto their Paths; Clot understood this from Mrs. Anders' stories. Torturous paths, choked with the messy, sweaty crowds of unsaved, who clamoured for the secret in your chest. Clot thought of the people packed between the sinks downstairs and decided that the first piece of advice he'd received at Slatterly was in fact the most important. He did not want to be Saved.

Clot waited for the rest of the boys to fall asleep before he snuck from the dormitory. If caught out of bed, the kid knew he'd face punishment through restricted food, Mr. Hollis's humiliations, and periods of solitary study in Mrs. Anders' office. The slick river-stone floors of Slatterly proved unforgiving at speed, but the kid knew how to keep quiet. He slid his bare feet along their dampness until he came to his destination near the heart of the orphanage, the single classroom.

Of all the locks in Slatterly, Clot knew the classroom's best. One day, almost a year before, his school assignment consisted of copying out passages from the *L* encyclopedia, particularly *Lock (types)* and the further *Lock (picking)*. The very same evening, Clot tackled the simple single cylinder of the classroom, and still found it most satisfying to pick. Each popped lock reminded him of that initial rush of awe and power.

Before he entered the classroom, Clot listened for Mr. Hollis. He wasn't sure what the man would do if he caught a boy out of his bunk, or worse, in the classroom, but raw instinct warned that the experience wouldn't be quick, nor kind.

He combed the teacher's desk for stray paperclips first, and bent a couple into tools. He slipped the replacement picks into the waistband of his underwear. He drifted to the back of the classroom and settled in a desk with the *C* encyclopedia.

Clot, he read, *a thick mass of coagulated liquid, especially blood, or of material stuck together.* His eyes glazed as he traced over the rest of the entry. Beyond the idea of healing through stemming, the biology and the vocabulary were incoherent. The kid had no idea why the dishwasher's people would call him a mass of liquid, and sought another meaning. The word, used as verb, came closer to an explanation: *form or cause to form into clots.* At least there, the kid thought, was a maker, an outside force. Is that what the dishwasher's people thought he was? Clot tried to imagine what it meant that he was verb and not a noun, but even these words, the more he thought on them, became jumbled, and eventually he closed the book and returned to his bunk without a clear thought in his head.

For several weeks, the people in the kitchen received his dishes without speaking. Clot meant to inquire after the word each time, but his voice failed whenever he met their eyes. He'd never seen such assortments of people before. After another month, Clot saw the man in his turtle-green vest, and his guts upset because he knew the man would speak again.

Sure enough, the man beamed through the window, then said: "Field's clear, Lord."

Clot dropped the grey tub of dishes and ran back to the dining hall.

The next week, when a woman stepped forward and told Clot her husband's name, he didn't run. He stood his ground while two men sang a song about an open field and a small gate. The following week, Clot stood before eight people who spoke at once. The spectacle of their need paralyzed him, and the dishes slipped again. A man who worked in the kitchen waved his arms to hush them, but their echo carried up the stairs into the dining hall.

When Clot returned to the dining hall, the second tray of dishes was waiting. Mr. Hollis held the third. "What a din my basement makes when you are down there," he growled. "Take me to the show."

Clot hoisted the next tray and set off without a word. He hurried his steps, thinking to get ahead of Mr. Hollis. If he returned to the dish pit quick enough, Mr. Hollis wouldn't hear the greeting over the din of the kitchen. Clot took one step, then two at a time. When Mr. Hollis paused to navigate the damp stairs, Clot scooted forward in a clatter of dishes. He heard a shuffle over his shoulder, the clamour of dishware sliding in alarm. Mr. Hollis's voice rang off wet walls: "Clot, wait!"

Clot sprinted. Hope overtook him. But in his haste, the tip of his shoe clipped an unsettled drainage grate. He fell forward, scattering dishes across the floor. His neck twisted sideways, and his head smacked on the slick cobblestone.

Later, he enjoyed imagining Mr. Hollis standing over his unconscious body while a group of strangers approached, each wailing the same word: *Clot! Clot! Clot!* What a frantic dance must have taken place. The kid woke in the infirmary, drunk on blood thinner. His head lolled from one side of the bed to the other, from Mrs. Anders to Mr. Hollis. *Clot*, the kid explained, was both a verb and a noun. Maker and the made. He evoked the jackrabbits, then, babbling through several experiences while Mrs. Anders paled. Was he Saved? He wondered. Did he save? Too late, Clot saw Mrs. Anders' expression. Her knuckles were white where she gripped the bed frame.

Incensed at such pagan flagrance, Mrs. Anders snapped a single word at Clot. "*Blasphemer*," she said, renouncing the matter.

Clot noticed, but didn't dare mention to her, or to Mr. Hollis, or to the nurses afterwards, the windows of the infirmary. They were left open all night.

In the morning, when Mrs. Anders checked on the disturbed boy, she found three dead squirrels curled amidst his blankets. She paused then, unsure if she should foster wrath at this attack of unsubdued nature, or seize the opportunity to redeem the boy's bewildered soul. She decided to let him make up his own mind.

Rattled at her staff losses in the kitchen, news that the city was scaling back funding to orphanages, and the threat of chaos within her congregation, Mrs. Anders became the kid's most direct agent of fate thus far when she shook him awake and asked him the single question Slatterly had prepared him to answer:

"Do you want to be Saved?"

CHAPTER 6

When the kid left Slatterly, the name Clot was taken back into
the kitchen's conspiracy of whispers, into the consternated
silence of Macy Sullivan in her mist-filled dish pit. But the kid
left with a more precious word tucked into the secret folds of
his mind, one gathered in his nighttime scrounging, a victory
of his stealth and patience.

It was Mrs. Anders who spoke the word, after she knelt
near the end of his infirmary bed long after midnight. The kid
controlled his breath, he kept his eyes closed. Her voice took
on the tone of prayer and the kid's attention wandered, long
before lulled into indifferent silence at the sound, but after she
finished, Mrs. Anders paused, before adding, "Lord, I yearn
for return." She repeated the phrase once more before a twitch
in the kid's leg alerted her to his wakefulness. The fury in her
eyes robbed him of the rest of his sleep. The very next night, the
kid's last in Slatterly, he let himself into the classroom and, after
padding his waistband with stolen paperclips, drew down the
final encyclopedia. Here he came across the word that he would
forever use to describe the feeling in his chest. *Yearn*, he read, *to
feel intense longing for something from which one is separated.*

The kid felt the immediate truth of the word. The definition
articulated what had bothered him about every other word he'd
tried, for not one of them explained the itch at the bottom of it
all, the lingering sensation that found no other description, that
only became clear in its definition: the want for completion.
Something solidified within himself as he peered into the

book, a confirmation of questions yet unasked. He felt a thrill, a widening of the world. A word for what he felt existed before he'd felt it. The thrill became a resolution, a secret uncovered; perhaps, he whispered in his quietest voice, there were other words, other stories, that could tell him more about himself, perhaps, even, their existence could confirm that he was not as unnatural as he felt.

So, he waited for the name of the noise the jackrabbits heard. Often, he wondered what sound the yearn made, what call reached their ears and tugged their hearts. For some time, he imagined they must feel the same, a shiver shared between him and the rabbits, one brought to fruition at the moment of touch. But as he grew older, the kid couldn't imagine crawling toward such confusion. No, he reasoned, it wasn't a feeling, it was a beacon, it was a noise.

He was seven years old when he was transferred to His Holy Rules, a co-ed dormitory for *hard-to-place* children. In his last days at Slatterly, Mrs. Anders called him a *siren*. Screamed the word at the infirmary after coming across a crow called to die on her flagstones. The kid supposed *siren* came close. A great, shrieking sound for all to hear.

In the second week at His Holy Rules, a raccoon crawled into the art room and died under the kid's drafting table. This was not before it pierced the flesh of Mrs. Pound's hand in five spots with its sharp teeth. She tried to shoo the creature back through the open window, but it snapped at her. Mrs. Pound sprang back and rushed to the paint-spattered sinks where the orphans washed their brushes. Before her hand gripped the spigot, she sobbed.

"O Moirai," she exclaimed. "I have rabies!"

None of the children registered Mrs. Pound's declaration, however, because after scrubbing her hand with a wire brush, she put her head under the faucet and gulped water. Mrs. Pound knew rabies caused a visceral aversion to water, leading to death by dehydration, and was trying to hydrate before madness mired her brain. Her students, unaware of this, were struck dumb by her frenetic effort.

The raccoon slunk toward the kid, unperturbed.

Orphans surrounded the kid that evening, demanding answers. Using as few words as possible, he told them about the jackrabbits, but not the yearn in his heart. They arrived, he said, and they died.

Sandy Bixby broke the silence. He'd heard of this before. He was smug in his naming, pausing before continuing. "It's called," he said, "an elephant graveyard."

The word washed over the children and crystallized in the air. The orphans understood that whatever name a kid entered the institution with was a mask that kid wore outside, when they needed to interact with a world filled with registration and tradition. Passage through the orphanage doors stripped each kid of such pomp, and the first task became choosing a name that exposed the kid's grubby core, a marker of evils and quirks upon which other survivalists could depend. Because of this, the orphans attended a kid's immediate weeks with a sensitivity to the connotations of any word. So, it was clear to the children what Sandy Bixby had done.

For the rest of the kid's time at His Holy Rules, the orphans called him Graveyard.

His Holy Rules maintained a small library of donated books and magazines in a room whose hallway provided plenty of warning of approaching minders. The library was therefore in regular use, but no one read the books. One year, some kids had ripped the last pages from every spine in the room, and nothing was replaced. When Graveyard entered and perused titles, onlookers rose. Two of the taller boys flanked him, a lank blond and his shadow, Rotten Smith. They told Graveyard he was too new to be trusted with touching anything.

"Ain't no use in reading books with no endings," the literate one, Smith, muttered.

Graveyard looked at Smith. He leaned towards Smith and Smith flinched. Every boy in the room saw Smith flinch. Most, if they were honest with themselves, would have flinched. Graveyard's touch was already the subject of much speculation.

Sandy Bixby watched with the detached wonder of one coming across a dog fight in an empty lot. Rotten Smith cracked his shoulder, his characteristic overture to a brawl, but Sandy Bixby raised his voice. "You'll not find your answer in any of these," he said. Smith halted, and waited for Sandy Bixby to continue. Graveyard noted this deferral.

"Let him look," Sandy said, and Smith and his lank partner drifted to their seats.

Sandy was right. A contingent of *Popular Science* magazines occupied the bottom two rows of all three shelves, above them a scattershot collection of fairy tales, Westerns, and an arm's length of mystery books with cornflower-blue spines. There was a portrait of two boys on each book, but their features had worn away.

Graveyard's shoulders slumped. He wanted to return to his bunk, but he realized that a show of defeat would feed Sandy Bixby. Before the room, Graveyard asked Sandy Bixby where he'd learned about an elephant graveyard. Bixby milked his moment, and then leaded his voice with indifference.

"Movie Seven," he said.

Several kids nodded. Discussions rose, orphans described jungles of the subcontinent and mountains of bones. Graveyard looked from kid to kid.

Movie Seven ran between Movie Six and Movie Eight. His Holy Rules had weekly movie nights, projected in the cafeteria, but only fourteen movies, stored in cannisters in the cellar. Movie Seven, Bixby said, was set in Africa, from which most things first came.

Graveyard waited three days for movie night; nearly every orphan in His Holy Rules squeezed into the cafeteria with a universal request for Movie Seven.

The movie was easy to follow. A boy, orphaned amidst apes, becomes king of his territory. This was the oldest story in the orphanage, told after a hundred different styles. Ivory hunters lusted for an elephant graveyard, but the orphan boy, now king, refused to guide them. In response, the hunters maimed an elephant and tracked its dying path back to the place of bones. The audacity of the act shocked Graveyard and lingered in his evenings for weeks afterward. He lay awake, afraid to feel the yearn.

The images of the boneyards banished his immediate fear, however. The ancientness of the piled spines, ribs, tusks, and limbs of proud bulls and hardy cows, their cycloptic skulls peering down from the painted frieze of the background, whispered to Graveyard. He felt a thrill at the truth they suggested: he was not alone. Generations of elephants had heard what the jackrabbits heard. To the kid, this leant a lineage. Thinking along the line of people who stretched back to deepest Africa, a warmth spread inside Graveyard, a satisfaction that equalled, to this point in his life, any human touch. He was, he realized, natural.

Bixby might be right about something else, Graveyard decided: the call came not from his heart, but from his bones.

Afterwards, the orphans watched Graveyard closely, but there was a vulnerability to his manner, his immediate silence and faraway gaze, which caused them to file out without bothering him. Graveyard sat alone for a lone while after, avoiding, in the last, the crooked glance of Sandy Bixby.

The orphans stayed distant, but this only increased Graveyard's anxiety. He was aware they awaited his word. Wounded jackrabbits, tailed to the orphanage by figures stark against the horizon, tormented his dreams. Graveyard screamed at night, but the sound went unmentioned by the rest of his dormitory.

After three days silence, Graveyard knew he needed to speak. There was no escape. The orphans expected him to confirm or deny Sandy Bixby's theory, but the longer Graveyard thought on it, the more precarious his answer appeared. Sandy was a burgeoning power, confirming his opinion was obviously beneficial. However, every kid could name at least one hole in Sandy's story. Namely, a person cannot be a place. To remedy this concern, Graveyard had an image to suggest to the orphans, one that had been with him since the boneyard of Movie Seven. He pictured her some nights, a woman who made her house of elephant bones; on other nights, he thought of a man. He visualized a family when he was happy or filled with hate. These imaginary people, born with Graveyard's yearn in their bones, were what the elephants sought. Graveyard had no name for them but *Ancestors*.

He worked at the image during his evenings, when he lay awake listening for the approach of others. He imagined sleeping in a house of bone, but could not picture waking in a room alone. The morning times comprised battles for space and food, along benches placed next to tables. He didn't even know that those who ate in homes sat at their own chairs. Many of Graveyard's imaginings were foiled in this way. He could imagine a hug only in an empty room and only for a moment before the noise and smell, and finally the elbows and knees, of other orphans overran such intimacies. The longer he lingered with aunts and grandmothers, uncles and cousins, the larger the horde grew, rattling walls, filling doorframes, blackening windows with their passing. He woke in an empty room, and before he was dressed, they were stepping on sheets that they'd scattered to the floor. After a week, Graveyard gave up; he couldn't picture a home that wasn't a variation of the institutions he knew. He couldn't even guess what a family felt like. He turned that thought over in his mind, over and over: he didn't know how to make home nor family.

When Graveyard described his ancestors to the orphans in the food hall, he knew Sandy Bixby was in earshot. "Imagine a home of bone," he began, using words rehearsed night after night. "Ribs for rafters and vertebrae at each joint." Supressed smiles, knowing nods, fumbled his explanation. Worried that the others had already detected his faulty architecture, he rushed his portraits of the family, and arrived at his conclusion too early. "The movie proves I'm no freak," he said. "Others like me have existed. If we listen to Bixby, then Movie Seven means I'm *natural*."

The room winced. A couple orphans whispered, a couple laughed. Sandy Bixby rose from his chair, quieting the room. His face was pink with fury.

"No," he snapped. "You are not."

Graveyard paled. He met Bixby's gaze, though he felt his insides turn to liquid. "Then the movie wasn't enough," Graveyard said to a room as quiet as a gasp. "I need a book."

CHAPTER 7

On a warm afternoon in June, Graveyard felt a shudder in his clavicle. His stomach sank. His Holy Rules occupied a converted malaria asylum on the edge of the southern river valley. Thickets of dogwood and untamed grasses encroached on the field behind the building. Graveyard knew it was only time before a dying animal emerged.

A jackrabbit, brown in its summer fur, stumbled from the distant grass line.

Dozens of orphans played in the field. They saw the hare as well. One by one, they looked to Graveyard.

Graveyard strode across the field. He clenched his jaw, his limbs moved, but he had not made these decisions. He watched himself reach out and stroke the creature. He watched the jackrabbit crumple, dead at his touch.

That evening, Slap Eddy, Hardnose, and Hives sat near Graveyard in the food hall. They didn't speak once. Later, after they'd cornered him in the bathroom, Hardnose laced his voice with disdain.

"Bet you've got to touch them, too, right?"

Eddy and Hives fell on Graveyard, but he knew to tuck his elbows against his ribs and curl. He had the patience to wait until the boys exhausted themselves.

When Graveyard came back to the dormitories with a limp, Sandy Bixby laughed. "Naturally," he said. When this wasn't acknowledged, Sandy searched the bunks around him, his gaze unmet.

Over the week, these small violences repeated. In the field, a rough girl named Alice Always doused him with juice she'd saved since breakfast. He dried sticky in the sun while Alice's gaggle snickered. That same day a boy named Snitch ate Graveyard's lunch piece by piece, sitting across from him. The whole table watched.

Graveyard grew suspicious of empty rooms and corners he could not see around. One afternoon, every boy, at one time or another, handed him a slip of paper marked with a cross and a semi-circle as an afterthought. Graveyard didn't know what it meant, but flipped over each paper and copied the boy's marks exactly, before returning it. When Sandy Bixby gave him a note inscribed with a simple question mark, Graveyard crumpled the paper in Bixby's face. He was sure they would have had it out then, but for the righteous hand of the English teacher, Mme. Estelle.

In the secret places of His Holy Rules, the dim nooks, unfrequented bathrooms, and lone hallways blocked by livid kids, the orphans found Graveyard and pummelled him. For nine days and nights. On the tenth morning, down a janitorial corridor, three girls and four boys had him on the ground with their kicking, when, at a natural pause in the violence, Graveyard raised his hand to ward off the next blow.

No kick came.

Graveyard opened his eyes to a boy named Slimes staring at his palm as one would an agitated snake. Slimes twitched as Graveyard stood. "*Watch watch watch watch watch*," whispered a boy over Graveyard's shoulder, his eyes, too, intent on that hand. Graveyard swung around and pointed at the kid who spoke. The boy glared with hateful spite, but refused to advance. Graveyard turned again. One of the girls dared a step. "I don't think he does," said the girl, but she couldn't goad herself into a second step. "There's nothing in his touch that kills," she sneered. Graveyard shuffled towards Slimes, and the boy broke the circle. Cautiously, Graveyard slid between the kids, then bolted down the yawning corridor.

Slimes's hesitation kept Graveyard safe for over a month. When cornered, Graveyard had only to hold his hand in the same erect posture and fix a glare. Children hurled insults, the cruder spat, but none breached the fear raised by Graveyard's body. After another month, the children settled into a begrudged stalemate, and focused their attentions on weaker arrivals.

Only Sandy Bixby was unwilling to let Graveyard settle. Graveyard's insistence on being natural was the second flouting of Sandy's authority. After a rash of older boys were sent to juvenile detention for racketeering, a power vacuum developed in His Holy Rules, and Sandy Bixby's brutes established him as one of the most feared kids in the orphanage. Day and night, Sandy Bixby plagued Graveyard with the sound a black bear made while it died only blocks away.

Huff huff huff, broke the silence. *Huff huff huff.*

CHAPTER 8

When Mr. Sze, a small man with the shoulders of a soldier, took over as director of His Holy Rules, he instituted arts programs, enforced hikes into the nearby river valley, and scheduled field trips to the local museum. With city support flagging, and gutting staff losses, the children and their minders tolerated these changes, well aware of how long idealism endured. The cultural programs soon fell to disinterest, the studio space was reclaimed by the janitorial staff, and the hikes were cancelled after a conspiracy of children used the chance to escape into the valley. Only the museum visits remained. The staff rotated through chaperone duty, while the rest enjoyed a few hours of solace.

During a visit to the Jacobian building of stacked brick that sat at the centre of the city, Graveyard lingered before a diorama of Blackfoot life. A man sat cross-legged in a natural corridor of the land. He wore a blanket over his shoulders and watched the horizon. He was called the buffalo singer, but the figure was passive, his mouth was closed. He waited in the open while the others hid. A tumult was painted on the wall, at the bow of the horizon — a thousand buffalo already mid-run, having heard the serene singer. The others hid. Only the buffalo singer waited in the open. This much Graveyard understood from the plaque on the wall. He wanted to ask questions, but the guide had moved past the exhibit without mentioning it, and all the other orphans had passed into the next gallery. Graveyard watched the man's face for a long time.

Unexpectedly, Sandy Bixby stood next to him. "Shut your trap, Graveyard," Bixby growled, "Don't make a sound." Graveyard checked the room. A reedy boy named Arch and the broadfaced kid called Guppy dawdled behind as well. Moreover, in the corner of the gallery, seeming a captive himself, was meagre Adam, a rat squealer of the widest renown. Adam's presence confused Graveyard. Neither Arch nor Guppy menaced him off, which meant he'd been invited to watch what Sandy Bixby planned.

Bixby pushed Graveyard toward the exit. "Across the park is every book you need," he snarled.

Graveyard's head buzzed as he followed the small group from the museum. A library of manorial sandstone occupied the far end of a garden dedicated to the war dead. The disc of the sun shone in each of its tall windows, obscuring the figures who moved about inside. Sandy Bixby held Graveyard's arm. Arch and Guppy were behind them, and reluctant Adam. Graveyard tried to read the quiet boy's eyes, but Adam didn't once look up from the ground.

Once they were inside, Sandy assured them of plenty of time. No one in their right mind, he said, could imagine that orphans would escape a museum just to run to a library. Graveyard found an encyclopedia, a folklore dictionary, and a picture book about the myths of Africa. He thought they would serve. Bixby's contention was Graveyard's belief in his own ancestors, in a line that proved he was natural.

Graveyard's visions of the family who lived amidst elephant bones had worn over the weeks. The imaginings, soon overfilled with other orphans, became onerous to maintain, wounding even, as night after night Graveyard could only sleep after blaming himself for his impotence in conjuring home or family. He could not even conceive of being tucked in, nor a weight at the end of the bed, until other boys, who'd had homes, discussed them in the bunks. The immensity of what he did not know dwarfed him, and eventually he abandoned the effort of imagining home.

He was exhausted, as well, by the petty violences inflicted over the past weeks. There wasn't a single orphan who offered comfort; all of them had suspect hands, springing up like surprised birds. He'd lower his head and receive a smack. He'd enter a room whose conversation turned cold. He knew it was a collective effort to break him down, spurred by his foolish declaration in the food hall. He wondered, some nights, how many of the orphans were aware of their actions, and how many imagined their words were simply thoughts come independently to mind. Other nights, he didn't know if it mattered. What he endured, Graveyard felt sure, was the fate of any indifferent to the herd.

Graveyard rested his eyes on the book in his lap in the library, but watched the boys over its top. He knew why Bixby brought Adam. Within hours, every boy, girl, and staff member at His Holy Rules would know what happened in the library. Graveyard saw what was expected.

Bixby caught him looking. Graveyard's eyes darted back to the book. Their careful histories revealed little more than what he had seen in Movie Seven. It was plain to him, then. Language was not meant to describe what was wrong with his heart.

Sandy made a show of rubbing his eyes and checking his bare wrist. "Well?" he said.

Graveyard closed the folklore dictionary and stared at the lights that hung from the ceiling. He knew it was important to portray regret, but he didn't expect the bitterness that laced his voice.

"I am unnatural," he said.

CHAPTER 9

After Graveyard's admission, the boys and the girls of His Holy Rules thrilled when a jackrabbit emerged from the river valley. The excitement of the orphans made Mr. Sze, the director, happy. Once, a boy named Peg grabbed for a beaver by its tail, but larger boys halted him. After weeks, this was the biggest ripple on the pond. Mr. Sze felt certain that His Holy Rules was the right place for the kid known as Graveyard, and he was glad the children of His Holy Rules had chosen to display independent rationality.

Small betting rings arose as the wonder wore off. Children marked distances from the tall grass of the river valley, quadrisected the open areas behind His Holy Rules, and charted with far more precision than in math class. Orphans pressed against windows in the mornings, hoping for a marred field. Winnings doubled if an animal reached Graveyard. Sandy Bixby made the outrageous claim that should Graveyard actually *heal* one, he'd bankroll double winnings.

Children became speculators, eyeing local animals with a scrutiny unsettling to staff members. "There's mange," one kid said to another as they stared into the bushes, or, "Worms like that'll hold for another week, wait 'til Thursday to put down your name." Side bets, hinging on type of death, became lucrative. A myth arose that girls had a natural talent for discerning health by eye, and soon they cornered the market on disease speculation, hiring out contractors to the scrupulous charting of the boys.

Mr. Sze watched the sober way the children gathered to watch the hares emerge, and congratulated himself for the consistency he'd bred.

Graveyard's days as a curiosity waned when a group of girls splintered from the speculative market. After proving accurate on several occasions, the group, led by Alice Always, changed its diagnosis. Alice Always claimed the animals were *healthy*. Not all of them, some were inarguably damaged, but once in a while Alice Always stated that there was nothing wrong with the hare who died. The question took root: *What if the jackrabbits were healthy?* Every kid knew what happened to the rabbits Graveyard touched.

After Alice Always's pronouncement, the staff noticed a relief in the orphans at a dead jackrabbit in the field. Dead, presumably, of its own affliction, rather than theirs. The day a skunk ambled out of the river valley while they were outside, everyone froze. Graveyard loitered near the grass, though far from where the skunk had appeared. His eyes widened, but he didn't move. Every kid stared at him. In the cold afternoon light, he saw how many believed Alice's rumour. When the skunk died, midway, relief flooded Graveyard, and he held his hands over his face.

The idea that Graveyard might kill with a touch prevented the kids from pummelling him, but hostility grew nightly. The betting dried up when the orphans unified over the *wrongness* of Graveyard. This alleviated their guilt and shame at wagering on the deaths of murdered animals. At first, Graveyard received a smack here and there, the orphans operating under the theory that he couldn't harm them if he didn't see them coming. There weren't nearly enough staff members to prevent violence. A large group of boys beat him one evening, and later claimed that his poison wasn't as potent diluted by so many, though most admitted headaches. The secret to dealing with Graveyard, His Holy Rules learned, was to round up a big enough gang.

Girls and boys spoke openly of their plans to corner Graveyard in the locker rooms, or the alcove in the food hall, and bragged about others already enlisted. They made no effort at concealment. Graveyard became, to the orphans, monstrous, as mutely inscrutable as the outside world. He knew the orphans meant to stamp him out.

On a late afternoon in the depths of August, Mr. Sze watched the children in the field behind His Holy Rules. Reports of abuse appeared consistent with the evidence on Graveyard's torso, although the boy would not confirm the staff's suspicions. Mr. Sze, unhappy with the inconsistency, stood at the window of his office. He couldn't spot a single supervisor. It was months since His Holy Rules had adequate staff, a situation that plagued every orphanage. The city had no industry, and was dying of the dust clouds that roamed the farmlands. The inestimable Council would one day, he knew, declare orphans an unnecessary expense and force him to turn his charges over to the compassion of the streets. By then, the orphans, Mr. Sze suspected, would notice little difference.

He pushed the speculation from his mind and tracked the field below. The children gathered in indistinct groups, their busyness a surface distraction. It was obvious from where he stood. When Graveyard began to walk towards the river valley, the others perked to attention. Those kneeling, stood.

A jackrabbit picked its way out of the long grass in the southwest corner.

Graveyard sensed the attention, Mr. Sze felt sure of it. The boy walked stiffly, consciously checking his flanks. A girl shouted a drawn-out word, but Graveyard didn't turn. Boys called out names. Graveyard advanced towards the hare.

Both girls and boys tried to prevent the injured hare from reaching its death at Graveyard's hands, but the animal pressed on. It crouched when the children closed, then sprang between their hands and knees. Mr. Sze watched the scene, wishing more whimsy into the children, wishing away the awful concentration on their faces. More and more orphans gathered in the jackrabbit's path. Mr. Sze's gaze darted to Graveyard at the other end of the field. He was enclosed in a tightening circle of children. Graveyard held out his arms, his palms pointing first at one kid, then another.

One of the older children led the movement. Mr. Sze heard their voices rise. He saw the expressions on their faces.

Graveyard's head snapped back, his knees bowed. Mr. Sze stared, dumb with shock. He hadn't even seen Alice Always's arm move.

As the circle collapsed on the boy named Graveyard, Mr. Sze ran.

CHAPTER 10

Graveyard kept his eyes closed for three days. The first evening he woke with a gasp, alone in the infirmary. The monitoring nurse was in an enclave across the hall, pouring a cup of peach tea, when she heard the sound. She suffered a strained ankle and a scorched thumb, but made the sprint in admirable time. Graveyard lay undisturbed, his eyes closed.

The nurse did not leave his side for more than a few minutes the rest of the evening. She explained the gasp to several people in the morning, and a bustle developed around Graveyard. He fought the flinch as they prodded up his legs and took stock of his fingertips. The doctor's voice dropped as she stepped away from the hospital bed.

"Coma," she proclaimed. "Unchanged."

He ached for a whole day. Pain welled in his shoulders and hips. His spine longed to curl forward, yet he kept still whenever he sensed another in the room. When left alone, Graveyard cried from the effort.

By the end of the third night, he could pace the infirmary fifteen times before collapsing. He deemed this strength enough. The next time the nurse limped out the room, Graveyard changed into the clothing he'd worn when the children battered him. Thin denim trousers, dark canvas shoes, and a long- and a short-sleeved cotton shirt. He stole a woollen coat from the nurse's cabinet. He ventured no further into His Holy Rules, caring nothing for what he owned. His final possession was the name Sandy Bixby had given him; but this, too, slipped away soon enough. The nurse who leaned out the window and shouted into the fields after him used a completely different word.

The nurse shouted several words out the window, but the kid wasn't attached to any of them. Names were merely the habit of a place, he realized, nothing more. A faint warning arose in his mind as he crossed the field, a familiar one, buried away as often as he could. If he left the orphanage, his birth parents would never find him. The thought was hateful to the kid, and he tried to strike it from his mind. There was no one coming. His parents were not looking for him. He was a mistake, and he would never know whose.

The kid waited, but the nurse only called for so long.

A tremendous shelf of storm clouds gathered above the valley behind the orphanage. The kid surveyed the land as the crescent of the moon slipped behind a thunderhead. Originating from a mountain in the west, the river entered the valley from the prairies, through the glades and wildflowers and tall grasses of decaying ranch land, before wending amidst deciduous forests interspersed with pine and spruce and larch, running alongside the long low plane of dogwoods that encroached on His Holy Rules. The kid sighed. The West was a mistake; he would become lost in the open stretches and decayed settlements, easy enough for any searcher to find.

He turned in the other direction. The moonlight shone last on the east, lingering on the broad brick sides of the Meriwether Fertilizer factories. From where he stood, the kid could read the famous boast that outdated the streets: *From dinosaurs to yesterday's nag: everything from the ground up ground up!*

The Meriwether patriarchs had anchored their factory in the eastern valley and mined the local hills for fossils, founding their business on the backs of the first creatures that fought for life. The factories made up a walled complex on the far bank of the river. Across from this, on a wide island tethered to the kid's side by unofficial bridges, a network of dim roads tied clusters of wood shanties, brick tenements, and corrugated-iron warehouses into the attempted town of Farrow. The pronunciation of the word remained the same across ages, but despoiled the intent of its coiner. Eldritch Meriwether, who had only ever heard his scripture spoken, insisted this was the proper spelling of the word Pharaoh. Despite Eldritch's wide local influence, the town was denied incorporation by the burgeoning city, which by then encroached a mere five miles away, and since, Farrow languished. Decay ate at all sides.

Rumours of the rowdiness of Farrow had penetrated every level of orphan gossip at His Holy Rules. Though the city had closed in the valley, Farrow was resistant to its regulatory moods, and retained its feral independence, considered as nothing more than an overgrown workcamp. The wildnesses required to survive the collapse and depression that ate at the city thrived in Farrow, and its quarters arranged themselves along lines of vice and need, slaughterhouses butting against speakeasies, brothels and betting rings foregoing the delicacies of façade and establishing themselves street level, proudly, declaring their freedoms with a frontier impunity. Tales of kidnappers and murderers, desolate gamblers, canny thieves, grand larcenies, and sweeping, ghastly fires emerged from Farrow and peppered the imaginations of every orphan who stood in the bright of day and stared upon its many darknesses. It was known that specific alley lanes wound underground, below the river, the tunnels of bootleggers and fugitives; the kid had seen maps. He knew the coiling passages by heart. Everyone said these were the best places to hide.

A light rain revived the kid. A thrill of wakefulness. The dry roar of excitement lit his heart. He slipped into the river valley.

CHAPTER 11

The kid woke to a flurry of knife blades, a hiss of hurried voices, strained and low. Hands grasped and spread his limbs. He was surrounded by the sound of boys. Unable to flee.

He sat up in a cluster of low birch. While the dream dissipated, he looked around for his path from the day before, but the grasses had long swept it away. The grass taller than he at points, the kid followed the undulating ridge, an ancient riverbank overgrown by birch. After two nights, he had no idea of how far he'd come from His Holy Rules, but he wouldn't climb to orient. Visions plagued him of cresting the ridge and finding himself only yards away, like a tunnelling prisoner in a paled comic strip.

The tension in his throat faded as the kid worked his way out of the birch and followed the descent of the land into dense clusters of pine on the valley floor. Thick branches scraped his face and drowned him in a scent of sap. He kept his eyes closed. He didn't need them open.

He pushed into a thicket of wolf willow surrounded by the pine. Small for his age, the kid knelt where others crawled. He followed the natural colonnade formed by the low canopy of silver leaves for some time, and then broke into the undergrowth that ran next to a creek. There, in a sunlit clearing, he found the young hare.

"Oh no," he said. "No no no."

Knives had been used on her. The kid was sure of that. Whoever caught the hare had used knives. Her ear hung, cut halfway. Stab wounds peppered her flank. She mewled when he knelt, the first time he had heard that noise.

"I'm sorry," he said.

His heart thundered with the yearn, but it was coupled with something else. Something he hadn't felt since the field of Slatterly. A rot. Seething with a sudden shame, the kid placed his hands on the jackrabbit, and she quivered and mewled again. White spots crowded his vision. The hare was a patternwork of its torture.

Exploring its skin, the kid felt each wound in turn. He leaned forward. He whispered. "I'm sorry," he said.

A gaunt boy kicked through the bushes at the edge of the clearing. The sudden clatter alarmed the kid, but he didn't flee. He couldn't bring himself to take his hand off the shivering animal. He cursed the chill morning breeze.

The gaunt boy, involved with freeing his foot from a creeping vine, did not lay eyes on the kid immediately. His face was plain, a smatter of pale blue freckles ran across his cheeks. His eyes were dark, however. He stamped his foot, seeking to sever the vine rather than shake it free, until the plant was finally overcome.

He stiffened when he saw the kid. His eyes went to the jackrabbit, then back to the kid bent low over it. The gaunt boy reached one of his red-stained hands behind his back and brought forth a curved knife that looked stolen from a kitchen. It was stained like the boy's hand. He waved it through the air, as though brushing aside flies.

"You leave my rabbit alone," he said, "or I'll cut your face."

The kid, who had raised his head to meet the gaunt boy's dim eyes, didn't move. He cupped his hands over the jackrabbit's shoulders and brought his forearms against each of her flanks. Still, she shivered.

The gaunt boy held the knife for a moment longer, but tired of it, and slid it away. "That's my rabbit you've got there," he said. "Can't you see my mark? Only you didn't know, maybe.

That there's a G. Stands for Greaves. There. Now you know. Now take your damn hands off my rabbit."

A fire welled in the kid. He glared at Greaves's hands. "You've done enough to her," he spat. But he didn't move. Terror shot through him, his heart and head pounded, but he staved off the encroaching dizziness by focusing on the shame he felt at Slatterly, on his resolution of refusing touch.

Greaves knelt, close enough that the kid felt the warmth of his agitated energy. He stared at the jackrabbit huddled under the kid's hands.

"What you doing to it?" he said in a quickened voice. "You think I'm scared of you? My mom's boyfriend killed my dad dead on her front lawn, and I wasn't once scared of him. And he knew it. I even said to him, Greg, you killed my dad. I wasn't scared. He knew. You think I'm scared of you?"

Greaves sprang to his feet, away from the gush of his voice. The kid leaned forward. The hare stopped shivering. She leaned into his touch and pressed her head against his hand.

"What do you have to hurt them for?" said the kid.

The knife appeared again. This time, Greaves held it like it were a snake trying to strike his wrist. He waved it again, but again he seemed unconvinced. The knife dropped to his side. Greaves arched his head on his neck and closed his eyes when he looked at the sky. He inhaled deeply, and then sniffed the air. "What is it, kid?" he said. "You got a scent about you?"

But the kid didn't listen. He felt the flutter between his hands, the jackrabbit leaned heavy and quivered, but its eyes stayed closed, and the kid wondered if it had moved beyond feeling.

A few feet away, Greaves knelt. "You better not let that thing die," he said.

The kid met Greaves's gaze. The hare was still. She was already colder. "You did this," he said.

Greaves smiled then. He seemed to better understand the kid's rage. "I promised I'd cut your face," he said.

A clatter of branches and bramble emerged from the woods behind Greaves. Boys' voices, raised in excitement, accompanied the noise. The kicking and thrashing done mostly for fun. A plant wrenched from its roots peppered leaves with clods of dirt. Greaves turned, surprised, yet with a smile. "Here," he shouted.

The kid flung himself backward as Greaves turned. Before the boy could swing his knife, the kid, short enough to scramble where others crawled, slipped into the underbrush and struggled beneath cover, wriggling, as the voices of the boys filled the clearing, into the low coverage of the wolf willow colonnades.

Three more boys came into view. The kid caught glimpses as they trailed in. The skin on their arms was weathered into tan but for the thin white scars from knife fighting. The one in front had a piddling chin and looked like an alert snake. Two stocky boys, dim and dimmer, followed the snake-face. Jackrabbit blood spattered their arms and chests.

The kid sank further into the wolf willow until he could just make out the hare. He shook uncontrollably.

The snake-face pushed into the clearing and laughed. "Told you we didn't lose it," he said to the others over his shoulder. "Greaves was born half a bloodhound."

The news excited dim and dimmer, and they crowded the clearing. Each proved able to draw a knife without elbowing another. Greaves stood aside while they knelt over the jackrabbit and stabbed downwards, three times. The snake-faced boy, who the others called Simon Sanderson, sidled over to Greaves and whispered something before snorting a laugh. The dimmer boy's head snapped up, and he glared at Simon Sanderson, but didn't dare speak. He returned to his work, his eyes darker than before.

The kid crawled deeper as laughter tippled from the glen. The sight left him numb. He drew his legs into his chest and curled around his knees.

Greaves knelt over the jackrabbit after the others had left it alone. He worked for some time. The other boys watched him, but from a distance, and over their shoulders, none daring anything longer than a glance. Except for Simon Sanderson, who watched openly, and displayed no surprise at what he saw. Greaves took first the intestines, the stomach, the lungs, and other organs, and strung them over the bushes around the hare like garlands. He knelt again, and worked again at the jackrabbit, but the kid couldn't see what so occupied his attention.

Later, the boys argued about building a fire.

The kid lay on his back, staring up through the silver leaves. He strained to hear the wind that moved them, but only heard the voices in the clearing. The laughter.

Motion took up in his peripheral, a quick flicker of knees and shins, of fluid ankles dancing. A slight boy came down a riverside trail with a lightness he wouldn't dare if he knew others watched. The path he was on led directly into the clearing.

The kid swept through the wolf willow as fast as stealth allowed.

He stepped onto the path with a finger held before his lips. The slight boy stopped short, about to yell, but his eyes fixed on the kid's finger. He wavered. The kid lowered his hand, ducked, then crawled under the pine and into the wolf willow. A moment later, the slight boy crashed in behind him.

"What the hell, buddy?" the slight boy whispered. Up close, he looked as old as the kid. His eyes darted from the colonnades to the blood on the kid's hands. Fear shot across his face, and he fell backwards. "What the *hell*?"

The kid couldn't speak. He opened his mouth twice, dredged for a voice. He crawled further into the wolf willow and motioned the slight boy to follow.

The boy paled when he saw the others in the clearing. *Sanderson*, he burbled with a frothy rage, and followed this with a steady stream of whispered curses. He never looked away from the industriousness, the cheer, in the clearing.

After a long while the slight boy turned to the kid and looked him up and down. He asked a question, but the kid didn't respond. He went back to watching the clearing.

"Best you head home, buddy," he said. "This world's done for."

CHAPTER 12

When the slight boy introduced himself as Sod, the kid couldn't think of a name to offer in return. None of those in his past felt right. He shrugged and shook his head.

Sod studied him. "You worried about some constable catching you up?" he said. "Some city worker with your name on a piece of paper? Don't. I've heard stories of things like that, church workers and such, candy and shelter on offer, but word is they get lost amidst the trees. Used to be people who'd snatch up kids for dollars, but orphanages ain't shelling out since the city stopped paying per orphan. Kids been living down here years and no one cared. No one misses kids that aren't their own. Trust me, buddy, you can have any name you want down here."

Still, the kid found silence the most comforting answer.

Sod led through the woods, marching out of sight at times, yet always returning to talk the kid though the intricacies of root systems, the snares of blackberries, or the shuffle-slide of moss-strewn rock faces. They came to an overgrown gully that wound inland and split like a stream, its outside track following alongside a hill that at times became a shelf overtop them. Here the air cooled, the light dimmed, and the wood became more of a tangle. Finally, after a disorienting crawl up a tunnel of naturally bent tree trunks, they emerged into a clearing at the base of the heavily wooded hill. Just visible were the decayed remains of a bricked structure, an abandoned utility station, and a huge culvert, taller by twice than the tallest kid, that disappeared into the hill like a throat. All was overgrown but what had been cleared by the children who camped in the ruins at the lip of the culvert. A large oven, built of river stones and appropriated brick, was incomplete but serviceable. The smell of carrot soup reminded the kid of the days since he'd eaten. Two boys and two girls emerged from around the camp and collected at the mouth of the culvert to listen to Sod.

Sod gave a breathless account of the boys with the knives, then pointed to the kid. "This is Chatter," he said. "Seeing how he never shuts up."

Though everyone was around, Sod spoke mostly to a boy named Briny. Briny's long thin neck and watchful eyes reminded the others of the deer that lived in the valley, the deer in particular who stood astride of the others, who would crest the hill first and be first to alert the others of danger. When he readjusted his weight, or prepared to voice a thought, the rest of the group altered its attention. He accepted this with a patience that marked him as the final word, and as a result, he kept still while he talked and thought. His sandy hair was grown past his shoulders; handfuls were tied back, but with no conviction. He asked Sod to repeat the part about the boys with the knives. Afterwards, he paced back and forth. "Shit," he said, "Goddammit."

The slender girl named Azalea knelt next to Chatter. She was tall for her age, taller, almost, than Briny, and either of them might have been the oldest; each could have been thirteen. Chatter, just nine, couldn't imagine how they'd survived so long. Azalea's voice, though calm, gave the impression of the first burst of water through the cracked flank of a dam. The rest of the kids didn't carry her frantic energy, but they listened intently for the answers to her questions.

She put her hand on Chatter's arm. She smiled, and, though it was an afterthought, Chatter blushed. Her skin was darker than he'd ever seen. His arm grew warm under her hand.

"Listen, Chatter," she said. "Tell us the truth. How long've you known those boys? You know where they sleep?"

Chatter, taken aback by her second question, shook his head. He was a while in dredging his voice, but when it came, he told of his escape from the orphanage and his hungry days wandering. He described the pitiful hare in the clearing, the boys with the knives, and the delight taken on the hare's discarded body. He did not admit his conversation with Greaves. He did not tell them about the sound his heart made.

Briny was motionless while he listened. "Holy shit," he said, and resumed pacing.

Azalea watched him, trying to set her expression. Briny's restlessness agitated the rest. Azalea picked up a bit of crumbled brick and hurled it into the forest. "There isn't nothing we can do about knives," she said.

"Don't tell him that," the brunt boy named Dirty shouted, pointing at Chatter. "For all you know, he's more them than us."

Briny walked between Dirty and Azalea. Dirty was a meaty boy, hardened by meannesses he couldn't predict. He didn't shy from Briny's height or Azalea's force. "We don't know," Dirty said, and with a gesture of his hand included the silent others. "We can't."

Fern, the pale girl with deep eyes and strawberry-blond hair, who stood nearest the ovens, made no movement at all. Though she deferred her attention to Briny, it was clear that Azalea was her point of focus. "There's nothing we can do about knives, Dirty," she said.

Briny knelt before Chatter. He searched the kid's face, the blemishes and scratches that made up the orphans' parting gifts. He offered no apology for his scrutiny. He was as still as the earth. His hands seemed huge to Chatter, capable of terrible strength. "Well, kid," he said, "What do you say? You more them, or you more us?"

CHAPTER 13

From his first morning at the culvert until his last, Chatter
was sent out to forage with Sod. Dirty went out with them
initially, shaking each boy awake with his rough grasp, but after
a couple weeks, Briny decided Dirty was needed for thieving,
and Chatter and Sod were allowed to awaken under their own
will. Sod, having spent every day he'd been in the gang with
Dirty, grew bold after this, awash in the freedom of the hills,
and sometimes the boys spent entire afternoons swimming in
ponds or daring one another deeper into the darkest parts of
the woods. "Dirty's fine," Sod would say at such times, his head
rocking in his hands, "he's just seen cruelty in too many ways."

After a couple months, after mornings and evenings
became routine, Chatter and Sod developed a coded language
that allowed them to converse all night, exchanging no more
than passing observances of nature, a darkening tree, the
fragrant moss, while maintaining their idle gossip. For another
month they believed themselves inscrutable; then, over dinner,
Fern giggled and spit soup over her stolen bread after Chatter
mentioned a settled fog. Fern never told the others of what
she'd discovered, nor took part in the exchanges, and never
again laughed, but always hung her head to smile. It was Fern
who made allowances for their afternoons dallied, concocting
a range of dishes around the potatoes that could reliably be
got from the beds Sod tended on a distant hill; Fern, who gave
Chatter grateful portions each day he played tether, naming

their responsibilities to Sod when he saw fit to waste whole days at the pond or wandered to Farrow and plotted burglaries.

When Sod spoke of Fern, his voice softened. He returned, time and again, to that day in early life when he returned home from selling papers and found his family gone, their rented rooms emptied. The neighbours claimed eviction, but could not say where they'd gone. No messages were left for Sod. He hung around the tenements for a couple days, but the neighbours grew cold, and he was turned away from their doorsteps until his pride could take no more. He slept in the valley after that, in the trees, until Azalea brought him to camp. "Fern," he said, "was the first who was kind to me. Kind without needing to be. And that just after I learned the old earth has no rule of kindness. Fern's soup was as warm as she, and that particular coal ain't ever faded."

Azalea was the only one who visited during the days, finding Chatter and Sod no matter how off course they strayed. She, too, ignored their delinquencies, instead striding to the highest point of the land, where she would stretch her legs and banter with Sod. Sod revelled in these moments, giving way to his sudden bouts of viciousness, his stream-of-consciousness ramblings that began with day-to-day gripes and climbed to atrocious heights of outrage, his compact frame bristling to curse the universe. And Azalea laughed every time, Sod's ferociousness overflowing, her surprised burble growing into guffaws. Even without Azalea, Chatter found the first belly laughs of his life in the face of Sod's rages, learning the charm of losing himself to the communal joke. Sod, who enjoyed Chatter's breathlessness, often wouldn't quit until the two were exhausted, neither able to stand for minutes after.

Azalea's wariness encouraged Chatter and Sod to sleep back-to-back in the maintenance sub chamber where the gang bedded down. They rotated nights; one watched the door while the other watched the rest — Briny and Dirty, and Azalea and Fern, who slept back-to-back in the same manner. Once in a while, Azalea slipped out of the tunnel in the dead of night, but only after whispering to Fern, and after a long time relinquishing her embrace. The first time Chatter woke and watched her leave, he felt Sod's head rise. "She'll come back," he said. "She does every time."

Sod and Chatter regularly passed the clearing where the boys with knives eviscerated the hare. They practised caution, making use of Briny's slipshods—a network of tunnel-like enclosures camouflaged amidst the underbrush—and the wolf willow colonnades discovered by Chatter. Briny was impressed at Chatter's discovery, and bragged about it for Chatter afterwards. Chatter smiled warmly whenever this was brought up, but he never had anything to add.

Near the end of August, Sod told Chatter they could avoid the clearing if they wanted. The grove of crab apple trees they frequented would soon be overripe, the apples good for nothing more than splatter-bombs. Chatter had suspected this for a week. The crab apples looked like a harvest of shrunken heads. They could shift their attention inwards, to the berries and onions further in the gully, or the potatoes and rhubarb that grew near the clearing. "You decide," Sod told Chatter in his goading voice. "You tell me if you're frightened of that clearing."

Chatter smiled at Sod's ferocity.

They stayed close to the culvert over the summer, sheltering from the gangs that riddled the valley, sprawling groups of kids who'd long claimed swaths. The prominent gangs—the Callaghan, the Grotto Nine, and Silver Wrists—scavenged through the woods and ruins and fought on sight, amidst countless other bands of savvy and violent kids. Chatter and the others hid at the culvert, or shuttered in the bushes, waiting in terrified silence. They contented themselves with subsistence. Even in this, they behaved cautiously. They didn't amass a store, fearful they would be robbed. The culvert offered shelter, and remained unknown to the wider valley. It was quiet at night;

the kids stayed quiet, and quiet the following day. Only Sod rattled the silence, rattling himself up for braveries.

"So?" Sod said, his eyebrows raised. "Afraid?"

Chatter grew comfortable with the feeling of Sod's body behind him at night, knew the relax and sprawl of his muscles, and could tell moments after the boy had fallen asleep. He'd wait a moment longer, but no more, and left the culvert whenever he felt the yearn. He travelled far into the dark, then settled to await the animal. Oftentimes he woke in the bare dirt, wet with dew, a magpie curled into the crook of his neck, or a pair of squirrels bunched between his ankles. These were the mornings he seemed to rise first to stoke the fire in the river-stone oven, to ready the meagre coffee grounds and set to boil the vegetable soup the children breakfasted upon; these were the mornings that convinced others of his selflessness.

Talk around the culvert centred on the Kin, a burgeoning gang developing in the marshlands, that included Greaves, Simon Sanderson, and the other boys with knives. *The Kin.* The name haunted Chatter. Valley-wide, rumours of their viciousness had become synonymous with the consequences of wandering alone. The others at the culvert kept each other awake trading new versions of the same cautionary tales, repeating the words nightly, as though this gave them power over fear. *The Kin*, came their voices across the campfire. *The Kin.*

A week later, Chatter caught sight of a gangly teen while tending Sod's potato patches near the clearing of the eviscerated hare. Another kid and another followed. Chatter fell back from his hole and scrambled down the hill.

Five. He'd counted five heads.

Sod worked the next hill over, secreting a trove of blueberries whose location he vowed never to reveal. Chatter knew a yell exposed them both. A throttling fury settled in his chest, as nameless as the call to the jackrabbits. Chatter's eyes

54

fell on the sixth head as it came into view. Greaves crested the hill where the potatoes grew.

Chatter fought the gasp. He crept into a cluster of trees nearby. A slipshod sat inside. Sod already crouched within, held his finger to his lips. Greaves shouted for Simon Sanderson while the other boys sauntered around the hole Chatter had dug, no more than thirty feet uphill.

Sod stiffened as Greaves knelt by the pile of potatoes on the hill. After a moment, he scanned the distant riverbank for landmarks. Simon Sanderson was the last to crest the hill, that snake-faced boy who grew further into the thickness of his limbs each time Chatter saw him, and it was immediately clear his was the largesse of leadership. He gazed at the hole, and the pile of Chatter's meagre harvest, before indicating his permission with a bored gesture. At this, one of the kids scooped a few potatoes at the boy next to him, and three of the numbskulls took up a game of stomping and kicking the yield into oblivion. Sanderson watched, smiling, but didn't take part. The others were careful to avoid him in their gambolling.

Sod knelt, perched forward on his feet. He clenched his fists so tight they shook. "They're moving in," whispered Sod. "They're goddamn closer every day. Rattail Gordon from Silver Wrists said the Kin overturned a whole camp. Cut their tents to bits."

Greaves left the others and continued down the hill. His eyes skirted the ground for footing, but always returned to the treeline. He drew close to the wooded cluster that contained the slipshod, and drew a curved hawksbill knife from his belt. He scanned the trees while he peeled a potato.

When Greaves was only a few feet away, Sod got to his feet within the chamber. Sod so small he could stand in a slipshod. Chatter noticed how still his fists had become, how assuredly he raised his chin.

Greaves bit the potato and gnashed it between his teeth. "Where are you?" he shouted. "We know you're here, little squirrels. We only want to talk."

The others on the hill laughed and shouted their own inquisitions. Greaves lingered a moment longer before ascending.

Sod watched the boys depart towards the blueberries. He spoke, but didn't turn from the field. "I've counted no more than ten of those pricks," he said. "We could scare them off if we joined up with Silver Wrists, or even the Grotto Nine. We *could*. But we don't. We don't even steal food from other gangs. We sleep in a sewer, and we hide in holes because Briny is too afraid to fight."

CHAPTER 14

The kids in the culvert greeted autumn with a watch schedule.
Regular duties were coupled with hour-long walks in directions
decided by Briny, reconnoitring the activities of the local gangs,
and charting the increasing expansion of the Kin, whose paths
were marked by slashed bark and hacked branches, the idle
swings of bored blades. The culvert was increasingly empty
during the shortening days, with Fern minding the oven
and food while the rest, leaving at dawn and returning after
sundown, wandered the forests with increasing paranoia.

Chatter bided his time. When, feeling generous in the
warmth of a September evening, Briny decided Chatter should
patrol with Dirty and himself, and more so, Chatter could
decide on their route, Chatter was ready.

Chatter bowed his head. He understood the expected
performance. He said: "There's a stretch of blackberry that
grows in the next hills, right alongside that ruined factory. Fern
said she's got enough flour for a pie."

He didn't clarify which ruined factory, though many
peppered the valley. Only the ruin of Forster's Tin lay within
a safe march. They rarely visited the crumbling chimneys
and chambers, however. A guard in a mismatched uniform
irregularly patrolled the grounds, and oftentimes brought his
eager hound. Neither Briny nor Dirty voiced opposition, and
soon the three of them left the culvert.

Amidst the trees, Chatter's dreams besieged him. He hadn't
slept properly in weeks. The latent threat of the Kin infested his

nights and picked him apart with fear. A different death waited each evening; he drowned once, the blades poked so many holes in his lungs; another time, the damage to his shirt concerned him more than his own cavity; and in another, the knives were sewing needles that sewed him closed as they opened him up. Often, he was in the forest, amidst the trees, death unseen until the first blade penetrated his chest. Despite the uselessness of his hands against their steel, he couldn't help raising them each time, so before all else, his dreams began with the mutilation of his hands.

Briny and Dirty were a murmur under his mind. Chatter stumbled on, not needing to watch his feet. He knew the way. He'd visited Forster's before.

The boys cut a wide swath around a cluster of stilted houses with corrugated iron shutters, the decaying community that never had a proper name. Briny located one of his earliest slipshods, and they crept towards Forster's Tin on their stomachs.

The major group of buildings lay distant from where the boys knelt, fifty yards away from the blackberry bushes. Ages before, a torrential rain had collapsed the shoddy ceiling beams, felled walls, and given way to the riotous siege of the natural world. Lichen and moss invaded the workshops and the workers' dormitories. Emptied floors of toil became fertile again. The grasses came next, unrelenting, overtaking the administration offices within a year.

Locals picked apart what remained. The mortar work of Forster's was recognizable in the bracing piles of the stilted homes and the cairn and keystone of their ovens and stills. Odd chunks served as doorstops and ashtrays. The rest of Forster's Tin was marked by remnant walls and joints and an eerie alley of free-standing chimneys, all enveloped in the growth of the river valley, the still visible brickwork stoic in the face of its unforgiving fate.

Briny watched the grounds from a stand of bulrushes. Dirty and Chatter crouched nearby. While he waited, Dirty snapped the thick reeds in increments, casual in his devouring. He didn't bother to make eye contact with Chatter.

When Briny urged them on, Dirty pushed past both and jogged to the blackberries. His hands full when the other two arrived. "These taste like shit," he said, but didn't stop eating.

For a while, the boys were quiet in their admiration of the blackberry bush. It grew over a quarter-acre of a huge and vanished warehouse, undulating through the fallen building. The grandeur of its silence and the bounty of its crop impressed the boys, but what struck each was the waywardness of its thorns. This seemed a good measure of violence. Serene, giving, yet approached with care. The boys reached out their hands, reverent, and ate even the bright red adolescent berries.

Briny was first to notice Chatter stray beyond the margins of the blackberries. The kid kept his hands in his pockets. He toed at the gravel before he knelt, scooped a few pebbles in his hand, then straightened again. Dirty stood next to Briny and watched, his hands stained with seeds and juice.

"Hey, Chatter," Briny said, "what did you say you wanted to come look at?"

Chatter approached the boys and held out his hand. In his palm were six or seven small grey objects that looked like thumbtacks with stubby stems. "Rivets," he said. "There are discarded rivets in the gravel. Millions strewn about. If you wanted, you could have a handful before half an hour."

Briny and Dirty swept their eyes along the ground.

"Hell," Dirty said, bending, holding the half-dozen he'd scooped with a swipe. "Been here lots, never noticed."

Briny didn't kneel. He narrowed his eyes and took a step towards Chatter. "You brought us here to show us something we've seen a thousand times before?" he said.

Chatter shook his head and scattered the loose rivets between his open fingers.

"From two handfuls of rivets," Chatter said, "I'll make you a knife."

Briny scoffed and shrugged, but Dirty fixed Chatter with a hard look.

"I needed to find something in a book once," Chatter explained, "so of course I had to read a dozen of them."

Chatter described how he hid in the library at His Holy Rules, holding book after book before his face, just low enough that he could watch the room. But there was one text he actually read, one that smelled of sawdust, whose spine was so broken it sat open at any page. He emphasized the shelves of *Popular Science* magazines. He wanted this image in their minds when he said the word *forge*. He trusted the word as concrete enough for their imaginations, bolstered by a row of spines. Briny scrutinized Chatter's words, his posture, and his tale. Chatter had stared long enough at the *Popular Science* article on *home forge(s)* to proceed, and banished insecurities from his telling. He could build a forge for the culvert, he felt sure of it. A machine wasn't any more complicated than a lock once all the parts were named.

Briny waited until Chatter had finished. "A forge," he said.

"Like in the magazine," said Chatter. "The valley is littered with junk. I've already seen most of what we need."

"You certainly keep your eyes open," Briny said.

Dirty narrowed his expression. "We could steal knives. I know where there's a hundred in Farrow. Hell, don't even have to go that far."

Chatter paused for a moment and watched Dirty. It was a moment longer than it should have been, and each of the boys felt it.

"There were these three kids at this orphanage I was at, His Holy Rules, Bill, Tom, and Percy, who plotted their escape," Chatter said. "A couple other boys were with them too, but I can't remember their names. Zeb? Pebble, maybe. Anyways, the other boys, the older boys, they had this plan, and they all were going to escape. There's this bathroom down the hall from where we slept, and the grills on the windows were so warped any kid could slip through. But they have two problems, first, they're on the third floor. And second, there's some guard patrolling, so they can't escape one by one, they have to go at once. So, each kid says no problem, right? Sheets and clothes make good ropes, everyone knows that. And what do you know? There's a window for each kid. So, each kid goes to work. Only, the night comes, and the kids meet in the bathroom, and Percy is so excited he forgot to strip his bedsheets, he's only got half his rope. But, no problem again. Greg's there, did I mention Greg? Anyway, he's there, and he's got an extra bedsheet, so he gives it to Percy. And there's Percy, stripping out of his own clothes and tying them to the bedsheet, so he's bare-ass coming out the window. But no problem, they're all out the windows, the dumb guard is nowhere around. No problem, only, problem. See, all the other kids make it down safe, but not Percy. See, Percy doesn't know that Greg cuts a hole in his bedsheet."

Dirty guffawed while Briny's face reddened. "So why doesn't Greg fall, too?" Dirty said.

"Because," Chatter said, "he knew there was a hole, he knew it would tear. He was ready for it to fail."

Dirty's mirth dried into a stale silence. He eyed Chatter with a guarded expression.

"You'll find kitchen knives out there," Chatter said. "Some carving knife chipped to shit on shank bones. Who knows who owned it? Or maybe we make shanks, every orphan's seen one of those. Something a little longer than your finger, so you have to get all nice and close. No. I mean we make a *knife*. A blade you build with your own hands. An edge you can be sure of. Somewhere you put your anger and fear, so it won't ever shatter."

Briny knelt and scooped some of the gravel in his hand. He picked out the rock from around the rivets.

"Before I built the slipshods, I slept in the dirt," Briny said, "I didn't venture into open ground. There have always been gangs in this valley. They are as ancient as trees. I learned the land down here by watching them pace out their territories. The Gnats, the Callaghan, Silver Wrists, and the Grotto Nine. I don't think there was a time when gangs didn't roam this valley. But if you've mind for it, you can stay out of their way."

"I kept to the corridors between lands," Briny continued, "I slept in slipshods. When I met Azalea and Fern, they slept there, too. Same with Dirty. Then one day Azalea was sick of slipshods. She decided we could take the culvert from a gang of rotten kids, the Scabs, who lived there before. Azalea saw how few friends they had. She knew no one else cared about that swampy area." Briny paused. "The culvert is good for us. It remains hidden."

"Not anymore," Chatter said, "It's a matter of time, Briny. The valley is full. So where will the Kin lie down? You like the idea of them wandering around while you sleep? Sod said they took out a Grotto Nine settlement a half a mile from the culvert. They're *coming*. Every night, I hear them. I close my eyes, and they stand behind every tree, I wake at a clatter down the culvert."

Briny stared at the ruin of Forster's.

"We've fought other gangs," Briny said. "Hell, most around here are up for a scrap, and it's rarely hard feelings. We got clubs and chains. Folding knives if something's serious, but who wants to kill a kid? You don't maim unless you have a point to prove. But you don't have to. This world allows those who'd hide to hide."

"That world is ending, Briny," said Chatter. "That was the first thing Sod said to me when we saw what those boys did with their knives. The Kin are changing the way it is down here. You know that already, don't you?"

"What do you know?" snapped Briny. "You ain't spent more than a season down here. Wait until winter, we'll see then who wants to hide."

Dirty stirred the gravel with his foot.

"Maybe he's right, Briny," Dirty said. "There's advantage here if we work fast enough." Suddenly, his face lit up. "Maybe it's not just us," he said quickly, flush with idea, "Maybe we make knives for ourselves, maybe we make them for the Grotto Nine. How much food do we give them to ignore the culvert? Imagine what we could get for a bucket of personal knives?"

"No, Dirty, the kid's wrong," said Briny, his voice thin as a blade, "The Kin are unreasonable. They don't belong to a system. They don't make deals. This kid named Beech ran into them couple days ago. He held up his fists, like you're supposed to, as has been agreed on for centuries. Here's his fists. But the Kin don't follow. They have knives in their hands. They cut Beech so bad he couldn't open his mouth without losing his jaw. What can you do against that?"

Dirty made to respond, but instinct stopped him. He sensed something in the sag of Briny's shoulders he dared not profane. Briny's anxiety turned inwards, his features darkened. He rolled the rivets between his fingertips, inspecting each as one would a skeptical coin.

"We don't take up arms against," he said. "We hide where we're allowed to hide."

Dirty shook his head and kicked at the gravel, but didn't speak.

"We make the knives ourselves," said Chatter, "We choose what goes in them, what shapes and lengths they are. We decide our own fates. We follow where Beech failed; our filled hands meet their filled hands. I want the same thing as you, Briny."

"No, Chatter. It's not an answer," Briny said. "Do you want your life to depend on the first real time you have to use a knife? Doesn't matter if we train every day, not if we forge the strongest knives ever. We won't become as cruel as the Kin, never as cruel. And cruelty is what they'll use to bury each of us."

Briny stared into the darkening sky. He told the boys they'd stayed too long.

CHAPTER 15

Dirty found Chatter and Sod amidst the Saskatoons. He grabbed a branch, dragged his hand along the limb, and sheared leaves at the stem. He palmed a cluster of berries and mashed them between clumsy teeth. Chatter and Sod watched. Neither said a word.

Chatter thought Dirty's arms looked like sausages, his fingers smaller sausages. But the gang didn't have enough food for overindulgence; Dirty was thick because his muscle outstripped his skin. He seemed to threaten a spurt of growth, but Sod said he'd always looked like that.

Chatter had the impression that Dirty bullied his friends because it simply hadn't occurred to him that there were other ways to control people.

"Stupids," Dirty said, he pointed at Sod, "Stupid One, you come with me now. Stupid Two, stay here and finish."

His teeth were mucked shades of blue from the Saskatoons.

Sod emptied his hands of berries into a discarded bag they used as basket. He wiped his hands on his chest.

"What are you talking about?" he said.

Dirty stripped more berries from another branch. He nodded his head towards Chatter. "Little crow is grown up enough to be out here alone, and there's a slipshod just a breath away," he said. "You and me are going to Farrow to get a couple chickens."

Sod paled and cast his eyes about, looking for a task undone. He stepped forward, then back.

"We're finished here, anyway," Chatter said. "I'll come, too."

CHAPTER 16

The three boys watched the Burrows from the birch skirt of its border. The homes closest, with their sloped roofs of natty wood shingles and stovepipe chimneys, descended from the squat cottages of the earliest quarrymen and prospectors who'd settled the valley. Beyond these, the dense bulk of the Burrows remained as undefined as its roads. Wood-frame tenements interspersed clapboard housing and pocketed courtyards shared by several families; scrap heaps, generations old, cluttered the open spaces. The boys stared into the back yards of the closest homes, the slim plots of land that boasted their self-sufficiency in an area without reliable power or telephones. Every yard contained fenced vegetable gardens and a few maintained beehives, and Chatter counted five chicken coops within an easy sprint.

Dirty eased into his old lecture about the dangers of the people who lived in the Burrows, the furthest extent of Farrow. Stories of chicken thieves who suffered fingers lopped off, or of boys dipped in honey and turned loose to the ants, were peppered with Dirty's dim wisdoms. He beat Sod and Chatter about the senses with his understandings, his voice fading long before it became useful. Chatter simply looked to Sod, and Sod to Chatter. A steeling look perfected in the dangerous territories of their foraging trips.

Sod crept into the tall grasses, towards the closest henhouse. Dirty took Chatter by the arm, and dragged the boy between the birches to the second coop. He ordered Chatter to get a chicken from the far property, then made for the nearest coop. He paused, and turned to Chatter. Chatter could tell it was a timed move, paced out in his mind.

"Hey, Chortles," Dirty said, "you damn better be as good as your word."

Chatter didn't back down. He faced Dirty. "I can make a forge," he said.

"I'll steal us seven knives this afternoon," Dirty said. "I don't need your forge. None of us do."

"What has anyone ever given you that you've relied upon?" Chatter said. "I haven't a thing. Not anything, Dirty. All I know, I know to be true because my bones know it true. I can rely on what I've made, because I was there the entire time. What else can you stand on? You tied your own shoes. Doesn't that make you feel safe enough to break into a sprint?"

Dirty set his jaw and said no more. He stamped grass in a show of boldness.

The henhouse sat near the middle of the yard, hemmed by the low-strung vines of a tomato garden nearer the home, and separated from the birch by piles of scrap metal and overgrown grass patches. Chatter crossed into the yard through a gap between antiquated sewer piping and the overturned chassis of a station wagon. He skulked through the debris and listened for sound ahead.

There were no chickens in the wired off exercise area of the coop, but Chatter sensed a rustle in the enclosure. He scanned either side of the coop, then swore under his breath.

The door to the enclosure faced the house. He'd have to open it in plain view.

He crawled around the coop and into the neat rows of tomato vines, pausing when the house came into view. The hothouse tomatoes were immature, so Chatter picked a couple cylindrical Romas and ate them while he watched the woman and the two little girls on the other side of the window. The woman kept busy at the sink, taking the separated vegetables one girl handed her, washing them, then passing them to the other girl, a bit older, who worked with a peeler. Once in a while they spoke, but seemed just as comfortable with silence.

Chatter allowed no sentimentality into his observation. He never believed the orphans who spun saccharine hopes into fantasy lives. For all he knew, everyone's life was as hard as his. He waited until the woman and the children turned from the window, then stole into their henhouse.

A tight, warm darkness enveloped Chatter. Straw rustled against his feet, dredging up an ammonia odor from the dried shit. Shelves ran along the walls, dim in the light from the wired-off area. A worried cluck emanated from the shelves, but each chicken Chatter approached maintained a stoicism that stayed his grasp. Later in his life, when crowds of people fell over themselves for his touch, Chatter often thought back to when his full attention couldn't even rouse a chicken.

Chatter knelt before an old hen who didn't bristle at his reach. Her indifference humbled him, the ferocious assertion in her gaze that his intentions were irrelevant. She was the one he took.

Sod and Dirty waited in a clearing two hills over. Dirty's chicken hung limp from his fist, but Sod's was alive. It hung upside down from his hand, warbling, flapping its wings slowly, a faraway look in its eye. Sod was delighted. He hooted. Even Dirty smiled. The chicken Chatter cradled quivered. He knew it drew no joy from the sounds its sister made.

And then, at once, Sod and Dirty's expressions shifted. Sod paled. Dirty's eyes went wide. They both shouted, at the same time, but there was too much panic in their voices for Chatter to understand.

The impact from behind sent Chatter sprawling. He tumbled forward blindly. His chicken arched through the air. It was on the ground for moment before one of the Kin caught it up and snapped its neck with a roll of his wrist. The reedy boy named Arch laughed.

Chatter scrambled up, but a different boy kicked out the arm he used for support. He rolled into a stamping kid, then another. A dozen Kin swarmed around the clearing. Eventually, Chatter was corralled with Sod and Dirty, who were stripped of their chickens.

Dirty refused to be cowed by the bigger boys. He straightened his spine, wrung out fists from his arms, but only succeeded in proving his own smallness. He blushed when Greaves separated from the rest and drew close enough to touch.

Greaves drew a knife with a curved blade. His grip pulsed on the handle, his thumb busy as though with a worry stone. He kept a constant motion in his fingers, a build and release of tension. Chatter felt Greaves's gaze rest briefly upon him, but the boy focused his attention on Dirty.

"Here we have criminals," Greaves said. "Some filthy rats."

Dirty bristled. He blushed again. "You thieve every damn day," he blurted.

The knife floated closer to Dirty's cheek. "It's not thieving if you already own it," said Greaves.

Greaves pressed his blade against Dirty's cheek and sliced downwards. Dirty cried out and shuffled beside Sod. Blood pumped under his aghast hand.

Greaves pointed next at Chatter, then Sod. "I've seen you rodents before," he said. "Scurrying around those hills. That where you live? Is that where you sleep?"

He smirked at their petty silence. Tears tipped from Sod's eyes when Greaves came close. Sod wiped his face immediately, but it didn't matter. The Kin saw. The clearing rippled with their laughter.

"Golly," said Greaves, as he sauntered to Sod. He rested his knife against Sod's chest, "*Golly.* You're sure scared. Does that mean I'm right? Now I know where you sleep?"

Sod belted a response, but his voice cracked, and then was lost in the laughter of the Kin. Greaves wiped Dirty's blood onto Sod's shirt, then shoved Sod to the ground. The boys laughed again.

Greaves rounded on Chatter. "I know what you are," he said, "You're scabs. If I want to find your home, all I look for is an open wound in the ground. Some shaking pile of leaves. Next time I see you, you better have better gifts for me." He turned back to the group and pointed to each chicken. "One, two, three," he said. "Three. So that's three for stealing."

The Kin fell on Sod and Dirty and Chatter. Chatter held his arms above his head and closed his eyes. He felt a flurry of motion around him, the gleeful hops of stomp-happy boys. He waited for his life to end, for the blunt impacts of the beating to turn into the bite of knives, but the Kin were content with what they could inflict with their hands and their feet. Chatter, during a moment of clarity, focused on the tooth he spat onto the ground. It was the last of his baby teeth. He found this a calm point of focus while he feigned unconsciousness, running his tongue over the gooey socket. Both Sod and Dirty screamed at times, high squeals that the Kin chorused. Sod went quiet after a while, and Chatter couldn't tell if the boy was unconscious or faking. Dirty, however, continued to scream.

Chatter didn't open his eyes until the Kin left the clearing. Blood matted the grass in patches. Sod knelt near Dirty, pale and bruised, but otherwise healthy. He couldn't hide his revulsion while he looked at Dirty.

As Chatter drew closer, he saw what the Kin had done with their knives. Three livid cuts disfigured Dirty's cheeks. It was obvious that Dirty had struggled, even while the blades separated his skin.

CHAPTER 17

Briny met them midway to the culvert. He shouldered
Dirty's weight and bypassed all slipshods to carry him
directly to camp. When Sod saw Briny, he exclaimed, "We
are surrounded!" then fell into an embarrassed silence.
Briny ordered Sod and Clatter to lag behind and obscure the
blood-spattered trail, but said little else. Chatter and Sod split
willingly, grateful for the time alone to cry. They didn't return
to camp for another hour.

Dirty lay unconscious in the maintenance sub-chamber
the children had converted to lodgings. Briny tended a meagre
fire and boiled scraps of cloth, while Fern sat with Dirty and
soothed him with her quiet voice. Fern, who usually wore loose
clothing because of her work before the oven, had changed into
thick denim overalls and several layers of sweaters. Amidst
the layers, Chatter noticed the collar of a black wool jacket. A
cudgel rested next to her thin leg. Briny wore layers of sweaters
and denim, but kept on his long shorts, for he was an ardent
distance runner, and wouldn't compromise his escape. Azalea,
Fern explained, had stormed off into the woods after seeing
Dirty settled. The snap and stomp of branches in her wake
lasted for almost ten minutes. Briny left soon after, to council
with the Grotto Nine, the gang whose territory bordered the
nearby marsh. After reflecting on this, the boys quieted and
found separate corners of the sub-chamber. Without speaking,
they fell into a rhythm of stoking the fire and changing Dirty's

blood-soaked rags while they waited for order to restore the outside world.

While he worked, Chatter's body was vacuous, his mind lost to silence. A primeval fear, deeper than language, rattled him until his elbows shook and his hands shook. Finally, he sat next to Fern, her hand on his, and she whispered to him as well.

Azalea emerged from the woods with knives in her belt. She clinked and clanked as she came down the culvert. The sound scared the boys witless, and left Sod unable to speak for several minutes. Azalea brought two blades for each boy, even Chatter, explaining she'd stockpiled for years, culling the broken and unattended from the surrounding homes and nearby scrap heap.

Briny arrived soon after. His entrance quieter, burdened with the news that no help would come. The Grotto Nine suffered the same from the Kin, so had Silver Wrists, and the Gnats. The whole valley was terrified into submission. Briny shook his head. "We never knew," he said, though the others were unsure to whom he spoke.

Azalea's voice rose and echoed dangerously down the culvert.

The arguments spun in Chatter's mind long after, the sub-chamber a cauldron of frustration and anger. Sod and Chatter repeated their versions of the story, but neither remembered Greaves mentioning the location of the culvert. Simon Sanderson wasn't with the other boys, though, and Sod swore this meant the gang had grown to contingents unseen. Azalea had Briny state the Grotto Nine's word-for-word verdict, and Briny had Azalea number the weapons in her arsenal. This, she did, but kept their whereabouts a secret. Sound spilled down the culvert, shushed for a moment, only to erupt moments later. No consensus emerged until Dirty hefted himself into a seated position, despite Fern's protestations. Dirty's face was swollen, ripe with bruises; his uncut eye closed from the stomping. A single malevolent orb swivelled above the bloody bandages on his face. He moved the lowest bandage to speak. Chatter glimpsed his teeth through his cheek.

"We got to make those knives," he said. Sod piped up in agreement.

Dirty remained unswayed by Azalea's offering. He scrutinized a stag-handled carving knife with its tip chipped off. He stabbed the air, then discarded it like trash. "Don't know who used to hold that," he said.

Chatter listened to Dirty recreate his own arguments. He told the story of the escaping orphans, though the others knew he'd never been at an orphanage, and altered it to feature Percy's death throes and a monologue of regret. He paused to swallow blood. When he spoke next, he didn't move his lips, and his voice slurred. He mentioned his shoes, how he'd tied them himself. "What Chatter knows," he said, "he knows in his bones." He paused, swallowed. War, he told them, was a natural answer to the question of Others.

"Go on," Dirty encouraged Chatter with the last of his energy, "tell them about *Popular Science*."

The vibrancy of Dirty's pauses, his slow collecting of words and lining up of arguments, allowed the unspoken elements of his advice to collect inside each mind, finding home amidst the fears and hopes that sheltered therein. Everyone turned to Chatter. The expectancy caused Chatter to flounder, but he remembered his own fear, the tormenting dreams, the hushed sound of trees unnaturally bent, their branches not enough to hold back any attack. Chatter explained how a forge could be made of a steel tire rim and some filched piping, and the method of forming the blades in molds made of river sand, lingering on the images of purely created weapons broken free from compacted earth, each shaped in light of the kid who would hold and wield, each reflective of the heart it kept unpunctured, the soul in the hand inseparable from the soul of the swing, the soul that lies along the edge sharpened to each kid's specification. The same way Fern needs a knife to slice radishes, he said. The same way Azalea needs a knife to keep us safe. Chatter indicated each kid in the chamber, pausing to intimate on the individual use each could apply to their tool, creating in each a specific hope, founded on all he knew about them. In each case, reflecting upon each image, Chatter paused, met the eyes of the kid, and convinced them that they, and only they, could craft a blade strong enough to save their lives. It was, he said, only natural. Simply scooping up the trash of the detritus-strewn world was, in Chatter's eyes, unnatural.

Azalea made him repeat the process three times before she and Briny agreed it would work, although Chatter knew his plan did not assure success. Briny and Azalea were as drunk on hope as the others. By the end of the evening, Chatter noticed that the children in the culvert looked at him with the same need as the dishwasher's people of Slatterly, and he lay awake until morning, sick with fear that he had forgotten how to fabricate a forge.

CHAPTER 18

Briny took Chatter to find the tire rim first. The rim would sit upside down on three supports and serve as the hearth. Briny knew the sight would improve morale. He mentioned this casually to Chatter while they hiked to an abandoned truck a mile from the culvert, and Chatter felt a thrill of conspiracy. All afternoon Briny addressed him as an equal, no matter how often Chatter slipped.

They returned with the rim and a length of exhaust that Chatter described as a bellows pipe. The name delighted the gang; kids became experts on the spot, explaining to each other, *This is a bellows pipe, it carries air to the hearth*, and, *Some dumb kid sits here and blows, and it is the crappiest job.* For days their pleasure was visible, as they stepped around the objects in the sub-chamber. Their longing glances sustained them through rainy days when only those on watch left the culvert.

Azalea brought Chatter to the scrap heap that served as dumping ground for the Burrows. They hid while groups of people shed themselves of dead iceboxes, soiled couches, and sodden bundles of newspaper and correspondence, but Chatter and Azalea acquired an oven pipe and the elbow joint that would complete the flow of air into the hearth. Before they left, Azalea broke into one car after another until she found a bottle of aspirin in the glove box of a silver pickup.

On their way back to the culvert, Azalea pushed Chatter into a huckleberry bush. Fear shot through Chatter until Azalea smiled. She burst into laughter. "Should've seen your face," she gasped before imitating his wide bulging eyes and gaping mouth.

Chatter smiled and sat up, but a moment later Azalea dove onto him. She pressed him down while she stared upwards. "Shut up, Chatter," she said, her voice urgent. "Go on and live up to your name."

Azalea rolled off Chatter and lay next to him. They peered through the undergrowth at the reedy boy named Arch plodding through the wood. He swept his wrist up and down while the compact menace of a butterfly knife spun around his fingers. White scars were scattered up his arms, and a few even showed on his neck. Arch marched forward with a blank expression while he mashed moss and fern underfoot.

Azalea and Chatter lay still until the boy disappeared. Azalea got to her feet and studied the boy's path.

"Only one of them," she said. "On his own. We don't know nothing about him, could be just some idiot. There's no need to tell the others about something so meaningless. Heard me Chatter? Tell anyone about this and I'll drop a rock on your head while you're asleep."

Chatter, mesmerized by Azalea's threat, merely nodded.

Sod and Fern, while foraging, secured a cradle for the tire rim, but refused to say from where. It was the central portion of a deck table. The glass surface was smashed away, so the rim rested evenly on the table's support pads, and the tripod of bowed legs provided support for piping. In a burst of activity, the children lifted the rim onto the tripod and fitted the oven pipe through the rim's centre bore. This met the elbow joint and fed into the bellows pipe.

Chatter traced his fingers up the pipes, describing the path of the air into the hearth. Here, he wiggled his fingers, and his voice grew high, reverential as he spoke of the fire. "Now," he said, and he beamed at the rest, "all we need is a bellows pump. So some dumb kid doesn't have to sit on his butt and blow."

A shuffle behind them disturbed the children. Dirty stood unassisted for the first time in days. "I'll get it," he said.

The others collected rivets at Forester's in the intervening time. The trips became pilgrimages, filled with solemn periods of silence and concentration, the gang reverent, pacing in careful spirals, bending to touch the ground, scattering should their sentinel whistle warning. Regular duties were interrupted for side trips. At nights, the kids spoke of their knives in the same tone the orphans spoke of their future.

In fallow hours, handle types were a common focus of conversation. Azalea favoured a pearled handle she'd salvaged from her other knives, while Briny saved some smooth wood, and Sod put away lengths of silver wire to wind round and round. Fern found an antler in the woods, and promised she'd share with Chatter. The sub-chamber filled with discussions of merit; of short and long lengths, handle friction, and blade maintenance. Piles of rivets increased. Then one night Dirty came back with a tall red bicycle pump. He dropped it before the others and proclaimed: "Now we'll never be afraid."

The forge failed twice before it sustained enough heat to melt rivets. The elbow joint clogged with ash the first attempt, but Dirty solved this by installing a grate made out of a .22-addled park sign. Azalea used a rubber glove to seal the bicycle pump to the bellows pipe, which caused the forge to heat too quickly during the second attempt, and smoke poured from the culvert.

This halted all progress. Terror settled into each kid as they watched the plumes of smoke reveal their location for anyone who cared to look at the sky. Briny hurried forward with a bucket of water and soaked everyone around the forge in his haste. A week passed while Azalea charted a system of chimneys, made of piping stolen from the house in the Burrows where Chatter thieved the chicken, that would funnel the smoke through the culvert and out its collapsed end. The pipes ran through a marsh, where the kids buried them and punched holes along their later stretches, so that the dispersing smoke might resemble nothing more than the natural fog in such areas. It became a rotating duty to maintain Azalea's chimneys.

Days passed before they found enough coal, in the ancient furnaces of the abandoned properties along the valley, to fill the hearth. The children lit and stoked the fire again. Excitement built as the coals maintained a steady glow and a few flamed. Smoke trailed down the faint suck of the chimneys. Briny paced, while Dirty, more comfortable with speaking, tallied his contributions to the program. The rivets dissolved. The children cheered and danced, and though they carried on for an hour, through the pouring of the liquid metal into the river-clay molds, Briny didn't once tell them to quiet.

"Hot damn!" Sod shouted as he danced. "We'll live forever!"

The kids made short knives first. Thin blades they filed and sharpened with rocks of different sizes and textures. A rich vein of mineral clay ran along the riverbed leading to the culvert, perfect for carving into molds, and soon the quarrying and carving of the clay, along with the collecting of rivets, became a part of every kid's day. Fern became an artist, and coaxed integrity out of wild, imaginative curves. Each kid happily lost themself to the oscillation of process. To the riverbed, to Forster's, to the woods for kindling, to the workshop, to the forge, to the bellows, to the molds, to the riverbed again. In the quiet of the nighttime sub-chamber, while the others rested, still thinking themselves through the paces of the process, Sod spun his blades between finger and thumb and tallied how many by the day, by the week, by the month they could make. He imagined buckets of knives for the Grotto Nine, for any gang who had it in themselves to ask, who could ante up the proper price. With a shine in the eyes of the others, Sod described how important they would be; he promised a place in the valley, vital where there had been nothing before. Like a magic trick. So each kid practised on the bellows pump, learning their own strength in relation to the fire. Too much oxygen sent sparks everywhere, and too little wasted coal without gaining heat. The children changed places, but the work didn't stop. No one wanted to consider what would happen when it did.

CHAPTER 19

Chatter cast a blade that was short, straight, and sharp on both sides. He imagined the distance from his wrist to a human heart, and used that as his measure. He was, in this case, merely extending his touch. His third casting was successful. They broke away the clay surrounding the cooled metal and the little knife gleamed. Chatter's fear dissipated. His first tooth. For a moment, he felt free of the world.

Briny made a longer and a shorter version of the same knife. They oscillated positions on his waist as opinion shifted on which hand was dominant. Azalea taught herself to throw with an unerring accuracy, and cast dozens of handleless blades. Her knives jutted from trees and fence posts for miles around. Fern contented herself with a series of functional blades, while Dirty tinkered for hours with the curves of a blade he claimed emulated the flame. The others agreed it was vicious; its odd shape assured it would not come out the same way it entered. Sod measured from the tip of his middle finger to the centre of his forearm, then his whole forearm, then included his elbow, and cast a blade Dirty said might as well be a sword. Sod out-practised everyone, including Azalea. On his own, in an unused corner of the clearing, Sod diligently swung and hacked, his passion getting the better of him at times, startling the others with bloodcurdling war cries.

Fern spoke of prospective meals while she sharpened her knives. The rest followed her lead, and their talk centred on what they could fashion from life, whispering at times, as though this were akin to prayer. Chatter worked his blade alone, waiting until the others were gone to retrieve his private whetstone.

Occasionally Briny's resolve gave, and the gang marched through their territory, their hands resting on their hilts. They kept to the heavily wooded ridge at first, but as summer wore on, they strolled through fields of wildflowers and chased the wind across swaths of ancient grass. They marched quietly, or in happy conversation. Sporadically, a swing sounded. A slash at a nearby branch, or a bunch of offending leaves, the thrash then curse at a knife not sharp enough.

Toward the end of August, the children followed a recently uncovered path through the marsh. Dirty strode ahead, his knife at hand. Often, he'd swipe at an unlucky bulrush, though with unreliable accuracy. The rest of the gang worked this into their rhythm, anticipating the roll of his shoulder, the *hack-swish-skein* of the downward arc, then the fallen bulrush, or the mad sway of the escaped. Dirty paused, and they looked up. *hack-swish-skein*. The kids continued forward. *hack-swish-skein*. And they continued forward.

Dirty paused.

Several kids looked up. Dirty's arm hovered above his head. First, his elbow slackened, then his shoulder. He lowered the knife to his waist, and the fearful expression he flashed over his shoulder terrified the others.

Azalea peered ahead. She pushed past Dirty. "Shit goddammit," she said.

Azalea, Briny, and Sod swept the clearing before waving the others closer. Dirty stayed with Chatter and Fern, but refused to meet their eyes. He entered last, he'd already seen. In the middle of the clearing, the Kin had strung a dead racoon over a structure made of twisted sticks. None of the children could bear the animal's expression. Around its neck hung a message scratched into a strip of poplar bark:

WHeRe ArE YoU?

The kids didn't linger. Briny forbade travel from the culvert for the next two weeks; the gang huddled in the sub-chamber around low fires at night. When next they crossed the boundaries of the culvert clearing, minuscule flakes of snow drifted down from the grey sky.

CHAPTER 20

Chatter could never remember how the day began. They were foraging. He and Sod. Same as they had countless mornings, over countless months. For the rest of his guilty life, Chatter hated his fickle memory for retaining nothing of the morning. Those so few hours. He only remembered the breach of timelessness, the routine of mornings sundered forever. His earliest impression of the day came like a point of impact.

He remembered the trickle of dread down his neck when Sod stiffened. They worked the potato patches in a fold of hills near the thicket of wolf willow. A grey sun hung overhead. Sod froze. Chatter knew at once that he'd spotted the Kin.

Sod knelt in the scrub and stared down the hill. A broad kid stood at its base, his back to them, watching the river crawl. He rocked idly on his heels.

Chatter reburied his potatoes, then slid along the hill on his belly. The nearest slipshod was a two-chambered pocket in a birch cluster thirty feet away. Sod, entranced by the broad kid, hadn't moved. Chatter resorted to a low hiss. He spat Sod's name.

Inside the slipshod, Chatter crawled into the second chamber, and kept an eye on the kid down the hill. A year or two older than Chatter, he had fair skin and a face not yet angled out of childhood naiveté. Content with his view, he didn't glance uphill once.

"Shit," said Sod as he crawled next to Chatter. "Shit. And he's alone, too."

Sod stood in the slipshod and stared uphill. "This is our chance. We've got him *alone*," Sod repeated. "Quick now. Let's beat him silly."

Chatter had watched the broad kid until that point. He looked towards Sod. "I don't know," he said.

"He'd do it to us," Sod said. "You know he would. Give him a chance, hell, go on out there and turn your back. I'm sure you'll find out. Where's a rock? Let's cave in his cheek."

"Sod."

Sod spun on Chatter, his eyes ablaze. "You want him to find the slipshods? They find the slipshods, we're all dead. They'll eat us up. They're wolves. You can hear them at night. They howl the same. You've heard them."

"I've heard."

"I'm sick of it, Chatter," said Sod. "Fear rots you inside. It tires you out, like a pain you can't shed, just taking away from every second something you'd never noticed. I hate it. Where's a rock? Let's cave in his head. There's two of us. It will be easier than you think."

"Sod," Chatter said in his evenest voice. "They didn't kill Dirty. I don't even know if they meant to hurt him that bad."

"Well, they hurt him that bad anyway," Sod said. "Are you questioning this, buddy? Don't turn traitor. You, of anyone. You picked Dirty off the ground. You heard him scream. We can't let that kid get away. Especially now, especially after we worked so hard. We have knives now, Chatter. C'mon, let's go cut his throat."

Chatter kept silent. Sod entered the slipshod pale, but a livid red now fringed his eyes.

"This is what we've waited for," said Sod. "This is who we are. We worked hard enough. But go on, if you're going to be a baby. *I'll* cut his throat, you just hit him with something first."

Chatter glanced down the hill. "Where's your knife?" he said. "I left mine in the dirt with the potatoes. I didn't even remember it until now."

"Couldn't gut a fish with that one anyways," said Sod. "Mine's up the hill. I left her in the stump that looks like a warthog."

Chatter glanced uphill. The knife jutted in relief against an enshrouded thunderhead. He met Sod's gaze again. "Fine," he said. "Go get your knife. I'll dig up a rock to bash in his head."

Chatter didn't move after Sod left. He sat outside his body, gazing across the slipshod at that little boy who would not move. He saw himself get to his feet, crawl about the slipshod, then return to his original position. He stared at his empty hands. He must have been searching the slipshod for something.

Laughter came over the glen. The kid down the hill stared at the river for a moment longer, then turned uphill. He smiled when he saw Sod. That slight boy now surrounded by knives.

Sod hardly moved. His eyes were rooted on Greaves, who stood off the top of the hill. Chatter craned his neck, but he couldn't see Simon Sanderson; just Greaves, just those boys who followed after his footsteps. Greaves ran his fingers along Sod's knife then eased it from the stump. He walked towards Sod, then past him, down towards the slipshod.

"Little rats," Greaves said. "Shitty rodents. This is where you've been hiding? The trees?"

Greaves swept down the hill, grasped the spine of the slipshod, and tore it open. The second chamber collapsed on Chatter, pinning him under debris, blocking him from view. Sod eyes fell on the emptiness of the slipshod, and a pure fury flitted across his expression.

"Looks like your bosom's screwed off," Greaves smirked. "Left you all alone."

Greaves kicked apart the slipshod. His voice rose in a genuine excitement, as though he'd found a new specimen. "You build forts in the trees, then hide when we come by?" he said. "Damn. And think, if it wasn't for you, I would have never learned how to find the next one and the next one after that."

He pointed the knife at Sod then held it up for scrutiny. "And this," he said, "The weight's shit, but it sure is sharp. You made this?"

Sod glared at Greaves. "Go leap down a well," he said.

"All the good it does you a few dozen feet away," said Greaves. "There's the first rule of being a knifeman, I suppose. Keep the goddamn thing close."

While the others laughed, Greaves jabbed the honed tip into Sod's chest. The wound wasn't deep enough to be serious, but Sod paled and stumbled backwards. He tried to staunch the blood with his hands.

"Keep the goddamn thing close," repeated Greaves, but the others didn't laugh. They watched him carefully, and carefully did they step while he stepped, each of them only half steps, but it kept them outside Greaves's range. Carefully they watched the knife Greaves displayed.

Sod wouldn't look, he stared at the blood on his hands. "I haven't done anything," he said.

"Haven't done anything?" Greaves mimicked. He held up the knife. "How about this? You sure did this." He closed on Sod. "Little rat is right, though. He hasn't done nothing. No, no; not yet. I haven't even given him the chance."

The knife landed at Sod's feet.

Greyson's own curved knife hung at his hip.

Sod ran his hand through the grass. When he stood, the rest of the Kin had their knives in their hands. They paused for a moment, and then converged.

"Oh, no," Chatter said. "No no no."

CHAPTER 21

Sod's eyes were still open, but he didn't raise his head at Chatter's approach. He kept his neck stiff while he cried, as though the rivulets of blood tickled his spine.

"Goddamn," Sod repeated. The one word his riddled throat could manage.

"I'm sorry," said Chatter and pressed his hands to Sod's wounds. The boy winced and swore, but Chatter pressed harder. He focused the warmth of his palms on the earthy tingle of Sod's wounds. He tried to push this energy, to imagine himself as the dishwasher's people in Slatterly had. In a flush of anger, he cursed the yearn, demanding with furious breath that it unleash its potential for healing, the reserve from which he was sure each jackrabbit could draw, but this quickly fled as the silence in his heart cowed him. Sod's pulse faded too quickly for patience. He cursed himself next, hoping humility would heal Sod. He pressed against the boy's wounds and imagined crawling inside Sod and sewing his skin shut. Chatter drew heaving breaths, and soon his chest ached and his head buzzed, which he took as a good sign. A throb in his head and his hands thrilled him. All else fell away as he tried to pass the upswell of energy in his blood to Sod.

Chatter looked up from the cluster of lacerations on Sod's chest. "What?" he said.

Sod lay still and stared at the sky. There was a faint emotion on his face, a grief at the exertion. He'd spoken only moments before.

"What?" Chatter repeated.

He placed his hands on Sod. On his chest, his arms, his neck. There were too many wounds, and Chatter didn't know which were important. His head buzzed. He waited for the dizziness to overtake him, make him swoon, but there was no warmth in his hands, the tingle had gone. The bleeding stopped. For a breathless moment Chatter studied Sod's face.

When the heat left the body, Chatter stood and wiped his hands on his pants. They were long dry, but he was able to flake off blood with his nails. He arranged the body in a formal position, legs crossed at the ankle, hands clasped across the chest. He collected the late blooms of the potato plants and scattered them on the body, saving the two finest flowers for Sod's eyes. He removed Sod's knife from his friend's torso and bent the blade until it snapped. He went further down the hill and flattened dirt over his own knife until he was sure the mound appeared no more significant than any other, and then he continued down the hill to a copse of birch that ran along the river.

CHAPTER 22

The kid roosted in an abandoned house on the distant end of Farrow. The houses there sat on cinder blocks half sunk into the marshy ground, each its own enclave amidst the tamarack and dwarf pine that bordered a swamp called the Gardens. Cautious, at first, of a whole house to himself, the kid built a slipshod in a cluster of nearby spruce. He spent his first nights in a chamber he'd built to Sod's proportions, watching the red shale road that linked the houses. During the evenings, no matter how warm the day, a fog settled in the Gardens, fostering the moss that undermined wallpaper and walls, keeping the area abandoned. Used to the wet drip of Slatterly, the kid was unbothered by the moisture, and after a week, he moved into the chattel house he named after the phrase scratched into the bottom of a roof beam: *tempest fugitive.*

The cheap locks of Farrow awakened an old instinct. Scores of empty buildings littered the roads, most boarded over. Rusted padlocks secured outside doors, inexpensive double-tumblers mass produced to a single key form. The kid jimmied a few, though he preferred the silence of a lockpick. He committed his burglaries in the dead of night.

It was during his first nights that the kid fruitlessly sought out the underground tunnels of bootleggers and fugitives that the orphans of His Holy Rules had so oft discussed. He'd carried the possibility of their existence through his time at the culvert, and, whether he acknowledged it or not, they were the reason he fled into Farrow. The promise of crawling underground, hiding in the hug of earth and the darkness of dirt, called to him so much stronger after what happened to Sod. He followed back alleys, shying from the sudden closeness of human voice, the brackish bursts of laughter and shouting, clinging to the huge pools of shadow in the unlit lanes. But every alley only led to another, these here and there truncated by dusty roadways. The kid was afraid to ask anyone for such secrets, and felt sure they were lies anyway. Everything the orphans knew about Farrow, he decided one night while he watched a bare-knuckle brawl from the depth of a shadow pool, was wrong. They'd lied to themselves and each other, but it wasn't for hate. The kid shuddered, and right there in the alley tried to shed himself of all the lies he'd learned. He tried until he felt empty again.

Because of his burglaries, the kid experienced for the first time in his life what could properly, in previous times, have been called a home. The rooms were mostly empty, with vestigial remnants of furniture, broken-backed couches, or three-legged side tables that the kid righted. He tried to imagine what once sat upon the scratched and discarded surfaces. Tattered clothing, cushion covers, and shoes missing their mates were simply left, bunched on the floor or scattered from room to room. In one house, the kid spent two hours staring at the skeleton of an upside-down ironing board, unable in the slightest to conceive of its use. In the empty kitchens and master bedrooms, he could not picture the lives of parents, only minders. In every room, orphans crowded and crowed.

Once inside the homes, he gathered items of interest and spent nights inventing the circumstances that led to abandonment. Some nights he was amazed at the disposability of people's lives. Once, he came across a pantry rife with canned beans, stews, fruits, and corn. In another house he found two boxes of letters, interspersed with photographs. Decades caught, printed, and preserved. For four weeks, he had a fire every night. He imagined the expression of the person who last looked at the boxes and decided the memories weren't worth the weight.

The kid spoke with Sod on the nights he heard the valley, the wind carrying sounds along the river's iced bank. Even after weeks, he paused at the sounds, awaiting response from the presence he felt as strongly as the yearn in his heart.

"Those clouds bring snow, Sod," he'd say, or, "Fire would only choke this room; blankets is what's called for, Sod."

Snow didn't settle in the valley, but the days cooled into a grey suffocation. Gusts of wind bit the eye, then froze the tear. Pedestrians turned their collars up, grateful to pass one another without looking. The sun rose in grey or painfully blue skies, but ceded early to a chill darkness, the natural state of winter. The kid slept during the piddling hours of warmth. Before he went to sleep, to break the quiet of Tempest Fugitive, the kid would ask Sod to wake him at sundown.

The kid endured the cold stretches. In his dreams, the kids of the culvert came in through the windows and the doors, and he woke gasping, crying out for Sod. He peered into the daylight, but the stark sunlight allowed no refuge, no comfort, despite the emptiness of the red shale road.

In a half-collapsed bungalow on the fringe of the Gardens lived a man who muttered his own name serval times a night: Ruddy Lou. He was tall, thick for a man so lanky and nimble. His shoulder-length hair, when tied behind his head, held streaks of distinguished grey, but Lou saved this effect for his ventures away from the bungalow. While at home, he let his hair obscure his face in a thick hanging tangle.

The kid circled the property carefully, even after Lou had gone, suspicious of snares and traps. A web of gutters and drains ran along the walls and through the roof, draining down into a huge cistern made of patchwork metal in a back room filled with buckets. Lou had torn the flooring out of rooms where the ceilings had collapsed, and worked a tilled soil from the sunken ground. The kid recognized, in the managed rows, the late sprouts of wild potatoes like those Sod had grown in the hills.

Ruddy Lou arranged his bunk near the stone fireplace in the front room. It was here that he collected potatoes, dozens of them, in large piles, and spent nights drinking a foul-smelling liquid and applying his nimble switchblade to the vegetables. He scrubbed the potatoes and cut them into chunks, swept these into the pots that he brought from the back room, and boiled them in the fireplace. Occasionally, he would fish chunks out of the pots, cool them with his breath, and eat them expressionlessly, but most of the potatoes remained uneaten.

The kid was mystified. Certainly, Lou's method was hampered by his drinking, but the processes were so haphazard that the kid had no sense of a goal. One night, Lou mashed pots of potatoes with a tool made from the overlong handle of a wrench, pouring water into the pot and mashing further until the froth spilled over his floors, another night he set this concoction to boil, but burned it after he passed out, waking to the smell and swooping the pot out of the house to dump it on his own front steps in a string of curses that would make Sod blush. The next night, he got a little further, adding a dark liquid to the potatoes, but he ruined this mixture in the same way. Another night, he was engaged in mixing yeast and sugar, but failed to achieve the harmonies he sought, howling out curses and kicking several buckets to bits. The kid, forgetting himself, laughed at the sight, and Lou froze, stood upright, and checked every window before circling the house. The kid watched him from nearby bushes, his hand clapped over his mouth, and never again laughed, though Lou often gave him cause.

No matter how regularly he watched, the kid could never envision what enterprise required such efforts. The kid tailed Lou several times, but always lost the man in the tangled corridors of the Burrows. Nevertheless, he looked forward to the nights when Lou worked with the potatoes. The scenes carried a domestic warmth he couldn't otherwise imagine. He stole several potatoes and kept them in a slipshod, eating some, letting others dry into the wrinkled faces of kids he'd known.

CHAPTER 23

One night, near the beginning of spring, the kid spotted Lou on a road called Clementine. The kid extracted his picks from a lock, and followed. Lou strode in a quickened manner, one arm stiffly at his side, and the other clutching his jacket closed. The kid wondered what would make him believe he hadn't time to button his jacket.

Lou passed through the dark district of the Burrows included in every orphan map the kid had seen. Blocks of converted tenements which were said to have housed the operations of rum-runners and moonshine syndicates during prohibition, abandoned in recent years, yet guarded still by angry dogs and sullen syndicate men in dark denim. The kid had already learned to stay away from these men, who prowled Farrow like bold badgers. Lou hurried along the series of brothel-laden blocks known as the Winks, and continued into the abandoned residential section of Farrow. The kid had never been into the area, and the quiet rankled his nerves. He couldn't help looking in the open windows of the clapboard homes.

Lou made his way to a mongrel house where several figures waited in the overgrown backyard. The figures, tall dirty men, including a couple syndicate men in dark denim, had started a fire with the loose underbrush. They sang to stave off boredom, a ruckus and light Lou stamped out. The kid circled a nearby house as Lou lambasted the men in a high stage-whisper. One, a burly man with a shocking red beard, admonished Lou for dragging his feet, and the others laughed, even after Lou shushed them with a strangled curse. After a tense moment, Lou unlocked a series of double- and triple-tumblers and let the men into the mongrel house.

As soon as the last man entered the house, the kid sprinted to the door and listened for an inside lock. The callous thud of a deadbolt disappointed him. He'd expected better security. He listened while the boisterous men moved further into the house, then withdrew a file from the inseam of his sweater and, with a long-perfected shudder of his wrist, worked the bolt from its cradle.

Empty chairs sat around four folding tables in the first room. Paintings with slashed and drooping corners, pasted advertisements from magazines, and cracked street signs were pinned to the walls in a half-hearted attempt at décor. The chairs, expectant, leered at the kid. In the next room, he found the same. The mongrel house had no hallways; rooms opened into one another, each containing empty chairs and tables set with the same irritating expectancy. The kid crept towards the noise and light at the back of the house mostly to escape the vacancy of the chairs.

The kitchen, an extended area stripped of cupboards but for the back wall, with only a sink remaining, bustled. Men stoked coal fires in tin buckets, set right overturned chairs, and lined up in front of Lou, jostling for position. One by one he opened the complicated locks on the back cupboards, the most advanced locks that the kid had seen in the area, and doled out draughts of foul-smelling liquid from the dark jugs collected within.

The first served, a small round man with dark hair and a light suit, who Lou called Mort, filled his flask with one cup and drained the second, and in a wobblily way saluted Lou's vast talent and toasted the others in the room, but it was clear they viewed him as an outsider, and he left without another word, taking his third cup into one of the back rooms. The kid knelt under a table as Mort passed, and the little man didn't notice him in the dark. Lou served six more men before he closed the cupboard and took off his jacket. He draped the coat over a nearby chair and turned to the next man, a pot-bellied warthog in dark denim who snarled for Lou's attention. "Dammit, Slim," Lou said in a firm tone. "I already told you. You don't drink no more until you settle your tab."

Slim yelled, kicked a chair. "Yer a gutter, Lou! I ain't the only who owes. Might bring myself to a legitimate establishment, yer not careful."

"Rub your shoulders with cops and presidents, right?" Lou shouted back.

The kid shrank from the anger in the voices. He hid amidst empty chairs.

Slim snarled, and slapped the porcelain of the sink. His rings clacked off its smeared surface. Lou stood his ground, while Slim gnashed his teeth. The other men paused their drinking to watch. "Yeah," Slim said, over and over, "Yeah. *Yeah?* Yeah."

With a wild swing, Slim punched the furthest cupboard door, leaving a craterous impression. He stared upon his destruction, mute in glory and apprehension.

Lou smiled at the man, laughed. His fist snapped out and caught Slim under his jaw. Slim staggered back until his knees buckled, then fell to the floor unconscious. The others watched the flat smack of Slim's head against the prised-up tiles. Lou adjusted the knuckledusters on his fingers. He scanned the room, measured the few that stood, outraged at the attack.

"Well, hell," came a gruff voice behind the kid.

A jolt of fear knocked the kid backwards. A red-bearded man in dark denim barrelled towards him, scattering empty tables and chairs in his wake. He lifted the kid off the floor.

The red-bearded man swept the kid up and kissed him. A musk of motor oil, rotten food, chewing tobacco, and stale ammonia emanated from his beard. The kid choked as the red-bearded man entered the kitchen and announced his prize. The man kissed the kid again. He declared the universe had given him a gift.

One of the others stepped away from the fire in the tin bucket. A mass of grey and black hair spilled out of his shirt. He ran his hand down his chest and rubbed his crotch.

"You, Giant?" he said. "Hell. Us."

The red-bearded man named Giant dropped the kid on the floor. Immediately, men bent around him. They tugged at his sweater and ran their hands through his hair. The kid struck out, but couldn't even kick over the coal before he was subdued. A man with wet hair stuck his nose in the kid's ear. The kid blinked his eyes to scatter his tears, but he wouldn't touch his face. He kept his mouth shut. He resolved to drown himself in the river when the men were finished.

Lou watched from the back of the room. He cleared his throat before sipping at a full jar and stepping closer to the coal. "Watch how you mark up his face," he said in a raised, yet casual tone.

Giant reared up, the men bristled. "What's you to tell me what to do with what's mine?" he snarled.

Lou grinned. He sipped his moonshine. "Well, you know me, Paps," he said. "I'm absolutely no one at all."

Giant stalked towards Lou, then back. He took the kid's jaw in his hand. "Why his face?" he said, the words issued around a mass of chew.

Lou walked back into the darkness. A jug tipped forward, tipped back. Lou sauntered into the light. "You leave his face the way it is on those reward posters, and I bet his dad pays you double," he said. "Maybe triple, your cards played right."

Lou drew a long draught. The kid felt a quiver pass through the men. Quick arithmetics took place. Lou assured them they'd seen the reward posters. Mentioned them twice more before a couple men echoed him, they *had* seen the posters, and then Lou fell quiet, and sipped from his cup. He agreed about the posters, agreed the boy in the picture looked just like the kid. He sipped at his cup again. Soon, the men swore the posters were scattered through the valley. Other details emerged, the kid uncertain of their origin. He became the great-grandson of an oilman, a hard-edged family that'd pay handsomely for the straightness of the prodigal's teeth. He acquired value.

Giant took the kid's jaw in his hand again. "He does look like a rich kid."

"A prince," said Lou.

The men gathered tighter and scrutinized the kid. They'd heard of oilmen, but only knew oil workers. Oilmen and their scions were a different stock all together. The demeanour of the men shifted, anger on some, softness in others. The kid kept his eyes open, even while the men rubbed his body.

"Of course," said Lou, and paused.

"What're—" spouted Giant. "Why're you saying of course?"

"Of course," said Lou, "I'm sure you know there's procedure before you. You'll get a tidy sum for that boy-flesh there, but only after you've passed through a den of wolves." Lou held his hands up, abstaining from judgment. "I'm just saying, send in your cleanest shirt."

Silence stole over the group. The man next to the kid swore.

"Yer—" said Giant, but he didn't continue. After a period of thought, he shrugged. "Suppose we're eating him, then."

Lou gazed at the rafters, lost in sums. "What's ten grand, eight ways?" he said.

"Seven of us," shot back an oily youth.

Giant laughed and nodded at Lou. "No records on you?" he said. "I'll bet you think us dumb enough to let you wander with our prize. You say you're a big man, slinging in your juke, but you don't have shit else. There ain't been nobody else here but us and Mort in weeks. I bet you turn on us in the precinct. Yeah, yeah, I bet you think we're stupid enough."

Lou waved off the nonsense and sipped from his cup. A long, drawn sip. "Best make sure all of him disappears, then."

The men hauled the kid off his feet and carried him from the room. With a surge of fear, the kid shouted: "Stop!" And to his surprise, the men did. They stared at the source of the squeak.

"Yew degenerates," said the kid. *Degenerates*, he suspected, was a rich boy word. He brought an inflection into his voice, an upper-class accent adopted from orphanage caricatures. "Dew yew know who I ham?" He demanded. "How dare yew? Mai father refrains sums in the *millions*."

The man with the wet hair cuffed the kid across the mouth and reminded him to be respectful. When he saw spite in the kid's look, the man knocked him unconscious.

The kid came to while they carried him into an adjoining room. At the first possible chance, he kneed the man carrying him in the crotch. The world went upside down.

The kid scrabbled to his feet, surrounded by laughing men. The oily youth marched forwards, his fists held up in response to the kid's. His terrible instinct to raise his hands. The youth feinted, and then hit the kid twice.

The men fell on the kid. Hands grabbed at the buttons of his trousers. Fingers probed his mouth. The kid kicked free and rushed to an empty corner. He swept up the base of an oil lamp and swung it behind him. The lamp cracked with the resonance of bone, and the man with the wet hair lay limp.

"Hey hey hey," said one of the other men. The kid couldn't tell which. Lou and Giant were in the other room, conversing in a low tone.

The kid held up his fists. Four men stood around him. One lunged and slammed him into the wall, but the kid stayed upright, despite the nauseous spin in his spine. The men converged.

Giant's voice intruded in the room. The kid lay spreadeagle. Two men pinned him down while another straddled his chest.

The fourth, the youth, lay nearby, dazed. "Quit it!" Giant shouted. He stood in the doorway, holding up a trifling box in his hand. Lou stood behind him in the adjoining room, never looking directly at the any of the men.

Giant held up the box again. "Look here," he said. "The sap's ponied up." He opened the box and displayed a small diamond ring. "Collateral," he said. "His great aunt's ol' shiner." The men climbed off the kid.

Lou leaned into the room, scrutinized the kid, and then swiped the box from Giant's hands. "No," he said, "I've decided otherwise. That kid isn't worth it."

The kid's guts fell through his feet. He drew a steadying breath. He made to scream, but wet fingers suppressed his tongue.

Giant and Lou adjourned to the other room, and argued. Giant returned with the ring, buffing it against his oily jacket. Lou followed, took the kid by the wrist, and dragged him away from the men. When the space of two rooms separated them, Lou paused. He pointed his finger at Giant.

"I'm back by sunup," he said. "No later. And dammit, the meanest bitch you'll ever meet laid a curse on that ring. I mean it. If any of the stones in that band are loose, the offending party will shit out his nostrils for the rest his life. Understand? Just don't say there wasn't fair warning."

This drew a dusky laugh from the men, though each moved further from Giant. Lou grabbed the kid's shoulder and led him to the back door, pausing only to tell Mort to screw off for the night.

When they were outside Lou smacked the back of the kid's head and pushed him into a full march. "Don't look so goddamn triumphant," he said. "You're an asshole if you don't think they're watching us."

The kid walked in silence until they were far from the mongrel house. "You aren't going to get that ring back," he said. "I don't know who you think I am."

Lou gave him a shove on the shoulder. "I know what you are," he said. "Mine. You aren't anything else. Do you see how cheaply I bought you? A ring and a box worth no more than a buck-fifty. Some sham story not even worth half-that. Great aunt? Nothing original there, it wasn't even a con. Some scratch version of the Glim-dropper. That's nothing. I keep a ring on me at all times. I've another in my boot. Hardly an effort at all. And now you're mine."

Fury rose in the kid. He couldn't stop himself. "You don't own me," he burst.

Lou laughed. "You owe me, kid," he said, "and don't you ever forget that. You owe me for that box, and that ring, plus interest. They're going kick my stock to bits when we don't come back. It took me the better part of four months to raise the money for that outfit, plus, I've been stringing those old boys for two weeks, clearing near thirty a week. You'll owe that, too. Now, I'm not the type to see a child eaten by wolves. You being so damn foolish with your sneaking forced my hand. So, you cost me my chance at an honest dollar, and you're going to make good. Hear me?"

The kid refused to answer, refused to look at the man. The sums spun his will.

Lou laughed. "Those men back there?" he said, "That's the world. That's what'll eat you up. For a single second there you showed a brain, though. A spark of something in your heart. Even if your accent was terrible. The instinct was right, however, and I can work with instinct. You're useful so long as you keep that mind working, kid, but don't let your brains go to your head. Brains, as often as hopes, can be dashed. Remember, if you're unhappy with me, I'll be happy to drag your skinny ass back to those mutts."

The kid kept silent. He marched forward, dragged his feet through slush. The sky lightened.

After a half mile of stamped puddles, Lou's voice softened. "Course, I fixed a roost for those birds," he said. "Anything on the raggedy edge is bound to be snapped off. I never should have set up shop that far from the Burrows. All these licenced establishments coming up now selling legal fare, there ain't the demand from the respectable folks anymore; business has gone to shit. But you pay for fancy space, kid, you can be sure of that. No place where people want to stand is free." He strode along under the brightening sky, clenching and unclenching his fists. The kid wasn't sure if he should respond. Before he could, Lou shook his head, his voice became audible. "Cost of that, sure, but costs anywhere," he said. "Hell, double the cost, we'll work it up on the road. There's double of us now. Then I'll have a place, something I could name after myself."

Lou punched the kid on the shoulder. "We don't have more than a few hours start on those men. Thankfully, they never root. They'll be out of the shine in less than a week. After that, those dogs will drift. A couple months in the country will do us fine," he said. "By the time we return, they'll be long gone." He stared at the kid. "You could stay here, sure, don't bother fleeing with Ruddy Lou. If you're sure of yourself. But I ask you, before you risk these streets with those mongrels around: would any starving man, allowed a glimpse at a meal, turn down a second chance at the plate?"

The kid stared at the mud. He thought of the men at the mongrel house. He looked at Lou. They weren't that different, once he stared past the grime and the charm Lou wore as easily as a coat. *All people are the same*, he thought, *dangerous in different ways*.

"If they're so terrible," he said, "what were you doing with them?" His throat tickled at his audacity.

Lou skipped forwards and swatted the kid. The blow was playful, but stung. Tears welled in the kid's eyes, and for the second time that night, he didn't wipe them away.

"Listen, kid," said Lou. "You don't ask me a question unless I volunteer an answer. Hell, here's your first rule: you ask me about my business again, in any way, and I'll string you up like a sheep and cut your throat. Fine?"

The kid's gaze fell to the road. The same grey slush as the sky.

"You don't know it yet," Lou said, "but you're the luckiest person who's ever been born."

CHAPTER 24

Lou secured the ladder outside the bungalow in the Gardens, while the kid teetered at the top. The kid inserted metal discs at all the junctions that led inside the house, redirecting the rainwater to the appropriate outside spouts. He climbed onto the roof and took down tarps that caught moisture from the nightly fog, and he removed the four false chimneys that hid large funnels. The kid begrudged Lou's ingenuity at the range of different methods the house collected water.

The kid's next job was peeling every potato Lou dug out of his back rooms, but Lou would only accept peels of a certain length. He displayed no patience at first, snatching overlong peels from the kid's blade and throwing them to the floor with such regularity that the kid feared he'd never get one right and Lou would turn him out right there. He made plans to squirrel the switchblade away had he the chance, but eventually he learned the technique with his wrist and became adept at cutting just the right amount free, just enough for a curl, with a little of the flesh left on the underside of the skin. These, the kid laid out to dry on Lou's bunk. The peeled potatoes he carefully kept in a pile at his feet. While the kid did this, Lou retrieved a large doctor's satchel that contained rows of empty glass vials, and two other peach crates outfitted to hold dozens of vials each. Lou sat across the room from the kid and polished vials. Later, Lou collected the peels carefully and kicked the peeled potatoes to mush, scaping off his boot out the front door.

"C'mon, kid," he said after, and let the kid carry the peach crates to the room with the huge cistern, crouched like a wrestler in the corner. Lou pressed his palm into its patchwork side, and ran his hand up and down as though it weren't interrupted by the amateur soldering. "This, kid," he said, "is the most magical thing you'll ever see. Every inch of metal here, all the different colours, the sheets, the valves, are made from the thousand melted idols of the world's thousand religions. There's not a scrap nor rivet here that isn't holier than both us guys together. The water, come from the sky, collected therein, is blessed with every ounce of grace mankind can muster. And it's all mine."

The kid filled dozens of vials from the apparatus Lou called the still, which was connected to the cistern, polishing them once again before placing them in the satchels. Lou inserted peels into some of the vials; others only contained liquid from the still. The kid wanted to ask Lou the purpose of the peels and the vials, but Lou's threat terrified him. He worked in silence.

Lou listed small towns and communities on the prairies beyond the city, mining towns, farming towns, unnamed towns indicated only by landmarks. A tour or two through, Lou assured the kid, and they'd make money enough for capital. Then, once he had a place inside the Burrows, or even Farrow proper, he wouldn't run into trouble with mongrels on the margins. He could bribe all the right people. His voice settled on this fact with such confidence that the kid didn't think to question it. *Lou's*, Lou said, spreading apart his hands like a banner. The kid merely nodded and continued with his work, invested with renewed vigour.

That night, when Lou leaned too heavily on the flask, he spun stories of crowds, of flashing eyes and pattering hearts; his voice took on the cadence of song, and he rehearsed speeches that sounded like they came from plays. "Not one of you is sick as I," he promised a blank wall, his eyes busy, cautious, never ignoring a returned glance. He practised revealing the satchel, the slow revelation of the stacked vials, emerging as they would from the sea, the first life-giving waters, rising as Lou opened the case at a slowed pace. The kid saw his future no clearer in these sporadic episodes, but sensed that such plans included him, and this excited him in a way that he could not name. He worked as hard as he knew how.

When Lou quieted, the kid paused in his work. The man watched him from the doorway. An incomprehensible warmth bloomed within the kid.

"You get it right when you work hard, don't you?" said Lou.

The kid dropped his head to hide his smile. He was glad for the busyness of his hands. He didn't respond, didn't want the conversation to move any further. When the warmth in his chest became obnoxious, he reassured himself that should he need to, he *could* outrun Lou.

CHAPTER 25

The sun rose while Lou and the kid made their way to the docks. The kid stumbled along, the events of the past couple nights whirling in his mind. He pictured the men from the mongrel house around blind corners or watching from rooftops. In each alley, the kid waited for Giant and his cronies to emerge from the fog, arms and mouths open. The kid angled behind Lou, just in case.

Lou secured them passage out of Farrow on an upriver barge, then retired to a pile of hoses behind the wheelhouse. He fell asleep before they set adrift. The surface of the river, a deep grey, almost black, bereft of reflection, rippled like an omen. Morning fog cloaked the homes of Farrow. Shutters were drawn in the Burrows, though life crept along its walks. The confidential hush of those roads carried into the forested hills. Gangly pine and birch jutted from the mist like spires in a crowded cityscape. The kid climbed the portside railing and watched the forest cover give way to the broken moorings of the dock outside Forster's Tin.

He held his breath.

No commotion of the air marked what began at the blackberry bush, no hesitancies of place. The kid's thoughts raced to Dirty in the grass, clutching at his face. The scent of potato blossoms skirted a river breeze. Awash with dizziness, the kid gripped the railing. His palms tingled as frost bound flesh to iron.

As he did when the world grew too quiet, the kid pictured the culvert sub-chamber when the news of Sod's death broke. Dirty's scream reopening cuts on his face. Briny pacing, *shit shit shit* rising and falling. Fern consoling Azalea with quiet, while Azalea would not quiet. The walls shuddering at the bristle of Azalea's knives, her impatient questioning of whoever discovered the corpse. But eventually these images became silent, and the kid knew them as his own creations. All he was sure of was the question that lingered on the brick like scum, the single question, echoing off the walls of their home: *Where is Chatter?*

The kid pulled his hand from the frost's puckered kiss and rubbed his eyes. He watched the ruins of Forster's until the barge turned with the natural curve of the river. He stared long after.

For the rest of the trip upriver, the kid couldn't shake the impression that amidst a field of standing chimneys, he'd spotted the ghost figure of Sod, eyeballing the kid's flight.

CHAPTER 26

Six weeks later, the kid kicked open the door to the beer hall known as Ails. Lou leaned on the bar across the crowded room. He wore a custard-coloured three-piece suit, his collar kept closed with a silver-studded corded bolo. He left his back to the room.

The kid stopped midway to the bar and raised his voice, louder than during practice. His throat thrilled at the jarring use.

"Doc Mari!" the kid shouted. "Doc Marigold! I need your help! Pa's sicker than cats."

Lou faced the bar. He spun the beer in his cup while others in the room turned at the noise. The kid shouted louder, his voice echoing amidst the timbered ceiling. "Doc!"

"Son, what's wrong?" A bulky RCMP stood up from a nearby table. The kid's guts tightened. The man sat with equally bulky men, all dressed in the similar wear of agrarians, long sleeves under flannels under sheepskin vests that fit beneath their coats. Lou must have missed the cop entirely when he gave the kid the signal to kick in the door.

The cop maneuvered his immense weapon around the low table as he approached the kid. "Son?"

A cold terror wiped clear the kid's mind, but for the single imperative Lou drilled into him their first night outside Farrow. He'd leaned over their tenuous fire and pointed to his chest with his broad hand. "The deadliest sin is hesitating, kid," Lou said.

The kid gazed up at the mountainous cop. "It's my Pa, sir. He's sicker than cats."

The cop nodded. "There's a call box out yonder, son. What's your father's location? I'll have a medic meet us there."

The kid scanned the cop in the fashion Lou taught him. *Intemperate Sweats,* the kid thought, picked skin along the nails meant, *Nervous Anxiety,* and watery eyes were *Sinus Tumour.* The kid dared glance at Lou, but he still hadn't turned from the bar.

The kid leaned away from the cop. "You sure, sir?" he said. "Maybe you don't want to get closer to Pa. You look like you're coming down with something yourself, sir. Don't mind my saying."

The cop's hand fell to his side. "Well, I just been tired, kid," he said.

"Sure, sir? No pressure in your sinus?" said the kid. "That's how it started with Pa. He got nervous. Couldn't relax, ever. You'd see him, unsteady on his feet, wiping sweat from his temples. Then he'd cough, sometimes for no reason."

"Where is your dad, kid?"

The kid pointed towards the door, an empty gesture, but it earned him a moment's respite from the eyes in the room. At the bar, Lou raised his head, but didn't turn. He watched the smoked glass behind the bottles. The doorway empty, attention returned to the kid. "Besides, sir," said the kid, "Why would I need a medic? Doc's standing right there."

This time, the kid pointed at Lou. Lou drained most of his beer, then clacked his glass on the bar, right next to his elaborate leather case that resembled a doctor's satchel. He revealed himself to the full notice of the beer hall.

Lou's voice developed a throaty resonance within the act. The tone reassured the kid that, despite the cop, little had changed. "Dear Isaac," Lou said, "Don't scream yourself hoarse. The noise will strain your throat. Stay quiet, child. Has your Pa the ringlets yet?"

Relief washed over the kid as they returned to the script he and Lou spent six weeks refining in beer halls, community centres, local fairs, and anywhere else Lou rustled up a prairie crowd. Nerves rankled the kid, however. He'd failed at his part too many times.

"Pa came home with a headache again," he said. "Told us he felt tired. That's all. This morning, though, Rawley went to wake Pa and next thing I know she's come out the room. Shouting. Even Liza screamed, and you know, Doc, she's quiet as a mouse."

"The ringlets are back," Lou said.

"Puckered," the kid said. "Half an inch maybe, maybe higher. There's pus now, too, Doc."

Lou's voice rose in anger. "This morning?" he shouted. "Half an inch, and you didn't go for help till now? Isaac, you dummy."

"I couldn't," the kid swore. "Not until now, Doc. How could any of us? That was four in the morning. Half-past sees us working the pens. I only now got off."

Lou shook his head and waved the kid off. "Get out of here, Isaac," he said. "I can't help you. You're wasting your time. Worse, you're wasting your pa's time."

Chairs thrust back from tables. A few more patrons stood than a moment before.

The cop's hands came to rest on his baton and his gun as they hung from his belt. "Hang on there, Buck," he said. "You're a doctor. You have an ethical responsibility here. You've treated this kid's dad?"

Lou wiped his hands on his vest. "I have," he said.

"He's your patient, then," said the cop with moral certainty. "You can't refuse treatment. I'll have you up. There's a cell not a pretty sprint from here."

The crowd emitted a sullen laugh. Neither Lou nor the cop flinched.

Lou glared. "You can go to hell," he said. He went back to the bar, but the bartender refused to serve him. Lou concentrated on the remainder of the beer in his glass. He argued over his shoulder that there were no such laws. Ethical statements are easy to make, he told the cop, because no one can enforce them.

The cop shook his head. "Buddy," he said, "Let's go."

"Dammit!" Lou shouted. "You've got no cause here, sir. The kid's mistaken. I am not, nor have I ever been, a quack. I'm no doctor, sir. My profession was somewhat different. *Doc* is a given name. That kid's pa was only a customer, and an old one at that. I've retired."

The kid gathered his breath. He treasured the moment preceding his last line. The burble of energy in his throat. "Doc!" he shouted. "Don't lie to the cop. He gave Pa a remedy that got him back in the field. Isn't that what doctors do?"

"What the hell, buddy?" said the cop to Lou.

Lou heaved a sigh, a resigned noise that calmed the agitated patrons. He picked up his glass and drank the rest of his beer. "As usual, the kid tells half a truth. I've no degree in medicine. I'm only human, and I only know what works. That's what I gave his pa, that's what I used to sell. A Remedy. But I never guaranteed against failure. Never once, did I, kid? I never did. Sure, it works for his pa, but who else is that lucky?"

The kid knew to make as if he was about to speak.

"Kid, stop," Lou said, "Isaac, don't let this go further." He unfurled his satchel's slatted cover. Rows of vials were visible for a tantalizing moment while Lou extracted two. "Take these to your pa, Isaac, and if Liza's cough drips again, give her some, same as Rawley's shin splints. Rub it on the affected. No, I don't want that grubby bill, go buy some bread, son. Go on!"

The kid took Lou's shout as the signal to run, and he pocketed the vials at a sprint. On a whim, he shouted out a peal of gratitude, though his garbled words sounded like a squeak.

Outside Ails, the kid flanked the clapboard building, and, still thrilled at watching Lou work the crowd, found an open window. The kid waited a moment before peering in, and left a space the size of Sod beside him. He stared at the empty ground for longer than he liked before he raised his eyes to the show.

"See that cop?" he whispered. "I stared straight in his face."

Lou held a full glass of beer at chest level and assured the crowd they were not interested in what he had to offer. The cop nearby, holding a Gin Rickey bought by Lou, spoke. The kid couldn't hear over the hum of the room, but knew Lou's script well enough. First, he let the crowd draw out stories of his failed travels as an itinerant vendor of Remedy, the empires and plains and mighty forests he crossed peddling medicine that fell from fashion. Then, Lou's head sunk suddenly, his hair obscured his eyes, before he brushed it back with the word that hounded his career.

"Charlatan!"

A murmur of consternation swept through the room. A man in the back called for Lou to open the satchel. More asked for the Doc's pitch, so they could test it against themselves. Common knowledge stated that the opinions of foreign parts couldn't be trusted.

Lou waved the crowd off, played up his gruffness again. *Retired*, he'd swear, *Of. No. Interest. To. You.* Then switched into his coveted character, the concerned man of medicine. "I hate, more than anything," Lou avowed, "the sufferings of mankind."

Lou followed such pronouncements with his collection of Everyman Affliction. Headache. Sore Throat. Exhaustion. Irritable Bowels. Sweating; too much, or too little. Shivers in the Night. Any symptom upon which the crowd could hang its guts. He and the kid turned the collection into a game, and killed time around cooking fires by naming the suffering of the common people.

"Corns," the kid would offer, but Lou's gesture at the nearby field told him that was too easy. "Gout," Lou said, "or, Splintered Arthritis." The kid held his hands to warm at the flames. "Insensitive Itch," the kid proposed, but Lou shook his head. "A tingle in the tips of our fingers," he said. "A persistence of the heart."

Lou nodded while he listed symptoms to a crowd. Nodded until others nodded. He asked the crowd if they were tired. If they woke up tired, if they could remember gazing out a window without thinking they were tired. Did their heads buzz, palms ache, ankles swell at the close of day? Sweats were a symptom, he said, same as irritable sleep, or unsettled digestion. Lou asked the crowd if they felt that no matter what they did, they never got ahead.

When he'd lent the room his nod, Lou grew serious, concerned. He looked around and told them that he saw, amidst the others, a dozen people who suffered from a fluke. *This*, Lou swore, was the reason for their unnatural tiredness. A parasite grew inside them, grew fat on the meat they'd meant for themselves. *This*, he said, pointing to his chest, caused their suspicions of unbalance, of inadequacy.

After a moment, Lou admitted to the crowd that he might be wrong—two-dozen people in the room could suffer from a fluke.

When Lou went over the script the first time, the kid scoffed. He said no one'd even *heard* of a fluke.

Lou gave him a smack. "Kid," he said, "You do this right, you can't even say fluke without half the crowd thinking of their guts." He grew serious then, dropped the story from his voice. "Don't mix these things up. You're not selling them on the remedy, you're selling them on the sickness."

The patrons of Ails raised their voices in question and Ruddy Lou countered with one of his own. His famous riddle. The kid called Chatter heard him clear over the clamor.

"What drinks your blood, but is never satiated?"

CHAPTER 27

Later that night, over paper plates of beans and garlic bread in a diner a few miles from Ails, Ruddy Lou asked the kid if he knew what the word *indenture* meant. The kid shrugged and spun the beans around on his plate.

Lou watched the kid. "Didn't notice that cop in there," he said with a laugh.

The kid shrugged again.

"Still," said Lou, "Sold him a half-dozen vials. Took them from me with a handshake. Sweaty palms, case you're wondering."

The kid scooped the beans onto the crust of his bread. He wasn't wondering.

"You did all right tonight, kid," Lou said. The kid, startled, tipped the beans off his crust. "You didn't crack," Lou said. "You stayed with the line, even when the cop shook you down. That shows me something. Shows you have something. A little spark inside you that'll grow. So, grow it, you dummy. Only one thing, call a cop *officer* to his face. They like that lie best."

The kid's vision blurred, and he stared at his plate. He focused on corralling beans. "Lou," he said, "what's indenture mean?"

The kid did his best to listen while Lou explained. The kid nodded. He understood most of the words. Some of what Lou said rattled him, but he buried these doubts beneath the swell of goodwill in his chest. One fact stood out: he'd be wanted for something he could do, not something he was. A verb, not a noun. Lou asked for an extra paper plate from the kitchen and scribbled some words for the kid to inspect. He spun the plate across the table and ordered them hot chocolate.

The kid buzzed. He'd never had hot chocolate before. His eyes skipped over the words, but he didn't read. His heart pounded. Every orphan knew there was paperwork before you left the orphanage.

The kid signed with a cross, then a semi-circle as afterthought.

CHAPTER 28

During the time he was on the road with Lou, the kid cried only the once. They were three months out of Farrow, in a flat district where the only landmarks were windbreaks, camping alongside train tracks, under the open sky, unafraid, for the spring rain was weeks away. The moon, full, spilled its pale light across the countryside, seeking the hollows and depressions that betrayed the static plain of the land, taking, for the service of its light, a degree of vibrancy from all it touched. The kid awoke in the stasis the moon cast, unable to rub the sense of dream from his eyes. The fire had long gone out, and the chill of night was breathable in the air. Lou lay, dead drunk, near the wood the kid collected during the gloaming, when at last he'd convinced Lou to halt their march. Every time they left a town, Lou assumed there were people after them, and forced nights of campsites hidden in the long liminal stretches of which the prairies were composed. Even two days later, Lou kept along at a pace, his breath growing heavier and heavier, casting glances over his shoulder at the direction of Stead.

Lou didn't stir when the kid got to his feet. He wouldn't wake until an hour after sun-up, when his snakeskin boots grew too hot for his feet. The kid turned a full circle; on all sides the horizon shirked out of sight. A couple hundred yards away, more visible than at dusk, was the patient shape of a grain elevator, those silent giants that haunt the prairies and watch over its towns. The elevator complex, including a smaller silo on one side, and few ancillary buildings, was dark but for a lone

light that shone on a wide patch of cracked asphalt. The kid
crept in that direction.

The kid skirted the outer dark of the light, careful to
avoid the caustic whiteness of its beam, which stole even
more vibrancy than the moon. On the far side of the elevator
complex, where its huge bulk blocked the breeze's chill, the kid
settled down cross-legged to wait. To occupy time, he played
Lou's game on himself. *Baited breath and shoulders stooped
with Robber's Spine*, he thought. *A persistence of the heart.*

The jackrabbit slowly became visible, materializing from
the pallid stasis of moonlight. Like the others, she did not alter
her path once she found it. She bore no external injuries, and
moved in the patient, practised way of the very old. At long
intervals, she raised her head, turned it from side to side, and
looked at the kid, but mostly she just continued forward.

The yearn swelled. He compared it against the nervousness
he felt before he burst into a crowd and shouted Lou's invented
names. The flowering in his gut and the dizziness of his mind,
his thoughts the flit of birds sitting along the same wire,
alighting before taking flight again, exchanging places in a
mad flurry of individual effort. Though the margins of their act
were firm to the kid, there were a host of contingencies, code
words, and casual shifts of stance that fled his mind as soon as
he shouted his first lines. He existed in a state of fear that Lou
would scratch his elbow or clear his throat, and the kid would
call out the wrong name, or invoke the wrong past. He had in
his hands, Lou reminded him, the ability to collapse their entire
enterprise. He was one dumb move away from revealing their
sham to the mob that surrounded them. One mistake from
ending every bit of the life they'd made.

In contrast, the yearn was resolute. It fluttered at approach,
and vacillated over distance and direction, but its foundation
never shifted. As soon as he felt it, the kid understood his role
in the process, understood, at least, what was required of him.
It stepped below scripts and stage names, below the words he

used to construct the world he could not see, into the realm of instinct, which did not share words, only wants, which demanded, in a voice that could not be denied, that his inner being respond to a reality unformed in any physical space. The closest the command came to his awareness was a tickle at his fingertips, a shift in his heart he called a yearn.

The kid reached out his hand, and the jackrabbit settled underneath it. She folded her front paws under her and rested, plumped up, against his forearm. A shock washed through the kid, then, an utter relief at the simplicity of her body, her warmth, the feel of her fur and the soft rhythm of her breath, a pulse that emanated out of her into the kid's hands, as undeniable as sunlight. The concreteness of her warmth, wearing away the tickle in his fingers, stood starkly against the shifting scripts in the kid's head, the stories that he and Lou told each other until the other believed it, the details they invented at a whim, congratulating each other on the closeness to reality. Happy, that they could fool even each other. The feeling against his hand, the kid knew, would only change once, the same change he'd felt over and again, the resumption of stillness in his heart, a stillness he would have assumed always still, had he not felt the yearn first.

The jackrabbit lay for some time under his hand. Her head bobbed like a distracted napper, but she never unfurled her paws or made to stand. A little bit before, she shivered, and opened her eyes to look at the stark pool of light upon the asphalt, and the shape of something colossal, beyond her comprehension, which stood behind it. Her silence remained resolute. She closed her eyes and shivered once more. Upon his palm and then up his arm, the kid felt her release, the disentangling of all her readiness. The kid pressed his face into her fur. He cried for a long while.

CHAPTER 29

Lou used the money they made on the road to rent a space in the Burrows that belonged to a retired cooper. The workshop was in a sunken alley behind overhanging timber-framed buildings. Cobblestones paved the courtyard, the work of those long under the ground. A mossy scent of ancient wood dampened the courtyard. Dimly lit shops — a barber's, a farrier's, a printer's, and a seamstress's — shared the ally floor; the farrier was their immediate neighbour. The workshop occupied two thirds of the basement level and bore no address but the four metal letters bolted above the timber door: C O O P.

For the first month, Lou and the kid lived in the workshop. The first order of business was to build a still from filched materials; then Lou taught the kid the process of distilling, giving him the responsibility of spotting the dead devils in a shaken proof vial, the beads of air that signalled the shine ready. They installed the still at the back of the building and cordoned it off with a wall of particle-wood panelling that Lou won at blackjack their last night on the barge.

The walls occupied their days until they'd bisected the space. The side with the still was left open for the shoddy wooden tables and chairs, while on the other side of the bisecting wall, a space Lou called the *clinic*, they built twelve scanty rooms. Lou brought in a squat stool and folding cot for every room. The next morning, he showed up with a spool of electrical wire, and the kid spent the day sitting on Lou's shoulders, stringing single-bulb lights throughout the building.

A few days later, they built a thirteenth room off the clinic. The room was cramped with a cot inside, and it stayed overwarm next to the still, but it had a door, and it thrilled the kid. It was the first room of his own he'd ever had.

After the saloon opened, the kid spent most of his time in the clinic. He performed a single procedure, on as many as twenty people, night after night. He showed the patients into a room, and administered a tonic of moonshine that Lou spiked with crushed sleep medication. During the patient's slow descent into unconsciousness, the kid entered the room with a tin bucket and a surgical knife. The knife, once he was sure it was seen, was placed on the floor, and when the kid warned them of the incision, he only pinched the thin flesh over the hip bone and let a little goat's blood slip out of the tiny flask he concealed in his hand. "You'll be unharmed when you wake," the kid assured. The dribble of blood into the bucket, timed properly, was the last the patient heard before sleep overtook them. The kid retired to his room for three quarters of an hour, then returned to wake the patient. He would present a curled and cured potato peel, tenderized into the rotted appearance of a flatworm, in a glass vial.

"Here," he said, "is the fluke that has drained your life." Sometimes, depending on the patient, the kid thrust his hands forward and exclaimed: "Live forever!"

The first patients came to the clinic after buying Remedy from Lou. He promised an *intensive treatment*, which was a phrase the desperate believed. The desperate, Lou said, don't need a cure, only the pursuit of one. The kid didn't understand, until patients, previously purged, maintained regular schedules. One, Mrs. Spinner, a line attendant at Merriwether's Fertilizer, maintained a standing appointment every second Thursday. By spring, the clinic was flush by referral alone.

The success of the clinic made the kid proud. If he worked for the five hours Lou kept the saloon open, he made nearly thirty dollars. His joy remained undiminished in handing Lou the full yield every night, as his contract stipulated, though he learned to hide his pride when it was clear he'd outperformed the moonshine. Those disconsolate nights when the only regular face in the saloon was Mort, the squat man who hadn't forgotten the moonshine Lou served in the mongrel house. The clinic became their staple, though Lou regularly threatened to knock down the rooms for more floor space if the kid didn't keep the copper of the still shining. The kid was almost sure Lou wouldn't, but scrubbed every week in case.

On nights the clinic closed early, the kid left the Burrows and went into the forest. Inside the treeline, he travelled in the direction dictated by the tickle in his chest. A shuffle of his heart that culminated in a crouched jackrabbit, a badger tattered from territorial defense, or a tricky encounter with a porcupine. The kid placed his palm across visible wounds and divined the source of pain; fear and hunger came from the natural world, but cruelty, the lacerations of blades, and the broken bones from snares and escape came from humanity. *Trapline*, the kid could say to himself, or *Pellet Gun*, or *Gasoline*. He waited until death with each of the animals, leaving when his heart quieted.

One evening, at the beginning of summer, the kid hiked to a marsh deep in the woods. A wide pond, surrounded by a tangle of poplar and birch, occupied the far end. Reeds grew in clusters around the bank, interspersed with the brash bulrush. The kid gingerly stepped onto a carpet of matted vegetation and crept towards the water. A colossal structure of fallen trees, harvested branches, and intertwined reeds sat on the far bank, channelling the water into a series of waterfalls. On the carpet of reeds, near the water's edge, lay an old grey beaver that had been savaged by a predator.

A solemn mass from the nearby colony attended the beaver, and six or seven other beavers slipped into the water as the kid approached. The animals swam a few feet away, then turned and stared. The young and the old of the colony kept watch from the dam, solemn in their rows, but this didn't perturb the kid. He'd never known a colony of beavers to act in any other way.

The kid placed his hand on the patriarch and waited. The others watched, and knew as well as the kid when the grey beaver passed. By the time the kid wiped his eyes clear, the colony had disappeared into the dam. He stayed next to the little corpse. He thought about his loneliness until it made him sick.

The kid tensed and stared at the reeds, disturbed by a breeze in the dark, then he relaxed.

"Oh, Sod," said the kid, "there you are."

CHAPTER 30

The kid raised his eyes from the mixing table at the back of the clinic and glanced down the hallway. Six closed doors alternated sides, and three at the intersection of the hall. A moment later, he refocused, and finished stirring Lou's concoction for the syphilitic in room four. "Has Mrs. Spinner woken?" he said.

Sod nodded as he came around the corner and into the mixing room.

"Good," said the kid. "Good."

Sod went to the door at the end of the tight room that led to the saloon. He put his hand on the broom handle that, wedged against the wall, kept the door closed.

"Best not," said the kid. "Patients are entitled to one free drink at the saloon if they want, but you gotta bring them here yourself, and as soon as they're through, you best slam that broom handle back in that groove. If not, half the beds will be full of drunks in an hour. And that's the least of your worries, believe me. Mort undresses fully before he lays himself down."

The kid checked the hall again, and, seeing it was clear, slid a panel loose from the wall. A store of fifty vials sat inside, a potato peel in each. He sifted through them with gentle fingertips.

"Mrs. Spinner's a regular," he said, "so I give her one of the best peels. A long, fat one, if you can find it. She keeps them. Some people don't, they'll leave them, and we can reuse them, but Mrs. Spinner always takes hers. Imagine that. The old ones all moldy and fallen to bits on her mantle."

The kid selected a peel that had the bearings of a face on one end and placed it in the centre of a small tray. "Can you take Four the tonic while it's still fizzing, then join me in Mrs. Spinner's room? Spinner's a happy old thing when it's over. There's a relief in her voice that will make you smile. It's as close to a benefit as this job offers."

Sod nodded and strode from the room with a cavalier air that made the kid smile.

The kid took the vial to Mrs. Spinner in room nine and cooed when he entered the room. "Here it is, Mrs. Spinner," he sang. "The vile parasite that has been drinking your life."

Mrs. Spinner was a large woman whose hair bore no traces of original colour. It sat above her head in a frazzled, sculpted, white-blond mess that appeared as an aura under direct lighting. She beheld the peel with an expression of revulsion, and then beamed at the kid. These were the finest moments, he thought, and was sorry Sod missed them. The transformative instant, when the peel became the fluke, and freedom from the fluke became freedom from pain, intoxicated the kid. The rawness of hope left him dizzy.

"Oh," said Mrs. Spinner. "Dear oh dear, glory, glory."

She slipped the vial into her purse. She shook her head. "I feel so much better," she said. "Lighter. *Free.* I don't know why I am so prone to flukes."

The kid commiserated, and then used the word Lou told him to use. "These things are insidious," he said.

"Flukes," Mrs. Spinner said, testing the word against her bulwark. "Ailment has beset my whole life. I've been in dim rooms such as this. Through my life, different men have called it different names, yet the pain never stops. But never," she said, her voice rising, fluttering and transparent, "*flukes.* That sounds like what I feel wriggling inside. Your Doc Sappho is a marvel.

I'm unburdened, child. For a few days, at least, living won't hurt this heart!"

Her face flushed at the pronouncement, and she swept the kid's hand to her breast. The kid dizzied at the sudden rush of his blood. Warmth poured from Mrs. Spinner's chest, a pure heat of her joy. A stirring of intimacy, coupled with a torturous curiosity, unsettled the kid; he couldn't move his hand, he wouldn't ever.

This is how they were when Sod came into the room.

The kid snatched his hand away from Mrs. Spinner's chest. "That's all for tonight, Mrs. Spinner," he said, then swept past Sod and down the hallway.

The boys waited until Sod locked the door of the kid's room to explode with laugher. Tension drained, and the kid couldn't remember ever laughing harder. Sod doubled over on the floor. The kid, in an attempt to hang onto the moment, told Sod the story twice over. His voice rang at each embellishment, until Lou abruptly opened the door. His eyes swept the room.

"Who in the hell you talking to, kid?" he snarled. When the kid didn't respond, Lou slammed the door. The music in the saloon rose after a moment, though the kid knew the place empty. The kid resettled himself on his cot and stared at the bare walls of his room.

He spoke again, but didn't expect an answer.

CHAPTER 31

For some time, the kid was aware that large sections of Farrow were devoted to brothels, competing moonshine jukes, and laundry-fronted opium dens, but recently the sensations in his body brought such places into finer focus. He'd spent too much time cleaning the boiling, stinking confines of the still, his lungs infused with the reek of mash, to find interest in drinking and the realm of dust inhabited by drug fiends, as Lou called them, which ate away its initiates with shocking speed, repelled the kid more out of compassion than fear. The brothels, on the other hand, endured in his attention.

Some nights, returning from the forest, the kid took the longer route to the clinic in order to pass through the district called the Winks. Seven brothels called the four cross-streets home, while another dozen peppered Farrow, but only three remained on the kid's continuous route. Each afforded a veiled stoop, covert overhang, or discrete alley from which he could observe their mysterious forms of life.

Shaky Slim's occupied the second floor atop a barbershop and grocer along Rue Elise. Sounds drifted out the windows into the Rue like perfume: laughter, shouts of passion, of anger, the uproarious jazz of the three-piece bands that played night and day. The kid stared upwards, unabashed, and at times wanted to dance in the street.

The joining porch of the Relegate Mercy, a block of redbrick tenements, brought the kid's gaze back to earth. The porch thronged with the women who worked in the Mercy, and the kid could hardly keep a steady pace while passing. Too often, the hot rush of a met glance sent him to studying the coloured lace hung in the windows, or the irregularly stacked brick.

Marian's, the long, low black building off Cleave Ave., lowered the kid's eyes to the murky dirt of the roads. Windows, painted dark and set just above the ground, tantalized with movement and flickered lights where the paint was worn away, but the kid was never brave enough to look. He couldn't figure out if the clientele was rich, or criminal.

The night Lou came into his small room, the threadbare vest and dress shirt he wore in the saloon sweated through, and announced a plan to expand Remedy sales to the brothels, the kid didn't sleep at all. A squirm in his stomach tormented him with visions and longings. Excitement fairly mixed with terror.

When he first entered the brothels, the kid imagined that they were the same as the palaces in Europe. He'd heard of such places, seen a couple in Movie 4 and Movie 9, and noticed no difference from those aristocrat-laden ballrooms and the receiving parlours that, at the command of an imposing matron, filled with prostitutes in fabulous costumes whose talk concerned the airy matters of a higher class. Splendour, he thought, looked the same in all ages, in all places.

The women were kind, or mean in that spirited way that felt like a kindness, a smirk after their acid, and, if he blushed deep enough, a shriek, a kiss, the lingering moment of the warmth of their palms on his cheeks. Not once did they beat him up or smack him. He felt an undeniable vivacity in their tones of flesh, the flush and rouge of their cheeks, the tingle-all-over their wobbly walk inspired. A laugh, a smile, a whisper, spun the kid dizzy. The brazenness of their dress, their language, the exposure of tongues, thighs, and stretches of skin he hadn't even known to covet rendered the kid speechless, locked within a tempest for which he had no vocabulary.

The kid's overexcitement had little effect on Lou's sales plans. Lou dispensed with the Remedy act out of respect for the women, who cultivated distrust of pretense, and kept his pitch straightforward: the Remedy protected against sexual disease, and more importantly, prevented eight of ten pregnancies.

Lou began with a back story of the kid's mother, Lou's wife, a famous madam from the southern swamps who'd passed on the Remedy before dying in a knife fight over the name of a horse. The women who worked in the brothels paid this little mind, however, and pestered Lou with questions of practical importance. Did the Remedy work retroactively, or was it preventative? How long beforehand must it be taken? Could it be used as a douche? Or, as some giggling girls asked, is it good as a gargle?

Lou responded patiently, while the kid marvelled at his calm, the consistency of his answers, which were nowhere else constant. "You choose one story and you never deviate," he told the kid. "Don't waste your time. No set of lives depends more on a network of shared information than those of prostitutes, kid. Don't forget it."

The kid, having little to do during Lou's presentations, spent his time as most did in the receiving parlours; he stared at the women with a mixture of fear and wonder. The women of Slim's were the most varied; often the kid saw the same faces for no longer than a month, then never again. At Marian's the women looked the same and spoke the same. When the kid caught a couple at a cigarette break on the curb, heard their real voices, and saw their real postures, he felt somewhat relieved. The kid found a range of comfortable beauty at the Mercy, women he was not ashamed to stare upon. He looked forward to going there the most.

One girl at the Mercy, a thin girl with strawberry-blonde hair and green eyes, emitted a coiled tension he found familiar. During his fourth visit, he forced himself to speak to her.

While Lou answered questions, the kid approached the green-eyed girl. She smiled, a smatter of freckles under her eyes. The kid's voice burbled in his throat.

"Are you Alice Always?"

She shook her head. She resembled the girl who had tossed her juice on the kid at His Holy Rules, but confidence had replaced fear, calm traded for aggression. "That's not my name anymore, Graveyard," she said. "I'm Alice Callaghan now."

Graveyard. The kid soured. He shook his head. "My name's changed too," he said.

"Yeah? What do they call you?"

The kid stared at the street out the window. "Chatter."

"Kid," said Lou. He stood across the parlour, his case held in both hands. A pack of men in military uniforms spilled in behind him, occupying attention with their shouts and laughter.

Chatter resisted. He hadn't finished looking at Alice, figuring out the ways she'd changed since His Holy Rules. "Can I see you again?"

Alice blushed and rolled her eyes. Chatter wanted to fall to pieces.

"Sure," she said. "But make sure you bring money."

CHAPTER 32

The question of Alice Callaghan's underwear troubled Chatter. No matter how often he played the interaction in his mind, he found no clues as to the colour of her underwear. Unsure why this inarticulateness ached, Chatter lay awake late for hours, feverish with imagination.

He guessed white first, then black, because white or black underwear was what he heard the girls at the orphanages wore. Next, rationally, came a beige colour, accounting for him not noticing a strap against the skin of Alice's shoulder. Prompted by a pin-up of a girl in a bikini in the saloon, Chatter imagined yellow. A burst of sunshine under her clothes. His mind wandered next through a forest of greens and blues, shades of the earth and the sky; he imagined lying with her on a bed of moss and watching the still heavens. After this he drifted toward the treacherous territory of reds, burnt colours that progressed into a silky, enveloping cover that caused him to twist and turn on his cot to no end.

The colour was pink, he decided, after a week of torture.

Alice Callaghan wore pink underwear.

Chatter needed confirmation. He couldn't wait the three weeks before they were due back at the Mercy, and wondered how much money Alice meant. He recalled a tone in her voice, a teasing, that made him think she might have been joking. This caused him no end of torment, either. What if he offered her money and it offended her? He imagined her anger until the pound of his heart silenced all else around him. After another anguished night, Chatter decided he'd better collect money in any case.

Lou kept careful count of the patients who came to the clinic, and expected fees each evening. Chatter didn't dare skim from these amounts—they were fixed, writ. He never forgot Lou's promise to cut his throat if he interfered in business matters. However, there were times when the patients, filled with gratitude, slipped the kid cash. A wadded, sweated handful of coins. Until then, Chatter unthinkingly handed these to Lou as well. *But*, he thought, here were blackberries he could collect.

The next day, Chatter wore himself out with enthusiasm and attentiveness to all the patients in the clinic, believing this the best route to more tips. The effort worked in some cases, but it alienated others, those wretched in their sickness, resentful of their reliance on street magic. Chatter gave these types distance, spoke gravely, and avoided eye contact. They tipped for silence, and a shared sense of misery. After three days, Chatter achieved an even keel, and gathered tips from one in three patients.

He gave Lou a portion of the tips so he wouldn't grow wise, but after the fourth day in a row, Lou accepted the wadded money with a suspicious pause. Chatter held back for a day, but this garnered the same reception. On the sixth day, he handed over all the tips, weary of the deception. It didn't matter; he imagined he'd saved enough. Squirrelled away in the hollow leg of his cot were six and a half dollars.

CHAPTER 33

The next night, Chatter left C O O P and made for the direction of the Winks. A tingle overtook his body as soon as he stepped into the night air, a constriction in his throat that he associated with excitement, and a dizziness at the prospect of fulfilling his nameless longing. He didn't even notice, until he was two blocks away, the feeling in his heart. He walked another block before reversing course.

Once inside the tall grasses beyond the Burrows, he spun and knelt. The sense of the animal was deeper, beyond the birch treeline, but a different silence had haunted his steps, seeming, at moments, to be just behind him. The dirt path that brought him out of the homes was empty. Chatter tore up a few strands of grass and tossed them at the path in an attempt to scatter the feeling.

As he entered the treeline, however, Chatter's focus shifted to what lay ahead. Regardless of what affected him before, he now felt the certainty of worry. The animal was close, in a nearby clearing, and the yearn in Chatter's heart had turned to a rot. Chatter sucked in a quick breath, and knelt again. Memories of the tattered hare at Slatterly made him lightheaded. He pressed his hand into the damp nighttime soil. He listened for a while, but didn't hear any movement ahead. The animal was still alive, but was static, and nearby.

A stoat lay a couple steps into the clearing. Chatter heard its laboured breath as he drew close. It raised its head and attempted to crawl to him, but its back end lay limp on the ground. A pool of blood seeped out of the large laceration that spoiled its side. The stoat huffed at Chatter's hand, but didn't avoid his touch. Chatter shivered at the trickle of the rot, but didn't dare take back his hand. It wasn't long before the stoat passed into motionlessness.

Yet the rot remained, a fading tone his heart would not relent. The unease diminished when he lay his eyes on the odd cluster of twisted sticks across the clearing. At first, he was struck by the utter unnaturalness of their assemblage, the sticks contorted against the grain of their growth, wound around each other, binding the odd shape that they, in their assembly, only half suggested. It was the work of human hands. Chatter shivered again. The strange silence of the grouping unsettled him, and did not disperse the rot completely. There was another source.

After a moment, the figure in the trees came into focus, pallid in the canopy-filtered moonlight. Greaves, motionless, stared back.

Chatter shot to his feet. His mind, at this time, went blank. A tremendous fear washed over him.

Greaves's eyes widened.

A sudden thrashing behind Chatter revealed two men, thin and thick, hewing through the tall grass and around the trees. The thin one was in front, and smacked every offending branch that stood in his way; the thick one followed, trudging as if on an open plain. Each of them wore dark denim with a sooty surface.

Chatter had seen them, or men like them, at Lou's saloon before. The syndicate men in dark denim who hid from the eyes of authority. They chose the dimmest corner and gambled at their table, refusing to speak to Lou or any of the regulars. Lou had brought them up a few times after he'd closed, as he dozed on clinic cots while Chatter attended the still. He didn't like the way the air settled around them. He'd hear whispering, but when he looked, none of their mouths were moving. Chatter searched the faces of the two men who came into the clearing, but didn't recognize them.

The thin one stopped short when he saw Chatter. "Oh, shit, Tuck," he said. "He's right here."

Tuck ambled up, finally pushing aside saplings to enter the clearing. His eyes darted from Chatter to the stoat. "Told you we were too close," he said. Then, after another glance around, "What in the hell is he doing?"

The thin man loomed over Chatter and looked at the stoat with disgust. "What in the hell are you doing, kid?" he said. "You do that? You out here in the dark being mean to animals? Don't have no weapon on ya. This something you do with your bare hands?"

"Lookit his hands, Drago," Tuck said. "Lookit 'em. All covered."

"Covered," Drago said. He looked at Chatter's hands. "I bet you came right out here to do that. You don't never sneak out but to come to the woods. This what you been doing all this time? Sick."

"Don't go tell him we're following him," Tuck kicked up.

"Well, he knows now," Drago said, "and now we know something, too. He come out here, and he does this." Drago's head came up and he scanned the clearing. His eyes fell upon the odd figure of twisted sticks. "What is this?" he said. He marched over to it. "You made this? What are you doing? You sick brained? I don't like this. You come out here, you do this." Drago's leg came up and hesitated for a moment, before he brought his weight downwards. He stamped the sticks until they were broken bits.

"Drago," Tuck said, "come on, leave off this round."

"I'll leave off," Drago said. "I'll leave off. This kid, he comes out here and does this. Sick. Sick shit. You out here doing this? Sick shit."

Drago rushed at Chatter and punched the kid in the mouth.

"Come on, Drago."

"I'm tired of this!" Drago shouted. "I'm sick of *reconnaissance*. We don't make moves ourselves, nothing's gonna move us. You listen, kid, you hear me? You and your partner better clear out your rinky-dink saloon. You're a mite, a leech. You got no cause taking Syndicate business. You don't leave town, we're going to stamp you flat."

But Chatter, stunned by the punch, only held up his hands. "It's not me," was all he could think to say.

Drago's lip came back in revulsion as he looked at the blood and strands of fur on Chatter's hands. He slapped them away. "You clear out," he shouted. "We don't want sick shits like you around here. You come out here, and you do this? This? Sick," he said in a calmer voice. "Sick shit. Sick sick shit."

Drago would not relent. He came forward too quickly. He beat up Chatter for what seemed like an hour. His words twinned with his fists, up and down, up and down. "Sick shit sick shit sick shit sick shit."

And for as long as Chatter kept his eyes open, Greaves remained in the trees, silent, as still as the moon.

CHAPTER 34

Chatter didn't pick himself up until after sunrise, when the grass warmed and he couldn't stand the glare in the sky. A fox at the edge of the clearing stood when he moved, and watched him groan and roll and fight to standing. Chatter stared at the animal for a while, but there wasn't anything in his heart. The fox was merely waiting for him to leave so it could scavenge the stoat.

Lou was awake but tipsy drunk when Chatter limped through the saloon on his way to his room. Lou's head kicked up at the commotion, and he peered at the kid through the tangle of his long grey hair. He looked Chatter over, the bruises on his neck, the scrapped cheeks, his tattered clothing. When Chatter opened his mouth, Lou held up a silencing finger. "I don't want to hear it," he said. "I don't want to know anything about it. Wasn't anyone I know."

"Lou," said Chatter.

Lou smacked his hand on the table, and he pointed at the kid. "Go to your bed," he said. "Hide that ugly face."

Before Chatter could leave the room, however, Lou spoke up again, issuing his words to the kid's back. "Listen," he said. "Keep the clinic closed tonight. Until at least the redness fades and you can walk proper. Ain't nobody going to believe in a healer who can't heal himself."

That night, Chatter slipped into the Winks. A tightness in his lungs suggested the nearness of a dying animal, but he ignored the sensation and the fear and guilt that rose.

Something burned inside his body, and he feared he'd die if it wasn't quenched.

When the Relegate Mercy came into sight, a chill invaded his bones and made him feel dislocated in space. Chatter hardly heard the music and voices that drifted from the tenements. Sweat seeped from his kidneys; he fought the urge to flee. Only after he considered the risk he'd taken stealing from Lou, and the inhumanity he'd shown to whatever animal died in the dark, alone, did Chatter decide that he had no other option than to enter the Mercy.

The atmosphere in the receiving parlour thickened with cigar smoke and cologne at night. Chatter sat near an open window to avoid coughing. He didn't see Alice amidst the girls circulating, and fretted in an uncomfortable bucket chair. A tall woman with beautiful dark skin and a high hairdo knelt next to him, but the cut of her dress distracted him from what she said. She stood, and a moment later came back with a thin glass filled with ice and a brownish-gold liquid.

"There you are, sweetie," the woman said. "That's a dollar and a half."

Chatter felt the floor fall away. He pulled out the bills he'd counted and recounted, and gave the woman a dollar and a fifty-cent piece. Her eyes lingered on his hand.

"Something wrong with the service?" she said, then, after Chatter handed her fifty more cents, she bowed, batted her eyes, and said, "The gentleman's generous tonight."

As she sauntered into the blur of the room, Chatter felt miserable. He sipped the drink, but the smell of alcohol reminded him of the confines of the still, so he left it on the windowsill. A couple of the circulating girls tried to engage him in small talk, but his focus was scattered. He did little more than nod his head. He counted down from four over and over.

When Alice Callaghan came into the receiving parlour, barefoot, she wore a dress of diaphanous taffeta. Her hair hung loose about her shoulders. An unkempt burst of life, exciting

Chatter with each tilt of her head. She came straight to him and drew up a gilded stool. "Hello, Chatter," she said.

"Hello, Alice Callaghan," he said.

She smiled, but didn't respond. She had a silver stud on the left side of her nose he hadn't noticed the first time they spoke. This banished words from his mind. In an effort to seem casual, he retrieved his drink and leaned back in his chair with the glass balanced on his hand.

Alice giggled. "Do you mind?" she said. She took his drink and downed half. Chatter swooned.

"How do you do that?" he said. "I couldn't stand the smell of it."

"Me neither," she said. "That's why you drink it quick. Don't give your tongue time to catch up."

Chatter nodded, and with no more hesitation tipped the liquor back into his mouth. The cold shocked his throat and stung his eyes. A sharp pain spread through his body before bursting into a mist of tender warmth. His eyes watered.

He drooled, laughed. Alice joined him.

"Why did you change your name?" he said, following a sudden burden of civility.

Alice shrugged, and gave him a smile. "The same year you left Rules," she said. "This woman comes to the orphanage and claims she's my mother. She has paperwork, too. She says she was young, scared, and stupid when she gave me up, but now she's lived her life, and means to make good on mine. Callaghan's her last name."

Chatter's eyes travelled around the room. "Does she work here, too?"

Alice laughed again, a different laugh this time. "No," she said, "I haven't seen her in years. We lived together for a while, sure. But things didn't work out. We're two different people, she and I. She wants her own life, but she needs somebody standing in the way of it. I was that for a while, I guess, but not as interesting as some man. So, my mom took off again. Before she left, she told me she'd owed her brother something, but now was free. She sounded happy at the time. I didn't know she'd traded me to him, to the Mercy."

Chatter nodded, but wasn't sure he'd understood. A blur spread from the corners of his eyes, the dimensions of the room grew fluid.

Alice laughed again and shook his leg. Delight in her smile. "The parlour is boring," she said. "Let's go upstairs."

Alice's room was larger than Chatter's at the clinic, but no roomier. A double bed occupied most of the space; a barren nightstand whose surface was covered in the dried rings of drinks past, a small lamp, and a squat dresser were squeezed into the room. Brash pink lace hung in the window, which Chatter took as a good sign.

Alice flopped on the bed without inviting Chatter, and he strolled around the room before he joined her. Water stains ate away the wallpaper, revealing cracked plaster underneath. A line of ants marched upwards in a corner. Turning to the bed, Chatter understood the low lights in the brothel.

Alice rose when Chatter sat, and rested her hand on his leg. She smiled, and inched closer.

"I don't have enough money," Chatter burst out, unable to suppress the knowledge any longer. He felt his face flush, and couldn't remember being so embarrassed. He felt like crying, and squashed the urge by standing and pacing.

Alice laughed her warm laugh. "What do you need money for?" she asked, her voice lighter yet. Her delight infuriated him without making him angry. He opened and closed his mouth several times. "Chatter," she said, "how much money do you have?"

Chatter froze. He reached for his pocket, but decided it would be a mistake to pull the money out. "Four- and one-half dollars."

Alice did him the favour of merely nodding. Her smile broadened, but she didn't laugh. "How much did you bring in the first place?" she said.

"Six-fifty."

She nodded again. When he looked at her, her smile hadn't shifted. "It's fine," she said. "I'll say you got nervous and hopped out on me. It happens with young guys. They'll forgive it. The first time, at least."

"Oh," said Chatter. "All right, that's fine."

Her laugh broke through him and shattered every plan he had inside. He wanted to run from the room. "Have you ever kissed a girl, Chatter?"

Airless, suspended, he breathed. "No."

Alice brought him to the bed. She kissed him slowly, and then let him kiss her heavily. She corrected the vigourous press of his lips, and chided him when pride made him hide his face. The Mercy, she explained, taught her that all life has rhythm, and then she showed him how to flutter his kisses and please her. Chatter sank into oblivion. In the end, Alice sat above him and traced patterns in his shirt with her fingertips.

They spoke for a while, but Chatter barely heard her voice over the beat of her heart in her thigh. Words, thoughts, belonged to a fractured place, inferior to the state they'd achieved. Alice curled in laughter; her palms lay on Chatter's chest. The soundlessness stretched indefinitely, time dissolved alongside language. Alice's hands, the small weight of her palms, contained the entire universe. Chatter imagined his bruises fading beneath the kindness of her touch, the fracture of his rib resettling, the dryness in his throat gone. He thought of bathing in the river with the others from the culvert, of pushing out from its silty bottom into suspension.

"Thank god," Alice said and rocked on top of Chatter then slid onto the bed next to him. He realized she'd concluded a story with her statement, but couldn't remember what she'd said.

"Really," she said, "Thank god. Maggie Allalong's cough was the nastiest thing. None of us could stand to be in the room when she got going. But after two weeks of her drinking your Remedy, I don't hear a thing. Some of the other girls say they do, but they don't."

Chatter nodded. An instinct caused him to suggest it also as a treatment to increase volume in the hair.

"Sure," Alice agreed. "You're going to get so many orders next time you come in. That stuff is way cheaper than other birth control."

Another instinct told Chatter to hold up a finger and chime the phrase *eight of ten*, but the thought made him feel hollow. Up through the floor came the happy clink of glass rims, the rising tone of a joke, the complementary chorus of laughter. One man shouted over another, over the hum of countless conversations. Groans, moans, and claps penetrated the walls and ceiling. Here frantic, there passionate, there angry. Cries of pain, cries of surprise. A wail of ecstasy nearby, drowned out by the call and response of one begging for a spanking. Chatter sat up off the bed and went to the window, but found it nailed closed. He stared at the ceiling, nervous, suddenly, of meeting Alice's eyes.

Before he left, Alice raised her head off her pillow. "Chatter?"

Chatter paused, the door half open. "Right," he said. He reached for his pocket.

CHAPTER 35

When he returned to the clinic, Chatter found half a dozen syndicate men kicking Lou's still to scrap. They'd collapsed the walls of the clinic, broken the furniture, and left Lou semi-conscious in a corner. Mort, brandishing a broken bottle, huddled in a corner, fled for the door at his first chance. Chatter hazarded a butcher knife, and the men in dark denim left him alone. He didn't recognize Drago nor Tuck among them. Numb with fear, Chatter sat next to Lou until the men left.

Later, at an uprighted table, Lou grew morose. He shouted at Chatter for not alerting him to men in dark denim, but the moment Chatter made to respond, Lou slapped him. Afterward, Lou, wobbled with whiskey, told the kid that it didn't matter. None of it mattered. The kid shouldn't cry, Lou said. He blamed himself. He knew the moonshine syndicates still operated in Farrow's wildernesses, squabbling over the last of the illegitimate patrons, and admitted the men could have come from any of them. They'd been cracking down on operations allowed impunity during the free-for-all of prohibition. He never should have allowed the men as customers, but he couldn't afford to be picky. Lou, after another drink, admitted to undercutting prices that very afternoon to revive business. The notion of such swift, retributive consequence scared him worse than Chatter had ever seen. "Thieves is worse than cops," he swore. He jumped at every noise from the courtyard, and when Mrs. Spinner knocked at the clinic door, Lou screeched at her until she fled down the cobblestones.

"We got nothing, kid," Lou said. "I've got no mind to fight an enemy who won't listen. No. Heard me? I said no, Lou. You ain't set yet for fine things. Kid, this isn't our game. Wasn't none but a dream anyway, and those are cheap enough to have every night. Thanking foresight, we have other lines in the water. Thanking goodness for the fine women of the Winks. We owe our whole lives now to those frail sisters."

"No," Chatter said, his voice a burble of acid inside him, "we don't."

Lou straightened in his chair. His eyes sudden and sharp. "What you say?"

Chatter sat as tall as he could. "I told Alice Callaghan our Remedy is moonshine," he said. "I told her about the cistern in the Gardens."

Lou didn't speak. He overturned their last table, and with every ounce of his strength, he beat the kid.

CHAPTER 36

Two days later, Lou remained tenuously sober. He and Chatter lived amidst the wreckage of C O O P, and they made no effort to clean. Chatter drifted in and out of sleep, keeping still for hours, pretending sleep, as Lou wandered about the space, muttering, shifting a pile of broken wood or bent copper. Once, Mort showed up, but Lou didn't even have a bottle to sell him. Pain clouded Chatter's mind; he was insensible to anything but the ache that overtook every movement. On the third day, Lou dragged Chatter to the house in the Gardens, and they dug up the potatoes.

For four days after, Chatter did nothing more than peel potatoes at C O O P. Lou's single consolation was to help the kid rebuild the walls of his room, but he left the door unhinged. He broke up the rest of the furniture and used it to fuel cooking fires. He roasted, fried, and stewed the potatoes. He swore he'd scallop, but never did.

Chatter sat on the wadded mattress in his room and peeled. He was certain the potatoes had contracted a disease in the plots, but when he mentioned this, Lou threatened to serve him nothing other than potatoes boiled in Remedy. During his waking hours, Chatter did little else but retrace the last day of Sod's life. The smell of starch infested his memories of Sod's death and heightened the guilt he felt at not hearing his last words. A haze grew in his head, a sick he couldn't shake.

When Lou told Chatter they had a show that evening, the kid shook his head. The swat from Lou knocked Chatter off his chair. "I hadn't realized His Majesty enjoyed the luxury of choice," Lou said. Wooziness clouded the kid's response, his words hurried against nausea.

Lou brought Chatter to a bar in the Burrows known as Captain Nimble's Gamble. The inside was dark, with fire-blackened panels absorbing the dim light of camping lanterns, meant to emulate a prospector's camp. Lou assumed his position at the bar and turned his back to the room. He signalled the kid.

Chatter kicked the door open. "Doc Mara!" he shouted.

The room swam. A tickle worked its way through Chatter's lungs. His throat itched. Tears flooded his vision. Lou spun with a theatrical flourish while the kid delivered his next line.

"It's Alice, Doc," Chatter said as he tottered. "She needs your Remedy."

Lou narrowed his eyes at the abbreviated script, but he didn't miss a beat. He waved the kid away. "Isaac," he said. "Kid, you'll get none of that from me."

Attentions rose, hooked on Lou's line. A righteous woman informed Lou of ethical provisions. "Yeah," slurred Chatter. He wiped sweat from his forehead and stumbled in place.

At the back of the room, a ragged man hopped aside. Others turned their heads, gasped. A chorus of whispers took up behind him, and Chatter turned from Lou. He stared at the door he'd kicked open.

Drool settled into the folds of Chatter's shirt. Warmer and heavier than he would have expected. He giggled, and then collapsed to the floor. He pressed his forehead into the coolness of the concrete. The yearn in his heart was almost unbearable.

When Chatter raised his head, a large jackrabbit, dark in its summer coat, crawled towards him. Mange marred its fur, and its limbs were wiry from starvation. Its head came up and down in caution as it approached, independent of its limp. Chatter slid along the floor. He reached out his hand. His mind was blank; a bright white light.

A gasp startled the stunned silence, then shuffles, exclamations. Pockets of sound blossomed. Chatter lifted his eyes from the dead jackrabbit. Some people stood on chairs; others were on their knees.

For a moment the room paused, then a wave of motion swept towards the kid.

CHAPTER 37

Chatter woke under an overhanging willow that shielded him and Lou from the rain. Their cooking fire lit the dome of leaves from beneath, and left a sky of a thousand moving parts. Chatter stared upwards, calmed by the quiver of each leaf, patternless in the breeze. What a fool he'd been, he thought, ignoring the yearn because of his pain, hiding amidst buildings. A sudden shame at the distance the hare crawled made him curl towards the scree surface of the willow's bark. He hoped Lou was drunk, that they were far enough into the night for him to be insensible, but when he checked, Lou sat upright over the fire, his eyes dancing clear and alert in the flicker of the flame. A storm moved across the prairie behind him.

Lou turned the spit, and then poked at the low fire. Embers rose into the canopy, and flared out amidst the wet leaves. "You heal animals?" he said after a while. "Shit. There ain't no angle in that."

"No," Chatter said. "Animals come to me to die. Jackrabbits, mostly. I don't know why. None speak to me. And there's no one else to ask. I can't heal them, even if I try."

"And do you try?"

"Every time," Chatter said. "Imagine if I could heal them. Maybe that'd make sense of it. But I don't know how to do anything."

"Sure looked like healing, kid," Lou said. "You took away its pain. Redeemed it of its life. You don't see that? There's not a single person in that room that didn't think you did that animal a favour. Pity it didn't have money."

"I didn't do anything."

Lou stared into the fire for a while, his eyes wide and unfocused. He nodded when he looked at Chatter. "Maybe the meaning isn't what you bring to it, kid," he said, "Maybe the meaning is what it brings you. What it brings us. I knew I felt something when I helped you from that mongrel house. Because I'm *due*. I've toiled in the gutters long enough. I was foolish to see my fortune in moonshine. Pleasuring my own pool isn't the right angle on business. But we aren't the types for that, right? Our hearts are on the road. What you have, well, *hell*. Drunks come and go with the fashion, but the world will never starve of sickness, nor of hope."

He stood, and watched the gathering of thunderheads over the prairie. His enthusiasm perked up Chatter.

"I tell you about Padre Ortiz?" Lou said. "Taught me when I was younger than you. Made a killing selling cures, numbers like you wouldn't believe. His goldmine, however, was the healings he performed in tents. He packed farmers and folk into a canvas tent of his very own and took money right out of their pockets. He sang them Lord this, and Life that, and then he shoved them on their asses. They loved him for it. He had the finest circuit through the summer prairies. I travelled with him twice myself." Lou laughed. "He had this saying he loved when drunk. He'd hold up his finger and he'd say, *Kid, every flock wants to be fleeced.*"

Lou's smoky laugh grew louder as he returned to his seat across the fire. "Every flock wants to be fleeced," he said. "We've been mistaken. No, the mistake is mine. I'll admit it. Sticking to flukes limited our afflictions. Now, this. I mean, what do you even call this? Hell. We'll claim anything we want. This is it, kid, this is our opportunity. We can take money from everybody."

150

Lou poked at the fire until smoke rose on the pitiful carcass. "And you never thought of eating the rabbits?" he said. "Never once figured it was your stomach calling food forth?"

"No," Chatter said. He turned back to the willow's bark.

"Guess you weren't ever hungry enough," Lou said.

CHAPTER 38

Chatter shouted at Lou over the sound of the highway. He yelled until his temples throbbed and his vision seeped red at the edge. Tufts erupted when he stamped his feet. Years of dust, stirred up by the nearby traffic, covered the defunct Starlite Drive-In. Chatter roused decades in his wake. He kicked a spray at Lou's ankles.

Lou laughed and danced away. He skipped from the kid's fury, and taunted the effort. Chatter stamped. Lou spun, and swept the kid into his arms. "Once more," he said. "Pay attention, now. Watch how I disconnect your body from your mind. Remember, you're an old biddy who's heard there's a healer in town. You've come to this canvas tent, and finally been called to stage. You're nervous and happy, thrilled to receive the attention of the audience. And here comes a high and holy man who has a hand charged with the Lord. You've seen others knocked over by his touch, only to stand healed, but when your turn comes, you're scared and you root your feet. Go on, kid, root. You don't think I'll knock you over?"

Chatter's head swirled as Lou touched the exposed skin of his lower back. Lou's other hand rose, hovering just higher than Chatter's sightline. Chatter rooted. Lou's little finger lifted from his lower back and stroked the kid's spine.

"See," he said, and broke Chatter's concentration, "Sometimes I'll stroke your spine twice, just until it tickles. Now, look at your feet. Where's your balance? You're already on your heels, leaning on my hand. See how much of your weight I carry? And here comes the touch."

Chatter's eyes darted back to Lou's descending hand. As his fingers graced the kid's brow, Lou released Chatter's weight.

A fine curtain of dust rose into the air as Chatter's feet shot upwards.

Chatter got to his feet in a wrathful silence. He turned from Lou and glowered at the corrugated tin fence that surrounded the drive-in. Stains ran its gamut, preserving soda splashes, exhaust burns, and the footprints of a thousand mid-movie hoppers, headed to or from the highway on the other side. The road wasn't visible inside the theatre area, but its presence was undeniable. The fence roared.

Sod's weary ghost hopped over the corrugated tin and walked across the drive-in, weaving around the waist-high white posts topped with dead speakers. He wouldn't come closer. Guilt rotted Chatter's guts.

He turned to Lou and brushed his shirt clean. "It's hot, Lou. How does shoving me in the dirt help with faith healing?"

Lou toed the dust. A cloud rose at the flick of his ankle. He watched it settle with the same patience he displayed with the kid, confident his will would endure all others.

"Listen, your job isn't faith, and it ain't healing," Lou said. "Your job is to build a belief. Now belief and faith ain't even near the same thing. A belief is the story you tell, faith is how much someone wants it to be true. Belief is the outside language we use, faith is the inside language they use. Faith is in the hands of your flock. It's damn near their favourite trick; they'll use it as often as they can, same as any kid with a new-shined rifle. It's their remedy against doubt. And each time they squash doubt with faith, your job gets easier. Belief is the house you build, kid, faith is the dance they do inside. You use words they know already. *LordHolyGod*, you say, and they'll nod and nod. Don't name names. Anything believed finds its proper name inside each believer. The Everyman Affliction is a belief, right? The tickle in their throat is faith. *What* you want them to believe doesn't matter. People will believe anything you build proper. Keep in mind, kid, you're not selling medicine, you're selling sickness."

Lou opened his face to the sun.

Chatter toed the dust.

"Padre Ortiz cured cancer by telling a tent full of people they had cancer," Lou said. "He swore he smelled the poison growing in their lungs. Swept his nostrils around the stage. Inhaling. Inhaling. *All of you*, he declared, *are dying this very moment.* Then he gave them his famous line: *My brothers and sisters, the habits that help you through life are those that kill you.* Isn't that great? He promised a cure to any who threw their cigarettes on stage. He told me later he hadn't bought a pack of smokes in three decades."

Lou's eyes glazed with memory. "I can count a half-dozen exorcisms I saw Padre conduct," he said. "Him holding down some writhing body on the rattling boards of his stage. Each a vagrant Ortiz found in the afternoon, paid before and after the show. Toothpaste helped them froth at the mouth, and no doubt did a favour to the terrified parishioners who kneeled over the tortured soul."

"And the Psychic Surgery," Lou continued. "Padre performed only a few public Surgeries. He pulled sick, cancerous growths from the abdomens of virgin farm girls and withered biddies alike. They were chicken kidneys, tattered with a steak knife before the show. When Padre scooped out those pulsing masses, the whole damn room believed. They found *religion*."

Chatter kicked the dust again. "I don't know nothing about Religion," he said.

Lou waved off the word. "Religion is nothing, kid," he said, "Just rules and rituals. Gold robes that make men feel like God. I said religion there, but I meant belief. Don't worry about religion, kid, rules and rituals are as empty as cups—they only exist because life is so long. Trust this, when their asses hit the floor, they'll *believe*."

Chatter shook his head. He held out his hands. "It isn't going to work," he said, "None of them are sick."

"Haven't you learned anything, dummy?" said Lou. "Every person in the world thinks they're sick. Ever since the invention of disease. One of the finest cons ever constructed, kid, believe me, I'll credit doctors with that one. Hell, have an old bird stand before a crowd. She's never had such attention in her life. If she sniffles, she'll swear she's dying. She'll see all those people needy to pray for her, and all of a sudden she's dead as death."

Lou stepped closer to Chatter. Danced his nimble dance. "At that point," he said, "you don't even have to be there. She's sewn herself up. You tell her you have the cure. You don't tell her what's in it. She already assumes she won't understand."

Chatter stiffened as Lou placed a hand on his back, and raised the other before him. Lou's palm moved towards the kid's forehead. "Your old bird leans back naturally," said Lou. "You rise up your hand and her head will rise, her body will take care of the rest. Feel her spine press into your palm. There. There? Feel your balance shift? You wait until your old bird is off balance, then tell her she's set to get what God intended. You grace her forehead with your thunderous touch. At the same time, you look her in the eye and slip your hand from her spine."

Chatter fell to the dust while Lou made merry sounds. Lou held out his hand, but the kid got up himself.

"Pay attention to what you experience now," he said. "Don't let anger get in the way, hell, don't let anything get in the way. *Feel* your spine release into my hand. You'll never be able to convince someone else if you yourself aren't convinced. Learn the feel of the body in suspension. Here is where you live. Here is where *we* live, the place between balance and standing. We have to be more vigilant than most, we have to see further. You've got to pay attention, kid."

A low sundog resolved itself into Sod. Over the fence again. His path a wobble. He gave each speaker post the solemn space accorded to headstones.

Lou snapped his fingers.

"People transmit their desires in the same manner," Lou said. "A throat touched in a nervous way. A shift or drop of voice. The sweat that breaks across brows. Eyes will widen at the sight of hope. These are languages you must learn."

Lou paced a distance, then sat amidst a cloud. Chatter waited for a while. Sod climbed the far fence and disappeared. Lou hunched forward. When Chatter sat next to him, Lou had sketched a map in the dust.

"We're heading into the country," he said. "No damn arguments. It'll be easier to attract rabbits out there. Then, when you feel yourself tugged, we find us a crowd, and you perform your trick."

Chatter felt cold in his chest. "It's not a trick," he said.

Lou turned to him. He tossed the stick he'd been drawing with into the dust and obliterated the map with a flat hand. "Sure, it is," he said. "We go into the country. You perform your trick, and I'll get us into the rest. That's how we start. Let me do the talking. You just look lost, and at my signal, you reach out your hand."

CHAPTER 39

In union halls and community centres, barns new and old, whatever venue Lou secured, Chatter healed with his bare hands. Lou touted their myth around town any day Chatter's heart buzzed with the yearn, his head cottony with an unrealized sneeze. At Chatter's signal, Lou led onlookers to a public place, and a crowd awaited the rabbit. Lou thrilled at badgers, beavers, and fawns, and charged double those evenings.

Once, Lou made Chatter wait for a hare in the midway of a harvest festival. More than two hundred people witnessed the kid lay his hands on the sick little leveret. Lou and Chatter couldn't perform that evening, however. A gang of incensed carnies chased them beyond the county line.

At the end of August, they bought a canvas tent and an old silver pickup to haul their gear. Lou paid extra for a tent with brass riggings. The support poles even had brass tips, though Chatter argued this was a useless feature for something driven into the ground. Lou paid him no mind. The possession of a tent, the same as Padre Ortiz had owned, cheered Lou considerably.

Lou started each night by suffocating the crowd. He led them in song after song, encouraged them to shout praise until they were dizzy. He put fury into a trembling crowd. The meekest old men hollered their lungs out at his request. *For the Lord*, Lou swore, *Per the Almighty.*

Chatter stayed behind him on the stage, playing the mysterious mute, while Lou, a silhouette before a sea of faces, shouted praise and humility. Some members of the audience refused to look at Lou, and glowered at Chatter the whole night. They'd twinned his silence with the silence of the sick inside, as though this were the first time they realized that the silences of hope and despair sprang from the same source. This didn't bother Chatter. He'd received similar stares as an orphan.

Lou quieted the crowd when they grew flushed. He churned their hearts into prayer. "Lord," he shouted, "need the sick beg you to remove sickness?"

By October, the nights were a blur until the moment Lou called the sick onstage. "Come ye," Lou said and stamped his foot. The stamp their signal. Chatter played pious and approached the front of the stage. Lou still handled the falls, giving the other half of the audience the show they came for, while Chatter performed moments of quiet intimacy with the frail and infirm, the suppurating and feverish, who would only suffer further from the fall.

The jackrabbits had prepared Chatter for the revulsion. Lou delighted in revealing tumours, bulbous growths, and gangrenous stains; he wanted the audience sure of what plagued humankind. When Chatter reached for a stretch of tortured flesh, the audience recoiling, Lou hiding his eyes in a theatrical manner, he didn't falter. He never forgot the shame of hesitating before the tortured hare at Slatterly.

One night, in late November, Lou and Chatter played to a crowd of fifty-seven. Farmers, families, hired hands, and over two-dozen townspeople from a local municipality named Mason's Ridge crowded into the tent, despite the light snowfall. Lou shouted his first line three times before they quieted into rows and gave him their undivided attention, their eyes settling on Lou's thrust hands.

"Live forever!" Lou shouted.

When Lou hearkened the sick to the stage with the four lines of ancient poetry he knew— "My children, you've made my heart pitiful. I cannot ignore your need, nor your sickness. Well I know what whittles your every hour. Yet sick as you are, not one of you is sick as I"—over forty people identified themselves as wanting healing.

Lou, in the face of the demand, fell to the contingency, and traced his and the kid's family history, evoking generations of itinerant healers who traversed Africa, Europe, and Asia, finding sickness by the pricking of their palms, descending to the father and son on display. The father blessed with voice, the son a mute since the death of his mother in a southern bayou. Both, Lou assured the crowd, healed with the same veracity. "We," swore Lou to a dizzied crowd, "are the natural gift of the planet."

Lou and Chatter healed two at a time, laying down bodies on the stage one after another. Chatter bowed his head to listen to the whispered ailments, but after the first few, he didn't bother, and placed his hand on the first stretch of flesh offered. Bodies rattled the plywood; Lou and the kid had long before worked out the timing. Two hours passed before the last person, a withered weaver, pulled off his shirt and revealed to the audience a globular tumour.

After Lou closed the show with a final pass of the collection plates, Chatter, in a daze, watched the crowd file out into the grey, snowy evening. He fixed on the odd movement of a teenage girl with braided hair. She made her way to a distant truck with her family. They were all dressed in the plain, hardy clothes of labourers. Chatter remembered the girl in line, but couldn't recall if he'd healed her.

She tried to make her gait seem natural, but she oversold it. Her leg was too stiff, she put too much weight on it, and it tugged her shoulders. Her braid bobbed. That was what caught his attention. The bob of her braid. She held onto her mother's arm, which was also held too stiff, bent to take her daughter's weight. Her brothers and father walked a few paces ahead, caught up conversing about the falls, but each of them, discretely, glanced back. And each time the girl pushed herself from her mother's arm and forced a few easy steps. Her mother caught her after. The perseverance on the girl's brow made Chatter nauseous.

He followed the family into the rows of cars and trucks parked in the foggy field. Twice the girl looked back, but she didn't stop. When Chatter caught up and asked if he might speak with the girl privately, the entire family, mother, father, and three sons, stared, flabbergasted. For a moment, Chatter returned their blank wonder, uncomprehending, before he shook his head, and added, "The Lord lends me voice when required."

Cautiously, the mother allowed Chatter to take her daughter's hand, then her weight, and lead her away from her family. Chatter staggered, as the girl leaned on him, and struggled to escort her far enough that their voices went unheard. Her fingers dug into the soft flesh on the inside of his arm.

"I noticed your limp," Chatter said. "You didn't have that when you left the stage. Do you want me to touch your leg again?"

The girl's eyes flashed, but she shrugged. With a pit in his stomach, Chatter noticed the girl's anger. She hid this, too, from her family. "What would be the point?" she hissed. "You think it stands a better chance working this time around?"

She pushed Chatter's arm away and squared her weight on both legs. A tear dribbled down her cheek.

"Wait," Chatter said, "I wasn't the one who touched you. There was two of us. Do you remember who touched you?"

The girl stared at Chatter for a long while. Finally, disgust creased her lip. "Doesn't matter," she said. "You all look the same to me." She wiped the tear away and walked back to her family, her step as confident as when she left the stage.

Chatter's eyes fell upon the brothers, who shot him wide-eyed glances from behind the barrier of their mother, and he felt small and cowardly. The sight of the girl taking her mother's arm, and the two of them fighting for her balance, made Chatter sick for a week. He felt glad when, a couple weeks later, Lou told him they were shuttering for the winter season.

"Goddamn cold freezes a man's soul," Lou said. "Leaves folks believing there's nothing left to heal."

CHAPTER 40

Chatter thought about the girl all winter. Lou spent a meager sum renting a single-room cabin on the edge of a mountain lake named At-Sun-Still-Shines. The rental included a shanty on the frozen expanse of the lake, seven hundred feet of fishing line, and a modest set of hooks and sinkers. Each day, Lou and Chatter hiked from the cabin to the shelter. Neither spoke, nor felt the need, the silence recuperating after the noise of the tents, the constant push of the road.

In their first week, Lou spoke just once, when he taught the kid how to gut a fish. "Get your fingers in there," he said.

The lake yielded rainbow trout and bull char. The fish were old, fat from the spawn, and ready to die. Chatter grew efficient at clubbing them as soon he freed them of the line. A quick, single jerk of his arm. That was all. Once, a sturgeon burst from the hole in the ice, a writhing moment of primordial chaos that almost knocked Chatter into the lake. He killed it after two or three missed attempts. Lou laughed and laughed. At the cabin, they smoked fish and fried fish, and Lou taught the kid the bliss of thin strips of raw fish. The rare delicacies were the perch, the slightly bitter grayling, and the vague consistency of mountain whitefish. The sturgeon was a freak occurrence.

They spent nights in the shanty when Lou drank too much. Chatter now came up to Lou's shoulders, but he lacked the strength to bear Lou's weight. Each time Lou passed out, Chatter, incensed, vowed to march back to the cabin, but never did. He dozed in his clothes under blankets, rising every couple of hours to tend the wood stove.

The ice shifted under Chatter in the night's quiet. He lay paralyzed, convinced he'd fall through if he moved. He tried to remember if he'd felt anything different when he put his hands on the limping girl. He pictured the knobbiness of her knee, the odd bulge of her shinbone. The prickle of her fine hairs on the inside of his palms. Later, he'd comfort himself with the certainty that he hadn't laid hands on her at all. Lou had handled her, and the pain she endured came from the fact that Lou couldn't heal shit. Guilt left him flat by dawn, however, shame pinning his shoulders to the ice. He'd let her right by him, she'd come so close, but he was too lazy to give her his hand. He called himself every terrible name he could think of. Again and again, he pictured her spite, soothing himself by calling it misdirected, picturing her face instead as he took his hand off her leg. Her happy skip off the stage to where her family waited. He felt ill at the thought, but didn't curl, for fear of breaking through the ice.

One night, the kid woke to the low crunch of snow. He caught a flutter of motion at the window, but when he peered out the frosted glass, there was no one in sight. He crept outside the shanty, into air so crisp it felt alert. Moonlight illuminated the vast plain of snow that lay on the ice. A single set of tracks led from across the lake to the window of the shanty. Chatter checked in all directions, but spotted no other life upon the silent surface of At-Sun-Still-Shines.

Chatter's voice came as a whisper amidst his crystalline breath. "*Sod?*"

In the depth of winter, when the days were only six hours long, Chatter listed the people he was *sure* he'd healed. Memories rose—relief broadening on the face of a clockmaker in Bingly, the gasp of an actuary in Gloaming's Resort, and the sudden quiver of a basket maker's thighs in the community of Crace—but soon left Chatter awash in murkier sensations he couldn't trust. He remembered when a seventy-year-old retiree licked his neck in Lister, the lingering wetness obliterating all else; he might have cured a few that night, but would never know. He longed for a night when he could vanish his doubts in the eyes of one sure heal. Then, he assured himself, he would know that the suffering of his affliction, the silent, wordless call that would never cease, was worth his pain and loneliness.

Towards the end of February, Chatter told Lou he wanted to handle all the healings when they returned to the circuit. They were the first words he'd spoken in months.

Chatter and Lou sat on either side of the folding table in the cabin, the only piece of furniture beyond their beds. A pile of maritime novels, left by previous renters, occupied most of the table, with space cleared for unwashed cups and plates.

Lou put down the book he was reading. "Wouldn't work," he said. "People know the story now. We're family. People don't want the junior version while the senior's on display. No one buys a masterpiece painted by an apprentice."

The phrase confused Chatter, choked his response. He picked up one of the books and flipped a few pages. Lou moved to his cot. He pulled out a pipe and smoked while he watched the sun set over the lake.

"You're struck by lightning," Chatter said. "We rub a dark grease on your arm until it stains, and then you hardly use it. Say it's a message from nature, a humbling; a sign that the next generation is able."

Lou shrugged. The cherry of his pipe cast a red light on his face. "Lightning kills," he said. "I'm dead as dolt if we use that."

"Not if I healed you," Chatter said. "Not if you're alive today because of the miracle in my hands. You can even use the arm again after a while, but we leave it marked. Think, you can wash that off whenever you want. Then we say healing you, I drew inside me both yours and mine. I'll do the healings, you tell the stories. Besides, a lightning strike doesn't kill a man, it makes him a god. Anybody will tell you that."

The light of his pipe fell away. Lou clouded his face in a silky exhale. He stared across the lake for spell. He emptied his pipe into the hollow leg of his cot, and then placed it back on the cold floor. "Kid," he said, "you're a natural."

CHAPTER 41

One night, a girl with auburn hair kissed Chatter as he helped her up from the plywood. A different yearning throbbed within Chatter, and he kissed her back. A howl rose in the tent, the steady rhythm of Lou's voice egging on the crowd. The girl swept off the stage, leaving the canvas walls to swirl. The dusky heat of May saturated the air.

When the hands of women and men lingered on his body, Chatter no longer felt aversion. His nights were whirlwinds, surges of emotion, rising and falling with the energy of the crowd and the inflection of Lou's voice. From one person to the next, Chatter's heart thundered, his hands grew warm, a whiteness clouded his peripherals. Sweat soaked his shirts. The world heaved as he laid his hands on an exposed stretch of skin. Women lingered in his arms, breathing promises into his neck. Months passed without leaving a single clear memory.

Freed from the burden of laying on hands, Lou focused on selling the Remedy and on his private, *intensive* fluke treatments. These treatments offset the healings, allowing Chatter to rest, while Lou worked patients for information, charting paths through prairie towns based on the whims of gossip and conjecture. Lou also performed psychic surgeries, although his proclivity for favouring young women saw them run out of several towns by posses of enraged fathers, brothers, sisters, and lovers.

Toward the end of their second year on the road, Chatter remembered the unimpressed chicken from the coop in The

Burrows. When the audience surged, he saw the bird's dead stare, that calm against the riot in his heart. The shade of the coop offered him a place of sanctuary, while the demands of the healings wore him down. He replaced the fervour of the faces in front of him with the impassivity of that chicken. At times, he could stand outside of himself, subject to the same lurch and shudder of the healing touch. When he wasn't careful, his aloofness grew, and he dropped people too quickly, from too high above the natural bounce of the stage.

Near the end of summer, Chatter introduced a convexity to his touch. He kept his palm lifted above the flesh, touching only with his fingertips. Just once or twice a night, at first, but as summer bore out Chatter performed this reflex with every second believer, meeting their eyes with his same intensity, but never once heeding the tingle in his hand, not once picturing the flow of energy from himself into the other. Still, they grabbed the back of his neck, still their fingers sunk into his shoulders. Still, they shouted. Still, while the plywood wriggled at their weight, they shot to their feet, their faces flush as the rest, and swore their bones felt warm. Some danced, some cried or kept quiet and ashamed at the straightness of their spine, the faultlessness of their step. Each of them *believed*. No matter how many struggled on their way out of the tent, they left the stage healed.

During the second winter on At-Sun-Still-Shines, Chatter thought of little else but the distance from the stage to the chair. Here all were healed. He worked the reason down to two factors: the touch of his hands and the flush of their bodies. The mute strength of the excited body; something as quiet as the hares, as internal. The mind, he decided, used the silence of the body to lie.

While the ice shifted below him, Chatter wondered at this silence. At first, even the questioning felt dangerous. All his life, Chatter had felt locked in a lightless room with an undeniable presence. This wild namelessness was calm unless confronted, at which it flew in unforeseen directions, each time coiling back to overwhelm Chatter with its no-presence, suffocating his thoughts against its inconceivable quiet. Over and over, Chatter tried to frame this presence, to corner it with questions or exhortations, but he remained unsatisfied. Did he owe it fidelity? Or was it his affliction, the same malignancy carried in each breast, which would, one day, entangle itself in the system that it killed? In the end, he came to two conclusions: the silence either sent the jackrabbits or it attracted them; but he came no closer to the truth no matter how often he posed the questions. Finally, defeated, he left himself to the silence, to its refusal, and curled on the ice, hoping to break right through.

One night, he woke again to the sound of steps crunching through hardened snow. He leapt to his feet and rushed out of the shanty, but found himself alone. Footprints approached and circled the cabin, yet no silhouette broke the moonlit surface of the lake. Chatter followed the footsteps out, until the bite of the wind became too much to bear, but he couldn't ascertain footprints' source. When he lay down in the shanty, he heard the water lap against the underside of the ice. That night, and for a month after, he dreamed of the culvert.

CHAPTER 42

When they took up again in March, Chatter noticed an acidy gurgle in his throat during Lou's pitch. In April, during a rainy night under a low oak, the accusation burbled, unsummoned, from the kid: "You're telling people the wrong stories."

Lou didn't indicate he'd heard. He sat with his back in a crook of roots. He inspected the jackrabbit on the makeshift spit, then withdrew his pipe and cleaned it, whistling through the chamber for an irritating spell.

"What did you say to me?"

Chatter ignored Lou's tone. By his figuring, he was fifteen years old. He couldn't count how long he'd suspected he could best Lou in a fair fight. But he knew Lou would never fight fair. Chatter stared into the fire and repeated himself.

"You're telling the wrong stories," he said. "It's all you talk about on stage. Nature this, natural that. You spend so much time convincing people we're some kind of normal, when you should be telling them we're *special*. That's how we make them believe. You don't tell them you're selling them dirt."

Lou studied Chatter until the kid's shoulders settled, then he leaned forward and drew a brand from the fire. He lit his pipe with a sigh. "Kid," he said, "you remember that story you told me the other night? You're talking about that orphanage, that afternoon you and them boys came across that manure and spent hours tossing cow chips like they were stones across the surface of a pond."

"So?"

"You had real shine then. Gazing across a cornfield while I'm slaving on dinner. And there you are, reminiscing."

"So?"

"So, you hated His Holy Rules. And Slap Eddy and Hardnose ain't never drawn a warm tone out of you. You haven't mentioned those boys in years."

Lou cut the kid off. "So, I'm saying anything we half remember becomes a paradise. That's a side effect of the human mind. Every single one works the same way, kid; that's what we call natural. People understand what's come before, but not what's before them if it hasn't, understand? One's natural, one's not. That's the line we walk, providing the service we provide. Natural is what people want. Special, but just so much as they recognize, just what seems natural. Guys like us work from the inside, kid, not the outside. Separate yourself from the crowd and you separate yourself from your profits. After all, people like to imagine money changing hands, not padding your pants. You think any of them know what natural means? Hell. They know a quiver in their parts; that's what we call natural. *Natural.* Doesn't mean anything, but it leaves a big hole. Big enough for guys like me, guys like you, to crawl through. People don't care about nature; they just like the idea of returning to it. Trust me, kid, natural is the same as religion, it's only there because someone built a belief. It's as much a racket now as it was then. *Nature*," he laughed, and drew another draught from his pipe. "Think of it this way: whatever they get, it's fitting. Fit comeuppance for those who have forgotten how vicious nature really is."

Chatter stayed calm, reminded himself of his own argument. "*We're* not natural," he said. "I can't heal half of the people I swear to."

Lou watched the kid. He let his pipe go out and reached for another match. "All the same, that's not a bad percentage," he said.

Chatter crossed his arms over his knees and stared at the nearby rail tracks. A bank of thunderheads massed over the wreck of a distant silo. Pressure built in the air, releasing in tight gusts that tattered their fire. Soon, a downpour would swallow light and sound from the air. Lou knew the tree wouldn't provide sufficient shelter. He snapped his fingers loudly, then pointed at the fire. Chatter turned the jackrabbit until the black smoke disappeared.

"All people are greedy for the same thing," Lou said. "And they lie to themselves about it. What's the problem with us lying to them too? They're just confused. Every single one thinks they're grander than decay."

Chatter nodded, but didn't respond. He was tired of Lou's voice.

CHAPTER 43

In late June, Lou's charting took them closer to Farrow.
He gloried Chatter nightly in his successes as a navigator,
presenting full tent after full tent. Some nights saw the back
walls taken down to accommodate the crowd. When he saw
such demand, Lou broke the nights into two, sometimes three
appearances. They once stayed for thirteen days in a town
called Flowerdale, where the kid pulled dust from the lungs
of coal miners while Lou sold their wives Remedy, swearing it
the best cough suppressant on the market. Thirteen days. The
kid hadn't stayed in a single place that long outside of At-Sun-
Still-Shines, but that was when winter shrunk the world down
to the cloud of your breath in the air. Chatter stared at the vast
prairie behind Flowerdale until he believed the world had but
one horizon.

Outside a hamlet named Riddled, in a field of harvested
rye, Chatter lay his hand on the warm neck of a woman with a
beehive hairstyle. He coerced her into leaning back, allowing
him her weight, then he slipped his hand away. Her arms
swung out, and she caught Chatter's shoulders, but her neck
snapped back, and the jolt served as well as a fall. Her eyes
twinkled as she regained her balance. She let her hand linger on
Chatter's cheek. She returned to her husband in the audience,
a squat man in a harried linen suit, whose face was obscured
by the upraised arms of the crowd, and the kid promptly forgot
them both.

Weeks later, Chatter noticed a growl in Lou's voice as they drew down the interior support of the tent. He knotted the door flaps then peered between them. "Malingerer," he muttered before kicking over a folding chair, "No good waste of." Chatter tried to tune out his gravelly voice, wet with whisky already, but Lou was insistent. He strode to the flaps and stared outside. "Still," he erupted. "Still!"

"What, Lou?" Chatter said. "Godsakes what?"

"Dummy," Lou said. "Shouldn't be surprised you haven't noticed." He brought Chatter to the flaps and pointed at the men scattered amidst the trucks still parked outside the tent. *In the suit*, whispered Lou in a slur of rage. Several men wore suits, but Chatter knew Lou meant the man in the harried linen suit who leaned against the grill of a silver model T. He was surprised Lou hadn't recognized him yet. "Man's appeared of recent," Lou said. "Never taking part, never raising his voice in prayer. Man in his *suit*." With a lightening-darkened arm, Lou reached into his vest and retrieved his silver knuckledusters. "Man wants something," he said. "Man won't leave until he gets it."

Chatter agreed to help, should Mort get the better of Lou in the confrontation, but he stayed in the tent as Lou slipped out. Chatter smiled as he knelt by the flap. Meek Mort, the soft man who curled up in the corners of Lou's saloons. Chatter had noticed him the week before, but hadn't mentioned anything to Lou. Chatter didn't mention anything to Lou anymore. The canvas muffled the conversation between the two, but Lou wasn't in the mood for talk. He drunkenly barked at Mort, who responded in his same old voice. His tone turned pleading as Lou grew louder. Chatter heard the muck of mud, Lou's rallying growl, and Mort's exclamation of a single word. Chatter stuck his head outside the tent to see Lou throw a monstrous swing and miss Mort completely. Lou's wet knees wobbled, and he toppled forward onto the man.

"Please!" Mort squeaked from under Lou. He clenched a small pile of muddied paper rectangles, several of which had scattered on the ground, alongside a trampled silver business card case. "Kid! Can't you reign him in?"

Chatter didn't make a move to help. "Not once in my life," he called back.

CHAPTER 44

Mort, Lou whispered at night, *Mort*. This became the river that carried Lou and Chatter back to Farrow. The promises of Mort, industrious Mort, flattering Mort, who'd somehow married himself into a slaughterhouse empire, who'd witnessed the country crowds and swore that greater crowds awaited in Farrow; established money who paid for regular services, and who weren't as discerning as rural folk. Crowds come for the other crowd, rather than efficacy. Mort, after climbing into Society, saw it needed gifts and amusements at every next step. And Lou, he knew, was a gift. Lou, swept along by Mort's visions, woke in the night bitterly muttering of riches already lost. He paced at all hours, like a mournful dog, pawing at his pockets, raising his voice in a restless howl. Mort says. Mort says. "We've finally found a class more in love with the walls than the show," he'd declare other nights, "You know how easy that would be to manage? Perpetual ecstasy?" Lou's eyes, moist with delight, with wonder, were the raft that carried Chatter home.

They stayed at Mort's Shambles and Dairy, the crown jewel of Mort's inherited empire, a corrugated tin warehouse that ran the length of a block, nestled amidst the cobblestone streets of the brewing and slaughter district. Mort offered a base of operation while they performed private visits and exhibitions around Farrow, and his reputation consequently rose. The invitations to the receiving rooms of the middling rich pleased Mort's wife to no end. One of the offices of the Shambles had been converted into a private chamber; although, drunk in the evening on Mort's largesse, Lou woke in a different spot each morning. Mort fixed a small room in a hayloft above the goats after Lou swore Chatter didn't mind the smell.

"Quarters," Lou reminded the kid at any sign of complaint, "can always shrink to nickels." His bray on par with Mort's rat-a-tat at such quips. Chatter heard them in the silence of the Shamble at nights, rehearsing the witticisms of the day. *"And then,"* Mort gasped for breath, *"And then."*

Lou's script changed for the new clientele. Here, he said, is the kid. And the kid is special. *Special.* He laid this word in the laps of the ladies who sat forward on the edges of couches, perched atop straightened spine, gloved hands folded before them. The kid was *special.* Even when they sniffed at the word, and their cheeks didn't flush, Lou swore it worked. These people were not the downtrodden afflicted. These were the chosen few, who, by virtue of nothing but their birth, the purest and most natural way to be chosen, led the elevated lives. The special lives. Nothing was more natural to them. "And rich ladies' cheeks don't flush," he said.

The men who sat on the sofas and chairs in the sitting rooms of Farrow wore double-breasted suits, the women light dresses busy with pattern. They smelled different than those in the tents, they sat with their mouths closed, and most refused to sing. Lou hypnotized them with rhythms of speech instead, wending their minds around and around in the way of song. Their wonder seemed the same to Chatter, hands alike quivered when he reached out his touch.

"You are *alive*," Lou stressed. "Your body knows how to be so."

Lou's custom of drinking half-full snifters of brandy at boutique healings, claiming it as tonic against the pain in his damaged arm, didn't perturb the guests. Chatter heard a woman with circular lenses remark to a man with oiled hair that such displays came part and parcel with finding redemption in the gutter. "And upon what pulp were Indulgences printed?" returned the man with a cagey wink.

Lou, said Lou when asked his name. *Ruddy Lou.* Lou had claimed a doctorate in the earlier days, but even this wore off as winter moved from Farrow, chased further north by the false spring of March. *Lou*, Lou said, without preface or explanation, without accommodating accreditations. In sitting rooms, bedrooms, foyers, and kitchens. "Ruddy Lou," he said, using his given for the first time in Chatter's hearing, "and this is my son."

Lou, said Lou now, when asked his name. *Lou.*

CHAPTER 45

In a market along the cobblestone roads of the Burrows, Chatter felt an anxious presence. The sensation often preceded one eager to touch his hands. Chatter scanned the crowd. He wandered through a fossil hunter's stall, then one offering scrimshaw on beaver bones, but noticed none of the stiff spines, craned necks, or quiet gossip that heralded such people.

He slipped into one of the muddy allies that led away from the market. Chatter passed a weaver commune in a cul-de-sac, then took a hard corner at a blackened house where vials of green liquid wept ammonia out the windows. Here, he spun, his heart thundering, but found nothing behind him.

A boy appeared out of the darkened doorway beside him. Chatter was stunned by the familiarity. Dirty had metamorphized into a young man. His shoulders had grown to the proportions of his torso, and his laterals rose aside his neck like honour guards. The old scar marred his face, tugging his eyelid where it had healed badly.

He took in Chatter with the stillness of a large animal. He smirked. "Your hair's getting long," Dirty said. "Wouldn't take nothing in a fight to find a handful and expose your pretty throat."

Chatter's spine went to water. Dirty's appearance dragged him back to that fearful kid in the culvert, whispering of boys with knives. Chatter opened his mouth, and then closed it.

Dirty laughed this time. A cruel, unpractised sound. "Still mute. Nice to see you're living up to your name, Chatter."

Chatter shook his head, not allowing Dirty's threat to rattle him. "I'm not fighting anyone," he said. "And no one calls me that anymore."

Dirty came closer. "Sure, they do," he said. He ran his finger down the inside seam of Chatter's flannel jacket. "You've gotten fat." Dirty stared at him. Stared at his hands. He drew a haggard dog-end from behind his ear.

Chatter patted his chest, his hips. He found a lighter and a pack of cigarettes in the front pocket of his coat, and handed them to Dirty.

The boy studied Chatter, then slid three cigarettes from the package. Two, and the dog-end, went back behind his ear. The spark of Chatter's lighter cast his face in a pale light, and for a moment, Dirty's contentment showed. "That's smooth," he said, languid in his exhalation. A long, slow stream of smoke poured from his mouth. "Damn. Goddamn."

"I heard you've been showing your face round town again," Dirty said. "Fresh as a daisy, they say, so I had to see myself. See the audacity."

Shame welled in Chatter. He glanced about for Sod's ghost. They were alone, however, Chatter and Dirty, rutted into the tight enclosure of the alley.

"They say you heal now," Dirty continued. "You've got a racket. You're sticking your hands up old ladies' drawers and giving them back life. I heard you cure cancer, gut-rot, and seizures. In fact, we're not sure just what you *can't* heal."

Chatter thought on the comfort of performance. The beginning of Lou's pitch rose to mind, but he rubbed his eyes instead, shoved his hands in his pockets. "Some I heal," he said. "Others I'm not sure."

Dirty nodded, his hand rose to his scar and traced an intimate pattern.

"Tonight," Chatter said, his words a blind tumble forwards, "My boss is set to heal a girl named Rosie Nostrum. He's going to reach his hands inside her at the Malcombe home and pull out the sick." Chatter cut himself off, his voice embarrassingly resonant in the air.

Dirty dragged the last of the life out of his smoke. He squeezed it out and scavenged the tobacco. "Sounds like something to see," he said.

CHAPTER 46

The virgin Rosie Nostrum pulled up her shirt to just under her brassiere and reclined before Lou. A stifled emotion spread through the great hall of the Malcombe byre dwelling. The cavernous ceiling absorbed the sound, echoed it muted. Voices emerged, none independent.

Dean and Sylvie Nostrum sat nearby, anxious at any wince from their daughter. Dean Nostrum flushed at the exposure and found solace in comforting his wife. Sylvie Nostrum didn't require solace, but tended to her husband's needs while she kept a supportive eye on Rosie.

Rosie Nostrum had been sick for six months. One night she suffered a dream in which she'd fallen in gravel, and the nurses in school couldn't remove all the stones. A grain of gravel passed through her body and lodged near her spleen. Here, the stone grew and grew until the pain was too much to endure, and she woke.

However, the presence of the stone didn't fade. Rosie couldn't lean forward without the overwhelming vision of her organs compressing around a jagged, alien entity. A silent, vitriolic object that pressed back and caused cramps and periods of retching.

When doctors explained to Rosie's parents that she had a bezoar, an indigestible object that had become a painful mineral in her gut, the Nostrums politely listened, then declined further service. The notion that her body could produce something that would prove harmful to it seemed wholly irrational to the Nostrums. Perfection cannot create imperfection, they reasoned, evil must come from without.

Lou's suggestion, at a social dinner offered by Mort's wife, that Rosie Nostrum suffered from a compounded ball of flukes, appealed to her parents. They suspected the malady organic, and the wriggling of a fluke explained Rosie's fluctuations. Sylvie Nostrum begged of her friend Agnes Malcombe the use of her cavernous home, and Lou agreed to perform a psychic surgery.

Chatter knew Lou was drunk before the last round of hors d'oeuvres. Lou's mistimed stories interrupted the preliminary rituals of their society. Right away he told a blue story about a gypsy love potion that turned a cluster of women off their canapés, and he delayed coffee for a full ten minutes while he demonstrated the proper procedure of flipping a cow foetus in utero.

"This far," he said, and held his hand halfway up his bicep. "The damn gloves come up this far."

Lou dozed through Francis Malcombe's introduction, waking with a start at the applause; he told stories of his and Chatter's itinerant past that they hadn't told in years; and when Rosie Nostrum raised her shirt, he flashed Chatter a broad wink most could see.

Chatter shot Lou an angry stare. The sight of Rosie's skin didn't give him the usual swoon, and for a moment, he imagined he could see Rosie's beauty objectively. His hands didn't tingle; his palms didn't itch. Chatter merely saw a girl in discomfort. He helped her into position on the table arranged at the end of the room and made sure she didn't disturb the tablecloth and reveal the bucket of goat blood and chicken livers hidden beneath.

Chatter placed a pillow under Rosie's head, and draped a blanket over her legs in case she writhed on the table and kicked up her dress. He secured her shirt under her brassiere and swept her bangs from her eyes. She watched Chatter with mounting nervousness, and relief flooded her face when Chatter stayed beside the table and held her hand.

Lou's breathing grew heavy, and for a moment he drowsed where he stood. Rosie squeezed Chatter's hand. "Will this work?" she whispered.

Chatter nodded with practised confidence and stoked her arm reassuringly. When he raised his face to the room, he kept his eyes wide and supportive, pools of mystical quietude in which the audience could drown. He didn't once turn to the attention that burned from the low, wire-laden French windows that rose to the ceiling, the squirming motion of faces just far enough from the light. He caught the flat sheen of light on Dirty's scar, but only briefly. He couldn't guess how many kids from the culvert were outside.

Lou spilled iodine across Rosie's stomach. Streams ran across her ribcage and trickled down her sides. Lou's blackened arm came up with a corner of the tablecloth, but his dabbing spread the stain across Rosie's torso and gave her a sickly pallor. He muttered apologies then puttered amidst the contents of his satchel. Chatter cleaned Rosie with the bottom of his shirt.

Rosie squeezed his hand twice, two quick syllables, the same as *Thank you*. She refused to look at Lou.

Lou's hands, sterilized with a rank liquid, travelled across Rosie's stomach. He hummed a melody with no refrain. His fingers dug into Rosie's side, near an obvious protrusion, and she groaned in pain.

Chatter held the tablecloth flat. Rosie's nails dug into his palm.

"Yes," Lou said, "Yes, yes. The evil fluke is found. A nest of vipers, squirming inside the belly of this dear girl. Yes. I have found the evil that afflicts you, dear."

Lou caressed her stomach with one hand, while the other, out of sight of the audience, jabbed Rosie's stone. Rosie shrieked. "That's right," Lou slurred. "Make as much noise as you'd like. What is inside you is unnatural, and it will not come without a fight."

Rosie's eyes snapped open, heavy with pleading.

Chatter grabbed Lou's wrist, and Lou jumped in surprise. Several people leaned back in their seats, shaken from the spell of their concentration. Lou gave a hearty laugh and shrugged. "Forgive my son the mute," he said, shoving the kid aside. "Sometimes he doesn't know when to shut up."

A natural laugh settled the room and Lou jabbed Rosie's side. She arched her back, bent her knees, and screamed.

Lou held his hands in the air. Iodine discoloured his palms. He sang a homily about a girl awaiting her lover under a willow tree, then a dirge in an old northern language.

Chatter met Rosie's eyes. He squeezed her hand. He imagined a flow of energy, unbroken, passing from his hand through her skin; he saw it move into her bloodstream, make its way to her heart.

Lou bowed smoothly despite his drunkenness. He kept an iodine-soaked hand in the air, quivering with the suggestion of his power, while his blackened one dipped into the bucket at his feet and came up with a small flask filled with goat blood. Before the audience, or even Rosie, noticed, both his hands hovered over the youngest Nostrum.

Lou lingered in rolling up his sleeves so the audience had time to consider his hands. He flourished his wrists, and the extension of fingers. Chatter stayed ready, and poured the perfumed oil over Lou's hands when offered. "When I reach inside this girl," Lou said, "this poor, dear creature, I'm going to pull the evil right out."

Rosie linked her fingers between Chatter's. "I'm sorry, I'm sorry, I'm sorry," she said, but Chatter wasn't sure whom she addressed.

The Nostrums kneeled and began to pray. The rest of the room joined, and a steady *please, please, please*, overwhelmed Rosie's voice. Only Chatter and Lou stayed quiet.

Lou took longer with the procedure than he should have. He circled round the initial penetration, whispering a parable, for almost three minutes. Tension wracked the room, and Rosie squeezed so hard her knuckles whitened. Finally, Lou pinched her. She gasped, and he slipped his fingers beneath her skin.

He squeezed the flask of blood and spilled it across Rosie's stomach. Several people in the room paled while he twisted his wrists inwards and emulated his hands entering her body. A young man stood abruptly, and ran from the hall.

Chatter wiped away the rivulets of blood while he surreptitiously handed Lou another flask. When the goat blood covered her stomach, Chatter unlinked his fingers from Rosie's hand and corralled Lou into finishing. He gave Lou a last flask, and then clasped Rosie's hand again. *"I'm sorry,"* he whispered.

Rosie pulsed her hand twice. She had understood from the start. She had seen her parents satiated by miraculous ecstasy, and received what she expected. Chatter squeezed back. "You are strong enough," he whispered to Rosie Nostrum. "We are so far above this."

Chatter brought up a handful of clean rags. Alongside these, he palmed Lou the shredded chicken livers.

"Ah," said Lou, interrupting the Nostrums' cycle of prayer. "Yes. Here is the source of woe."

Rosie's eyes fluttered closed. She gritted her teeth. She cried out when Lou dug his hand downwards.

Lou rolled his wrists again, bent his elbows. To the audience he appeared up to his forearms in Rosie's abdominal cavity. Rosie arched her back. "Yes," Lou said. "Yes."

Lou bent his elbow at a sharp angle, and scooped out the vile mass of chicken livers as Rosie groaned. "Here," he shouted. He squeezed the livers, and they pulsed before the crowd.

Lou laughed and displayed the mess, delighted at the horrified expressions, but his grip slipped. He'd pinched too hard, and the livers spilled over Rosie Nostrum. Lou did not bother to gather them up. He wiped his bloody hands on his shirt and staggered back a step.

"Who's the parents?" Lou bellowed.

He focused on the mice that presented themselves. He stepped into the audience. Others scattered as he closed on Sylvie Nostrum. "Mater," Lou said. "Pater." He held out his blackened hand. "Let you not neglect my fee."

Several people rose to their feet. Francis Malcombe looked ready to yell.

"We—" stuttered Sylvie Nostrum, "We thought this was by donation."

Lou's laugh battered the windows, roosted in the cavernous roof. "Donation!"

After his next laugh, as he pressed his pockets for some tobacco, he became aware that he'd outstripped his goodwill. Nine other men were on their feet in support of Dean Nostrum, and Sylvie had shrunk back to Agnes Malcombe's embrace.

"I must take my leave," Lou growled. "Other appointments demand my skill set. *Paying* customers and all. I'll leave my boy to mop up. He'll straighten out the details of your *donation*."

Lou swept his blackened hand behind him and the blood on his forearm sprayed Chatter and Rosie. Lou took one last look at the confusion on the table, telegraphed Chatter another drunk wink, then stumbled down the path that cleared before him, and out into the cobblestone streets of Farrow.

CHAPTER 47

Suddenly, Chatter felt the sheet of his skin pull back from his muscles. The sensation tore him away from Rosie Nostrum and the Malcombe sitting room and left him wanting to wretch. The sensation struck again, a clean sheet stripped from his frame, and he was only prevented from falling by Rosie's tight grip on his hand. The strangeness of the pain obliterated Chatter for a moment; he was lost in the shattering wholeness of it. The people in the room became phantoms, figures of an insubstantial world, but for the certainty in his hand. The clamour of the shocked audience watching Lou's clumsy exit faded into Rosie's touch. She let go only to bring her hands to his cheeks, to wipe the sweat from his brow. Chatter staggered back from the table, his knees hardly up to the effort. He felt his neck, his arms, he stuck his hands into his pockets, though nothing was in them but a bit of gravel.

Rosie sat up but Chatter reached for her. He lay her back on the table, calming the wild fright in her eyes with his serenest expression. He moved his hands across her stomach until the tingle in his palm reached a pitch. Heat rose up his arm and intermingled in his chest, he pictured waves lapping at the shore of the riverbank, the over and over and over of their gentle force meeting again and again the softness of earth, drawing the sand into silt, the silt into grains, which, separated from their source, were borne along the current as easy as a seed in a breeze. Chatter pressed his hands flat, with as little pressure as he could manage, until he felt no separation of their skin, and if he closed his eyes, he could not be sure of the outer extents of his body. Rosie kept still, her hands rested on his wrists, her breath, in easy draughts, rocked them both. Chatter's dizziness increased as the tingle in his palm reached a crescendo, cresting and cresting again, twinned to the beat of his heart, before dissolving in single exhalation. He fell forward, gasping, and took Rosie's hands in his. He pressed something into her palm. When she looked, she cried. It was a single piece of gravel.

Rosie Nostrum shot forward and kissed Chatter. He was ready for her, he'd seen the intention in her manner, but he was overwhelmed by the bliss that surged through him. The softness of her lips was like a hug, her scent as comforting as a room with a lock on the door. Chatter kissed her back, more of him dissolving the further forward he leaned. A roar arose in the room. Lou was gone; the audience had turned back to the stage.

Rosie held Chatter's face close, her hand gripped the back of his head. For a moment, the suspension lasted. Chatter brought his loosely closed hand between them. "Live forever," he whispered. He let his handful of gravel fall on the unbroken skin of Rosie's stomach.

Rosie caught her shaking breath. She kissed him again.

Pain shot through Chatter as Dean Nostrum and Francis Malcombe mounted the stage and separated him from Rosie. Chatter's knees weakened, and he leaned into the grip of the men who ushered him through a room filled with aghast faces. He was thrown, spinning at the odd pain, into the uncaring street.

For a while, Chatter's fury at Lou transcended words, numbing, almost, the wracking pain and delirium, and keeping him from feeling the rot that rested underneath it. But he could not deny the yearn.

The gummy smell of wet jack pines outside Farrow woke Chatter to his cause, and he gained a better sense of direction.

Beyond the pines, a grass field sank into a marsh where the ground became a bed of trampled reeds. Skeletal larch, still naked in the early season, perched around basins of water, awaiting giving Spring. A swell caught up to Chatter here, and he dropped to a knee. His head spun. The reeds the horizon the sky the horizon the reeds

After its swell, the yearn deadened. The intensities of the emotion trickled through Chatter's fingers, into the reeds, into the cool water beneath. Its timbre remained, however, a clear beacon of where the animal faced its final trauma.

Chatter followed the trace to a cut-bank sheltered by overhanging willow, a socket of dark in the moonlit marsh. An iron-waft of gore blew outwards on the breeze. He stared into the branches and waited. Nothing emerged but the play of shadow and the rustle of leaves.

Several small structures littered the inside of the hollow— hewn twigs and branches, tied at their tips to form teepees or cubes, tied together again in abstract geometrics. Attempted structures, snapped, nested in snarled string, outnumbered the successes. Chatter stepped with care, fearful of the broken and unbroken alike. Piles of shredded muscle sat at the back of the space. Tendons hung like streamers from the branches, their whiteness catching latent light. Chatter imagined them torn from his legs: his knees, ankles, limp against gravity. In a corner, Chatter discovered a midden pile covered in dried bramble. The space reeked of panicked animal sweat. Amidst the midden, tumbled over itself, as though tossed without care, Chatter found the body of a young jackrabbit, its head removed midway up its neck. He found another body, after a moment, but neither of their heads.

Chatter collected the bodies and brought them to where the jack pine sweetened the air. He dug into the hard earth with a rock carried there by a glacier, flaking layers of frozen clay. The work allowed him to suspend his frustration with Lou, his lust for Rosie Nostrum, and his incomprehension at what he'd found. Only when he'd buried each animal in a grave did he notice the quiet observation of the forest, the vacuity of the landscape, as if awaiting response to a question posed before he'd arrived.

"Greaves?" Chatter said when he couldn't stand the silence.

Chatter rooted the travelling stone halfway in the dirt, between the two graves. His hands ached, his back ached. He spoke no words, performed no ceremonies, bashful before the whisper of the trees, the gossip of the grasses.

CHAPTER 48

Chatter straightened his back, spread his shoulders, and continued towards the Shambles. A disturbed step, a harried glance over the shoulder, would betray that he knew he was being followed. The streets busied closer to the Shambles, despite the wee hour of the morning. Goat and swineherds drove their charges along cobbled passages, calling and clicking to their animals in the half-language agreed upon by both. Chatter felt better in their midst, the livestock smell dissolved his agitation. Reaching the stiles that marked the entrance to the Shambles, he stepped free from the bustle and approached the doors.

A flicker of light along the corrugated tin tunnel that led from the front entrance to the holding pens caught his attention. The scent of his brand reached Chatter, but the boy who approached, smoking one of Chatter's own cigarettes, was not Dirty.

There was a similarity in the shape of his face, but the boy's cheeks were gaunt, and he'd outgrown his clothes years before. Chatter tried to imagine which of the kids from the culvert had grown into the figure that now sauntered forth.

Another inhalation. The red glow of the cherry. Chatter smiled, his fear abated. "Briny," Chatter said. "You could've said something."

Briny drew another long inhalation from the cigarette. He shrugged. "Wanted to see how wide your eyes got in fright," he said in an even tone.

"I'm square," Chatter returned, slipping back into the constants of war outside the civilized world, the endless spars that reified peace. "Weren't for the hogs, I'd of smelled you down the block."

Briny's smile, dull white in the dark, unveiled. Chatter brought out his cigarettes, offered two to Briny. The boys smoked in a conspiracy of silence, each eyeing the other. By the time they'd tossed their cigarettes into a puddle around a clogged drain, both wore smiles. Warmed by goodwill, Chatter noticed late that the humour didn't reach Briny's eyes.

"Dirty has a story," Briny said, "about you laying on hands."

Twice Chatter tried to respond. He held up his hands. A chill seeped down his neck. "It's true."

Briny stared at Chatter beyond humour, beyond anger and goodwill. "Chatter," he said, "Azalea is sick."

CHAPTER 49

Briny and Chatter scaled slopes grown frosty in the night, then dropped into patches of unrelenting pine, larch, and spruce. Not once did they use a trail from the past.

Chatter only thought of Lou to distract his mind from what awaited at the culvert. When the sky lightened, he pictured Lou wheeling across the kill floor towards his private chamber, racing to beat the early shift of butchers. Chatter listened to that uncertain walk every night. Lou wouldn't wake for hours, until the heat and smell of the Shambles roused him to a torturous headache. Perhaps then he would miss Chatter. The word rattled Chatter's mind. He might be missed.

When the sun illuminated the ridge, Briny directed them out of the light, into the cool of the woods, where they followed the overgrown riverbed that led back to the culvert.

Fear shot through Chatter at a bend in the riverbed. Two girls and a boy sheltered in a natural crook of the bank, near two shillelaghs and a studded axe handle. They girls wore heavy clothing sewn with strips of what appeared to be chainmail, while the boy wore a leather cap with sewn strips of flattened tin and an armoured vest. Briny raised his hand in a wave, returned by the taller girl, but they exchanged no words. A nervous tension gripped the kids. Each cast suspicious looks at Chatter, though avoided his returned gaze.

The sun hadn't risen above the birch when they arrived at the culvert. A haze rose from the grass as morning warmth met the night's frost. Dozens of children occupied the open area before the culvert. Networks of camouflaged lean-tos, built from knolls and natural gullies, displayed a surprising industry. Chatter spotted a cluster of forges near Azalea's chimney piping, two different greenhouses, and a large open-ended shelter dug waist deep into the ground.

"Who are all these kids?" Chatter said.

"Us?" Briny said. "Let me remember. Most kids came from the Gnats. The early days of the war near obliterated Silver Wrists and the Grotto Nine, and their survivors hid with us. The culvert was the only place the Kin couldn't find. Still is. Now us here? We call ourselves the Prissies."

"War?" Chatter said.

Briny stared at him for longer than comfortable. "The war you started," he said.

Chatter opened his mouth and closed his mouth. Starvation marred the kids of the culvert, a hollowness in their eyes the same as the people come for a healing. The wariness that haunted the armoured kids in the riverbed darkened the faces of all those gathered. Conversations stopped at his appearance, kids paused in their activities, and their eyes followed his path through their camp. "War?" he repeated.

"After Sod died and you disappeared," Briny said, "we blamed the Kin, Azalea blamed the Kin, and she got quiet in her way of being quiet. We attacked any we found alone, and when the Kin struck back, they struck wide, and we pulled in a lot of allies from the other gangs in the valley. A lot of these kids came to us because we made knives." He swept his hand towards the row of forges built beneath birch and spruce shelters. Chatter counted four lit forges, and several kids at work, constructing the chainmail, alongside components for weapons, tools, helmets, and innumerable batches of nails. "We're long past *Popular Science*," Briny said with a degree of pride.

"You made knives for all these kids?" Chatter said. As they strolled through the camp, Chatter lost count of how many kids bore knife marks on their arms necks and faces. One girl, who carried two armfuls of firewood, had nine horizontal scars from her forehead to her chin.

Briny shook his head. "Not knives," he said. He reached to his waist and held up the metal-capped truncheon that clipped to a pewter hook on his belt. "Not after we made a bushel for the Grotto Nine and two kids got cut up so bad they couldn't be told apart. Azalea decreed an end to edged weapons. They're too destructive. And a knife isn't as much use as you want against the length of a club, believe me."

Briny entered a forge and handed Chatter a length of chainmail. The linked surface was smoother and lighter than Chatter expected; he fought the urge to hang it over his heart.

Briny stopped to speak with a couple of ashen boys by the oven, giving Chatter the chance to inspect the planking at the mouth of the culvert. Walkways of plywood beams nailed to birch trunks ran down either side of the tunnel. A stream trickled out of the culvert between the walkways and pooled in a wide reservoir outside. A platform sat to one side of the pool, while the opposite side became a network of troughs that ran to the kitchen next to the oven, the forges, and a half-dozen other places in the camp. Chatter didn't have time to trace them all before Briny returned.

"Fresh water," he said, "Diverted from a creek in the marsh. Azalea organized the whole thing when the Gnats arrived. The reservoir, the walkways, the troughs. She figured it'd sew us together. And it damn near did."

Chatter nodded. He dipped his hand into the water, and then tasted his fingers. "Cold," he said.

"Damn straight," Briny said.

"Briny," Chatter said, "are you still at war?"

Briny sighed. "No. Well, not yesterday."

"How did the war end?" Chatter said.

Briny turned, but Chatter could still see his face. "Fern had a bad death," he said. "Even those vile pricks were shaken by it. You remember Simon Sanderson? He and that crazy kid Greaves caught Fern alone. They wouldn't leave her alone after she was gone either. It rattled the whole valley. I'm surprised you didn't know anything of it. It split the Kin in two. Sanderson and Greaves took their contingent of kids into the woods, dispersing like coyotes in the trees, and the rest of the Kin followed this girl called Harmony, of the deep dark eyes. It was she who came to Azalea with the idea of the accords. She offered a truce, and Azalea knew just how to build it. All the valley made the Peace, and it's been that way since. Even the Kin follow Azalea's rules. Sanderson eventually settled in the marsh near us, and Harmony took the east, making home in the ruins of Forester's Tin. Since then, it's been calm waters. No more violence than is natural to surviving."

Briny scooped water into his palms and washed his face. "We do all right," he said. "There's bunks along a half mile of the culvert. Some shanties. An old electrical chamber has two floors of rooms built in. Stinks, though. Our crops of potato and berries grow well. Over half the valley uses the tools and armour we make. The day we made those accords, everyone started their lives."

He stared into the culvert. Chatter made a show of inspecting the reservoir, the planking that ran into the culvert. "It's impressive," he said. "You've done a good job sheltering your people."

Briny fixed him with a hard stare. "If you can heal with your hands, why didn't you heal Sod?" he said. "Or Dirty's face when those scum cut him up?"

"I tried," Chatter said. "With Sod, at least. Believe me Briny, I tried. But it didn't work. When I was older, I met a man who showed me how to use it. I didn't understand before I met Lou."

"So, you know now," Briny said. "And if that happened to Sod or Dirty now, you'd help?"

Chatter felt his pride rise. "Sure." Then, "Briny, is Azalea cut up?"

"No."

"You said she's sick."

"She is," Briny said. "Hell, I *hope* she is. Then at least we'd have an explanation. A name of some sort."

Chatter shook his head. "What happened, Briny? Where is Azalea?"

Briny indicated the yawning mouth of the culvert. "Yesterday morning, Azalea left camp early. A few kids saw her, but their stories don't match up. She's calm in some, stops to chat with Ronnie Scourgebottom or helps Greta gather firewood; others report her as angry, cold with that look she gets when you know to stay out of her way. Anyway, she doesn't come back until the sun is gone. Just some light in the sky. Just enough to show us what she'd done."

"What did she do?" Chatter said, as Briny paled.

Briny pointed again. "He's in here," he said. "We've left him in the sub-chamber. Remember where we used to sleep? That was the only place we thought to leave him—none of the kids wanted to look at him."

"*Who?*" Chatter pressed.

Briny proceeded into the culvert. Kids crowded the walkways that ran into the depth of the tunnel. Chatter straightened his spine, pushed his chest out. Most teenagers were taller than him, those younger tempered by a harder history. None were ashamed of their open scrutiny. None afforded him space on the causeway. Several, after looking at Chatter, glanced over their shoulders, further into the culvert, where the sub-chamber and its occupant waited, weighting the very air with their presence.

"A crazy kid called Greaves," Briny said over his shoulder, "the murderer of Fern and Sod. Azalea dragged him through our camp last night, him screeching and kicking and crying. The both of them covered in blood. Though turns out only Greaves is hurt. And he's hurt real bad, Chatter."

Briny caught the quiver in his chin and paused on the walkway. He stared at the stream that ran beneath them until he could control his expression. "Seems Azalea's carrying knives again," he said.

CHAPTER 50

The sub-chamber gurgled like a badly stoppered throat. Greaves muttered and sobbed within, but his voice never rose to words. Chatter and Briny stood outside and listened.

Briny rocked on his feet, heel to toe, toe to heel. "So," he said, "you don't need me in there."

Chatter shook his head. "No."

Briny nodded. "Don't let him take you hostage," he said. "Or at least scream if he does."

The sub-chamber had shrunk. Chatter couldn't believe he'd slept comfortably amidst six kids on the ledge that ran along three walls. Coal fires burned in low tin buckets at opposite corners. Greaves curled in the darkest corner, where the floor sank to a drain. Its concave echoed his sobs, the chortle of a single pipe run underground. Chatter chose the unoccupied corner.

Greaves lay with his legs curled under him, his head resting on crooked arms. A liquid inflection dogged his voice. "Why're you here?" he whispered.

"How do you feel?" Chatter said.

Greaves rolled over. He'd shed the frame of a child and was lost in the agelessness of his teens. His skin was pale, mottled from undernourishment. *Malignant Hunger*, Chatter thought. *Restless Suspicion*. Old blood blackened his clothing. His left arm hung awkward, swollen and dislocated, his fingers twice their normal width. His nose jackknifed, and one of his eyes was closed over a broken socket. Four ugly gashes disfigured his crown.

Greaves tracked the motion in the room with his good eye. "*Why're you here, Greaves? she says to me,*" he uttered. "*Why're you here?*"

Greaves flinched as Chatter's hands came out of his pockets. He cowered at Chatter's approach.

"Why're *you* here," Greaves said when Chatter retreated again. "So, I said, *Why're you here? Not your land anyways, yet there you're standing, demanding. Why're you here?*"

Chatter knelt. "Azalea said that?"

Greaves paled at the name. Shuddered behind his mangled hand.

"I'll help," Chatter said, and reached for Greaves.

Greaves yowled. "Sun's up," he said. "*Why not a walk?* you say. So out you go. You go for a walk."

Chatter shrugged. He clasped his hands and recited a blank prayer, which was what Lou did when people babbled. "O Lord," he intoned, "forgive us ourselves, our very created selves, in past, in forgiveness, in future, until almighty kingdom come, O please O Lord, forgive us ourselves."

Inside Chatter's jacket, conspiratorial against his breast, three vials of Remedy pressed. Chatter presented a vial, his fingers tip tapping the stoppered top. "Are you in pain?" he asked.

Greaves managed a laugh. He looked around the room. "Guess I found out where you sleep, huh?" he said.

"This comes from around here," Chatter said as he shook the vial. "Hell, maybe you've even seen this place. A farm owned by a man the name of Harlo Grace. His first year on the land he augers here, he augers there, and he can't draw water for a well. Doesn't make sense to him. His neighbors have wells on the same line, but Harlo can't find water."

"Finally, after three months," Chatter continued, "Harlo had a hole that burbled with the rush of an underground stream. So down he runs his pipes; by afternoon, he'd installed a pump. The first time he used it, the pump hacked, gurgled, but nothing came out. The second time he pumped and pumped, and it shuddered with a rise. After twenty more minutes of work, a tattered, beaded wristband emerged out the mouth of the pump. The next time Harlo tried, finger bones rattled out, all fingertips, like large teeth lying in the dirt. After that, a cough of water."

Chatter placed the vial on the floor between him and Greaves. "By this time," he said, "Harlo is dog tired from working in the sun. He scooped some water from the puddle on the ground and took a sip. Instantly he felt revived. Another gulp, and he was ready for a day's work. The water gave back energy, strengthened sight, taste, and even healed cuts. When Harlo's neighbours, who drew from the same underground stream, questioned how this could be, Harlo offered the bones and the beaded headband as explanation. He'd bored through the grave of a holy person, he'd said, and the lingering remains sanctified the water as it passed."

Chatter held up the vial again. "This water here, in this vial, comes from that pump. It's near here," Chatter said again, words he knew to be crucial. "You could visit if you wanted."

Greaves's expression didn't shift once during Chatter's story. His eye moved from Chatter to the vial, and back to Chatter. "Indians didn't bury their dead," he said. "They wrapped them up like presents and left them in the trees."

Chatter shrugged. He slipped the vial back into his jacket.

Greaves raised his unbroken hand. "Here," he said. "Didn't say I didn't want it."

Chatter handed him the vial. "Take sips," Chatter said. "Only half now. It's powerful."

Greaves unstoppered the vial and smelled its contents. He shook a drop onto his finger, and licked it. He brought the vial to his lips and tipped the Remedy into his mouth. Once, twice, then his good eye fluttered closed, and he leaned back against the wall.

Chatter retrieved the vial from Greaves's limp grasp. He stood and backed up to the door. "I'll leave another with your guards," he said. "They'll bring some in a couple hours."

Greaves nodded his head, but didn't open his eye.

Chatter left the sub-chamber and motioned Briny to follow. "Get some kids to tear up bandages," he said. "Get someone with a strong stomach to cut the swelling over that eye. Fold a bandage and put it over the eye, then wrap up his head. All those broken fingers need wrapping too. And you're going to have to pop that arm back in. Nobody's going to enjoy that. Here," Chatter handed Briny the Remedy. "After all that, give him the whole vial. Might help. Might not. Won't hurt him any worse, though."

Briny turned the vial over in his hand. "I don't know, Chatter," he said.

"What do you mean?"

Briny shrugged and tucked the Remedy into the pocket of his trousers.

"Briny," Chatter said, "that kid in there dies if you don't help him."

"Why do you think you're here?" Briny said.

"Then *listen* to me," Chatter said with more violence than he'd intended.

However, Briny made his indecisive face. He stared over his shoulder, then down at the light in the mouth of the culvert. He shrugged again. "Don't know if I should," he said. "Probably should check with Azalea first."

"Fine," said Chatter. "Let's go. Where are you keeping her?"

"Keeping her?" said Briny. "We aren't keeping her anywhere. Greaves is *hers*. She brought him back here, slept all night; she left thirty minutes before we arrived. She's down by the scrap heap right now."

Chatter's face creased in confusion. "Free?" he said. "This starts a war. If Greaves dies, I don't care how many treaties you have, Simon Sanderson is going to march right through here. Those two were always tied to each other, I remember. And you're letting her walk free?"

Briny stared at Chatter, bemused. "I don't let her do anything," he said. "No one does. You look at our entire camp and what you're seeing is her. We are here because of her, Chatter. Azalea's genius gave us this place. She imagined what none of the rest could, me included. I built what she described, but I never had her mind. Not one of us does."

His voice verged on a laugh. Briny shook his head. "It isn't like the old days, Chatter. The Prissies aren't my responsibility. Azalea is our leader."

CHAPTER 51

Azalea knelt inside the chassis of a gutted Model T, the teeth of her file busy against the coil springs in an interior wheel well. Chatter wandered up and down a distant corridor of the scrap heap until he saw the bob of her hair. She cursed abruptly, and the Model T rattled at her kick.

She stood and watched his approach with an impenetrable expression. She'd grown taller and come into her features. Whereas before, her skin seemed barely able to cover her skeleton, Azalea's gauntness now stood as testament her survival; taut muscles stood out from her shoulders and forearms, and the heave of her chest emptied Chatter but for a humble shiver in the pit of his stomach.

Azalea bent back into the Model T, sawed for another moment, then stood again. She pointed behind Chatter. "See that refrigerator over there? Get me the heating element from its back. Go use your big strong arms."

Chatter nodded, and without a word fought loose three rickety rods from the appliance's yellowed husk. He dumped them before the car with a measure of pride, although he found his yield inferior to the harvested steel that sat around the Model T.

"What are you collecting these for?" he called into the open hood.

Azalea stood again. Sweat dripped down her face from the tangled crown of her hair. "I'm making a special knife," she said. "May I have your blood?"

204

"My blood?" Chatter said.

"A knife isn't ready until it's drawn blood," she said blankly.

"I know that," Chatter said. "*I* taught you that."

For the first time, Azalea smiled. "Hello, Chatter."

"Hello, Azalea."

Azalea knelt back into the Model T. It rocked from side to side at the effort of her file. Chatter watched though a reverie, enjoying the vacant moment in the warm spring sun. His gaze shifted beyond the scrap heap, to the low plane of the valley floor, the long grasses, hyacinth, and prairie violet softly in motion.

A dull *clunk* brought Chatter's attention back to the Model T. The wheel well on the driver's side had sunk, and Azalea proudly held up a thick coil spring. The steel in the coil alone, Chatter knew, would provide for at least three knives. Azalea tossed it atop the heating element from the dishwasher, then ran her eyes over Chatter again.

"So?" she said.

Chatter realized he was staring. "What?"

"Can I have your blood?"

Chatter tried to hide the smile that crept across his face. "Sure."

Azalea bent into the chassis, and made a show of poking through the remains. "What are you doing here?"

Chatter's mind stumbled, he stared forward, mute.

Azalea stood up again. "Briny went and got you from your throne of shit in Farrow," she prompted.

"They're worried, Azalea," he said. "They want me to heal you."

Her eyebrows shot up. "Am I sick?"

Chatter shrugged.

"Are you a doctor?" Azalea said.

"I'm no doctor." Chatter gained an interest in the ground, in the tufts of grass that grew from the mud.

"Your hair is long, you grew up," Azalea said. "Living indoors suits you."

Chatter felt a flash of guilt at this. "Your hair is a mess," he said.

Azalea smiled. She reached into her hair and pulled a few more strands up. "I'm not sick, Chatter. Must have scared those kids bringing Greaves back like that, but, dammit, he fought so hard. Punched me like I was a man."

"Why'd you bring him back, Azalea?"

Azalea scowled and paced away. "He was there when Fern died," she said. "Everyone knows Greaves was there when Fern died. Him and Simon. And sure, I knew it too. Even though I've seen him more than half a dozen times since. I was even close enough to reach him a couple times. But did I? Even though I knew. Even though I've seen him walking where she can't. Then, yesterday, I'm in the marsh, and I see Greaves, making his way. First, I won't lie, I didn't think anything. Imagine that. I didn't think nothing more than one would on seeing a snake slither by. Then. Well, Chatter, don't look at me sideways when I say this—and don't you dare tell the kids at the culvert—I saw something. Fern came around a tree just a few yards ahead of me. She didn't look any older in the wind, her face hadn't changed once since. You'll tell me it was someone else, but you're wrong. I know that girl's face better than I know the moon's. It was Fern, quiet as she always was. Have you ever seen a phantom, Chatter?"

Chatter shook his head. "Never."

Azalea nodded. "Suddenly, right after Fern slipped behind another tree and out of the light, I had this thought, clearer than any I'd had before. I saw Greaves and I thought, *As though a gift*. The thought rattled me. It wasn't even in my own voice. A gift. Like the world offered such things. I imagined any of the Prissies in my place. I imagined their terror at coming so close to the Horror of the Kin. How they'd shake. But I wasn't afraid. I wasn't angry. I was calm. A *gift*, I thought. Because those kids deserve space, grass, a chance at not having to put their shoulder into every goddamn minute. But they're afraid, and they'd never reach out their hands. Not once. I would, though, Chatter. I would. I saw that in that moment. I didn't have no problem with it, either. And I realized that that is how I help them: I reach out my hands. I wasn't angry. I was calm."

"He's hurt bad, Azalea," said Chatter, "and the kids are too scared of you to bandage him up."

Anger flashed in Azalea's eyes, a sudden ferocity that caught Chatter off guard. "Thought you said you weren't a doctor," she said. Then, softer, "Those kids aren't scared of me."

A grim girl and six boys came into sight at the end of the lane. The girl, her hair drawn tightly back on her head, led the boys in their cautious approach. They clung to the side of the lane, occupied with its other direction, the direction closer to the office where the scrap yard's owner conducted his business, and moved as a coordinated group.

Azalea crept down from the Model T and felt in the grass amidst her pile of refuse. She withdrew a large lug nut and hefted it twice in her hand. Not once did she break sightline with the girl. Azalea drew a calming breath and then planted her feet. She threw the lug nut on a direct line at the grim girl's head.

"*Go go go*," she implored as she broke into a run, sweeping Chatter into her wake. He stumbled, and almost tripped grabbing the coil spring from the ground. "*Go go go*," she repeated, dragging them over the crest of a hill and behind an outcropping of pine. Chatter all but fell over Azalea when she slid to a halt.

The grim girl, who screamed when the bolt hit her neck, clapped her hand over her throat and gurgled a command to the others. The boys, all six of them, hollered, finally allowed to run in the sunshine.

Chatter made to bolt, but Azalea wouldn't move. "On my own land," she hissed. Chatter shook her wrist for her attention.

"We have to go, Azalea," Chatter said. He pointed across the valley floor to a pocket of pine and spruce that ran along the river. "Azalea!"

The boys hooted and stamped towards the outcropping. Two carried stunted machetes and hacked at the long grasses. One paused to kick apart Azalea's piles of scrap.

"*Azalea*," Chatter hissed. She pulled her wrist from Chatter, glowering past him, to the cowardice in his heart. Azalea turned back to the girl, and met her eyes in impudent defiance.

"Run!" Azalea shouted.

CHAPTER 52

Chatter drove deep into the pine. Azalea kept close behind, weaving crazily to throw off pursuit. The boys of the Kin stomped into the trees with unrestrained abandon, and trampled the undergrowth as Chatter and Azalea rushed uphill.

Chatter brought them to a thicket of birch he'd sheltered in when he first descended into the valley. Perched on a shelf of raised bedrock, it was already grown flush in the spring sunshine. The growth muted the howling Kin. Azalea fell to her knees in the moss beds that grew between the birch, the green the orange the brown, moist from dew. Chatter knelt next to her. Azalea wiped the moisture from her hand on her forehead, and Chatter held his breath as it dripped down her temples.

He waited until he could draw air with a regular rhythm before he decided on the flutter in his stomach. A small excitement broiled his gut, a sudden feeling of fragility, as though no matter where he moved, he would crush grass or stone, or his bones would collapse in the effort of supporting his weight. He realized, quickly, that it came from his proximity to Azalea, their sudden intimacy, and a fear that it would be over before he could sort out what to say. He felt as nervous as he had at the Relegate Mercy, on the stairwell up to Alice Always' room. A terror, wholly wordless, arose whenever Azalea shifted, or settled herself more securely on the ground.

When he could move again, Chatter peered out from the edge of the thicket. He came back and lay down next to Azalea.

"Gone," he said. "A couple straggle, but they aren't looking for much."

Chatter stared up through the leaves. The thousand moving parts of their sky. Then, a trickle in his heart. A lightness. He raised his head but saw nothing in the branches. "Do you really think Greaves is a gift?" he said.

Azalea eased back onto the moss. "When I lie in the culvert," she said, "I wrap my arms around myself, because I've elbowed others, my toenails have scraped shins. I can't remember if it was like this last year, last month. Winters have always been tough, all us cooped up in the culvert, but this year hit every kid there. Riley Longshanks spent a week this February stone naked, stamping up and down our stream. I heard him all night. *Stamp stamp stamp.* All winter we were cramped. Stunk like rot. Like armpits and feet."

Azalea shook her head. "I once believed the Prissies would end. Never told anyone that, but I did. After the war, after the peace, after years of the peace, I imagined life after the Prissies, when we'd get grown, get too old to stay in the woods, and get lives in Farrow, maybe even an occupation in the city. Every kid knows that's where they're headed. Even after the snatchers and orphan-sellers gave up dragging kids back, there wasn't any question where we're headed. Once in a while a kid will get pregnant, and we'll lose her early, to the missions, to the world of adult cares, or some kids see survival in the street means sharing less of your loot, means you can sell yourself for every penny you think you're worth, but most kids stay, most won't be pushed out until their bones grow too long for the culvert. I felt the growth in my bones, those pains that shoot up and down. I feel it all the time. But there is no end to the Prissies. Kids keep coming. Where do they all come from? Now, I can't ever see an end. Now there's too much future, too many kids. I'll be grown, and there'll be kids found in the woods, kids following others back to the camp. And who in the hell is going to take care of those kids? Other kids? C'mon. They don't know nothing."

Azalea sat up. "So, yes, when I saw Greaves, I saw clearly. I saw a gift. The land next to ours? Room for our elbows, our knees, and our toes. Room to grow our food. We don't have any plots left right now, we can't grow enough food to feed ourselves. Kids steal from Farrow, and get themselves locked up. Or they starve, waste away before our eyes. And that's a terrible sight. It's not fair. It's not fair what the Kin took from us, Chatter. And it's not fair what Greaves did to Fern."

Chatter met Azalea's eyes. The yearn in his heart rose. "You knew Fern before the valley," he said. "You and she were first, after Briny."

A breeze moved through the birch. The trees swayed at their roots. Azalea nodded and rested her chin on her knees. "I met her in the last foster home either of us had," she said. "I'd have been lost without her. Fern was always the smarter one." Azalea smiled. "My favourite story of her happened at the foster home before ours, before we'd met. When Fern arrived, there were already two other foster girls there, Leslie and Erin, terrible girls. Leslie pulled hair and bit, and Erin liked to punch, slap, and smash. The three of them stuck in a single room with a bunk bed and a single bed. Leslie slept on the top bunk, and Erin on the wide single. Fern, of course, was stuck with the bottom bunk. Meaning she's subject to Leslie and Erin's abuse, not just during the day, but all night long. Erin flung her limbs across the divide while she slept, smacking and slapping Fern, while Leslie spun and grunted and twisted above, and two, three times each night, she climbed down onto Fern's mattress on her way to the bathroom. Fern didn't once sleep through a night. After three months, she was exhausted."

A smile played across Azalea's face as she stared into the swaying birch. "So, one night," she said, "while Leslie's snarking up above, and Erin's thrashing on her bed, Fern creeps from her bunk, quiet as Fern could be. In one quick motion, she tugged the sheet away from under Erin's chin then swept upwards and smacked Leslie across her open mouth. Fern dove back into her bed while Leslie shot up and stared downwards at Erin, awake and staring at her shifted sheet. Do you see what Fern does? Who'd suspect her? Leslie snapped at Erin; Erin, bleary, snapped back. Soon enough, the foster's sticking his head in the room and hollering *Shut Up*. Erin and Leslie go quiet, but they don't sleep."

Chatter raised his eyes to the trees. He traced a path along several intertwined branches.

"Fern waits, three nights, until Leslie and Erin fall asleep again," said Azalea. "Then she switches targets. She tugs the blanket from Leslie, and smacks Erin's fat face. This time, Erin's up without an angry word and gives Leslie a cuff. The foster's in the room again, and breaks them up. And, of course, there's poor Fern, huddled in her bunk." Azalea chuckled. "Poor Fern, horrified at violence. Wasn't long after that Leslie gave Fern the top bunk, so she and Erin could watch one another at night. And Fern? She slept fine."

Azalea turned to Chatter and crept across the moss until their knees touched. "Fern pitted Erin and Leslie against one another," Azalea said. "I always admired that. I wouldn't have thought of that. I'd have just gone and taken the top bunk, no matter the scrap."

Chatter watched her silence. He noticed the bruises on her hands, her swollen knuckles and tattered skin. She treated her left wrist tenderly, holding her forearm against the warmth of her belly.

She brushed the hair back from his face and met his eyes. "Do you really believe you can heal with your hands?"

Chatter looked down at his lap. He shook his head. "I don't have a name for what happens," he said. "I never asked for it. I've been saddled with it as long as I can remember. But the meaning was never clear, and I haven't ever had anyone to ask."

"You've never seen Greaves in your garden."

A flutter amidst the leaves above resolved itself into a brown and red sparrow. It hopped back and forth on a diseased branch, spying on Chatter and Azalea with either eye. After a moment's consideration, it descended into the moss, landing once, twice, until it was close enough to hop into Chatter's cupped hands. Once more it looked at Chatter, then Azalea, with each of its eyes. It furrowed its feathers, settled, then its head tipped forward on a loose neck.

Azalea watched with a flat expression. Chatter held the bird through the end of its life. He let out a sigh, glad, as always, that the bird found him. When he looked up, Azalea's eyes were wide.

She shifted in the moss, leaned forward, and touched Chatter's face.

"What did you do?" she said in a shaken tone.

CHAPTER 53

Back at the culvert, Azalea ordered Greaves bandaged up according to Chatter's direction. Chatter supervised, but didn't help. The children were practiced at mending one another. A boy named Rodney straightened Greaves's nose with a surgical precision. No one inside the culvert escaped the jarring pops of Rodney's trade. Greaves only moaned, beyond screaming by then. Chatter gave Greaves his last Remedy, and the boy swigged the entire vial at once.

During the process of binding Greaves's stamped fingers to one another, Chatter sat on the walkway and watched the progress of the water. Azalea moved through her camp, her Prissies, visiting groups of children. Chatter spotted the reassurance in her body language, the careful way she touched others, her smiling, nodding, remaining open in the face of concern.

That evening, after dinner, Azalea brought a tin bowl of soup into the sub-chamber. She helped Greaves onto a stool, so he faced the wall opposite the entrance. He had nothing else to focus on but her bowl of soup. Azalea hummed as Briny, Chatter, Dirty, and a few other kids entered, all of them staying behind Greaves. A couple of the kids looked as though they'd like to throttle Greaves from behind, but most of them carried in the nervous worry that unsettled the camp. None of them would look at Chatter.

Azalea scraped the spoon as she stirred the soup.

Greaves's first sips were timid, but he soon trusted Azalea with entire spoonfuls. He even slurped after a while. Azalea tipped the spoon up up up, foregoing the last drip down his chin. More than half the soup disappeared before Greaves shook his head and Azalea placed the spoon back in the bowl.

Greaves glowered at her. Colour returned to his face, a pink, virulent red. "Guess I found where you sleep, huh?" he said. But Azalea didn't respond. She stared at him until his smirk disappeared. "Why the marsh?" he slurred. "Not my land there. Not yours. A waste of wet socks and shit fish. That land's anybody's."

"Except when the Prissies walk there," said Azalea. "They get thumped by your people. Everyone knows that."

Greaves smiled. "You think I have anything to do with that? You damn screwed up, girl. I got no say over the Kin's rights and wrongs. *My* people. They ain't mine."

Azalea watched him. For a moment, Chatter worried that she'd strike him, but she lifted the spoon instead, and allowed him a sip. "Harmony and her slugs were at the scrap heap today," she said. "*My* scrap heap."

"No one wants your scraps. She came to take a swipe at you."

"She's after me, no doubt," she said. "Or after you? I ran into the bush, but she saw me. Saw me with someone else. And what does Harm do when she sees me with someone else? Kill them both, she shouts. Kill Azalea. Kill Greaves."

Greaves shook his head. "She didn't."

Azalea nodded. "Pointed with that long damn knife of hers. Both of them, she says. Azalea. Greaves."

Greaves laughed. He shook his head. "Why'd she think I was with you anyway? Unless your little rabbits are running around with stories."

Azalea held the spoon to his lips, but dribbled the last of it down Greaves's chest.

A cruel smile spilt Greaves's face. The soup had revived him. "Ransom?" he said, "That your plan? You think Simon Sanderson is going to trade you something for me?" He spat. "Sure, he'll give you something."

Azalea drew some more soup into the spoon and placed it against Greaves's mouth. He hesitated, and then parted his lips.

"Can't imagine you're worth much," she said. "Ransom isn't the plan, in any case. I'll just keep you for now. There's a lot of stories in the valley about me bringing you here, but no answers on why."

"You kidnapped me," Greaves blurted.

Azalea shrugged. "Some say," she said. "Others, well, maybe they're not clear. Some of the kids here start to talk, tell about how happy you are, how free and giving you are. Here, with me. More and more of my own will be spotted in the marshes. My soldiers with them, bashing *your* people on *your* order, because that land is ours now." Azalea placed the soup on the floor, bent to meet Greaves's eye. "What do you suppose Simon Sanderson will think then?"

Greaves glared. "Won't bring any good. He'll come after me, then he'll come after you."

"I know your boys and your girls," said Azalea. "We live so close. And the accords have given us the chance to know them. No. They won't cave without a fight. And they'll get a fight. We'll stir them up. Let Sanderson's army ready itself. Let them make no secret of it. My kids will get word to Harmony's camp, too. Word of an army brewing, word of you, emissary of the marshland Kin, bringing us into the fold, building war machines for Sanderson's war, a great effort to take back from Harmony what was rightfully yours."

Greaves laced his laugh with derision, but there was doubt in the sound, as obvious as the rain. "They won't believe nothing," he said. "Not Simon Sanderson. Not Harmony. No one's going to trust your little mice. No one listens to your shit."

"Sure," Azalea said. "No one cares about the Prissies. No one listens. But you bet ears perk up when the name Greaves arises. Everyone listens when stories of crazy Greaves are passed around."

"Don't call me that," snapped Greaves. "You don't know nothing."

But Azalea smiled a small smile. "You bet they're going to listen," she said. "Greaves comes here and spills all Simon's secrets, we'll say. Or, Greaves comes here with an invasion plan for Harmony's realm, we'll say, bearing the seal of Sanderson's intentions. Don't matter what we say, really. They'll believe us. You know they will. No one trusts Greaves around here. No one ever will. We all know what you are. Crazy Greaves, muddled in the head and the heart. Mad Greaves, mad as rabbits in March. You know what you are. Sick. Crazy as they come."

A smile broke Azalea's face, a wide, joyful dart that made Greaves flinch. Each of the children at the back of the room watched the tension rise through Greaves's back. His shoulders flattened, his thighs swelled with anticipation, his feet slid towards firmer ground. Chatter cried out as Greaves leapt forwards, but the rest of the children remained silent, their faces hung, left to the dark. None met Chatter's eyes.

Azalea swooped the soup out of the way and spun as he hurtled past. Greaves doubled over the concrete rise, Azalea's hand on the back of his head, guiding it faster and faster downwards. He went limp with a wet smack and slid onto the floor. Azalea watched blood stream out of his nose for a moment, then turned to the room. She hadn't spilled the soup.

Azalea met the eyes of each of the kids. "So, it's a plan then," she said, still smiling.

CHAPTER 54

Azalea sowed her war amidst the Prissies. She spent the day in counsel with separate groups, rising early with the launderers and the bakers, and abstaining from the communal dinner to confer with older kids in chainmail back from patrol. Azalea broached the manner of war in the same way. She told kids she was kicking up dust, and they'd have to shield their eyes for a bit. Those who stayed in the culvert, Azalea explained, would face little more than regular danger. She knew where to recruit *Gnawers*—those kids who would brave open attack—so vital to her strategy. To some, she undersold the danger; to others, she amplified it, sketching, on the spot, the contours of a plan otherwise unworkable, until each kid recognized their duty, their longing, or their fear within, and volunteered for the front offensive. Her voice, joking, cajoling, or flat with patience and understanding, haunted every space in the culvert. She smiled and nodded. She touched the kids who required closeness, and left alone the others, who met such treatment with suspicion. Easily she sorted these, and spoke in a manner that made her words appear unchosen, natural.

Each time Chatter emerged from the sub-chamber to take the air, the camp was changed. Industry developed in the kids, the excited noise of their voices rose and ran down the culvert. "Fern," Chatter heard. "*Fern.*"

After dinner, Chatter found Azalea braiding the hair of a young boy while a girl braided hers. She spoke in a soft voice until Chatter drew close.

"Greaves still suffers," Chatter said. "I need more Remedy. At least, fill up these bottles again."

Azalea's hands didn't pause. "No, no," she said. "We need more than three bottles. Take a guard of three. In a dream last night, I saw you chased through the woods like an animal."

Chatter protested, and Azalea upped his guard to five. With another few words, Chatter's escort was ready to leave. Nothing disturbed the march to the Gardens, but Riley Longshanks walked so close to Chatter that their thighs touched.

Chatter halted the march at the red shale road into the Gardens. He swore the location of the Remedy so secret even Azalea didn't know. No one protested. That far from the culvert, the kids were happy to leave the mystic to his secrets.

The house sighed when he opened a window. Chatter checked each room, positive that Lou waited in ambush. "Sure is something to be alone again, hey, Sod?" Chatter said. The cistern in its room at the end of the hall had the same quiet as the forest. Stacks of peach crates, each with two layers of stoppered vials, lined the wall. Chatter's eyes blurred when he tried to count them all.

It wouldn't be a thing to take one, Chatter thought. It wouldn't hardly be a thing.

CHAPTER 55

Seven children—three boys and four girls—dozed on beds of moss in the culvert's newest enclosure. The infirmary nestled in a far corner, at the end of a specially diverted reservoir trough. Henni Axehandler, a tall red-headed girl who attended to the sick and wounded, specified the enclosure be double wide with two rows of moss-lined beds. Construction took four days. The first wounded, a boy named Francis Francis, whose collarbone had been broken in a skirmish, arrived before they were finished. They tied down the ceiling of the infirmary over Francis Francis's unconsciousness.

Chatter knelt near the end with his hand on a sleeping girl's ankle. Six of the seven had suffered wounds from the war. Simon Sanderson's faction had set angrily at the Prissies in the early days, mercilessly attacking children in the marshlands, but the arrival of Harmony's Kin, and the subsequent infighting, lessened the attacks. The girl under Chatter's hand was one of the more recent, having fallen into a four-foot hole dug by the Kin. She stirred when Chatter removed his hand, but didn't wake.

Henni carved a reed flute near the door. She kept her head lowered as Chatter passed, reserving her energy. Briny wouldn't be in for another few hours to spend the night with her. Her voice rose as he left. "Sleep for a stretch," she said.

Greaves slept on the raised concrete of the sub-chamber, his head crooked upwards on his arm. An angry bruise discoloured his face. His distressing injuries had healed, the swellings decreased, and his bones had set, which Azalea viewed with increasing dismay, but the sourceless bruise persisted. His eyes fluttered as Chatter entered, but did not open.

Chatter sat in the opposite corner. He knew he wouldn't be bothered. The sub-chamber had become a sanctuary away from the pleading, confused, suspicious, or melancholic eyes of camp, and the only place Chatter could sleep. No one wanted to see Greaves, despite the successes in the war. Chatter watched the sleeping boy. He leaned his head against the wall.

Greaves stirred, but did not move out of his position. When Chatter opened his eyes, Greaves was watching him. Chatter met the boy's gaze. Often, they watched each other, but neither had spoken. Greaves's voice, dredged from disuse, was thin in the quiet of the sub-chamber.

"I saw you," he said. "I saw you in the trees. Those two guys, they beat you up bad. But it wasn't even your fault."

Chatter wrestled with a calm expression. "Why did you do that to the rabbit?"

But Greaves only shook his head. "Shouldn't have done that to you, those guys. They shouldn't have. You didn't see their faces like I could. You should've. They were real scared. Both of them. But they shouldn't have done that. So. It's not your fault."

"Didn't even hurt," Chatter said.

"Sure it did. I saw it. Had to hurt. And I'm sorry about it. Anyway. I'm sorry that happened to you. Wasn't your fault. He shouldn't have called you that, sick."

Chatter couldn't form a response.

After a while Greaves's sullen voice emerged. "I saw you in the trees before, too. Even before that. You remember. That day, on the hill. You and that kid digging potatoes. I saw you in those trees, hiding in that collapsed shelter. I saw you there, but I didn't say anything. Isn't that hilarious?"

A coldness, unaffected by the nearby coal fire, washed over Chatter. Greaves's voice sounded from thousand miles away.

"What was that kid's name? The one with you that day."

Fury choked Chatter's voice. He wanted to explode across the room and pull Greaves off his ledge. He wanted to dash the boy's brains over the softly gurgling drain.

"Sod," Chatter said.

"Sod," Greaves said. "Sod."

A sudden clatter of words came down the culvert. A rush of voices. Whispers. Gossip. Shouts. Tense shocked voices passing the same phrase, like a prayer. Slovenly Pasture. Slovenly Pasture. *Slovenly Pasture.* The walkways rattled with footfall. Kids stamped down the stream. Slovenly Pasture, they said. *Slovenly Pasture.*

Henni burst into the sub-chamber, the colour drained from her face. Her eyes settled on Chatter immediately.

"Slovenly Pasture," she exclaimed. "There's been an ambush!"

CHAPTER 56

"Again," Azalea said.

Chatter let the fire-blackened hammer fall toward the flattened coil spring. The impact rang out in the forge with discordant *clang*. He grinned, sheepish. He'd missed the blade and hit the anvil once more.

Azalea shook her head. "Again," she said.

Chatter hoisted the hammer. He did his best to control the descent. The clap of metal against the anvil rewarded his effort. He smiled. Sweat dripped, stinging his eyes.

Azalea swung the coil spring, at the end of long tongs, into the forge, nestling it back into the glowing coals. She turned her head, her expression expectant.

"Shit," Chatter said. He dropped the hammer, returned to the bicycle-pump billows, and curled his tired fingers. He lifted his hands, lowered his hands.

Exhaustion welled across his shoulders. He tried to maintain a pace that would not distract Azalea, but increasingly devoted his attention to staying upright. He grunted, heaved.

Azalea watched the fire, the warm colour of the metal that revealed malleability. Chatter suspected her patience was less about compassion and more driven by need. The war against the Kin had entered its fourth week, occupying most of the children, who toiled in various parts of the camp. No one, however, would help Azalea make her knife. The presence of Greaves unnerved the gang, whether they admitted it or not, but the Prissies protested outright at Azalea doubling back on her declaration against blades.

The industriousness of the early days intoxicated Chatter. He maintained a regular schedule of visiting the wounded with Remedy, but found middling success as a nurse, and left these duties to other kids. During the day, he helped bake bread at the ovens, tear pilfered sheets into bandages, or work the vegetable plots at the back of camp. He thrilled at watching the yields of the day coalesce into the mechanics of war. The forges and smith shops buzzed with preparation. A cluster of huts near the treeline commanded the construction of armour, and dozens of children were engaged in the industry of sorting, shaping, and sewing the bits of metal brought in from the valley. Magpie piles grew around the clearing, metal stolen from an already forged realm. Larger kids brought back felled trees for rendering into the hafts of weapons and the reinforced spines of slipshods. Chainmailed soldiers stayed busy; squads endured a never-ending cycle of combat training, reconnaissance, and maintenance missions to the existing slipshods in the valley. The conviction of purpose enlivened the days and assured nights of exhausted recuperation, nights spent around fires, kids congratulating one another on the smaller victories of the day.

Azalea's return from the scrapyard with a coil spring from the Model T dampened the preparations. Work continued in the forges, but the Prissies left Azalea alone. Kids drifted over, in twos and threes, for confirmation. Azalea greeted each of them, smiling, as though she couldn't see their expressions.

Chatter's assistance allowed Azalea an escape into explanations of how the process had developed since the earliest molds. Together, they cut the coil spring into palm lengths, then drew out the metal to almost twenty inches. They flattened it, and Azalea worked one end into a toothed point, then the other into a wide spine for the handle. This took the better part of four mornings.

One morning, while they were alone, Chatter asked her what she needed the knife for. Azalea paused for a moment, watched the heat roil off the coals, then answered him. "I'm going to put it through Greaves's heart." Chatter didn't know how to respond, but Azalea didn't seem to mind the silence. Neither brought it up again.

"*Chatter*," Azalea's voice shook him from his reverie. He blinked sweat from his eyes and leaned into the bicycle pump. Heat was vital at this point, and Chatter didn't want to compromise the blade. He focused. When the metal glowed, Azalea brought it from the coal to the anvil and hammered it herself. Chatter fought the urge to collapse. His eyes blurred over the subdued motion of the camp.

A lanky boy holding a bent buckler entered the forge. He kept his face turned away and moved to the furthest forge.

Chatter raised his hand in a half-hearted wave. "Hey," he said, "Riley."

Longshanks didn't return the greeting. He glanced at Azalea's forge, but didn't let his eyes focus. He left with his buckler, his business uninitiated.

Azalea lowered the hammer. Her eyes followed Longshanks' retreat. "Ignore him," she said, "It's only natural. We've been too successful in battle so far. We were bound to run into a defeat like Slovenly Pasture."

"No," Chatter said, "It isn't Slovenly Pasture. It happened the first time you sent me to retrieve Remedy."

Azalea smiled. A haze blown away from her eyes. She knew the story.

Hours after he'd escorted Chatter to the Gardens, Riley Longshanks claimed he felt a tingle in his legs. Notorious for his knobbly legs, Longshanks complained nightly of shooting pain in his shins. He kept others awake with his whine, and the vigourous scrapes and slaps he thought would allay the pain. No one paid attention, then, when Longshanks first spoke of his legs. The children noticed only later, when Longshanks shut up.

He outperformed his squad in sprints, hikes, and long-distance running, and at night slept so soundly that his bunkmates shook him awake, worried he'd died in his sleep. As word spread, Longshanks stood by the fact of his recovery: on the long walk, when his leg touched Chatter's, he'd been healed.

Other stories rose in the wake of Longshanks' claim. Children swore toothaches, cricked necks, and swollen knuckles disappeared after brushing past Chatter. Bolstered by these evidences, Riley was Chatter's biggest proponent, boasting of the miracle that fixed his leg in the voice of one who'd narrowly allayed death.

"Then the other day, when I'm on my way to the infirmary, a dozen other things on my mind," Chatter said, "Riley steps before me and he says, *Hi, Chatter.*"

"You're a wretched person for not recognizing him," Azalea said, unable to hide her smile.

Chatter shook his head. "In front of his squad, too. I tried to make amends, but he avoids me now. He's gone back to limping."

Azalea stared out at her camp for a long while. "A show," she said. She returned to the blade on her anvil, cooled to a depthless black. She held it up and gauged its straightness against the treeline. "Give them a show. They deserve it. Hold out those hands of yours and heal Riley Longshanks."

CHAPTER 57

The next day, after an early rain, Chatter stood on the reservoir platform before the assembled children and raised his voice. He declared he would heal Riley Longshanks, and any others who dared. Blank stares greeted him. For many, it was the first time they'd heard Chatter speak.

In his loudest voice, he railed off the Everyman Affliction.

The wounded from Slovenly Pasture were brought to watch. Cheers and whistles greeted them as they found their places, and soon they intermingled with the rest of the kids, until Chatter was unable to distinguish the sick, the hurt, and the healthy. Every kid in the audience displayed naked skepticism.

Dirty and a few others refused to join the audience proper, and lounged at distant vantage points around the clearing. Chatter spotted Azalea amidst the kids, tending to Sylvie Task, a young girl who'd broken her ankle while fleeing the Kin. Briny lingered near Dirty, but wandered to the audience when Chatter repeated his promise.

Chatter took off his wool jacket and rolled up his sleeves. He bowed to a smatter of applause. A girl at the back shouted out something to the amusement of those around her, but her words were lost to most.

Chatter cleared his throat. He sang a song to the Lord.

The children refused to sing. They stared him with the same hapless expressions that haunted Mrs. Anders' sermons at Slatterly. The *Lord*, he thought, chastising himself, there is no Lord beyond the society who invents Him. The children of the culvert had little use for pacifying homilies; they couldn't eat prayer. Holy water was no better than the river at cleaning their clothes.

Abandoning Lou's pitches of betterment, Chatter seized the attention of the culvert by inviting Petror the Giant to the platform. The tall boy lumbered up, a dim concentration buried deep in his eyes. Chatter raised his voice and exclaimed the power in his hand. A moment later, with the touch of a pinky, Chatter knocked Petror the Giant on his ass.

The children exploded. They laughed, hooted, and cried for a repeat performance. Again, Chatter talked Petror into a trance, the way Lou taught him, and again Chatter knocked Petror the Giant on his ass.

The kids around Dirty moved closer. A few joined the line that formed next to the stage, their faces screwed up as they cast about for symptoms. By the time Chatter abandoned onstage diagnosis, the margins of the clearing were almost empty. Even those tasked with work left their tools and wandered into the mirth. A last few lingered at the edges, resolved not to join what had become, for the rest of the camp, a feat of strength.

For two hours, Chatter had them all, from the stingy attentions at the fringes to those in the front rows who leapt in excitement. Every heart beat upon his palm. Matchstick Darcy swore she'd stand her ground, but Chatter's hand graced her brow and she fell with a surprised whoop. The culvert uproarious. Again and again. Chatter lost his voice in the noise, in the sheer weight of others, and a whiteness ringed his vision.

Chatter lost count of how many crossed the platform during the healing, and of how long he seduced people to fall. Riley Longshanks happily fell like the others, and hopped away on two good legs, hollering Chatter's name with the rest. A number of the kids quivered when he touched them, and he saw how unused they were to intimacy. It seemed a betrayal, at times, to drop them from their first embraces, but Chatter promised himself that it was in service to his performance.

The children, he thought, more than anything else, needed to believe.

Every kid fell to his touch.

The last in line, a red-faced boy named Garters, with an actual sniffle, fell before Chatter could touch him. Garters' knees folded as Chatter reached out. Despite themselves, the children gasped. But Garters bounded up after a moment, and they burst into applause. Chatter helped the kid off stage amidst the hollering, wiped his hands before the crowd, and concluded the healing with a heartfelt: "Live Forever!"

CHAPTER 58

The next morning, while mist clung to valley, Azalea and Chatter climbed a ridge to meet the sun. Grasses grew waist high around pockets of spruce, black in the early morning light, and thin grey cottonwoods. Dazed from his successes the day before, Chatter meandered behind Azalea, partially listening to the reports from the marshlands. Harmony's Kin had arrived in force now; dozens of kids were spotted every day, making their way into the western territories, dressed for war. Azalea recounted the battles and ambushes the Prissies had witnessed. Slovenly Pasture, she reminded Chatter, only happened because retreating Kin had stumbled upon a scout group of Prissies.

After this, Azalea was quiet for a while, watching the sun climb out of the leaves. When she spoke again, her tone had changed. "I hadn't—" she said, "I didn't expect the retribution to fall on others. I thought so long as we kept Greaves, and our plan wasn't revealed, the Kin would keep the violence mostly within themselves. I'm ashamed of myself for that, Chatter."

Chatter shook his head. "What do you mean?"

"Roscoe's Cove has been terrorized," said Azalea. "It's a cluster of fishing huts by the river where a group of kids named the Wallows live. Past few nights, fires start nearer and nearer their camps. Each time the kids go and put out the blaze, they get attacked. Big dumb idiots come out of the bushes with their big dumb fists. It happened at Caspar Falls too, and when they got back to camp someone had come and killed all their chickens. No other communication."

Unbidden, the socket of misery beneath the willow arose in Chatter's mind. Sweat beaded on his cheeks as he thought of those tortured hares. The weight of a hand pressing their necks downwards, their hind legs clawing against the dirt. How many times, he questioned himself, had he felt the yearn in his chest the past week? Or worse: how often had the warmth of the fire, the voices and closeness of the other children, deafened him all together? Shame burned hot across his mind.

Chatter floundered for response while Azalea bent forward. She disappeared into the grass for a while, then emerged holding a small black stone the size of her palm. She waved Chatter over and pointed to a hollow in the ground. A blasted rock emerged out of the land, and beneath it flakes of minerals glinted in the sunlight.

"Fern and I had the same foster father," Azalea said. "Allister. He hurt both of us. But I knew the nature of Fern's character from that very first day I arrived. Of the other three girls there, Fern was the only one who warned me what happened when Allister took you into his study. That trembling girl, unafraid of her huge secret." Azalea turned the stone over in her hand. "I was frightened of Allister when we went into his study. He was bigger than I was, he had this belt wrapped around his hand, and the boiled cabbage smell of his body suffocated my mind, but in the end Fern's strength made me unafraid. Soon Fern, and Allister, came to know the nature of my character, too."

Azalea handed the stone to Chatter. It was smooth where it had cleaved from the rock; its convex side fit nicely in his palm. "Quartz," she said. "You'll find a few of these rocks jutting out of the tops of this ridge."

"Quartz," Chatter said.

"Fern and I left Allister's together," Azalea said. "Those other cows wouldn't come. They figured they were *safer* at Allister's. Imagine that. Fern and I stayed on the street for a while, but there's only so long one of you can stay awake while the other sleeps. After a few weeks, Fern wondered if those girls weren't right. That's why I brought her into the valley, so we could live away from the terrible world people made." Azalea watched the mist rise out of the valley. "But we found it down here, too."

Chatter handed the stone back to Azalea. "What is the quartz for, Azalea?"

Azalea hefted the stone, let it settle in her palm. "Maybe we were safer," she said with a wry smile. "Quartz is best for a whetstone. It will make my knife sharp enough to cleave dreams from dreamers."

"Azalea," Chatter said. He meant to continue but found himself echoed by the mist, the valley, and the low ghosts of shrubs just in sight. *Azalea! Azalea!* The cry grew closer, frantic, separated by heaving breathing and the crack of a pubescent voice. *Azalea!* A boy in an ungainly helmet tumbled up the hill towards them.

"Azalea!" he shouted, "Greaves has escaped!"

CHAPTER 59

At dawn, the children from the culvert crossed the river on rafts of birch. The biggest kids pushed the rafts across the slow current east of Farrow with poles of year-old poplar. They worked hard, and quietly, and soon the entire attack force of thirty kids waited on the other bank.

Chatter tried to match the steel of their expressions, but terror roiled his guts. Azalea rode with him on the last raft across the river. She assured him he need only come for the wounded after the fighting advanced, but this didn't make him feel better. He thought of each kid carrying a vial of Remedy, and grew sicker.

Greaves hid from the Prissies in the marsh for a day before he was spotted by a short girl named Natty, who gave chase but lost him somewhere along the river. Natty said it looked like the boy had never learned to swim, but he was frantic enough to stay above the surface and ride the current out of sight. All agreed that, given his injuries, Greaves's ability to evade them in forest was near miraculous. Stories took up of him sprinting on creaking bones, of blood trails vanished, or ascended into unclimbable trees. Kids better at sniffing trails followed his path across the river, trailing him to an abandoned grain elevator on the prairie shelf. The elevator was known to the kids, and routinely avoided, as a nest of vipers, where drug users, vagrants, and fugitive members of the Kin took shelter. Prissie scouts reported a fortification program—at every entrance prairie fencing was repurposed into bulwarks wound with barbed wire, and boobytraps littered the concrete pad where rail tracks used to sit—but the efforts remained unfinished, and the scouts never saw any work performed. Greaves was seen on the second day, walking from the collapsed silo to the main building, and the next day excited reports of Simon Sanderson's presence raced around the culvert.

Azalea smiled at such reports, responding with fierce cries of confidence, or readying orders, but Chatter saw these for the show they were, flush with his same confidence of the stage. Azalea, whenever he found her alone, bristled with a nervous agitation. She was afraid Greaves had revealed her plan to Simon Sanderson, that this would then make its way to Harmony, and that the whole culvert would be surrounded by a nest of hornets she kicked up. She didn't sleep until Greaves and Sanderson had been located at the elevator, and after she immediately organized an attack. *Both of them*, she would say, pounding her fist into her hand and grinding her knuckles into her bones. *Both of them.*

Azalea's outward optimism was the only sound on the birch raft beyond the grunt of the oarsman. She carried a lithe ball club of the type made in the valley for thousands of years, a fist-sized stone affixed to a haft with thick strips of leather. The knife she'd made sat in a horizontal sheath on her belt.

Before they reached the bank, Azalea drew her knife and handed it to Chatter. He accepted the weapon, bashful at her earnestness. "You promised," she said.

Chatter remembered Lou's cardinal sin. He didn't hesitate. He drew the knife across the back of his left hand, marking the blade with his blood. He needn't apply much pressure; the edge of Azalea's knife was the sharpest he'd ever felt.

Azalea took back her knife and slid it into her belt without cleaning the blade. "I remember these times the best," she said. "The air before a rumble is always crisp."

The elevator sat at the edge of a small settlement retaken by the prairie grass, abandoned after the city pulled up the railway tracks for scrap. The complex at the elevator's base, a scattering of independent sheds, wore an odd camouflage of branches dragged from the valley, hacked into brash new forms, jutting from the bulwarks in senseless clusters. The whole structure felt like a scar on the land, a pock, virulent in its waiting. No noise came from the building, no motion revealed life.

The attack force amassed in a coulee out of sight of the elevator. The three kids with the best eyes kept watch in the early light, while the rest circled Azalea. A tired group joined, the vanguard that'd camped at the elevator for three nights. All told, almost fifty kids stood shoulder to shoulder in the coulee. As one, they took a knee before Azalea.

"I know that I broke your trust that day I brought Greaves to the culvert," Azalea began. "Don't think that I didn't see your faces, that I didn't hear your voices. The accords were what kept the sky above us. I know it. And I ended that. Then, I asked you for your trust, I asked you to fight a war no one wanted. And you did. Because you, like me, are growing big in a small world. You know the Prissies can't stay in the culvert; we can't keep hiding in the trees. We'll all be gone soon enough, and what can we say will last? Our names? No, none of us will be remembered like that. They'll only remember what we've done, what we did on this day. They'll remember the Prissies, they'll remember the day we broke the Kin.

"We have broken the Kin. Not I, but you. We. Sanderson's territory is scattershot, overrun by scavengers from the western Kin. Each one of you has stretched your legs on his grasses. Not his. Ours. Yesterday, I walked a favourite field of Fern's, and I can't tell you how much that means to me. You gave me that. And Harmony's Kin? They are not what they were; made more of our stories than their might. More than half grew and left, and nobody wants to join her smelly ass. She's punching in the dark. Just spinning around in blind circles. We have done this. Not I, but you.

"We *will* be victorious," Azalea said, her voice alight. "There are sixty kids here. All Prissies. All sturdy. Simon Sanderson doesn't have those numbers. Our spooks have spent four days setting fires in the bush and blowing reed whistles all night. Not a person in there is more awake than you are. Half are mad. Last night, a dozen kids abandoned the elevator. There's nobody there, only Simon Sanderson, only Greaves, holding each other in fear."

Azalea smiled, but none joined her. "Ten of you go east and barrage them with stones and arrows," she said. "That'll flush the kids inside out front, where we'll be waiting. While that happens, fifteen of you breach the west. Defenses are weak there, so once you're in, we'll have them surrounded. Then all we do is knock over kids until we find those snakes."

Azalea rubbed her hands together, but the business hung in the air. A few shuffled in the ranks, neighbours whispered. "What the hell is wrong?" Azalea said.

Eventually, a thick-necked girl suggested, "They got knives."

Azalea blinked, stunned. "Look, I like it as much as you," she said. "I loved when the worst you could expect from a fight was a loose tooth. Remember when a scrap told you who you were, who you were with, and who you weren't? You needed everyone standing, just so they'd know who won. But it isn't about that anymore. We're not fighting over what we share; we're fighting over the idea that we have to share. And that means this isn't an act of war, this is an act of nature.

"The world we live in is passing. You know it, I know it. I remember the sunshine from when I was young, but all last summer, I don't recall the sunshine. Seems like every day is grey now, every meal is soup. There's no more sunshine than what we hold in our hands. But that's where it is, remember that. The sunshine is in your hands. We can do something here. We have the chance: one good act to wipe the skies of grey. Today is in your hands. Remember that. You can wash them after."

She looked at the kids around her. "I'm scared of their knives, too," she said, "And it might seem unfair that I have one with me, so I promise you now that this knife has only one use, and it won't be in combat. I won't need it. Because I trust our armour, I trust you who threaded this mail, who balanced my club. I trust the Prissies. And I trust Chatter, I trust what Chatter gives us."

Chatter hung his head. He saw how many turned his way, how many hands slipped to stowed vials of rainwater Remedy.

By the time the children climbed out of the coulee, Kin stood behind the battlements. Seven were in sight, though early reports went as high as thirteen. A few of the Prissies recognized their handiwork in the stolen chainmail. Jeers from the children of the culvert drew no response.

Buoyed by the inferior force, the Prissies grew crude. A few bared their asses, while others took up a song about errant mothers. The song died quickly, as more and more soldiers filed out of the grain elevator.

"Twenty-nine, thirty," Briny counted next to Chatter. "Hell," he said. Then he smiled and punched Chatter on the shoulder, and Chatter felt something settle in his chest.

"Hell," Chatter said, but he couldn't think of anything more to add.

Briny turned with the rest and watched a squad of armed Kin march out of the elevator into the open ground. Bats and staves and brass knuckles in plain view. "I always thought there *had* to be more rules than there actually are," Briny said. The mallets he carried bobbed in his hands.

Dirty stood amidst a squad of big kids, embroiled in preparation. They screamed in one another's faces, their cheeks red, their eyes bulging. Dirty rubbed mud on his face and his arms in insensible patterns.

A tall kid with thick glasses and a heavy canvas coat marched out of the massing Kin and held up a fist wrapped in several feet of chain. "Azalea Handle-hurler," he shouted, "this is a cowardly attack. We call you out on the rules of a Rumble. Ten-on-ten, twenty-on-twenty, or pick your best five. You got no cause for anything else here. This is our only offer."

A silence as great as Chatter felt inside fell over the elevator. Azalea strode from rank into the open ground. She already had the rock in her hand. "Here is my offer," she yelled, but it was only to distract the boy. The rock clipped him across the jaw, and he fell to the ground moaning.

A staccato blast of reeds, at several shrill tones, took up from the eastern side of the elevator. The swaying grasses shrieked in a wild language.

Briny shook his head. "Imagine listening to that for a week."

The Kin fell into an agitated state. A number clapped their hands over their ears, a couple threw stones into the unresponsive prairie. The offensive quieted the reeds quickly, and the squad in the open ground tightened, nervous at easy victory.

A kid appeared in the east, a badger up from the grass, mid-stride, his mouth wide in a yell. His torso hurled forward in a calamitous arc. A blunted javelin soared into the squad before the silo.

The kids at the centre of the squad collapsed around an unconscious girl. The rest scattered as stones, sticks, boomerangs, and spiked balls made of roofing nails rained down. Many made for the elevator, but the eastern assault herded the kids towards Azalea's line.

Chatter couldn't see beyond his terror. He held a studded billy club, given to him by Briny. The weight of the weapon in his hand had felt good in the coulee, but it tugged his shoulder now, and made his elbow ache. He considered leaving it on the ground, but when Briny broke into a sprint next to him, Chatter followed, his mind an overbright blur.

The two sides met with a gasp. Crazed Kin swung haphazardly, felling one another as often as others. The Prissies remained calm, targeting the isolated and the wounded before moving on. The earthen smell of turned dirt thickened in the moist air.

A girl hurtled past Chatter, fixed on one of the larger boys behind him, and their shoulders collided. She grunted and grabbed at him, but he twisted away. He spun, lost his bearings, and fell into the grass. The field a chaos of a thousand separate parts.

Chatter couldn't locate Briny amidst the fighting, but Dirty and his squad remained easy to distinguish. They fell upon the Kin with a chilling ferocity. None carried weapons; Dirty's squad remained content with mailed gloves and studded caps on their boots. When Dirty chortled, the scars creased his face in a disorienting way.

Azalea's voice broke above the clamour; she shouted instructions to the younger kids, hurled abuse at her foes, and cheered the children of the culvert towards the elevator. Comfortable in her armour, she threw herself into the ranks of the Kin, swiping, punching, biting, and kicking. While he watched, Chatter felt a thrill he could not name.

Chatter caught a flurry in his peripherals and flinched, lessening the blow from the croquet mallet. He toppled, his sinuses flooded with stinging liquid, and he dropped to his knees and threw up as the mallet swung again for his temple. He dodged and rolled, pushing himself away with his feet. A crazed, red-eyed kid from the Kin swung the mallet downwards and caught Chatter's ribs as he rolled.

Chatter flung a handful of mud and clambered to his feet. He ducked the next swing and brought his club down on the red-eyed kid's thigh. The kid roared, then charged. Chatter brought up his club and set forward.

The impact sent both boys sprawling, but they were soon at each other's throats, neither able to gain advantage. Club and mallet abandoned, each boy relied on fists and elbows and teeth. The kid yanked Chatter's hair; Chatter dug his thumb into the kid's eye.

Chatter was surprised at what came back from his fights at His Holy Rules. His hands, free from weapons, grew nimble and hard. He leaned into his punches, finished them, and did not allow the red-eyed kid any blind chances. Success came not to the strong, he reminded himself, only to those willing to endure.

The kid called Chatter drifted. The bodies on the field blurred; those standing became vagaries of the breeze. A distant sensation rose, a cry from the west, a sweeping motion across the foreground. Eventually, the bodies cleared. Chatter blinked.

"Dammit," Dirty said. He shook Chatter's shoulder again. "Get your head right, Chatter," he said. "What are you supposed to save with those?" He pointed to Chatter's hands.

Chatter stared downwards at his swollen fingers and split knuckles. Beneath him, the red-eyed kid groaned. Both eyes were swollen shut, his lips split. "Shit!" Chatter exclaimed and climbed off the boy.

Dirty looked Chatter up and down. Dirty's arms were spattered up to his scarred shoulders. "What the hell you waiting for?" Dirty said. "You're up. It's showtime."

The field behind Dirty had emptied of combatants. Nearby, a group stood around a fallen kid. An unsettling sound came from their midst.

"What happened?" Chatter said.

"We did fine," Dirty said, as they jogged to the group, "but they were waiting in the west. Azalea took everyone to push through. Greaves ain't here, though. He left days ago, they say."

Chatter's head spun. His mind blanked as they approached the group.

Riley Longshanks lay on the ground in a pool of blood, his hands clasped across his inner thigh. "No no no no," repeated Longshanks as he forced his palms down on the ugly gash that revealed the bone. He raised his head, saw Chatter, and then laughed. "Thank god," he said to the kids around him. "Thought I was a goner."

Dirty gave Chatter's shoulder a push. "Go on," he said.

Chatter nodded and knelt next to Longshanks. He nodded again. Blood, already cold on his hands, flaked when he flexed his fingers.

"Chatter?" said Longshanks. His voice dropped away. He raised his head and repeated himself.

"What?" Chatter said. He held his hands over Longshanks' thigh. A moist heat rose from the injuries. Chatter glanced up, but Longshanks' head lolled backwards, his eyes fluttered.

Chatter pressed his hands onto the wound on Longshanks' leg, a thin pulse detectable against his palm. Riley's skin paled to a flat grey as he watched. The change startled Chatter and a throb at his temple overwhelmed him. His hands moved clumsily from wound to wound, his fingers insensate, the yearn in his heart gone cold.

"Chatter?" Longshanks said.

Chatter raised his head, his attention returned. "Yeah?" he said.

"Am I doing something wrong?"

A few of the kids watching stifled laughs, absurd noises for their absurd world. A murmur ran over the heads of the boys on the ground.

Chatter took his hands from Longshanks' leg. "No," Chatter said. "Riley, you're not. We're almost there. I swear. Just lay your head back. Close your eyes. You'll be better in no time."

Kids scoffed, but Longshanks focused on Chatter. His face stayed calm. He winced when Chatter pressed too hard. Eventually, not even then.

A few kids broke off and ran towards the west side of the elevators. Another couple followed. Chatter focused on Longshanks. He tried to feel the press of energy. He focused on his heart. He held his breath. The kids nearest Chatter muttered to one another, then headed after the rest.

The throb against Chatter's palm ebbed. A further gush of blood spilled out of the wound when Chatter loosened his grip. "All right, Riley," Chatter heard himself whisper, "that's all right. You're ready now. Now we can begin."

He raised his eyes to rouse support, but only Dirty remained.

Dirty inspected Longshanks' limp body then met Chatter's stare. "It's almost better it's a lie," he said.

The noise of battle rose on the west flank of the elevator. Dirty didn't tarry. He left Chatter alone with Riley Longshanks.

The blood cooled on Chatter's hands. He lowered his head. "I'm sorry, Riley," Chatter said. He was glad he was alone, so he could cry a little.

Bodies of kids littered the ground before the elevator. Most lay still, unconscious, their breath blowing bubbles in the blood on their mouths. Others wriggled like worms in dry dirt, desperate for a reprieve. One kid, with two broken ankles, crawled in a direction that was neither the elevator nor away. She let out a keening that Chatter felt in the roots of his teeth. He saw a Prissy rock himself off a pinned arm. His functioning arm freed, the kid poured Remedy over the wound that ran deep in his chest. He hummed a homily Chatter had sung on the reservoir platform. By the time Chatter drew close, the boy was motionless.

Chatter came to a quiet area in the field. Children lay in a scatter tableau, ragdolls insensible in the rising sunshine. Dazed, Chatter wandered into their midst.

Huff, huff, huff, came the breath of a girl who'd fought for the Kin. *Huff, huff, huff.*

The image of Sandy Bixby imitating the dying bear came back to Chatter. He knelt next to the girl. She'd suffered one of the flails made from bike chains. The offending flail lay nearby, but Chatter couldn't tell who had wielded it. Bodies were everywhere.

Huff, huff, huff, said the girl, her skin spilt in several places. Chatter didn't know how she was still alive.

The girl watched Chatter, then looked back at the sky. *Huff, huff huff,* she said.

Chatter reached out his hand. The tack of the blood on his forearms tingled. A light breeze disturbed the dirt around the girl's head. He laid his hand on her calf. "C'mon," he said, "C'mon."

The girl's eyes found him once more. After a while, she rolled over.

With the crack of a flung door, Simon Sanderson stumbled out from the grain elevator. The Prissies had stripped him of his shirt and his socks. His emaciated form displayed several fresh wounds as he spun to confront the pursuing Prissies. He tried to sprint, but the kids coming from the east grasses corralled him as they approached. He spun clumsily, goggling at the enclosing kids. Even at a distance, Chatter could see Sanderson's stumble, the glazed eyes and pocked arms of a morphine junkie pulled prematurely from his fever dream.

Chatter took his hand off the girl's ankle and joined the group before the elevator. Wickedness lit the eyes of every child, a blaze of life at the battle-glory, the battle-gore, and the confident knowledge of survival. The surging adrenaline provided a rush of camaraderie; sweaty, steaming kids clapped Chatter on the shoulders as he merged with their mob.

Azalea entered the circle and shouted Sanderson's name. Blood matted her hair and covered her face. Her eyes blazed from a mask of wrath. She slid the knife from her belt and tossed it at Simon Sanderson's feet.

Sanderson ignored the weapon.

"Pick it up," Azalea growled in a voice the beleaguered Sanderson couldn't help but obey. He bent at the knee and scooped up the knife. "Now give me the rest," Azalea said.

Wobbly, Sanderson brought the blade of the knife to his trousers. He unseamed one side, then the other, then stripped the pants off. Catcalls and wolf-whistles emerged from the crowd, but Azalea glared them quiet. She motioned to Sanderson to continue.

Next were the waffle-fabric long johns, dispatched easier than the pants. Several people laughed despite themselves, even Azalea cracked a smile. Simon Sanderson wore little boy underpants.

"Go to hell, all of you!" Sanderson slurred. He slashed the knife through the air while the Prissies laughed at the impotence of this rage. A second unmet swing toppled his balance.

"Shut up," Azalea snapped at her crowd.

Sanderson's focus returned to her. "You mad bish," he said, "You've no idea what yer done."

Azalea's voice dropped to a fearsome depth. "You stupid little boy. This is what you've done with yourself? Got yourself stuck up a tree you can't climb down? Maybe you think dope wipes your mind, but it won't never get it clean, I can tell you that. There is no escape from this. There is no escape from what you've done. Now, keep going," she said, "you aren't done yet."

Sanderson dropped his eyes and slipped the knife under the elastic of his underwear. He flung the crumpled fabric to the ground, then the knife. He tried to hide himself.

The Prissies sang a song about size, exchanged jokes, and several kids tossed sticks and rocks, trying to lodge them in Sanderson's buttocks.

"Shut up!" Azalea screamed. The Prissies fell into shocked silence and shifted uneasily. Several shivered as the adrenaline left their bodies.

Azalea turned back to Sanderson. "Pick up that knife," she said. "I told you. You aren't done yet."

Sanderson stared at her uncomprehendingly. His head shook from side to side. "No, there's nothing left," he said. "There's nothing left for me to give."

Azalea took a step forward, and Sanderson retreated. "I bet you're proud of the stories you told," she said. "I've pictured the look on your dumb face while you told it. That pig joy. You couldn't help but include all the details."

Azalea steadied Sanderson with her gaze. She stared at him until he retreated again. "That's how I know," Azalea said. "That's how we all know about what you did to Fern. No, you aren't done. Remember? First, you took Fern's clothes. Then, you took something else."

Sanderson whimpered and gave Azalea a horrified look.

"Either you do it, or I will," said Azalea, "But I won't be gentle. So. Go on," she gestured to the knife on the ground, "You aren't finished yet."

Sanderson glared at Azalea. He turned, but found no quarter. The silence of the Prissies had solidified into a physical presence. He cried for a moment, and then collected himself. He took a weaving step, then another. He scooped the knife off the ground. He inspected the blade, blew it clear of particulate, then grabbed a handful of his own hair and tugged upwards. He cried again. He pressed the knife into his hairline until the blade separated his skin from his skull.

CHAPTER 60

Chatter returned to the culvert amidst silent children. No jubilation greeted them at camp, only wary stares. A numb count of who walked back, who was carried. No one spoke of what Simon Sanderson had visited upon himself.

Azalea knelt next to the reservoir at the mouth of the culvert and washed her face several times. She ignored the tentative remarks of others, intent on replicating, over and over, the silkiness of the water meeting her skin. Afterwards, she sat on the lip of the reservoir and washed her arms, chest, and neck in the same way.

The sight mesmerized the kids in the culvert. Chatter stood nearby, at the ovens, in the hope their latent heat would shake the chill that deadened his body.

Briny approached Chatter. He'd suffered several broken ribs, and a virulent bruise spread up his neck from under his clothes. He stared through Chatter. "Aren't you going to heal her?" he said.

Chatter hung his head. He drew a helpless breath. "I can't," he said. "Didn't you see? In the field? I can't, Briny."

Briny fixed Chatter with a plain look. "Go on," he said, he waved his hand to indicate the clearing. "All these kids can see."

Azalea didn't acknowledge Chatter's approach. She remained focused on her own silhouette, indolent in the water. "Go away, Chatter," she said, "I'm tired. I want to sleep."

"So, sleep," Chatter said, "But you aren't alone in the world right now."

She looked up at him, uncomprehending. Her eyes travelled around the camp. "All right," she said. "We'll go into the culvert. But I want to lie down."

Azalea brought Chatter to a deep chamber in the culvert where the Prissies kept the crates of Remedy brought from the Gardens. Chatter wanted to tip over the towers of peach boxes; he wanted to stamp every vial. He placed his hand on a stack, tested its balance. Azalea lay with her back to him.

Chatter lay next to Azalea and wrapped his arm around her. She made no motion to accommodate him, but when he moved to shift his weight, her hand clasped around his wrist.

They listened to the progression of the attack force along the walkways to their bunks deeper in the culvert. A few spoke, but most stayed silent. Chatter buried his face in Azalea's hair to suppress the frenzied episodes of his heart. His forehead met the back of her head. He held his breath for as long as he could, but blood and sweat still matted Azalea's hair.

When he rolled away, Azalea didn't move. "Azalea?" he said.

"Yeah?"

"When the war is over, and everyone sleeps at night, will *this* all stop?"

Azalea stayed quiet while she considered his question. She stared at the peach crates before her. "You tell me," she said.

CHAPTER 61

Chatter slipped out of the culvert, and made his way back to Farrow. A persistent tone haunted his walk, and he attributed it to the aftereffects of the mallet. He felt nothing else. He didn't stop for rest or water, and arrived at the Shambles as the workers clocked out. Mort sat at his desk, behind the green door that proclaimed *OWNER*, but didn't raise his head as Chatter passed.

Lou stared out the breakroom window that faced the street. He was unsteady at the knees, and leaned against the pane. Chatter's reappearance after weeks made little impact on the man. He turned watery eyes to the boy in the door. "They're laughing out there," he said.

Exhaustion came over Chatter. His chin dipped. He sat at the table Lou liked to sleep on. It was closest to the faucets, and, if needed, the drain. Chatter wanted nothing more than to curl up in the loft above the goats. He rubbed his eyes, leaned his tired weight on the table. "What are they laughing about, Lou?" he said.

"What you goddamn think, kid?"

Lou came and slumped at the table. "I feel like a barnacle," he said. "I always thought if you felt like a barnacle, well, that's the day you die. Hitched to a single place. I know what you'll say: *But, Lou, barnacles grow on ships, too.* So, sure, the earth moves around a little, but you've still no choice in the matter. That's still death, kid. And here, with our appointments, our hosts, our manner, we've settled into dying."

Lou stared at Chatter. "Don't roll your eyes at me," Lou said. "Those people out there are laughing at me. *Me.* To my own name. Dammit, half the draw of being a con is having a self to walk away from. I've a wallet of them. But I screwed up. Giving my own name. Damn pride. Damn damn pride. You go out in that street, and you ask them what they're laughing at, and they'll tell you: *Ruddy Lou.* Shit, kid. That's what they'll say."

Chatter shook his head. "I'm not leaving, Lou," he said.

Lou smacked the table. "How does His Majesty enjoy the luxury of choice?" he asked with a cruel smile. His hand slipped inside his vest and soon he fanned himself with a folded paper plate. "Your mark is right here, kid," Lou said. "You want an impression of how you looked that night?"

Chatter scowled and pushed his chair back from the table. All of the illegitimacies of his birth arose in his mind, every thought he'd suffocated.

"That doesn't mean anything," he said. "You had no more right over me than those goons. You aren't any better than them." Chatter's voice quivered into a yell, "You're a kidnapper!"

Chatter was aware of a nervous ringing in his body. He knew there would be no return from the line he'd crossed. His ankles, his wrists, felt loose, as though he were improperly put together. At any step he might collapse.

"I can't leave, Lou," Chatter said. "There's a fight going on in the woods, and it's my fault. I convinced a boy he was bigger than he stood, and I started a war."

Lou snorted a laugh. "What use is a con in a war?" he said. "No, kid, guys like us have no place in that business. We keep the pond calm, we don't smack the surface to see what rises."

"Not me," Chatter said. "Not anymore. Lou, I can *feel* this. It's my fault Sod died. I've thought back on that day every hour since, and I know I could have stopped him. If I hadn't been so afraid, I could have saved him. Godammit, Lou, I didn't do anything. I was too busy keeping the pond calm."

Lou waved his hand. His balance shifted and he grabbed the table to remain standing. The plate smacked flat on the surface.

"I believed the world would leave me alone if I kept quiet enough," Chatter said. "I'm guilty of that, at least. But you have to be ready to fight. Running won't help. You can leave, but I am staying. I have to make amends. Somehow, Lou, I can mend this wound."

Lou shook his head. He unfolded the plate on the table. "Look, kid," Lou said, "you've not got a grave to stand in. *Kidnapper?* You're into me for thousands. Maybe more. Every minute you aren't doing my bidding, you are *stealing* from me. I ought to kill you for the nerve. You leave here, acting like you have a damn choice. Sure, I figure you found a girl. Sure, I figure the kid could use a break, we're set up here right fit. Sure, I figure, because I'm a goddamn saint. You take two weeks, three, sure, why not? But goddammit kid, when I say we leave, we leave. You've been a problem in my hind since the start. Quashing perfectly good deals. For what? An ache in your chest? You dummy. After what I done for you? You aren't ever going to be free of what you owe me. Kid, listen, you have no idea—"

Lou's gesture had left the plate unattended. Chatter's heart gave a calamitous heave. He kicked the table into Lou's gut, and the man wheezed and collapsed. Chatter snatched the plate from the floor, but Lou was already in motion. He smacked Chatter once, twice. "Dammit, kid," he said.

Chatter tackled Lou into the cupboards. The two of them thrashed around on the floor, each lashing inexpertly, passionately, crying out ungodly sounds in lieu of words. Lou tried to lift Chatter, but the boy had grown too big, and used the opportunity to regain his feet and aim a kick at Lou's knee. Lou dropped to one leg.

"Dammit, kid," he said again, spitting a wad of blood onto the floor. He patted the pockets of his vest with shaking fingers, but he already knew. Chatter wriggled his fingers into the knuckledusters.

"Shit," said Lou. "Kid, you've got to listen."

CHAPTER 62

Two nights later, Chatter woke to a gurgle that started in his guts and travelled to his lungs. The whole of his torso tingled. He mistook the sensation as hunger, not having eaten since he'd fled the Shambles, and tried to force himself back to sleep. But the gnaw wouldn't allow him peace.

He rubbed his eyes and shook his head of the past days. He lay behind a small Laundry in the Burrows. He remembered the occasional gusts of warmth and fragrance from the venting, but little else. He supposed rain. A slick of moisture covered the alley and soaked the cardboard around him.

A white-coated jackrabbit approached down the centre of the alley. She was late, inappropriately coloured. Chatter saw a target. A blatant, easy mark.

Tire treads frayed the tips of her ears. One of her eyes bulged a virulent red. Chatter felt the impact of the car. At each step, she seemed uncertain how to continue.

Chatter leaned towards the jackrabbit, but she flinched and pulled from his reach. He rested back against the brick. His fingers swelled inside Lou's dusters. A sick yellow crept up his skin, the rust earned by his sweat, by the lonely clasp of his fingers. Pain spread along his hand, as though he'd clenched his fist for days.

Chatter slipped the dusters off his fingers and massaged his palm until the jackrabbit crept closer.

Chatter reached out his hand.

CHAPTER 63

Gus, the boy who brought the offal to the incineration pile behind the Shambles, told Chatter he'd missed Lou by four hours. He acted out each part, Mort storming out of the Owner's office in tizzy, and Lou calm as ever in the face of flurry. Gus worked up an impression of Mort's distress. *Huff, huff, huff,* said Gus.

The door to Lou's house in the Gardens, with the cistern and the long-abandoned beds of potatoes, hung open. Chatter slid inside. Lou sat on the stool next to the cistern's spigot. He wore an overcoat Chatter hadn't seen before. The room once contained dozens of peach crates, each with two layers of empty vials, but a paltry six remained. Chatter felt sick at how much he'd taken, and he spent several moments staring at Lou in a miserable silence.

Lou's face was still swollen, but the colour had gone back to normal. He held his neck stiff, and a large bruise marred his throat. He grimaced when he noticed Chatter, and continued filling vials.

"Getting's good, I guess," Chatter said.

Lou shrugged.

"Mort's heart's got to be broken," Chatter said, finding silence no better than his voice.

"Mort's the sort of guy who finds something good, and he says to himself, well, damn, if I can make this last, then I'm good," said Lou. "He believes you find one answer and you don't look for another. What can you do with someone like that? They're fodder, nothing more."

Chatter's eyes travelled to Lou's satchel. "Where you going, Lou?"

Lou filled another vial, placed it in his bag, then stood and flexed the fingers of his blackened hand. "Feels good," he said, "I been clearheaded two days now. I'll see if I have more in me. But I can't stay here. It isn't healthy. There's a bout of hay fever going on in the southern communities. I'm heading there now. I'm going to blame the sickness on a serpent. Guy I know in another town has an angle on a stunted python. I'll have her cheap, then I'll sell a stroke for a nickle apiece."

Chatter kicked at a rise in the floorboard. "I have to stay here," Chatter said. "It's — It's my fault. All of this. I thought I knew better than others what my name was."

Lou laughed. "I made that mistake young, too."

Chatter's hated hand slipped into his pocket and retrieved Lou's dusters. He offered them over, but couldn't say any of the things he'd practised on the walk over.

Lou laughed and waved his hand, his tone cooler, crueller. "They're yours," he said. "I tried to tell you before, but you weren't listening. I think that's the problem, neither of us have listened for a while, now, and I've been too drunk to notice. But, see, kid, it's what I said before. I'm a barnacle. I am. Only, I didn't mean you are too. You and me, we're different. I'm the barnacle, you're the boat. You have a course before you, but you have to choose it. As for me, I've had it with this life. I run it into the ground with the others, and like the others, I'll leave it there. Ruddy Lou is dead, kid, his debts are cancelled. I, whoever that is, am not responsible for Lou anymore. And you? You have something to do now. That's what makes a man, having something outside you to do. Makes you halfway a person."

Lou shook his head, then returned to the stool. His hands busily filling, corking, and stowing vials. "Kid, I told you right off," he said, "You're lucky. I never had something to do; I always had to make it up. When nothing's calling, you have to use your own voice. But hell, maybe you weren't worth nothing. Yours is a fine story. I'll eat on it again, I assure you. I'll find benefit in the lies of your life yet, kid. There's something at least," he scoffed, "even if you didn't give me nothing else."

Chatter bristled, surprised at the instinct to stamp his foot. He wouldn't, however. Lou couldn't goad him anymore. Chatter relaxed his shoulders. "Lou," he said, "I gave you the same thing you gave me."

CHAPTER 64

Chatter wandered out of the Gardens and across Farrow. He drifted through the Winks, stared feverishly at the Relegate Mercy, and thought of Alice Callaghan, formerly Alice Always, the first girl he'd kissed. He spent an hour studying the shades of lace in the windows, but couldn't remember which Alice slept behind.

A rot in his chest penetrated the reverie, an irritation of his senses. Chatter stumbled along mud roads in blind pursuit, then beyond the knotted cottages on the furthest edges of the Burrows, and out into the tall wet grasses. Clear of windows, Chatter fell to his knees.

He knew the source of the rot. The suspicion had haunted him for years, resting in the silence, rising to the surface of awareness only when he felt alone. But the bloody socket in the forest and the two headless hares rarely left his mind. Sweat dripped down Chatter's temples. Twice, he retched, but he hadn't eaten for days. He dredged bile, finally, unsatisfied.

Chatter moaned and raised his head above the grass. Lou's dusters hung heavy in the front pocket of his trousers. "Goddammit," he growled.

The rot intensified as Chatter descended into the valley. He barely acknowledged the paths, and when the trail ran counter to the rot, he chose the rot, stepping into the brazen growth of the forest. A swell of pain, a straightening gash, unseaming, forced him to pause and gasp until he could continue.

In a marshy clearing of decomposing reeds Chatter stumbled and fell to the ground. Tangled around his foot was a structure of sticks tied together with knotted twine. A cube topped with a triangle, the triangle topped with another horizontal twig. The hide of a muskrat was under his heel, still wet.

Chatter, unperceiving, stared at the mess until he noticed other figures nearby. Taller, and more angular, the construction was the same. A scaffolding of cube, triangle, and horizontal crossbeam. Draped over this skeleton, gaping with eyeless sockets, hung the hide of a raccoon. Six figures, grouped in couples of tall and short, interrupted the clearing.

In the dim light of the wan moon, Chatter located the flayed animals, the racoon cold, the muskrat still warm, dead, yet emitting the ache of the last seconds of its life. He stayed with the muskrat until it cooled, apologizing and apologizing, while rage overcame his revulsion.

When the muskrat was gone, Chatter continued toward the location of the rot. The sensation of his skin lifting was too much to bear, dissolving the boundaries between his body and the thin air, and wracking his bones with a breeze-borne pain. Chatter pushed through the delirium, unsure at each step if his foot even met the ground. He crossed the clearing, to a section of the marsh sunk under stagnant water. On a sodden bank a boy knelt over a jackrabbit, his arms bent, sawing at the animal. Chatter couldn't help himself. He gasped.

The boy raised his head, his face met moonlight. Greaves narrowed his eyes.

Despite the knife Greaves held, Chatter rushed him, and shoved the boy away from the jackrabbit. Greaves stumbled backwards, and slipped into the moon-slick water up to his knees. A film of particulate marked the surface's high reach on his pants.

"What in the hell, kid?" Greaves said.

"What you gotta hurt them for?" Chatter shouted.

"Who's hurting them?"

"You're torturing those animals," Chatter said. "That muskrat died of pain and terror, not nothing to do with your knifework. And you left it on the cold ground. Who else would do that? I don't know what I thought of you before, but I'm sure of it now. You got to be sick."

Fury twisted Greaves's expression. He lifted his sopping legs free and charged out of the water. He brought his fist down in a hammer blow on Chatter's nose, and sent the smaller boy sprawling.

"Don't you dare," Greaves snarled. "Don't you dare. Not you. Never use that word with me. Don't never. You don't know nothing about that word."

Pain split Chatter's focus for a moment, but it washed away a haze, and when he felt able to stand, he charged back at Greaves, and shoved him back into the water. "You left that muskrat alive!" Chatter shouted. "And this rabbit's hardly dead, either. You're skinning animals before they're dead. What other name do you have for that? It's monstrous."

Greaves stuttered. "I didn't," he said, then paused. His fist flew up before him like an angered wasp, and he punched the surface of the water. His face darkened. "What do you want me to do? Didn't nobody teach me how to skin an animal, not how to trap one or kill one. I tried to break their necks proper. I never had no one to ask. Everyone around here is just some dumb kid. There's no knowledge, just the things we figured out. You don't just go around finding dead animals. I don't mean to leave them alive. It's a mistake, kid. I ain't doing it on purpose. Sometimes I rush myself, I get carried away."

"You gotta kill that one, buddy," Chatter said. "Stick your knife in its heart now. It's the only kind move you've got left. You know where its heart is?"

Greaves shook his head. "Can't," he said. "Can't. That wrecks its coat. Its coat can't be wrecked. There wouldn't be no point otherwise."

"There's a point to this?"

But Greaves only stared at him. "What is your name, kid?"

Chatter opened his mouth.

"I know what they call you. But what's your name?"

Chatter stood as tall as he could. He set his jaw. "You gotta kill that animal, pal. You like watching it suffer?"

Greaves walked back to the muskrat, stepped over its body, then righted the figure Chatter had knocked over. He placed the hide atop the structure, settling it near the racoon, precise about their places. He was careful in his consideration. He stepped back and evaluated the figures in the context of each other. "Don't nobody like watching suffering," he said.

Chatter knelt next to the jackrabbit. He folded its skin back over its muscles, like he were tucking it in to bed. He held his hand against its flank. He imagined the happinesses hares share, he whispered them to distract the animal, but it didn't listen. Its eyes were closed, its ears pressed back against its body. Chatter hushed himself and willed all of the jackrabbit's pain into his hands and up his arms.

Greaves didn't move. He kneeled the whole while Chatter whispered to the animal. "Watched my mom die," Greaves said, "and she suffered. Puked and spat up and shook like electricity shot right through her. She got so hot her brain boiled, I guess. It was this drug did it to her, she had too much, and then she was dead as dirt. Weren't a year later the cops killed Greg, my mom's boyfriend. Killed him in our living room, same place my mom died. Greg didn't suffer much, just gurgled while the bullets were in his lungs. I was alone after that, for a while."

"You blame them, then?" Chatter said. "Mean ol' Greg?"

"Ain't no blame, kid," Greaves said. "Ain't even anyone to point the finger. Do you think anyone cares what happens down here? No, there's no blame. There's only what happens. What stumbles before you." Greaves nodded to himself. He took a swipe at the surface of the water. "I didn't ask for any of this. I don't want to feel what I feel. You think I asked for this? I don't take their skins to make them suffer. I wish I found them dead. I take their skins because I don't know how to say what I have to say any other way."

"Bullshit," Chatter said. His hand had grown cold.

"Screw you, kid," Greaves said. "You don't know nothing. Don't blame me. You want to blame anyone, blame Simon Sanderson. It was Sanderson who gave me the first knife I didn't have to steal. His idea to come to the valley. The homes down here are easier to rob from, he says. Six of us, I think? Seven? I remember this one night we're walking along the tracks the other side of the river, and this nasty thing come along the rail, walking in these wobbly lines. Was this half runover fox. We'd guessed the maintenance truck that we'd seen an hour before. And this damn thing is wandering around like that for an hour. It was a sight. Sickened every one of us. And the sounds it was making? *Huff huff huff* And this pitiful yip. I had a folding knife, so I stuck it in its throat. Died quick enough after that. I remember, there's Sanderson and this huge grin. *You just did that*, he said. *Didn't even think at all. Didn't stop once. Didn't bother you at all.* And the others are looking at me too, so I say, *Yeah*, because I thought it sounded tough. So, Simon stole me a blade from the pawn shop he knew to steal from. Things changed after that.

"Or maybe I thought things would change, felt like they did, but they just shifted, then settled again. Only, each time Simon needed a blade stuck in something, he'd remind me, saying, *Greaves, now, who gave you that nice knife?* I could have taken my own knife; I did, but it didn't change; Simon still said, like I still held the same knife, *Who gave you that nice knife?* The only way to shut him, shut up the others, was to stick what needed stuck. They're all silent after that, always. Sometimes I hated it, sometimes I didn't. No one had ever needed me before. I never minded a knife fight, either. I was never afraid. My mom's boyfriend shot my dad on my front lawn, and I wasn't even scared once."

Chatter kept his hand on the hare. "You don't care about suffering," he said.

Greaves punched the surface of the water. "You think you don't owe me?" he said. "You've been thinking that this whole time. I'll bet. Bet you blame me for Sod's death. Bet you have this whole time. And you're not wrong. It was my fault. I'm the one who did it. I'm the one who took away his suffering. Maybe you couldn't see, so busy hiding in the bushes while your friend was on his own."

"You were the first to hurt Sod," Chatter said. "I saw that much. I saw that."

Greaves watched the surface of the water for a long while. "I stuck the kid the first time," he said. "Stuck him for surprise, stuck him for some blood. Stuck him so his eyes would go wide. But it wasn't deep enough to wound. I knew that. I'd done it a dozen times before. Stick a kid and they get all compliant, *yessir yessir nosir nosir,* they'll do what you damn please. I stuck the kid the first time, but I didn't stick him the second. Some other kid then another kid does the same. They were behind me at first, so I didn't see their excitement. I couldn't see their eyes. They started in to Sod, too many of them, too quickly, all of them rushing forward, no longer scared, no matter the blood. And I saw them, kids who wouldn't ever, giving Sod a jab, and I saw they let themselves feel all right about it through me. I saw all that. They let their hearts run away under my name. So, I set on Sod again. I saw him bit all over, saw him suffering, saw how scared he was. And then, without knowing, I knew where his heart was. That's what I did for Sod. I pushed all those kids off him, and I found his heart. It was a miracle, I saw him suffering, and my hand went right to it." Greaves shook his head. "I hate those kids. All of them. I didn't never talk to them, and they didn't never talk to me. They're happy as hell to stand behind me, though, happy as hell to rush around me. I didn't think they would until that day, being honest, I didn't know how quickly we can lose control. Scared me, being honest, but you tell anyone that and I'll cut your face."

The rabbit's hind legs, held close to its body, loosened and lay flat. The emittance of pain, as it disappeared, clawed the inside of Chatter's skin.

Greaves watched without a word. The moonlight left his face pale. His eyes widened, picking up glints from the sky. "You taking them?" he said. "Those little lives? Do they settle on you, too? Even the little ones that slip out, I've found, linger. I imagine them heavier than air, because no matter the wind when they flee the body, even twisting around as crazily as leaves, they remain, they settle, and cover your skin. All those little lives. But you don't feel anything, right? Layer after layer settles, and you can't feel anything anymore. Not hate, not warmth. Nothing."

Greaves approached Chatter, stretching his legs into overlarge steps. He knelt for a closer look at the jackrabbit, but kept his distance.

"I'll have this vision, sometimes, that I'm clear of it," he said. "Everything I've done but didn't mean, every consequence of getting carried away by my heart. The film wiped off my skin. And then I'm better again, I got better. I picture it so perfectly. But I don't even know how to get it off my skin, no matter how I wash. I think it settled for so long it bled inside, maybe it coats my bones. This mud of consequence, a mark of how wrathful my heart is. And I can't get rid of it myself. I need it wiped away, I need someone who can wipe it away. Do you understand me, kid? Can you feel it on your skin too?"

Chatter got to his feet, but didn't move. He stood over the jackrabbit.

"Didn't mean for Fern to die like that," Greaves said. "That shouldn't have happened. Simon Sanderson was worked up, and I knew he was worked up. Seen that clear as a bell before, and I saw it then. We saw her first through the trees. Simon Sanderson said he wanted to hunt her, like sneak along, and

I thought that sounded fine. I knew he was worked up. But I never let him undress her, not even her socks. Smashed him in the face when he tried. That's why he took her hair. He's mad at me. But I didn't care. I stopped her suffering, too. Both her and Sod. Fern and Sod. Sod and Fern."

"I don't know anything about it," Chatter said.

"That's right. You were fled, too."

Chatter didn't respond. He kept still as he could. Greaves had gotten too close while he was distracted by the hare. Chatter's hand crept towards his front pocket.

"Let me ask you something," Greaves said. "What does it feel like to watch cut-up kids pour moonshine on their wounds?" He shook his head. "Never mind," he said. "Shouldn't of asked. I know already."

He stood abruptly, then crossed to the figures. He resettled the hides over their structures. He moved the muskrat closer to the racoon, then the racoon further away.

"Can't never get these right," he said. "Not ever once. I see them so clearly in my mind, the one, then the other, and every time I convince myself I know enough to make them, but here they are, as close as I can make them, and I feel the same. The one, then the other. Sod, then Fern.

"At first, they didn't have names. At first, I didn't know enough to know. Sometime in the past I bent one stick back against the other, and another stick back against that, and saw, where I had never seen before, the shapes the spaces between made. It wasn't just the weakness of nature, these scummy sticks that couldn't stand my strength, it was something else. I understood that I had made a vessel. Didn't do anything else with it after that. In fact, pretty sure I stomped it for speaking back to me the way it did. But after that it didn't ever go away. I saw in the natural twist of underbrush the better shapes for my vessels to take, the cruel way to choke the joints, the shiver of spindly sticks that hold huge tension. I made more, more and more, and each time I felt the swell in my heart, the need

I didn't know I had until the means to fulfil it were right in front of me. But it never worked, it never scratched what itched inside me. I made more and more until I realized again, these were vessels, not shapes but spaces that needed to be filled. And that's when I came upon the skins. A vessel can't contain nothing if it doesn't have sides. And I knew the vessels I made were to contain life, so I needed skin. Came across a dead badger, mauled in the wood, and used its skin first, but it was so tattered it wouldn't stay right, it made a mockery of what I'd done. But even still, wrong as it was, I learned its name, after the life it would contain. That first one, I called Sod. So, they needed skin, they called for containment. I understood this to be the truth because they better quieted my heart than anything else. I felt controlled, like it couldn't carry me away anymore. My heart was almost still, silent, free of that sting, that want, that urge."

Chatter nodded, unable to hold himself back. "The yearn," he said.

Greaves watched him carefully. "That's right," he said. "That word sounds right."

He reached down, moved the muskrat away from the racoon, the racoon closer to the muskrat. "Made thousands of these now. This figure, then that. I tried to stop for a while, but the agitation grew in me, my mind got unsettled again, made me want to run in every direction my heart leaned. It was only these, this figure, then that, that quieted me. I can't never get them right, though. I know that's what's wrong. I see them so clearly in my mind, these perfect vessels, that, if I get right, will carry some of what I carry, until, eventually, I won't have to carry as much. The life I have on my hands will be passed back into them, and I'll be able to wipe them clean. It has to be these. They speak stronger than anything else in this flickerworld. May they say better than I what is in my heart. So, I make them night after night, whenever I can catch an animal. I don't mean to be clumsy, I don't mean for more suffering than this world demands. I'll twist each of these straight growths into my very own vessel, and I'll fill them up with the quiet of the world. Then they'll hear me. Sod, then Fern. Then I can say what I want to say."

Chatter nodded again. His hand moved slowly. *Ritualism*, he thought. *Unconscious hyperactivity.*

Greaves spent some time staring at the dark sky. He watched the tops of pines wave in an up-high wind. His stasis lasted longer than a pause, and after a while Chatter felt like he was intruding with his observation, and lowered his eyes to the jackrabbit.

"Hey," said Greaves suddenly, and Chatter's hands shot into the air in surprise. Immediately, Greaves's gaze grew cold, and he narrowed his eyes and stared at Chatter's hand. Lou's dusters were firmly settled over swollen fingers.

"You wouldn't," Greaves said. Then, after a long look at Chatter, "You would."

Chatter opened his mouth, but couldn't think anything to say beyond excusing his actions. He kept his hands in the air and walked backwards, slowly, watching Greaves pace with the knife, until his vision was swallowed by pine and wolf willow.

CHAPTER 65

Azalea met Chatter as he returned from Farrow, a bustling pillowcase slung over her shoulder. "We're late," she said, striding past him, and soon distanced herself outside the range of talk. They marched west of the culvert, along the base of the ridge for half a mile, taking advantage of the clustered birch and poplar to shake off any tails. Azalea was used to the route, and stopped at practised intervals to inspect the path, although nothing presented itself in the languid heat of the late afternoon.

While they walked, Azalea switched the pillowcase from shoulder to shoulder. Chatter guessed at knives from the shift of metal inside, but kept his suspicions to himself. When he offered to carry the bag, she laughed, and then her expression clouded. "I have to carry this, Chatter," she said, and no longer appeared burdened.

Azalea followed the unlikely rise of bedrock into a sheer cluster of pine, and then pushed onto a mud path that wound through the overgrown chaos of the forest. At each turn, Chatter imagined they would crest the hill into the wide field of His Holy Rules, but Azalea kept them true to the ancient path that hung just inside the lip of the valley.

Overgrowth swallowed the path for a spell, before receding around the remnants of a brick utility shed perched on an exposed shelf of rock. Two full walls remained, as well as portions of a third, which suggested a bisected room. The back half of the building had crumbled into the ravine below the shelf. The valley undulated for miles beyond the collapsed end. Folds of green and early spring yellows hugged the distant meander of the river.

Azalea crumbled off the corner of a rotten brick and hurled a spray of gravel into the ravine. The smack of rocks into the leaves sounded like a smatter of applause. "I'm worried about you, Chatter," she said. "Here you're bringing in crates of your Remedy, and you haven't taken a dollar from us. I'm worried Lou is going to kill you."

The name gave Chatter pause. He pictured the man on the road, a gust of prairie breeze chasing him indoors, where rooms of people had never heard his name. "Lou is gone," Chatter said, surprised at the deadness in his voice. "He won't return."

"Gone?" Azalea shook her head. She hurled another spatter of gravel into the void, then walked to the lip and sat, dangling her legs over the edge. She indicated that Chatter join her. "We are losing so much these days, Chatter. Too much. I try to tell the kids that's the way of it, the day starts dark, and it ends dark. All the rest is passing. But those kids at the culvert, they don't listen. They act like the sun don't move at all. They believe the Prissies will never die. Like they don't know the way to Farrow. Like it isn't just day after day after day.

"I have pains in my legs. I know my socks are getting further away. I'm not a kid, Chatter, though I don't know when I stopped. There was so much running during the war, so much hiding and fighting, we lost so much. I wonder if I outran it then, and didn't even notice. I didn't see its passing, I only knew it was gone. One day, looking around, I knew it was long gone.

"When I was little, and Fern and I were shivering through nights in the city, I remember saying to her, *I can't wait to be an adult,* and her saying to me, *we won't have any problems when we're adults.* It seemed so secure, the world adults inhabited. A place free of the chaoses in a kid's life. I even buoyed the years I've lived down here with that idea. *When I'm an adult.* But I don't know nothing about it. There's no one I could ask. I don't know, Chatter."

"What?"

"You ever pictured yourself an adult? Thought, really, about how it feels? I've tried, but can't summon convincing visions. There's a house, but I can't tell you if it's got a lawn. I don't see myself, but someone taller. She's got clean skin and she smiles a lot. Do adults smile? I ain't hardly seen it. I thought I knew. I saw Farrow in my mind, when I thought of it, a job in a kitchen, or cleaning the homes of the rich, finding, even, some of my friends from before, kids from the culvert who've gone and done, but we never hear from those kids, and I don't know if I'd recognize them grown. It does strange things to a person's face. Problem is, every time I picture a home, picture myself knocked up, or dusting my fine drapes, I'm never alone. As quick as I can picture it, the room is full, there's kids all over, dirt from the culvert all over their feet, too many of them jammed in my bed for me to sleep. I can't even imagine the quiet of an empty house; I think I'll have to keep my windows open all the time. So, I'm starting to think I don't know nothing at all. I worry that Farrow is going to eat me all up. I know how mean the world is, and I don't know if that's going to end. Maybe it'll pass with our age, but I don't think so. I think that meanness is rooted right to its core. It's the dark that spits out and swallows the sun. But I don't know nothing else; I don't even know for sure I saw Fern in that marsh."

"I see Sod," said Chatter. "Sometimes not at all. Sometimes he sleeps as close as a kid in a culvert."

Azalea smiled as she searched Chatter's face. "Is he here now?"

"Sure, just over there. Kicking rocks over the edge. He pretends not to listen, but he does all the time."

"Sod," she said. "Guess you've heard us talking about you, then."

Azalea searched the crumbled wall, then looked back over the valley. "You ever heard of Love, Chatter?" she said. "You felt it?"

"I don't know. Didn't know if it was when I did, I just felt different."

"Often?"

"No. Not even really once I was sure of."

"I heard of it. Every kid talks about it, or asks for it in their way. Some shy, some not. Love. Like the word itself was story enough. But I don't think I'm picturing it properly. Not sure if I know how to form it in my mind. See, I love some of those kids in the culvert, think I do, have proper feelings. I want to keep them dry from rain, sort of thing. Haley Limerick plays this song on a reed that makes me want hold her forever. Thom Po can't do nothing right, but he brings back bouquets of wildflowers that make everyone happy. I'd name a dozen kids who make me dizzy with care, but I know I'm not doing it right. I know you're not supposed to feel this much anger alongside."

Chatter shook his head. "Lot of anger in love," he said.

"Not this much," Azalea said. "So much it rots in my chest. I'm awake at night and I feel it, wriggling inside me. Anger knotting up, year after year, until it took the place of my heart. It outran me, and I didn't even notice. All the love I felt spoiled by anger."

"Why?"

"There's a graveyard we keep in the woods, just some sticks nailed together, a couple big stones some kids rolled in there. Sometimes it's just a flower picked and left in a crook of bark. No name, no nothing, just that fact that someone is missing and someone else knows about it. I don't ever go there, I don't have to. You ever seen the flu take someone away? The colour goes out of them. Like glass on a window slowly fogging. Every time you come back, there's less of them there. That's something you don't ever forget. Six kids in there we found over so many years, frozen in the morning. At night, there they are, flush in the fire, and in the morning they're gone. Clutched up the way you'd think they would. And it makes me so goddamn angry. You know how much noise the world makes when a kid dies?"

"None at all."

"None at all, and it makes me so goddamn angry. I can't get over it. I need it, now, that anger, it burns up everything else, all the worry and fear. Gets me closer to sleep than anything else. I burn so white hot every night, filled with love, but the world is too huge, too uncaring, and nobody knows what the next sun spits up upon. I feel sick inside. Wrecked already."

Azalea drew a deep, steadying breath.

"We can do this together, Chatter," she said. "The Callaghan are the most powerful gang in the valley. Hard to even think of them like us anymore. Before we were even born, they figured out the problem of aging, staying a family like, the young becoming the old who join their syndicate. They have more of our metal than we do, and far outnumber the Kin. They don't involve themselves in lowland struggles, but I know I can convince Arabella Callaghan to lend her weight to our war. She's got a stake in it now; she'll come to see. And with her, Chatter, we win this thing. We crush the Kin, we clear the valley for every kid to stretch their legs. No more Longshanks stamping up and down the culvert. No more sore shins. Imagine that. Before I'm gone, before I'm tall enough to survive Farrow, I can build this one last thing for the Prissies. Peace enough to last forever. I think I can do it, Chatter. We can do it."

"What can I do?"

"The ninth night you were with us, do you remember?" Azalea said. "You thought you were slick, thought you were so silent. Waking after midnight, quiet as you could, and leaving the culvert. I followed you through a swamp, up and down hills. I thought, this kid is lost, but you weren't, were you? Because, finally, you come up on this dam at the end of a marsh, and you put your hands on a beaver pup. I'm sure I heard the sound it made."

Azalea leaned against Chatter. "What do you think they hear?" she said. "Those animals you call. Are they glad at the noise, or sad? Tired, maybe. The sound must be loud, for them to notice across such distances, though I can't catch a strain. I wish I could, though, sometimes, if I'm honest, Chatter. I wish just once I could hear what they hear. Is it a song? Does your heart sing to them?"

A longing opened inside Chatter, so acute he dizzied, and he stared into the depth of the ravine to steady himself. He glanced at Azalea to determine if she had seen his swoon, but her eyes were trained on a distant hollow in the trees.

"Do you think my enemies can hear me coming?" she said.

Her shoulders slumped; she rubbed her face with both palms. She sat upright, and Chatter caught himself, unaware of how much of his weight she bore. "Chatter?" she said.

"Yeah?"

"Can you heal me?" She stared across the valley. Her eyes, only once, darted sideways. "Can you unknot my heart?"

Chatter didn't respond, but moved behind Azalea, cautious of how close she was to the edge. Visions of her plunging downwards sweated his palms. He brushed her hair upwards and rested his hand on her neck. The tips of his fingers rested against her jawline.

Azalea's head bobbed forward. Her chin tapped her clavicle. The cold sweat of Chatter's palms sent shivers along her ribs. His breath found her neck quickly, however; she never stayed chilled for long.

Still, Chatter felt no tingle, no healing rush as he had on stage. He sniffled in agitation. He stamped away from Azalea. A rain of gravel shot out over the ravine.

"I feel better when you're around, Chatter," she said. "Clearheaded. I can focus on what my hands are doing. My knife is strong and sure. Hell, the whole camp is better with you around. Kids pull shifts around the clock in the forges and the kitchens. Three construction projects the lazy butts left for months are finished. And that healing? That was great. Nobody has seen anything funnier than Petror dropped on his ass."

She imitated Petror's surprised cry, and laughed. She made the sound once more, but didn't follow with a laugh. Her eyes skipped from the treetops to the distant wend of the river.

Chatter returned to Azalea. His hands explored her neck. Her shoulders. Her skull rolled forward at the insistence of his fingers. Under his concaved palm, her pulse throbbed.

"Damn it," Chatter said, and he stood. He kicked the nearby wall and flung a stone into the ravine. "Damn it. *Damn it*."

"Why are you upset?" Azalea said.

"It's not working," said Chatter, "I can't make it work. Maybe if you lie down, or we sang something."

"What do you want to sing?"

Chatter shook his head. The brick crumbled and bit into his palm.

Azalea ducked as Chatter's wild spray sailed out into the air. She stood before him and cupped his hands in hers and brought them to his chest. "How does it work?" she said. "What do you feel?"

"Hold out your hands," Chatter said, slipping into Lou's script, "an inch and a half apart. No, wait. An inch." He put his hands on hers and adjusted the distance. "Stare at that space between your palms. Look at your fingertips. Can you feel the breeze between? Focus on the tickle. Do you feel your hands drawn together?"

Azalea laughed. "What is that?" she said.

"Energy," said Chatter. "That's the energy your body gives off. I'm not the only one who feels it, so can anyone else. I think I'm just more sensitive. The sickness in someone gives off an energy, too. That's how I find it. I hold my hands on them until I feel a cross-vibration. And then I *pull*."

"Pull?" said Azalea.

Chatter shrugged. "Maybe push," he said, "Doesn't matter." He held his hands an inch apart. "Because it's not working. I can't feel anything."

Chatter cut off into an uneasy silence. Tears glassed his eyes, and he lowered his head, ashamed and silent. He moved his hands two inches apart, two and a half, three. At last, a prickle moved up the fingers of his left hand and he gasped with relief.

He blinked, returned to the shed over the ravine. Azalea held her hand between his. His fingers curled to meet hers.

"There it is," she said.

CHAPTER 66

Azalea and Chatter hiked for another hour along the tree-laden ridge before they climbed up onto the prairie shelf. A stretch of overgrown grass and thistle greeted them in the hazy evening, its surface hallucinatory in a cross breeze. Chatter wavered, stricken. Across a distant expanse sat his second orphanage, Slatterly.

Azalea nodded at Chatter's gasp. "That's right," she said. "That place was abandoned years ago. But the Callaghan scouts are fastest. They claimed the building, and ain't no one tough enough to take it back. Imagine. Finding that."

Despite the heat, the river-stone sides of Slatterly retained a dark wetness, a moisture too intimate for the late afternoon, as though the bashful building were caught shedding skin. Chatter's eyes fell to the long grasses that once were tall enough to hide him from the other children.

"Careful," said Azalea, "walk where I walk. The Callaghan boobytrapped this whole stretch." She continued to praise the Callaghan as she stepped carefully into the tall grass. It was clear she meant to emulate the Callaghan success with the Prissies, but she always returned to the one fault the Prissies could never surpass. "We're no family," she said, she repeated, "we don't share any blood." This fact seemed to doom the Prissies to eventual dissolution, with all else.

An ache arose at the back of Chatter's head as Azalea talked. Azalea brought them through the field, towards the back door of the kitchen where the cooks slipped out for a smoke. Battlements built of prairie fencing, guarded by three girls with poleaxes, formed a border across the tall grass. A number of kids, linked by a musky likeness, milled behind the battlements. The door to the kitchen was propped open, and the ghastly smell of rotten yeast wafted forth.

The tallest of the guards handed her poleaxe to another and stepped around the battlements. Her vest of chainmail hung open informally, her manner relaxed. "You want to go around front, Azalea," she said. "Believe me, the smell only gets worse." She smiled, until her eyes fell on the pillowcase Azalea carried. "I'm afraid of what you bring."

Azalea brought the pillowcase from her shoulder. "Will you have a look, Tallulah Callaghan?"

Tallulah shook her head and looped her thumbs under the shoulder of her vest. "Not me," she said, "but Arabella Callaghan most certainly will. Only, we can't take you to her just right away."

Azalea bristled. "Why not?"

"Arabella Callaghan isn't the only one who wants to listen to you," Tallulah said. "Envoys from half the other valley gangs have come, too." Humour crossed her face at the slump of Azalea's shoulders, and her voice became teasing, "What? You thought war was a silent business?"

A shout from near the kitchens cut off Azalea's response.

"*Chatter*?" A thin girl with strawberry-blonde hair detached from a group of kids smoking cigarettes. She wore a thick black smock like the rest. She blocked the sun from her eyes and shouted again. "*Chatter*?"

Chatter couldn't help his sigh. She'd taken the stud out of her nose and cut her hair short, but was still recognizable as the girl he'd kissed in the Relegate Mercy. "Alice," he said as she approached.

Alice swept in a drag of her cigarette and rolled her eyes. "It's Alice Callaghan," she said. "First the one, then the other. It's a mark of honour around here if you're family."

Chatter performed a mock bow. "Alice Callaghan," he said.

"Chatter the witch," she returned. "We've heard of you around here."

"Now, then, Alice Callaghan," interjected Tallulah, "matters such as these are best left to Arabella Callaghan."

Alice nodded. Dragged from her cigarette. "Of course, Tallulah Callaghan," she said.

A rattle of metal as Azalea shouldered her pillowcase. "Right," she said, "I'll go through the front entrance. Tallulah Callaghan, collect your envoys, and, please, bring Chatter when it is time." She turned without looking at Chatter, and marched around the old stone flanks of Slatterly.

Alice brought Chatter to meet a few of the others behind the battlements. They curtsied and called him Chatter the witch, to general delight. The Callaghan enjoyed their easy humours, and Chatter soon felt accepted. When Alice noticed his face pale, she handed him a cigarette. "Here," she said. "It helps with the smell."

Alice told Chatter she'd lived at Slatterly for two years. She left the Relegate Mercy a few months after Chatter last saw her, and shared an apartment with six other girls in the city. She got a job in a flower shop, but saw too many of her former customers. Same thing in the coffee shop, and the oil office where she worked as a copygirl until she was discovered underage. "Was there," she said, "in the mailroom, where I was trying to set a fire, that I met Davey Callaghan, who recognized me because I had the face of my mother. She was a lapsed Callaghan, never a part of the family's business, lost for years in the morphine houses of Farrow, but Davy Callaghan saw my face, he knew my blood. I was born into family, Chatter, I was born into inheritance. I meant something larger than myself. Davey Callaghan brought me here, and I haven't ever left." She worked in the laundries first, she told him, before moving to the kitchens. "When we *can* work," she said, glancing at the open door.

Chatter followed her eyes. Kids stood inside the kitchen wafting baking pans. The smell oscillated as a result, first burnt yeast, then an underlying sulphur, both of which Chatter recognized. He stared into the kitchen. A row of large copper bells squatted in the depths, the telltale copper cap-arms meeting worms that spiralled into wooden barrels. To the amusement of the others, Chatter stepped towards the kitchen and inhaled deeply.

"Moonshining?" he said. "But it's coming out cloudy, shiny on top like an oil slick, with bubbles lazy to form?"

"How in the hell did you know that?" asked a kid in a floppy hat.

"Chatter the witch has experience in poisons," Alice said with a sharp smile. "Ever since they moved into this building, the Callaghan have been trying to make moonshine in the kitchen. We brew beer in dank corners, sure, and it sells, but our whole family knows that profits lie in spirits. We just can't get it right. Kids in the kitchens spend more time fanning the smell and cleaning up mash puked out of pipes than making anything worthwhile."

The kids around Alice laughed, then chimed in with their own stories of batches gone wrong. Instances of exploded barrels, imploded bells, burst pipes that whistled requested songs, and batches of whiskey that caused kids to lose their hair, turn taupe, or speak in tongues, were related in the breathless, competitive manner of the Callaghan storytelling. Soon, most of the kids who worked in the kitchen were involved.

"*Chatter!*" A call rang over the clamour. Bernard Callaghan, in the midst of a story about the batch that turned two kids albino, ignored the interruption and raised his voice.

"*Chatter!*" The kitchen workers parted reluctantly. Tallulah Callaghan pushed her way forward and glared the kitchen Callaghan into silence. "Chatter," she said, "we're ready. I'll bring you to Azalea." She turned to the rest of the kids and raised her voice. "Callaghan," she said, "there's business to be done. If you'd hear and partake, come to the hall."

Chatter followed Tallulah through the kitchens with a large group of kids, all holding their smocks over their noses. Alice walked next to Chatter until the kids bottlenecked at the stone stairway that led to the dining hall. Swept up the stairs he'd sprinted down to escape Mr. Hollis, Chatter dizzied at the overlay of memory and presence.

Azalea met him at the top. "Screw up your strength, Chatter," she said, "this is going to be unpleasant."

The Callaghan had squared off the dining hall into semi-open apartments, all fronting a large communal area. Low folding tables, salvaged from Chatter's time, scattered around the room, hosted numerous kids busy with private tasks.

Chatter noticed Arabella Callaghan right away. She had the rays of radiant suns tattooed under each of her eyes, and all action in the room deferred to her. Callaghan raised their heads as she passed; a group of young girls, flitting between the apartments like butterflies, seemed always after her attention. A light, black chainmail hung to her knees. Across her bare calves she wore a pair of greaves forged by Azalea herself.

"Azalea," Arabella said, after the kids from the kitchens filed into the hall. The space stilled to an immediate silence at her voice.

Six kids sat on chairs arranged at the end of the room, three on either side of an empty chair. These, Chatter assumed, were the envoys, as none bore the hardened resemblance shared by the Callaghan. Arabella walked to the empty chair, but did not sit. She turned on her heel. "Let me see," she said.

Azalea lowered the pillowcase to the floor where it settled with a *clink*. A tine of foot armour poked into view as the pillowcase fell open. Private conversations buzzed around the hall.

"Do you have his body?" Arabella said.

Azalea did not waver. "This is all we recovered," she said.

Arabella took each piece of the armour from the bag and arranged them in a line on the floor. A tattered chainmail vest, a pauldron, trampled gauntlets, and a single, bent greave. A sob came from the far side of the hall.

"Will you agree, Azalea," said Arabella, "that each item here is armour made by the Prissies?"

"I will."

"And you will remember how you promised the safety of our brother Callaghan? Dear Harlan," Arabella's voice rose into an inflection of Azalea's, "*A stream pure and clear*, you said, *right in the middle of a marsh*. Water clear enough for our brewing, and a water diversion project for the Prissies. Will you remember your offer?"

"I will."

Arabella nodded. She picked up Harlan Callaghan's saddle-shaped pauldron and inspected both sides. "We let our brother down there to taste your pure water," she said.

"Harlan Callaghan will not remain unavenged," Azalea said. "Prissies scour the marsh. Our best trackers. The Kin will suffer. They are weak, and we will purge them in Harlan's name, in Fern's, in the dozens of names you hold in your hearts. They will all rest when we dismantle the Kin. Not I, but you. We."

"We," said Arabella. She stepped from the line of chairs to comfort a young girl of seven who wept softly. When Arabella stood again, she met Azalea's eyes. "*We*, you say. Yet you made the decision to snatch up Greaves. And now you parade our dead, your dead, to justify your actions. Azalea, *your* actions. And, if this weren't enough, you've found yourself a witch."

Chatter stiffened under the room's circumspection.

"You wanted to see him," said Azalea.

Arabella nodded. "I did," she said. She stepped towards Chatter. His knees weakened for a moment, he wanted to bow. "Can you hold out your hands for me?" she asked.

Bewildered, Chatter displayed his palms to Arabella. She studied the creases across his fingers.

"Is it true you healed Sylvie Marcade when she was whipped to death and dying in front of Simon Sanderson's grain elevator?" said Arabella.

"No," Chatter said. "I don't think so."

Arabella cocked her head to the side. "Are you calling Sylvie Marcade a liar?"

Chatter held up his hands. "I don't know Sylvie Marcade."

Arabella fixed Chatter with a glare, then turned back to the girl who had not quit crying.

"Combined," said Azalea, "we can scatter the Kin. I've proven they're broken. Their power *relies* on us remembering their power. But it doesn't have to be this way. It never did. We only believed it. You think a year ago I could have taken Greaves? Or, here is a better question: would the Kin allow this if they could stop it? Imagine, no collars around our necks. I mean to live peacefully, Arabella Callaghan, I want fairness and happiness for the Prissies. I believe we can beat the Kin."

Arabella picked up a gauntlet and returned to her chair. She sat, and rested the armour in her lap. "You, Azalea," she said, "not we. You went to war with your neighbour. You decided to fight over a swamp. Why should we be involved? You are the one who cost us our brother. Everyone here will nod toward the Prissies, everyone knows the name of the Prissies, and has for years, and that's because of you. No one will deny it. You did that, too. But it's you that's done this, you who stirred up war, and it's you that's going to have to settle this."

"Arabella Callaghan," Azalea said, "I won't win this without the might of the Callaghan. I'm not asking for blood to be spilled, only the gesture of it. With your support, the Kin won't dare. We can purge them from our swamp, we can clear the riverbanks. Let Harmony keep Forster's. I'm sick to death of blackberries anyway."

"Blood has already been shed, Azalea," Arabella said. "The Kin were falling to bits before you roused them. Simon Sanderson was sleeping away his life, there was so much in-fighting on his side, they were going to be scattered to the wind, nonetheless. We knew this. Harmony was planning on taking hers into Farrow, settin up in an empty neighborhood. She's outgrown Forster's. We knew this. But now she's tromping all over the marsh, because she's cruel and stupid and can't help but leap at any opportunity that flashes. She's shedding blood because she sniffed out an opportunity. The same opportunity you're here offering us. And worse, even, than those other two, you've unleashed the Horror on our valley. Greaves hides in the trees out there, unkept by borders, mad as an animal."

"I haven't word of Greaves since he fled the elevator."

Arabella shook her head. "The valley is riddled with word," she said, "stories no matter where you turn. He ignores food, grudges, rational targets for his rage. He upsets nowhere places. One night he comes across the Harried's cooking fire. He sits, he eats of their food, friendly as a snake, then leaves. He even gives them two skinned hares in return for their food. In the morning, the Harried wake up to a coop of neck-wrung chickens. It's senseless. The Harried. Those kids don't have shit. Why torment the silent?" She shrugged. "Makes as much sense as going to war over a stretch of swamp." Arabella paused, her stare challenging Azalea. After another moment, she added, "It's soggy. There's nothing it's good for but getting your socks wet."

"We'll find him," Azalea said quickly, "I'll find him, and put an end to this. Kids aren't scared of the Kin, they're scared of him. If he's gone, the Kin are as weak as Harmony on her best day. I'll leave here right away and take my best kids. We'll find him. We'll stop him."

"Azalea, you have already made me a promise. Do you remember? You stood in the field outside our home, and you told me you'd come rather than sending a messenger, that you wanted to look in my eyes and tell me our brother is dead. Then you made me a promise. Do you remember the promise you made? You best trackers, you said, all after the killers of Harlan Callaghan."

"I meant it," Azalea said. "And I have, I have. We've long suspected Greaves. Who else? He's fleeing from us, and he ran into Harlan Callaghan. Poor Harlan, dear Harlan. If only he'd told us he'd gone to the marsh that day, I would have sent a guard with him. But out there, alone, and he runs into the animal Greaves. Well, I don't need to tell you what Greaves is capable of."

"Then take your army, Azalea, and wipe away this stain from our valley," Arabella said.

"I can't," Azalea said. "I can't leave the culvert undefended. I need your help, Arabella Callaghan. I need some of your kids as reserves. Not even many, twenty, maybe thirty. Just forty kids will help me take what's ours."

"No, Azalea," said Arabella, "This was not our trouble. The Kin grew on your side of the valley. You left the other gangs to cope on their own, and now, the Prissies will have to do the same."

Azalea diffused her temper by bending at the waist and retrieving the pillowcase from the floor. She folded her every spiteful response into a tight corner, a crisp line, until a tightly tucked square sat in her hand.

Anger built inside Chatter, and he felt the room drift further away, as though he were once again watching Lou from an outside window. Whispers and rustles from the crowd became detached noises, uninvolved in the outcome of what they observed. Greaves prowled from the back of his mind to the front, stepping careful over some young growth, while stomping on others. But this was the degree of violence that Chatter could imagine, and when he pictured what the boy was doing at that moment, he could only conceive of flight. The horror attributed to him seemed so foreign to Chatter, spun out of fear and lies, as conflated as a campfire shadow. And for a brief moment, holding up the fears of others to his interior

282

light, Chatter felt a twinning, the rise of an otherwise intangible notion that he was linked to Greaves, that he, better than anyone else, could speak against the horror. He saw in Greaves's scurry his own. He knew then, that if left alone, Greaves would flee the valley; he'd sensed as much the night before. A surge, then, overwhelming Chatter's anger, brought the hope that Greaves was already gone, that the rising sun had seen him out to the prairie and beyond. But just as immediately, Chatter thought of the rot in his heart, the tinge he felt amidst all the deadness. Chatter looked at Azalea, and the anger rose again. He thought of the kids in the culvert, of the single action that would make home home.

Chatter shook. His voice rattled up his empty throat. "Don't ignore the yearn in your chest, Arabella Callaghan," he said. "This was my fault, my crime. When the Prissies accepted me, it was the first time in my life I wasn't just around the kids I was forced to be around. So, for the first time in my life, whenever I felt a rot in my chest, and knew it was Greaves laying hurt into an animal, I ignored it. That was my crime, I let Greaves continue, so I might have comfort. His wreckage is my fault, not Azalea's. I didn't tell her; I didn't want to. I found acceptance. A home without walls. Can I be blamed for staying?"

Arabella sat in her chair. "There is no yearn in my chest."

"A constriction," Chatter pressed. "A rot. A faintness of breath. An unsureness, like walking along a ledge. It coats my sinuses with a bitter fluid. Last night, when I followed the yearn to the point where it grew strongest, I found Greaves. Two miles from here, maybe closer."

The hall became silent with private conversations. Arabella sat back in her chair, her eyes narrowed.

"I will find him, Arabella Callaghan," Chatter announced. "If you'll agree to reinforce to the culvert, I will take Azalea to find Greaves."

Arabella shrugged. "Save your spells, witch," she said. "The answer is no."

Chatter didn't flinch. "Your moonshine reeks," he said. "I smell it even now, drifting up that back stairwell. How many days is this very room inhabitable? How many days do you lose to kids in the kitchen waving their pans about?"

"Azalea," Arabella said with a wave of her hand, "Quiet your enchanter. He doesn't know his place."

"I can fix it for you," Chatter continued, "I'll solve your basement brewing. Your mixtures are imbalanced, and you're cooking mash at too high a heat. It's a damn mess down there, but the remedy is easy enough, if you've been shown. And I have been shown. Promise to send soldiers, and as a show of good faith, I'll make your stills natural producers."

Arabella's eyes travelled the room. "Azalea brings a witch," she said, "and she asks us to believe in witchcraft. I suspect some of you do, as well, the way you quiver. Azalea's opinion is obvious, but who else believes in spells and magic words? Is there a Callaghan who will speak for the witch?"

A strawberry-blonde girl emerged from a contingent of kids at the margins of the hall. Alice Callaghan raised her hand. "I've watched him calm the deaths of rabbits. I've seen his face when he felt one approach," she said. "And I've drunk his mixtures. The witch speaks true, I've always known him as honest."

Arabella stood from her chair. She returned to the armour on the floor and placed Harlan's gauntlet with its pair. "Reinforcements, then," she said to a buzz in the hall, "while Azalea works magic."

Azalea stepped forward in the hushed hall. Chatter caught her eyes, just once. He spotted inside a spark of life previously dark.

She all but bowed.

CHAPTER 67

Dirty sat upright, exposed by the fire. The light shone white on the scar that tugged his eye closed. Around Azalea, around Chatter, he didn't mind as much. At the culvert, he kept his head bowed.

During the night, he'd pull his face from the heat, turn it to chill in the dark air. Chatter imagined the air cooler on the scar, a depth of satisfaction unallowed to him and Azalea. His refreshment earned. The memory of Dirty's scream, in the field distant from the coop, banished such sentimental thoughts from Chatter's mind. Yet, he reasoned, that trauma was the reason Dirty accompanied their party, while teams of better trackers scoured the valley. Azalea's sentimentality. Dirty held the fact before the camp, before all others: Greaves had been careless with him first.

The hunt, Chatter corrected himself, was what Dirty had earned.

Azalea kept busy with her whetstone. Her blade at a specific angle up one side and down the other. The whetstone she clutched even during the day.

On the second night, Chatter brought them to the husk of a mill. Only the great grinding stone remained, and the shelf where Chatter imagined the miller slept. Chatter leaned back out the door and whispered to Azalea and Dirty. "Fine," he said. "It's nothing."

It wasn't nothing. An aged badger eyed Chatter with undiminished malevolence. The animal bared its teeth as Chatter sat, but didn't have the heart to bite. Eventually, Chatter ran his hand over the creature's matted fur.

A figure in the door behind him blocked the shaft of moonlight.

Chatter looked over his shoulder.

"He's not here," Chatter said to Azalea. "It's nothing."

The dewy grass of morning masked the smell somewhat. Intestines, hearts, and an immature gizzard were strewn about the clearing. At the far end, near the path leading onwards, were two skins stretched on skeletons of sticks, with skulls of rock and moss. On one, the largest mushroom the children had ever seen served as skullcap, while empty sockets yawned.

Dirty knelt before a marmot skin draped over pine scaffolding. A crown of magpie feathers alternated in black and white behind its head. He crooked his finger and collapsed the structure.

"I don't understand," Dirty said.

Azalea, across the glen, inspected the hacked marks of flaying, the ridges of flesh left, and the tattered and punctured hide. "Don't think Greaves does, either," she said.

At Roscoe's Cove, there was a kid blackened with ash. Her eyes wide green pools. The skin of her lips was dried and peeled in strips. She growled before she spoke.

Dirty discovered her, self-entombed in a cavern of old tires and gas cans. She wielded the blade of a sickle, broken off at the handle. Lengths of torn clothes, wrapped round and round, made it bearable to hold. She almost caught Dirty, too, leaping wildly at his sudden appearance. Dirty dragged her out at the end of her weapon.

She stared at the burned husks of the homes with a faraway curiosity. She swore wind was responsible. A breeze of calamity.

Of teeth. "The wind has left us alone," she said, in response to questions.

On an unburned wall, behind a shack with white wood panelling, Azalea came across a rabbit skull, a cottonmouth skull, and the hastily plucked head of a magpie, impaled on ancient nails. Feathers still crowned the beak. Thick streaks of blood and flesh clung to the skulls. Below this display, two hides wrapped conical structures. On top of each sat a rotted pear. The bow of the rot gave them a contemplative air, their observance sanctifying the sight above.

The ash-covered girl knelt before the wall. Azalea, Chatter, and Dirty kept a distance. The girl crept to the nearest figure. Her hand went towards the bloodied hide, as though she would stroke the fur. Instead, she plucked the pear off the top and bit around the rot.

"Any you got food?" she asked while she chewed.

They hiked until the sky darkened. On the crest of a hill sat the facade of a pioneer home. The ancient logs were split, and hosted growth that would unsettle the structure. Infant pines and lilies sprouted at unlikely heights.

A single floorboard remained in the squared space. A knee-high back wall, overgrown, ran longer than the dimensions of the front wall. The limbs of a coyote, disarticulated at each joint, littered a still-standing corner. Its head was missing. Then, after a moment's inspection, Chatter dug a tooth from the packed mud.

Azalea trailed her fingertips through a pool of blood. She stood straight up; her eyes skipped across the ground. "Warm," she said. "Despite this chilly air."

"Hell," Dirty said. He walked from one side of the squared ground to the other. He peered into the blackness. "Hell!" he hauled Chatter up by the arm. "Still warm," he repeated.

Chatter stared at the coyote remains. "I know," he said.

"Well," Dirty said. He grabbed Chatter's arm again. "Where are they? Which direction did they go?"

Chatter walked to where Azalea knelt, from corner to corner, from the back wall to the edifice of a home. "It doesn't work that way," he said.

Dirty shoved Chatter from behind. Chatter's chest met the wall first, then his hands, and then his head. His brow smashed into the ancient wood and his knees buckled. Behind him, Dirty spouted a litany of kids who lay wounded at the culvert. Chatter raised a hand to fend off the next attack, but none came. Azalea shoved Dirty until he tripped over the back wall.

"You think he doesn't know their names?" she shouted. She advanced. "He's looked at every injured kid there. He watched them when the rest of us wouldn't, and now he's out here, sniffing out Greaves. It's not his fault we've got what we've got."

Dirty picked himself off the ground and stomped into the night. Azalea watched long after he'd gone.

At sunset, Chatter and Azalea built a fire. They kept quiet afterwards, each tracing private shapes in the flames. At times, the longing to speak rose, and Chatter turned to Azalea, but words, he figured, had failed since Slatterly. Chatter caught Azalea's eyes.

Her focus shifted back to the centre of the fire, where the wood became wisps of flame. Her jaw pulsed angrily. "Sometimes I see Fern," she said, "still. Walking through the woods with me."

Chatter nodded. "Sod was around a couple days ago," he said. "But I didn't talk to him, I don't know why."

Azalea adjusted a crumbling structure in the fire with a blackened stick. "Fern never answers."

"Neither does Sod."

Azalea rocked forward, then back. Her hand slipped behind her. After a moment, Chatter heard the specific angle, up one side and down the other, of Azalea's mind at rest.

Dirty returned to the fire an hour later. He brought a duck he'd killed with stone-throw, and Chatter plucked it and cleaned it. Twice, he paused at his work and watched the dark. The silence at the fire was terse, however, and he didn't want to disturb Dirty and Azalea's reconciliation. After the duck was cleaned, he sat further from the fire, nearer the outer dark.

Chatter told a story about a pioneer love potion that hypnotized a village for six months, and then Dirty repeated his same old scare story about the roaming ghost of the pioneer preacher Gardner the Throat. He'd almost reached the part where Gardner fixed the sun on the dying side of the horizon for seventeen days, when the jackrabbit hopped into the firelight.

Dirty leapt in surprise, startling Azalea and shocking Chatter, who slipped off the rock he sat on. He'd felt the yearn, but imagined he had more time. Dirty's face twisted in disgust. "It's bleeding!" he shouted.

Chatter stepped in front of Dirty, rougher than he ever had, and took up the hare. He cradled it to his chest, but couldn't stand the way Azalea watched him, and he quickly strode into the dark. The jackrabbit didn't stir. Chatter rolled it slightly; it had a single puncture wound in its torso, and was breathing heavily. It wasn't in much pain.

Moonlight filtered through the forest and settled on an old stump, still exposed in the tall grass. A small figure, twisted out of twigs that still seeped sap, sat atop the stump. Its head, a curious curvature, was turned to meet Chatter. Bringing the jackrabbit closer to the heat of his chest, Chatter continued forward.

A little further along, Chatter paused. Greaves stood next to him, near enough to grab him, still as a ghost amidst trees. By the time Chatter met Greaves's eyes, the hare had died.

Greaves, colourless in the moon, nodded toward the animal. "I'm getting better," he said. "Only one swift stroke, that's it. I knew what I was looking for, without even seeing it. I didn't know I could do that. Wouldn't have imagined if I didn't try. But you see the insides of something enough, you really learn it. Soon they won't suffer at all. Not," he said, his smile only a flash, "unless I need to find you, I guess."

Chatter tightened his arms around the jackrabbit. "Listen," he said, "you gotta come with me, Greaves, or you gotta get out of here. There's an army coming across these hills, and they got your name. Get out of here. Get out of the valley. Won't nobody out there remember what you've done here. Imagine that."

Greaves drew back. "I don't see anyone out here. Just you on your own, and me, right here."

"It's not just us," Chatter said, "the Callaghan are involved. Azalea's convinced them to her side. We come out here to find you."

"What for?"

"I don't know."

"You know." Greaves looked at the sky. "Feels like it's getting closer," he said. "Waking up to my breath blowing back on my face, yet I'm sleeping under open sky. Can't you feel that? There's nowhere else to go. I can't get free, anyway. I couldn't get out of the valley before Hardnose and his crew caught up with me. I can't shake them. We ran into a coyote, and it bit Pancake bad. He's talking silly, and the skin around the bite has gone the black of dead things. They know about the hunting parties. They ain't going nowhere, and I can't get shed of them."

"I can heal him."

"You can't."

"I can. I have."

"I've heard. Sylvie Marcade." Greaves paused, he cocked his head to listen to a distant noise. "Are you really out here alone?"

"Chatter!"

Greaves jumped at Azalea's shout. His eyes widened. He lunged, suddenly, snatched the jackrabbit from Chatter, and disappeared into the dark. Moments later, Azalea stepped into sight. Her eyes rested on his empty hands. "Where is the rabbit?"

But Chatter only shook his head.

"Did you bury it?"

The next morning, before the early mists rose, Chatter, Azalea, and Dirty knelt in a distant birch stand. Azalea spotted the dead jackrabbit first, a tiny corpse folded over itself in a patch of grass, and hurried the boys into the birch. As the sky lightened, they kept watch for a trap.

The jackrabbit was on an undeniable bent towards where they'd bedded down. Even Dirty agreed on the line. It was less than half a mile away when it succumbed. "If it hadn't died there," Azalea whispered with a terrible certainty, "it would have reached us while we slept."

"Why did Greaves leave its skin?" Dirty asked, burrowing his cudgel into the loose dirt at his feet.

Azalea shrugged. They wouldn't know unless they got close enough to read the tracks left around the body, she explained, and they weren't going any closer. She pointed to the surrounding treeline. "Imagine eyes in all of them," she said.

They remained in the birch for another hour, until the mist evaporated and the tree-lined clearing became visible. While they kept watch, Azalea and Dirty planned. Hardnose's crew, they said, numbered no more than four, plus Greaves. Neither of them liked the numbers, but they weren't deterred. The proximity of their prize intoxicated them, and they spoke as though the result of their plans were assured. Ambushes near the river, traps dug and covered in prairie grass, or funnelling wildfires, became momentary solutions, invigorated by the thrill of discussion. Eventually, however, their plans required knowledge of Greaves's location, or his destination, and Azalea and Dirty would turn to Chatter, who'd given up watching the trees, and they'd fall silent and return to staring at the dead jackrabbit.

When Azalea made the decision to leave, she apologized to Chatter. "We have to leave the rabbit," she said. "You can't go out there. There's nothing you can do."

"It doesn't matter," Chatter said, his first words in hours, "I can't feel anything after they've died."

Azalea and Dirty walked ten paces ahead of Chatter. They had fallen back into the certainties of their planning. *If this then this and this*, they'd say to one another. Azalea skipped at times, but never Dirty. The sighting of Greaves energized them both, reminding Chatter of the light in their faces when he'd first sworn he could craft knives.

Chatter dawdled. Azalea's optimism seemed at odds with the inevitability in his chest. Only at a distance could he order his thoughts. He didn't mention the small figures, woven of twisted sticks, that appeared near their path, and neither Dirty nor Azalea seemed to notice. Next to him, through sun-soaked fields of grass, and the dim, chambered cathedral of the pine forests, walked Sod.

Neither boy spoke to the other.

"Chatter!"

Chatter, Dirty, and Azalea knelt behind the moss-covered trunk of a fallen tree and watched Pancake scream Chatter's name to the indifferent forest. His voice had rung out for almost an hour before they found him, propped up on a long-abandoned anthill, near a stream wide enough to leap across. He was pale, almost bone-white, but for the dark spots of long dried blood.

"Leave him," Azalea said finally. "Dying in a quiet place is more than Pancake deserves, anyway. That out there ain't anything but a trap."

Dirty agreed, and made to resume their march, but Chatter shook his head. "It's my name he's screeching," he said. "I can't think with that noise, I can't notice anything I'm supposed to notice. I'll just go out there and shut him up. I've got some Remedy; I'll trade it for his silence."

"Fine," Dirty said. He got into a crouch. "I'll come, too. I'll shut him up if he won't stay shut up."

Chatter stood. Dirty stood. "Wait," Azalea said. She grasped Dirty's wrist and tugged him back behind the fallen tree. "Hold on."

Moments later, Chatter emerged from the brush alone. Pancake didn't react to Chatter's presence other than to choke off his next scream. He watched the boy take cautious step after cautious step towards him. His only movement was to dip his maimed arm into the slow-moving water. The forest around them was quiet, still.

"Stream might be corrupted," Chatter said. "But I've something pure as thought. The great Pioneer Preacher Gardner the Throat wouldn't speak without it. He swallowed a vial before each sermon to pave the way for the Lord abo—"

"Don't believe in much," uttered Pancake.

"Well," Chatter said, "that is a problem."

"Give it anyway. I'm going to make you give it to me."

"How?"

Greaves and others were close, closer than Chatter had imagined. Two stout boys and a kid Chatter barely recognized as Hardnose emerged from the other side of the stream. They'd rubbed their skin with mud, and it dried dark, and clung in clumps.

"How?" Hardnose echoed. "How? How? Greaves says you'll fix Pancake, here. Bet you've just got to touch them too, right?"

Greaves stayed apart from the others. Chatter glanced at his face, but couldn't read the emotion there.

"Easy," Chatter said. "I could fix you, too. Looks like you bit off more than you could chew with that coyote. Those fingers of yours are swollen, and I can tell you wrenched your shoulder. Should I shed you of that pain?"

"None of us believe your shit."

Chatter reached out his left hand. "Go on," he said. "Make sure you're sure. You don't have to be afraid."

Hardnose laughed. He stepped forward. "Yeah," he said. "Yeah yeah yeah."

Chatter waited until the boy was within reach. He swung his right hand quickly, but planted his feet and smashed Hardnose's jaw with Ruddy Lou's knuckledusters. Hardnose collapsed, sprawling at the feet of the mud-covered others.

Immediately, one of the stout boys shouted and grasped his eye. He bent double and dizzily fought for balance. Another rock, following on the heels of her first, came from Azalea's charging figure. Greaves ducked, and the stone throw missed.

Dirty charged at Greaves, but the other stout boy stood in his path and met him with a ferocious yell. They collided near Chatter and fell over top one another, clawing, punching, biting. Dirty kept his fists clenched tight as stones and when he could, used the terrible strength of his arms to shut up the stout boy. The second stout boy recovered during their struggle and set at Dirty's turned back.

Chatter shouted a warning, but was interrupted by a lunge from Pancake. His unwounded arm wrapped around Chatter with a surprising grip and took them both to the bank, then to the water. Pancake became a busy flurry above, growling and trashing, spraying water and the thin scum that sat atop, trying to force Chatter's head below the water. But Chatter kicked and wriggled, and he started to speak, but the words, caught in an interior surge, became bellows and hollers and bawls. He swiped at Pancake's face with a stream stone, he rolled in the murk, and, finally, he thrust out his hand and grasped the wounded flesh on Pancake's arm. He squeezed as hard as he could.

Pancake screamed.

Azalea vaulted Chatter and Pancake and tackled Greaves at full speed. They tussled on the bank, neither able to gain the upper hand. Greaves scrambled free, only to be caught again;

Azalea punched, only to be punched. Azalea fought free her knife from her waist, but Greaves slapped it out of her hand, and the two dived across the ground, fighting for a grip of the soaked handle. Neither gave the other a chance at such final statements.

Pancake screamed. Screamed and screamed amidst the bustle. He smacked at Chatter's hand, but Chatter was resolute, his arm, his hand, was not shaken. He squeezed until his whole body quivered, until, in spite of the brawl, a calm resilience informed his arm, his hand; and Pancake, out of breath and fight, fell unconscious to the water.

Dirty screamed. He was pinned by one of the stout boys while the other pounded him mercilessly. Azalea kicked Greaves in the face and set at the stout boys, colliding with the one on top with her full weight. They went sprawling while Dirty clambered up from the ground, woozily setting upon the stout boy closest. In a moment, Chatter was next to him, bringing Lou's dusters up in a calamitous arc. Once they were certain of the boy's unconsciousness, they turned to Azalea, but she didn't need their help. She stood over the boy she'd knocked to the ground. She held, above her head, a huge rock she'd fought from the suck of the shore. For a moment, she paused, and she and the boy on the ground exchanged a glance that Chatter and Dirty could only guess at. Azalea dropped the rock on the boy's leg, where it landed with a sickening crack.

When she turned, her eyes did not fall upon Chatter or Dirty, but on the already small form of Greaves, as he sprinted along the bank of the stream and slipped into a distant copse of trees.

"Goddammit," she said.

Dirty tried to echo her statement, but blood dribbled from his mouth. His nose was badly broken, and angry bruises seeped up his skin like a soiled pond. He stood for another moment, and tried to speak again, before he collapsed.

Each time Chatter paused, Dirty encouraged him on, his commands issued between heaving breaths. "Goddammit Chatter," he kept repeating.

Azalea directed them into a nearby gully, then sat at a shallow stream and washed her fists in the clear water. She took Dirty's other arm when Chatter stumbled, and the two of them brought the half-conscious boy to the bank.

Dirty remained awake enough to swat away Chatter's hands. "*Goddammit Chatter,*" he swore repeatedly. Azalea scooped water on his face until he woke fully. She gave Chatter her knife and he shredded his sweater into strips for splints. When he split the seams, a half dozen lock-picks fell to the mud at his feet. The pieces of bent metal, artifacts from another life, tired Chatter. He left them where they fell, and helped Azalea bind Dirty's broken arm and ankle as tightly as he could manage. Exhausted by the effort, Dirty swore once more at Chatter, then lost consciousness.

"Azalea," Chatter said, "Dirty can't stay here. He needs the attention of the culvert, and Henni. If you take him, you should make it by tonight."

"We can get him back there by supper," she said. "Pick him up."

Chatter shook his head. "I'm staying," he said. "Think of it. You need Greaves. Give him to the Callaghan and you will win the war. You'll keep all those kids safe. If we don't stay on him, though, who knows what damage he'll cause, what you'll be blamed for?"

"You take Dirty, I'll go after Greaves."

Chatter shook his head again. "Greaves knows how to track me, and he will. I know that. We have something to say to each other. I'll lead him on a chase. I'll go the long way, through the marshes along the river, give him a soupy path. I'll stall the night, then bring him in the morning to the hill where Sod died. Meet me there, with as many kids as you can."

Azalea smiled. She took Chatter's face in her hands. "Enough," she said, "for a proper show."

Chatter felt the yearn in his heart as the sun slipped below the trees. It was, by then, so twinned with the rot that he didn't notice the absence, and spent an hour avoiding a magpie that looked no older than a year. When the bird finally landed on the deer trail ahead of him, skipping back and forth in the last light of day, Chatter felt the unmistakable yearn, despite its seeming health. It came right up between his legs, brushing his ankles with its wings, and died before he reached out his hand. Greatly disturbed, Chatter picked up the bird and held it to him. That was when he felt the rot, faint and far away as its attendant yearn. The feelings, again twinned, moved in his direction.

Once, in the waning moon's light, Chatter spotted Greaves moving through a gully bottom. He was a vision only, wholly silent at distance. He walked without hurry, trailing a jackrabbit. Chatter sat and watched the boy until the jackrabbit corrected its course and led Greaves directly toward him. He wished the hare would just die, that it wouldn't have to suffer until morning. He realized, afterwards, that he still held the magpie.

Chatter rested in a nestle of dogwoods that ranged across a wetland and watched the moon move across the surface of a pond. Thoughts of the magpie clung to him and prevented him from dozing with half-conceived questions, empty propositions. He assumed the animals who came to him were dying. At His Holy Rules, Alice Callaghan, then Alice Always, had accused him of killing healthy animals, but he hadn't let himself consider the option; he blamed Alice's fear, the fear he knew that was natural to life, and the willingness of the frightened to form a mob. He thought he knew the yearn in his heart, imagined it as an echo of death, a promise of peace, a prelude to his comforting touch, the last, and perhaps only, compassion offered by the quiet earth. But as he traced the moon's path across the pond, he wondered if it wasn't instinct that brought some animals to him, but instead their want to die.

While he navigated the collapsed slope of a pine ridge, he worked through, moment by moment, the calamitous arrival of the sturgeon in the shanty on At-Sun-Still-Shines. Chatter couldn't recall the condition in the shanty before the fish's appearance, but attributed it to the timeless stretches of silence and companionship between him and Lou, the forgotten hours that merely supported existence. His memory began at the shattering of such peace, collecting his dissolved self into centrality of a moment's demand. The yearn had rose in his heart with a quick ascension that tickled his throat. He sat up from where he'd slumped on a blanket-covered cot. Lou dozed across the small space, near the simmering stove. Chatter brought his legs off the cot, and again looked around, he checked out the window. His heart gave a lurch. The surface of the water, visible through the hole in the ice, gulped, the hole gasped, and for a moment further it was silent. Then the sturgeon, longer than Chatter was tall, burst upward with a harrowing roar.

In the next instant, all the silence went out of Chatter's heart. The huge fish crashed down on the cot, sending Chatter to the ice, where it then landed in a great hurricane of trashing and bellowing. Chatter flung his arms and legs around the fish as freezing water soaked his clothes and restricted his movement. He clasped his hands together and didn't dare let go as the fish rolled over top him and upset the stove with the flail of its frenzied tail. Lou hooted and hollered and scooped the stove back into place before it set the shanty ablaze. He kicked the fish back over Chatter to keep it clear, but Chatter lost his grip and he and the sturgeon found themselves again on equal plane. Chatter scrambled for the club as the fish's fins raked his skin and he spun and swung and swung and swung again.

Lou laughed and laughed. First, he impersonated Chatter, then the sturgeon. When Chatter took up the pliers to wrestle the hook from the fish's lip, Lou waved him off. "Wasn't one of mine," was all he said. Lou's rod lay snapped on the ice, its line still sunk in the water. Chatter stood over the fish and admired its enormous body, achingly unfamiliar, yet immaculate, once filled with a strength so large he could only comprehend it for the instant it was held against his body. As he stood there, the silence returned to Chatter's heart.

Near morning, sick with shame at the endurance of the jackrabbit that patiently tracked him, Chatter bent his route back to the heart of the valley, towards Farrow, towards the culvert he'd come to think of as home, and the hill where Sod died. He took the same ridge he walked along the night he left His Holy Rules, and surprised himself at immediately recognizing the clearing where he'd slept. The second night, he remembered, had been moonless, the dark inside the clearing complete when he woke. Disoriented by the dark, he'd felt an immediate fear as a sudden yearn coupled with the sound of something massive moving through the bush toward him. Instincts flared, surges of decision ran along his legs, but Chatter was paralyzed; he couldn't even clench the soft soil beneath him. Nearer and nearer the noise came; fear surged and frothed inside Chatter, yet he remained still, even when the animal, with a wash of its musk and the force of its breath, the steadiness of its lungs, the coarseness of its nostrils, entered the clearing and stood over Chatter, radiating heat and power from its body. With deliberate care, the animal settled next to Chatter, touching him with its torso and rocking him with the depth of its breath. It wasn't until dawn, after the breathing stopped and the animal grew cold, that Chatter felt safe enough to look. Next to him, curled as tight as it would in a womb, was a gigantic elk, just old enough to grow antlers.

Chatter slowed his pace as the yearn in his chest faded. Greaves's jackrabbit, he figured, was close to succumbing. It was morning, the sun's colour disappeared from the sky. Chatter backtracked, following the yearn, and then, when he felt close enough, snapped branches and stamped underbrush. He left a trail easy enough for Greaves to follow. He made his way along the river, to the dirt path he and Sod took every day. Here he stopped leaving signs, though the jackrabbit had died an hour before. Greaves, he imagined, making it that far, knew exactly where Chatter was headed.

Chatter crawled inside the wolf willow colonnades while he waited. He was still able to move about without disturbing the upper reaches of silver leaves and yellow flowers. He sat in a chamber that allowed him to straighten his spine, and watched the path. Over and over, his mind replayed Sod coming down the trail, unaware that ahead of him Greaves and Simon Sanderson were already making use of their knives. Again, Chatter traced the path, the instinct to dart ahead, to warn Sod, but found no surety in his memory. Was Sod unaware, or did Sod look into the colonnades when he came around the corner? Was it seeing the boy's eyes that spurred Chatter into action? He couldn't remember. He wasn't sure. Was it the yearn of his heart that Sod, too, recognized? The slight boy came along the path, he paused, he glanced into the wolf willow.

Chatter shot forward, hardly aware of the crawl between where he sat and the flat dirt path. He scrambled out of the bush as Greaves came into sight, airily following his feet. Chatter froze, as overwhelmed, for the moment, as when the elk pushed its way out of the dark. Greaves didn't pause, though; he continued down the path. He held Azalea's knife. He smiled. "Now," he said. "Now, now."

Chatter bolted. He was sure, as he leapt through the underbrush and narrowly avoided trees, that Greaves would follow, and felt an indescribable thrill when he glanced over his shoulder and saw the boy bounding after him. Chatter ran until he could see the treeline, the petering out into the wild field and slope where he and Sod had harvested potatoes.

His pace flagged, but he continued, responding to the rush of fear at Greaves's close approach. The fear resolved itself into a deadening disappointment, and then a deeper terror, a lost feeling in which he felt wholly unmoored. He wanted to scream in frustration. The field, the hill where Sod died, was empty of others. Azalea and her army were nowhere in sight.

Chatter ran out into the open space, his legs churning in lieu of thought. Greaves followed him into the field, then slowed. As he slowed, Chatter slowed, until both of them were merely walking, lifting their knees higher than usual to march through the thick, tall grass. Finally, Chatter stopped to catch his breath. Greaves closed in on him, but kept his distance. He looked at the hill, the field, the quiet run of the river whose banks were still so near.

Greaves's eyes narrowed. "You can't feel them, can you?" he said. "You don't know where they are. When it comes to people, you're as blind as anyone else."

Chatter couldn't stop himself. "Not all people," he said.

Greaves tapped the blade of the knife against his thigh. "Couldn't believe you assholes tumbling over each other like that," he said. "Sure, I laughed. Sure, I stood there and laughed. You splashing about in that water."

"Trying to trap me," Chatter said.

"Not you," Greaves said. "Azalea. Her in my hands ends this as soon as me in her hands. Least Hardnose seemed to believe. I hate that kid, can't stand the stupid way he breathes when he eats."

"Not going to breathe the same way anymore," Chatter said. He was surprised at the tone of his voice. He'd meant to sound tough.

Greaves laughed. A surprised, honest sound. He stared at Chatter until the colour faded from his cheeks. "Was going to leave the valley," he said. "Ran away from you wrestling assholes and didn't once care about the screams I heard. Could've been gone, long, long now."

"You weren't going to leave."

Greaves stepped toward Chatter. The knife, forgotten for a moment, tapped on his thigh. "So, say you know that," he said. "You're sure of it. But how do you know that?"

Answers surged in Chatter's mind, but he was unable to match any to words. He reeled at the force of his urge to answer, and it shook him worse than any hunger he'd experienced. He opened his mouth; he closed his mouth.

"Maybe I came to give Azalea her knife back," Greaves said, shrugging, "but I'm guessing she made it for me." When Chatter wouldn't return his smile, he shrugged again. "Let me ask you something," he said. "Few months back, nighttime, there I am alone. In my alone spot, off that soft ground outside Farrow. It's been my alone spot since I was old enough to name it. And there, few months back, I'm working at nighttime, trying to wrap my mind around what my mind is asking, and I hear these clumsy footsteps, this mucking around of the soft ground outside my alone spot. Few minutes later, while I go stand in the trees, what do I see but some dumb kid come kicking his way through like he knows exactly where he's going. Some dumb kid who fiddles with my work. Some dumb kid who stands in the open and only says one dumb thing: my name."

Chatter watched Greaves. He remembered, then, that Lou's dusters were still tucked in the back pocket of his trousers. "That a question?" he said.

"How did you know it was me?" Greaves said. "Sure, you sow death for critters. I'll accept that. You felt some dying, and you wanted your take, sure. I see how you'll follow them to where they lie, no matter how wet your socks get. So that puts you there, explains the mess you made of your hands after, but it doesn't say anything about me. It'd been years, kid. More'n five, at least. How in the hell am I supposed to remember you? And yet, there you are, standing in wet grass, calling out

Greaves to the trees. So, here's your question: why'd you say my name?"

"It was a guess," Chatter said. "Just something I said."

"No, it wasn't," Greaves said. "Wasn't even an instinct. You *knew*. You didn't say anyone else's name, no second guesses."

"There's a rot," Chatter said quickly, "something inside me that turns over when you work. I don't know why."

"What does it feel like when others work?"

"It doesn't," Chatter said.

Greaves nodded. He seemed about to speak, but only nodded his head further. A pensiveness came over him as he turned and stared at the river for some time. "Sure," he said. "You've a sense of death, and I've got it laid all over me. It's soaked into my skin. I wish it wasn't. I wish it hadn't. But it has, it did. Maybe you can feel me. Suppose that's what seems right about the animals too, my work, the shedding of skin. Like I could lift it off and say, *That's it, that's all it is. See how thin it really is. How can that contain all of life?* But it does, it can. You ever feel that? Like life is wider than our sense of it?"

Chatter shook his head. He watched the knife in Greaves's hand. "You gotta get out of here," he said. "There's kids coming. The hills are crawling now."

"Those kids you live with," he said. "Those kids you give moonshine to? What do they give you?"

"Home," Chatter said. "They give me as much family as I ask for. Ain't ever had it elsewhere."

"Never?"

"Never."

"Probably why you think so much of it then," Greaves said. He sucked in a violent breath. "I remember the first kid I punched in the mouth," he said. "Wasn't older than first grade. I remember how much it hurt. I didn't expect it to hurt, but it did. I clipped his teeth with my knuckle, cut my hand open. Missus James asks me why I hit the kid, and I tell her it's because he called me unnatural. Funny thing is, until I told the teacher, I didn't know why I hit the kid. He said what he said, and I hit him. That was it, but thinking back on it, I knew why I hit him, though I didn't tell Missus James. I didn't hit the kid 'cause what he said bothered me. I didn't care about that kid. I hit him because a few nights before, Greg, my mom's boyfriend, found me in the crawlspace at home. I'd brought down a cat that was killed in the road. I wasn't doing anything. Didn't want to. I just wanted to look at it for a while. But Greg hauled me out of there. He beat me up bad. And it was him who said it, he said it first. He called me unnatural. That's why I hit that kid. But it wasn't something I was called at school first. It was something they called me at home. My family. Well, Greg."

Chatter didn't respond. A sheen of sweat rested on Greaves's neck, and his heartbeat, steady and sure, could be seen in the pulse next to his throat.

"Those kids at the culvert treat you like that?" Greaves said. "Like family? You ain't ever once felt like a charm, or a pest, something they keep around or can't get rid of? You always just felt like yourself? No. No, I know. Here's the shitty secret, kid: you're only family if the family feels it too. What you think they feel about you?"

"I haven't asked every kid," Chatter said. "I didn't set out to measure that."

"But you know it anyway," Greaves said. "Same as I know it. Same as I felt for all those years. The Kin. What a joke. I suggested that name, me. I meant it as a joke, but Simon Sanderson, Harm, they ain't ever understand my jokes. We weren't the same. But you and I, kid, we are the same. I know it, because same as you can feel me, well, I feel the same. I don't feel much, not with my skin so covered, but it's there, this sense, something not come from the outside, but something from the inside. I feel that, if I don't feel anything else."

Chatter shook his head. "I can't help feeling it," he said. "It isn't my choice."

"You think I asked?" said Greaves with a laugh. "Choice. You think most of what happens to you is by choice?" He shook his head. "Listen, how's this for sense? You, your whole life long, been haunted by animals who're looking to die. And I been haunted my whole life by something I can't say but with the skins of dead animals. Right? It's silence the whole way down, but what I know and what you know, what I say, and what you say. I don't know much else, but I know what I feel, I know what you feel. I know neither of us is going to outrun our ghosts, and I don't know if either of us can. I know I'm sick, and I know you heal. I know what I want you can't help but collect. I need the animals, but are too clumsy in killing them. You kill animals, but don't want to keep them. Can't you see that? You and me, we're the same. Maybe not even the same, maybe it's more I'm empty of something you have, and you're empty of something I have. Maybe there's no name for it yet. Maybe no one's ever heard of this. It's like we're two parts of a natural process. You and me. Some system closed down to just you and me. I don't understand it any better than you. I can't tell if this is really old, or brand new. Is this older than us?"

A silence slid over Chatter's body. He found an openness in Greaves's eyes that he didn't expect.

"We could leave," said Greaves. "You and me. Don't need those kids back there, who'd only look at you like the dog anyway. We'll look out for each other. I'll keep watch while you tend to your animals, and after you've made your ablutions, you can donate the carcass to me. Then I'll make it speak again. Like you did, giving me that jackrabbit two nights ago. Carried it from your fire right to me. How did that feel? I could show you what I did."

"I've seen what you've done," Chatter said. "I saw Roscoe's Cove."

Greaves shook his head. "That wasn't me," he said. "Sure, I was there, but I didn't do any of that. That trash. It was Hardnose, Pancake, and the others. They're copying me, think they meant to impress me. I find kids do that a lot. The sick I have on my skin rubs off. But they become vicious in their own way, and I can't stop that. It's this whole valley, all the kids are sick already."

Chatter let his hand slip away from the dusters tucked in his back pocket. "Where would we go?" he said.

Greaves started, then stopped. He smiled. "Anywhere we want," he said.

"Won't work," Chatter said. "Azalea won't stop, she won't settle. She needs you for her peace. She needs you gone, not missing, but surely gone."

"We won't come back," Greaves said.

"Not good enough," Chatter said. "We need a show. Something to show them all."

"Let's just leave, kid."

Chatter scrambled midway up the hill. He swept his hands through the flattened grass, searching for an aberrance of land. Finally, he lowered onto his stomach. There, on his belly, he recognized the angle of the hill against the sky. Again, he ran his hands through stalks of grass. Then, he dug.

His hands shook as he unearthed the first knife he'd made. His tooth, short, straight, and sharp on both sides. The blade the distance from his wrist to the human heart. He measured it, and to his dismay, the handle fit his grip just as perfectly, and the reach of the blade remained the same.

"Here," Chatter said. "Here is what we do. I tell Azalea you caught me up, you met me here, and we tussled. I'll make it a big one. You start kicking up the earth, stomp a few bushes. I'll tell her I got the best of you, that I killed you and your body went down the river. She'll believe me. I can make them believe me."

"You wait a night, tell your story around camp," Greaves said. "Then you'll meet me? I'll wait across the river."

"Two nights," Chatter said. "Or three. Odd numbers are convincing."

Greaves shook his head. "They won't believe it," he said. "Won't believe you killed me with that little knife. Won't believe it without seeing my blood on the grass. Won't believe not a scratch on you."

With the same suddenness he used to stab Sod, Greaves stuck the tip of his knife into Chatter's shoulder, just below his collarbone. Warm blood ran down his chest and arm, his hand tingled and grew numb. Chatter gaped in open shock.

"I don't know why I did that," Greaves said. "I'm sorry. Don't know why I did that." With the same impulsive quickness, Greaves brought the knife to his forearm and sliced it open.

"It's fine," Chatter said. He pressed at the wound. "It'll help."

"No, it won't," Greaves snarled. "I'm sorry. I couldn't stop myself. I can't ever. I'm sick. I'm a monster."

"You're not a monster," Chatter said. "You're just sad and mean. You've been alone too long. I've seen it before. There was this kid in a half-dead town, named Bailiff, who dreamed her teeth were covered in skin. It was the middle of winter and her family had frozen to death, and she just couldn't, no matter how hard she tried, break through their flesh. But she was so hungry."

Chatter stepped closer to Greaves. "There was a day when she woke with a ringing in her senses. The sort where you feel your blood vessels exposed to the air. Her teeth *ached*. Pressure changes unbalanced her, and whenever she sneezed, her lungs, her neck, and the backs of her eyes seized with the worst pain. It wasn't until three days later that the thought occurred to her: before she felt bad, she went for a swim in the river. It was obvious what happened, she told me. A parasite from the riverbed had worked its way under the nail of the smallest finger of her left hand."

Greaves quit pacing. He watched Chatter.

"This girl knew a parasite tunnelled under her nail because, on six separate occasions, her finger throbbed with no outward cause," Chatter said. "Soon, the throb was all she could think of. She pictured this worm wrapped around her bones, feeding off the scrapings of flesh under her nail from one end, while the other end spiralled towards her heart. She knew it would suck the stems from her eyes and lay eggs in the channels of her brain. There was a bulge at the sides of her knuckles that wasn't there before. So, she decided, the next day, to use a pair of her father's needle-nosed pliers to pull the nail out of her finger. Even then the parasite didn't die. Her sinuses were still shot with that bleeding, seeping pain. Her knuckles still bulged."

Chatter looked at his own palms. "The very morning, I met her, she'd smashed her finger between two concaved rocks. Three times. Yet the throb hadn't stopped. *I'm so hungry*, she said, *Please, I'm so, so hungry.*"

Chatter showed Greaves the emptiness of his hands. "I laid my hands on her head. First, she was feverish, and she fought me. She wasn't one to give up a fight. But her fever cooled, her nails didn't dig so deep in my arms. It was in those raw moments, after she was purged, that I knew her capable of an honesty I wouldn't find elsewhere, and I asked a very important question."

Greaves face darkened. Finally, he growled: "What?"

"What drinks your blood but is never satiated?" Chatter said. He smiled, and took another step forward. "I know what haunts you, I can feel the pall on your skin. And I know how to wipe it away. I learned it from a mad girl in Bailiff. I can wipe it all away."

"How?" said Greaves.

Chatter stepped toward the boy, the soft grass folding before him. He held up his hands. They were as empty as safety, one bloody, one covered in dirt. Greaves watched him for a while. He shivered, despite the lack of breeze, then kneeled.

Chatter placed his hands on Greaves's brow. He applied pressure to Greaves's temples. "Dear Lord," Chatter said, "is this thy servant?"

Chatter shushed him when he tried to speak, and dug his fingers into Greaves's flesh. "*Fear*," he whispered, "*is natural to life.*" He massaged Greaves's scalp, his hands pulsating a warmth beyond contact. He felt a lightness, a trickle spread outwards from his spine and nestle in every empty spot of his body. The spread of this energy, the give and take between the thin layer of their skin, the intermingling in a place that had not existed separately, was as natural as breathing, felt as normal as a yearn in the heart. Chatter quivered, and lost sense of Chatter, lost, even, the notion of his standing, of his arms pressing, the pain in his shoulder faded, the feeling in his fingers returned, and for a moment, a pulse of energy, colourless and silent, filled the incoherent space between his hands.

Greaves gasped. He fell back from Chatter's hands, gaping upwards. A wild terror crossed his face. Chatter noticed a flicker, down by the river, an inconsistency on the bank. Sod ascended the hill.

Greaves scrambled to his feet. His lip quivered in rage. He stared over Chatter's shoulder. "This was a trick?" he shouted. "This was a *trick*?"

Azalea collided with Chatter and Greaves at a dead sprint. The three of them tumbled down the hill on separate trajectories. Chatter's path took him across an exposed patch of shale and into a depression of a caved-in burrow. Shards of shale dug into his skin. He felt cold, despite the warmth of the blood.

Azalea scrambled on top of Greaves and pinned his arms down. Greaves raised his head, only to have it beaten back again. Azalea fell into a rhythm, rolling across her shoulders, bringing her gauntleted fists up and down in a hypnotizing pace, a *smack-smack, smack-smack* that banished all other sound from Chatter's mind. Greaves struggled beneath Azalea, but couldn't free himself. Her ferocity was terrible to behold.

Prissies soon enveloped her, and she climbed off Greaves to give the mob a turn. The crowd of kids allowed Greaves to pull his broken carcass up and stumble down the hill, but only to feel the thrill of chase before knocking him to the ground and stomping him.

Azalea climbed the hill to Chatter. She pulled off the cloth that bound her hair and pressed the balled fabric to Chatter's wound. "Listen to that," she said. "The Prissies are chanting your name."

Silence returned to Chatter as he watched the sight down the hill. He wavered in shock. "That isn't my name," he said.

Azalea frowned. "He hurt you bad? Can you reach the wound?"

Chatter sat forward. He couldn't stop watching Greaves appear and disappear in the swirl of kids. "Live forever," he said. He stood and stretched his hands in the sky. "Live forever!" he shouted.

Several kids stopped. More and more once they noticed the others. Chatter held his hands in the air until the tension of their stillness commanded every kid to look uphill.

"It is over!" Chatter shouted. "We will all live forever!" His hands swept downwards and grasped the bloody crown of Azalea's head. Her neck stiffened, and she held her head in place. She closed her eyes.

"Lord," Chatter said, "Lord." But he couldn't continue. Something inside him shook to the degree that he couldn't form any other words, nor continue using the word that rolled around his mouth like a rock. He hummed the stolen melodies of several hymns while he pressed his hands tighter, seeking that silent still place he found with Greaves, but his concentration was spent. He tried to keep his eyes closed, but they kept snapping open. He felt the sweat on his palms, the ache in his knuckles. A tiredness, more profound than he'd ever felt on the road with Lou, came over him. Greaves, down the hill, behind most of the mob that stared uphill, finally got to his feet. The kids next to him didn't appear to notice, and for a moment, he steadied his balance, he wiped at the blood trickling from his nose. He, too, looked uphill, but his eyes didn't rest on Chatter. They didn't focus on anything but the sky. Sensing the distraction of those nearest, Greaves turned and began to lope toward the river, only a couple dozen yards away. His first few steps went unrecognized, and briefly Chatter believed he might cross the distance, but quickly the kids around him tore their eyes from Azalea's healing and returned to their sport. Their hollering snapped Azalea's eyes open. Abruptly she pulled out of Chatter's hands and stood. She rolled her head on her neck.

"Thanks, Chatter," she said, "I feel much better."

"That's not my name," Chatter said.

But Azalea didn't hear, she never even knew he spoke. She'd already run to join the kids who tore Greaves to bits.

CHAPTER 68

The Prissies made a lot of noise. Even years later, their stories of the day are replete with hoots and hollers, and often near the climax of the telling, one who sat out of sight will smack their hands as loud as they can. Their story of origin; the war entire is credited with forging the Prissies into the force that rose and fell over decades. It was their first great collective act. But the war is too large to tell in a night, so most stories focus on a kid called Chatter, and, moreover, on the Mob at Sod's Hill. They relished their memories of this, hundreds of kids claimed to have been there, and by the time they'd grown old, the collective vision of the hill contained thousands. Ask a Prissy, if you ever come across one. They'll speak of the noise, the shouting and screaming, the sound of so many voices shouting one name, the multitude of opinion spun into a single clamour in which every mouth recognized itself. They'll brag about it, even, as though this were their achievement, as though every campfire story weren't told to suppress the silence of the nighttime wood.

Chatter didn't say a word. He wavered as he stood. He watched the mass of kids down the hill. With his eyes on a blur, the separate kids became indistinguishable, as numerous as strands of grass blown into a single fabric by the prairie wind. They reached over one another, shoved and pushed and picked each other up, the few who formed a tight circle around Greaves at the centre informing the wider motions of the rest, and those who stepped to avoid the blood Greaves vomited caused ripples to which the kids on the outside responded. A lurch, a grab at a scrap of Greaves's clothing, and a host of kids surged; any empty place was immediately filled, a frenzy at these moments, the bare desire of kids' faces revealed, then eclipsed by the strange motion of what they had become. He could not name any one kid, no matter how plainly he saw their face: the notion of difference dissolved in their turmoil. Chatter watched their mouths move, but he didn't hear a single sound.

Perhaps it was the stretch of the landscape—the busied horizon that reached beyond the valley, past the plots tended by farmers, and became lost in the fractious maw of mountains— that swallowed the commotion, or perhaps it was the still of the trees, the calm complacency of the grass, the patience required to endure a thousand lifetimes, that dwarfed the calamity visited upon Greaves. Perhaps the sky is too wide for our voices. Whatever the reason, from Chatter's vantage near the top of the hill, silence suffocated the sight.

Chatter rubbed the soil off his hand, then pressed his palm into the blood that seeped from his wound. He rubbed his hands together until both were covered. He found, by flicking his fingers, he achieved effect he needed. He spread blood all over. Every kid there swears to it: Chatter's blood was everywhere. His early knife was found, alongside Azalea's. The Prissies saw enough to see the scurry of a knife fight. No one told them the story, they told it to themselves.

Discolourations of the bark stain the trees of Sod's hill. You can see the curves of palms, the clench of fingers, charting the course of Chatter's bloodied hands through the birch. The marks, larger where he leaned for balance, or to catch his fleeting breath, withstood the seasons, and endure to the present day. Trampled grasses reveal where his knees gave, and he lay and collected himself. His path wavered, but he never ascended. He continued downwards. This much, the Prissies will show you.

Chatter passed into the high grasses, where the thick grass grew, and the pocked land dropped without warning. When the ground dipped underfoot, Chatter thought of Lou. That large man, over-graceful, wandering prairie backroads, fostering the con that would carry him through the end of days. Chatter imagined saloons warmed at a central point, heads buzzing, swirling in Lou's artful lies of the kid's life. Chatter called himself *the kid* then, and afterwards discarded both names. He continued through the high grass that would erase his path.

He would, of course, only follow the yearn. He'd pressed his hand to his wound so often it clotted, and left the last of his blood on a thin birch near the edges of a huge thicket of wolf willow. Afterwards he skirted the wolf willow, allowing more of himself into the yearn than he ever had, and the trickle of longing spread into his bones and quelled the fear that he had so long sworn was natural, the fear of his parents' silence, the fear of becoming the inchoate, the form the silence desired, the vessel, the namelessness contained therein. Near the dirt path next to the river's bank, he knelt. Just inside the wolf willow was a female jackrabbit, thin with spring sickness. She quivered, and at first was reluctant to move closer. Her foreleg shook as she extended it, and she was a long time in shifting her weight forward, testing the reliability of limbs held stiff as porcelain. She froze when he reached out, and only continued when he withdrew his hand and didn't give any indication of help. He wanted to alleviate her worry, but he had no words; in all his life, he had never learned the language of the jackrabbits. So, he waited. He kept his presence there. Eventually, she crept close, and leaned her body against his forearm. She was cold already. She watched his hand rise off the ground, watched it eclipse the sunlight mottled by wolf willow, but closed her eyes before it settled. Her breath was frail, shallow, inconsequential, yet he fell into her rhythm, easing and controlling his breathing until there was no difference between their bodies, until, at last, there was quiet inside her body. He pressed his face into her fur. And then he cried for a long while.

He left his head on the jackrabbit after. A deep silence had settled over the wolf willow, and he stared at the colonnades that ran though the thicket, lending sense to the tangle. The leaves, he realized, would keep the rain off the hares. He lifted the jackrabbit into his arms and carried her deeper into the wolf willow, nestling her near its centre. When he crawled out, he went to the river and washed off his hands, wiped the blood and muck from his face until it was as blank as ever. He returned to the wolf willow, watched the breeze through its leaves, rustling a sky of a thousand separate parts. His heart was silent.

ACKNOWLEDGEMENTS

I am exceedingly lucky to have had Naomi K. Lewis edit this novel. Without her guidance, and unerring grasp of character, structure, and oddness, the work would not have been able to find its scope, nor compassion, nor its porcelain limbs to stand upon.

I would like to extend my gratitude to my graduate supervisor, Aritha van Herk, whose patience and encouragement supported me through several years of study, and several more drafts than years. Her unfailing commitment to the craft of writing, the practice of reading, and fidelity to clear, substantiated thought remains a source of admiration and inspiration. Without her discipline and compassion, I could not have accomplished this novel.

I am grateful, most of all, for my family: my mother, Jane; my father, Mike; my sisters, Elizabeth and Patricia; my brother-in-law, Brendan Bakay; my nephews Rory and Hugh; and my niece Fiona. Your love and humour sustained me through lonesome years of artistic growth, and your support ensured that I never quit for long. My father taught me to locate love and life in storytelling, and my mother taught me that all forms of life deserve equal love and compassion. I could not write novels without these lessons. And I am deeply grateful for the patience and open-hearted acceptance of John and Helen Bubric, my sister-in-law, Laura, and my niece Emma. You all mean the world to me.

And to my wife, Katherine Bubric, who revealed a life worth living: your unfailing stride beside mine is a constant source of strength and energy. I fear the composition of this novel weighed as heavily on you as on me, and I am in awe of, and indebted to, your patience and unflagging confidence in my ability to complete the work. If I succeed, it is because your love has given me the will to do so, if I push forward again — again and again — it is only so that I might keep pace with you.

Photography by K. Bubric

CHRIS KELLY worked as a butcher, a bouncer, and a bartender before resolving himself to the bloody business of fiction. He is the author of *On Quiet Earth*, and winner of the Kaleidoscope Award. Chris lives in Alberta, in the shadow of the Rocky Mountains, with his wife and a feisty rabbit.

BRAVE & BRILLIANT SERIES

SERIES EDITOR:
Aritha van Herk, Professor, English, University of Calgary
ISSN 2371-7238 (PRINT) ISSN 2371-7246 (ONLINE)

Brave & Brilliant encompasses fiction, poetry, and everything in between and beyond. Bold and lively, each with its own strong and unique voice, Brave & Brilliant books entertain and engage readers with fresh and energetic approaches to storytelling and verse.